KNOCK KNOCK, OPEN WIDE

KNOCK KNOCK, OPEN WIDE

NEIL SHARPSON

NIGHTFIRE

TOR PUBLISHING GROUP

New York

This is a work of fiction. All of the characters, organizations, and events portrayed in this novel are either products of the author's imagination or are used fictitiously.

KNOCK KNOCK, OPEN WIDE

A Nightfire Book
Published by Tom Doherty Associates / Tor Publishing Group
120 Broadway
New York, NY 10271

www.tornightfire.com

Nightfire™ is a trademark of Macmillan Publishing Group, LLC.

The Library of Congress Cataloging-in-Publication Data is available upon request.

ISBN 978-1-250-78542-8 (hardcover)
ISBN 978-1-250-78547-3 (ebook)

Our books may be purchased in bulk for promotional, educational, or business use. Please contact your local bookseller or the Macmillan Corporate and Premium Sales Department at 1-800-221-7945, extension 5442, or by email at MacmillanSpecialMarkets@macmillan.com.

First Edition: 2023

Printed in the United States of America

0 9 8 7 6 5 4 3 2 1

To Anna

My mother, my teacher. Who gifted me a love of Irish folklore, and whose only relationship to the myriad horrible mothers in this book is as their absolute antithesis. *Gach grá is buíochas, a Mham.*

To Aoife

Jaysus. You were right about just about everything with this one.

KNOCK KNOCK, OPEN WIDE

Is it over? It certainly feels like it's over.

In the space of a few weeks, Etain Larkin has gone from being the most famous woman in Ireland to . . . well, admit it. You had to remind yourself who she was.

But why worry? She's back, safe and sound now, which is a better ending than any of us expected (myself very much included, dear reader. I can confess that now).

Poor Barry Mallen has been vindicated and we can even hear the tinkle of wedding bells over the horizon. A bit soon after such a horrific business, you might say? To hell with that, I reply. What has this whole grisly affair taught these two young people other than that life is cruel and arbitrary and awful and you have to seize your happiness and hold on until your fingernails bite your palms and draw blood?

Marry, you crazy kids. Build your shelter and fill it with fat, happy babies. We wish you every joy. You deserve it, and the interest.

Is it over?

Nothing is ever over, but, if anything, we know less now than we did before.

We've gone from one, fairly straightforward mystery ("Where is Etain Larkin?") to dozens, if not hundreds.

Feidhlim Lowney is still presumably at large, whereabouts unknown.

We still don't know his motive (though, of course, we can guess).

We still don't know why his farmhouse burned to the ground.

There are questions regarding the body found in the ashes. There are questions as to how Etain Larkin was brought to the Lowneys' home in Scarnagh.

There are questions about the Garda investigation.

Why did they home in so relentlessly on Barry Mallen as a suspect despite the absolute lack of any evidence? Incompetence? Force of habit? Or was someone telling tales out of school?

There are, likewise, questions about the media coverage of the

disappearance. We of the press need to take a good, long, hard look at this job. Corners were cut, lads.
Shoddy work. A stiff breeze would bring it down.
There are questions, in short.
And there are questions about the questions.
So no, dear reader. It's not over.
Mere preamble, the lot of it.

"SCARNAGH AFTERMATH LEAVES MORE QUESTIONS THAN ANSWERS"
PATRICIA SKELTON, *THE IRISH PRESS*, NOVEMBER 29, 1979

Yes, darlings, Mummy has been drinking. Don't worry, it won't affect my writing (never has before). Yes, darlings, Mummy has been crying (that probably will).

I come before you like Cassandra to warn you of the impending tidal wave of shite that is headed your way.

"Patricia Skelton, legendary journalist and our longtime colleague, is departing our paper for pastures new. We wish her every success and have no doubt that blah blah blah . . ."

What was it that Thackeray said about eulogies? I can't find the book. They're all bollocks, that's the gist. But the professional obituaries of your humble narrator will be world-beaters in bullshit, you mark my words.

I am *not* "leaving for pastures new." I am *not* "pursuing exciting new opportunities." I am *not* "a respected and beloved colleague," because I've seen what it takes to gain love and respect in this industry and they don't pay me enough. And I am most certainly *not* leaving of my own free will.

I have fallen from respectability. But check the eggshell for fingerprints, darlings. Mummy was pushed. Why did the bad men do that, Mummy?

Did you ever see Punch and Judy? What a little horror. Like they figured out how to stage a nightmare. He beats her, he kills her child. He gets away with it.

Punch laughs. Ha Ha Ha Ha.

We laugh. Ha Ha Ha Ha.

The show only works if you don't see the hands.

It's all a puppet show.

And I saw the hands, my darlings.

"GOODBYE"
PATRICIA SKELTON, WRITTEN FOR THE *DUBLIN HERALD*,
JUNE 6, 1999 (UNPUBLISHED)

OCTOBER 1979

The clock that hung on the wall of Mrs. Maude Pygott's shop was of the same make that could be found in schools and offices across the world: a large metallic ring with a curious mechanical quirk that caused it to run efficiently throughout the day until it reached half an hour before quitting time. At which point the entire mechanism seemed to wind down, and the arms would move like an ant crawling through thick honey.

One of the reasons that Mrs. Pygott approved of the new girl was that, unlike every other college student who had taken part-time work here, Maude never found her staring at the clock when she should have been sweeping the floor or taking inventory.

Right now the girl, a short, pale, brown-haired twenty-something named Etain, was trying to wrestle the sweeping brush back into the cupboard without upsetting the Rice Krispies.

Mrs. Pygott had gotten the impression that the reason Etain was never to be found staring at the clock and cursing its dreamy languor was that she didn't like to be reminded that she would soon be returning home. Etain did not seem to have a happy home life.

Trouble with the mother, Maude guessed.

The shop was not a place to work if you were claustrophobic.

In terms of the goods it sold, it was a decent-sized grocer's, offering canned goods, tobacco, fruit, vegetables, cleaning products, newspapers, and toiletries. However, the size of the shop was better suited to a small newsagent's and this meant that the shelves were crowded together and laden down with goods from the floor to the ceiling, which gave the place the close, stuffy atmosphere of a library.

The girl placed the broom back in the cupboard and turned to where Maude was leaning against the counter leafing through an issue of *Ireland's Own*.

"You can leave now if you like, love," Maude told her, gesturing to the clock. "Not much in it."

Etain simply nodded. Not much of a talker; another point in her favor in Maude's opinion.

"Oh, and would you mind telling him his tea is ready?"

Etain nodded again and headed through the back entrance into the Pygott home that abutted the shop.

In the living room, Maude's youngest son, Tom, was watching television, cross-legged on the carpet and still wearing his school uniform.

Etain gave a rare smile. She liked the Pygott boys. They were both quiet, and often painfully shy (Tom in particular), but they were sweethearts. Good kids.

"Hiya," she said gently.

There was no reaction.

Glued to the box, she thought to herself. She looked at the screen.

Bloody hell, she thought. *Puckeen? Is that still on?*

Memories returned, unbidden, of long, purgatorial afternoons after school with the rain washing the world outside. She and her sister, Kate, had watched *Puckeen* religiously; that is, as a joyless ritual that neither of them fully understood. It was one of very few television programs that Mairéad Larkin had allowed her daughters to watch. It was not, certainly, the biggest grievance she had against her mother. And yet, Etain mused, it was a lot higher up the list than it should be.

On the screen, a young, bland-faced man in a white Pierrot costume was explaining different shapes to the audience in English and Irish:

"And this is a square. *Cearnóg.* Four sides. *Ceithre thaobh.*"

The costume notwithstanding, he looked and sounded like a man announcing the profits for quarter three, which were broadly in line with the profits for quarter two.

Behind him was Puckeen's box.

They really haven't changed a thing, she thought to herself. She wondered if this was a repeat, and they were simply airing an episode from her childhood. But no, the presenter was different. Very similar, certainly. Same affect, same costume (in fact, quite possibly *literally* the same costume) but nevertheless a different person.

Growing up there had usually been a male and a female presenter. And of course, Puckeen himself. At least in theory. Puckeen lived in the box that dominated the center of the set. The box was plain and black, and rectangular. It was always in sight, always visible. Sometimes, one of the presenters would be "bold." Loud. Disobedient. Argumentative. Overly inquisitive.

And the other presenter would remind them, sometimes severely, sometimes nervously, sometimes more in sorrow than in anger, that if they didn't behave, Puckeen would be cross and come out of his box.

For children watching the program for the first time, it became a game. Waiting for the episode where Puckeen would finally emerge from the box. Where they would finally see what he looked like. Episode after episode, they awaited a revelation.

But it never came. The offending presenter would inevitably repent, apologize to the other presenter, and be forgiven.

She realized with a jolt of dark amusement that the nation's taxpayers had been funding a decades-long practical joke on their own children, who spent hours watching a program whose main character had never appeared, and would never appear.

Beckett could have learned something from the RTÉ children's programming department, she thought. Even he never tried to make *Waiting for Godot* last fifteen years.

Only fifteen? It was already running when I was a child. How long has it been on . . .

Suddenly, her train of thought was broken and she remembered why she was here. She laid a hand on Tom's shoulder and the boy jolted like he'd just been woken.

He looked up at her, blearily, as if not quite sure who she was or where he was.

"Your tea's ready," she told him, and left through the back door to the yard where her bike was stashed.

The call came at twenty minutes to seven, which was enough to tell Etain that it was from Kate.

It was the perfect time for Kate to be sure that Etain was home (which, technically she was, as she wearily wrestled her rain-slick bike through the narrow front door while trying not to send a family of porcelain cats on the hall table to an early grave).

But it was also the perfect time to ensure that Mairéad was *not* there, as she would be at evening Mass regardless of the torrential rain outside. Or indeed, anything else up to and including a full-scale war. Since Kate had graduated and moved out of the house she had not said two words to Mairéad, either in person, by phone, or by post. Kate refused to acknowledge her, speak of her to friends, or even admit that she had been born to anyone. Kate had, to all intents and purposes, killed her mother. Etain looked forward hopefully to the day when she could do the same.

She picked up the phone and answered, her voice still husky and wheezing from cycling across town in the rain.

"Hi, sis," said Kate on the other end.

Her sister had a plummy, almost aristocratic South Dublin accent and she seemed to come by it effortlessly. Etain had spent a lifetime trying to force her own voice into that kind of shape, but had only ever managed a neutral tone lodged somewhere in the riverbed of the Liffey. When she was upset, or stressed, she lapsed into a nasally northsider twang that she hated.

"How is the cave, and where is the dragon?" Kate asked.

"She's at Mass," said Etain, trying her best to juggle handset and handlebars. *But you knew that,* she thought, *or you wouldn't have risked calling.*

"How is she?" Kate asked. Not a query as to her mother's well-being. A request for an update on an ongoing crisis. A casualty report.

"Same as usual," Etain wheezed, stripping off her soaking mac one-handed and dancing as the sleeve gripped her left wrist like a hungry beast and refused to let go.

"You poor thing," said Kate.

"Thanks," said Etain.

"You should come down," Kate said. "No, you *have* to come down. That's an order."

Etain sat down on a chair in the hall, too tired to stand, and tried to remember where "down" was. Since leaving the family home, Kate had led an almost gypsy existence, house-sharing with one set of friends for a few weeks or months and then moving on somewhere else. In the last half year she had been living in Clontarf, Rathmines, even a brief spell in London. Then, Etain remembered. Her sister was house-sitting for their aunt, who was away doing missionary work in Uganda. For the last three weeks Kate had been living alone in a tiny

KNOCK KNOCK, OPEN WIDE

cottage in the wilds of Wexford and, by her own admission, being "driven mad by all the fucking peace and tranquility."

"You want me to come down to Duncannon?" said Etain.

"I do."

"Why?"

"Because I am throwing a party and it is going to be the best party of our miserable lives."

"When?" Etain asked.

"Tomorrow night."

Oh, fuck right *off,* Etain thought.

"I can't," she said.

"You can," said Kate. "You will. You shall."

"I can't, I won't, I shan't," said Etain irritably. "How am I supposed to get down?"

"Borrow the car," said Kate.

"She won't let me," Etain replied.

"I didn't say 'Ask if you can borrow it,' I just said 'borrow it.'"

"I have work the next day."

"So don't stay too late. Leave around eight and you'll be back home in plenty of time."

Etain did not share her sister's optimism. Her aunt's house lay at the center of a labyrinth of winding, brambly, unlit country roads and Etain was not a confident driver. She had never even driven outside of the city.

"Kate, I can't," she said.

"Etain—"

"Sorry, I—"

"Etain. Barry's going to be there. He is traveling a lot further than you are. And I promised him you'd be here. And, one way or the other, I think you owe him a face-to-face."

Etain very nearly slammed the receiver down right there and then.

Bitch, she thought, *fucking interfering bitch how* dare *you* . . .

But she was too tired even for that. And after the first flush of anger had passed she realized that she was more angry with herself than anyone else.

Barry Mallen had been her . . . no, technically still *was* her boyfriend legally and in the eyes of God. Ever since he had completed his

degree in agriculture he had gone back home to the family farm outside of Bantry and they had tried to make a few phone calls every
week take the place of seeing each other every day, kissing at house
parties, walking arm in arm around the lake in Belfield. He was a big
lad. Good for sheltering from the wind. Strong arms to get lost in.
Sweet as chocolate. She had thought him a joke when she had first
met him, with his wild, unkempt ginger hair and thick Cork brogue
that reminded her of a barking sheepdog. As an arts student, she'd
instinctively thought herself better than him until the night she had
gotten blackout drunk at a party only to wake up on Barry's couch
the next morning, having been safely escorted through the midnight
campus past foxes and worse. He had made her a cup of strong sweet
tea, and spent the morning patiently listening to her tell him why
she hated her mother. A few weeks later he had invited her and a few
of his Dublin friends down to the family homestead and they had
kissed in his father's barn while the rest of their friends sat drinking and singing softly in the darkness and chased the bats with their
flashlights.

She loved him, she realized with a start. Which was why she hadn't
done the honorable thing and cut him loose.
    She had to break up with Barry. If she didn't show up to this
party, that would be as clear a signal to him as anything. But he deserved better than that. Kate was right, the absolute unutterable
hoor.
    "Fine," she said wearily, and hung up the phone, because if
she had to listen to Kate celebrating her victory she would have
screamed.

It was a bright, cloudless October day, cold as a razor's edge, and
as she drove Mairéad's ancient baby-blue Ford Cortina down the
coast to Duncannon, she reflected on how much more she would
be enjoying the journey if there wasn't heartbreak waiting for her
at the other end. The Irish coast spread out before her in all its
wild, rough-faced beauty and she had a mad desire to stop by the
side of the road, strip naked, and leap into the sea until she was
too cold to think or worry. The sea air made her senses sharpen
and she could almost feel layers of Dublin grime and funk lifting

off her skin and lungs and eyes. It felt like she was being scoured, cleaned and made brighter.

The road to her aunt's house was little more than a dirt track running through a near-impenetrable forest of blackberry bushes that seemed to wind and twist like an intestine for half a mile. The road was so narrow that Etain could hear the thorns of the bushes clawing hungrily at the doors of the Cortina as the tiny car bravely pushed deeper into the brush. Etain winced, not wanting to even imagine what this was doing to the paint. Mairéad would kill her. Ah well. That had been inevitable since she had left the note on the kitchen table breezily informing her mother that she was borrowing her car, as if that was something that one simply did.

Even more worrying was the thought that she might meet another car coming toward her. There was no room for two cars to pass, there was barely enough room for one car to move. The thought of having to reverse all the way back through the blackberry jungle filled her with dread. But, at last, the road widened and there was her aunt's house, a small, cozy-looking two-story that would have been quite pretty had it not been painted in an absolutely despicable shade of orange. There were five or six other cars parked haphazardly in the weed-speckled driveway, and she tentatively squeezed in between two before turning off the engine, gripping the steering wheel, leaning her forehead against it, and whispering, "Okay, okay, okay."

She took a few deep breaths, and got out of the car, not bothering to lock it.

She knocked on the door, which was opened by a tall vampire with a black plastic rubbish bag awkwardly tucked under his collar as a cape.

He threw his arms open joyfully at the sight of her and said something completely incomprehensible.

She stared at him.

"What are you wearing?" she asked him incredulously.

Keano Flynn sheepishly removed a set of plastic fangs from his mouth.

"It's Halloween," he said, a little hurt.

* * *

It was indeed Halloween, but thankfully no one else had bothered to dress up. Keano, the least threatening vampire in Europe, sat sullenly in the corner, nursing a beer. He had helped Kate to arrange the party, but whereas he had wanted a Halloween party, she had been adamant that it was simply to be a party that happened to take place on Halloween, and she had won.

Only a dozen or so people had made the journey down to Duncannon, but the house was small enough for that to feel like a crowd. Etain wandered, adrift in the mass as always. She knew all these people but she couldn't work up the nerve to talk to them. She had an irrational fear that no one would remember who she was. Suddenly, she felt a hand on her shoulder and she spun around to see Barry smiling at her.

His face has changed, she thought to herself. It had been so long since she'd seen him that he looked noticeably different. He had moved back home, and his mother's cooking had broadened his face slightly. His arms and torso were bulkier too, as he was working full-time on his father's farm. And he'd gotten a haircut. The haystack had at last been tamed and he looked almost clean-cut. He leaned in to kiss her and she kissed him back, even as she thought that she really shouldn't. *You're here to break his heart, remember?* she told herself.

Just his. Sure.

"Heya, Tain," he whispered.

"Hi" was all she could say.

He gestured for her to follow him and she did. They left the living room, through the hall, and Etain found herself in her aunt's guest bedroom, which was crammed with books and boxes of clothes and a small wire settle bed. Barry closed the door behind them, muting the ruckus of the party to a low background hum.

She realized that he was sweating. What was going on?

"How are you?" he asked. His breath was strained, as if he was about to break bad news.

Just do it, she told herself. *There's no good time. Tell him it's over. Just . . .*

"I was in Youghal," he said, apropos of nothing.

She decided to let him finish.

"I was in Youghal and I was passing Cotter's and there was this . . . I saw this in the window, like."

Etain would remember for the rest of her life how the sound of the party suddenly seemed to drop away and all she could hear was Barry's voice and the sound of her own breathing. For at this very moment, Barry had reached into his pocket and taken out a small navy-blue box.

Oh. Oh Jesus.

He was stammering. He was so scared.

"And I thought . . . I just . . . I wanted more than anything to just go in there . . . and buy it . . . and give it to you . . . I could see it all, like. What it'd be like. You and me. And I wanted that more than anything, Tain. It just. I couldn't help myself. So I . . ."

He looked at her and suddenly he lost his nerve. The look of shock and (he thought) horror on her face killed his courage stone dead.

He had been about to pass her the box but now he put it back in his pocket.

"Sorry," he mumbled. "Sorry. It's stupid. It was stupid. Tain, I'm sorry, I don't know what I was thinking. It was stupid."

And, realizing what was being taken away, something in her, greater than her fear of Mairéad, greater than her fear of anything, rebelled and she blurted out:

"Yeah!"

Barry looked like he'd been stabbed.

"Yeah," he said softly. "Yeah. I know. Stupid."

He reached for the door handle to escape and her hand shot out and grabbed his wrist. She gazed into his eyes.

"No, Barry. 'Yeah.'"

Realization slowly dawned.

"You mean . . . yeah?"

"Yeah."

"Yeah?"

"Yeah."

"You . . ." His voice was cracking. "You will?"

"Yeah." And she was laughing and crying at the same time. "Yeah. I will. I will. I will, yeah."

And then came a kiss. A kiss bigger and vaster than any kiss that had come before. A hurricane of a kiss. A typhoon. A kiss that could blow you off your feet and knock you to the floor. Or onto a nearby settle bed.

NOVEMBER 1979

Afterward, they slept like stones buried beneath the earth.
When she finally flickered awake, blanketed in his arms, she realized that the house had stilled and the room was in pitch blackness.

Shite. I have to drive back to Dublin tonight.

Every aching muscle, every inch of warm cozy skin, every buzzing, euphoric nerve told her to stay here, wrapped in the arms of her . . .

. . . her fiancé . . .

A grin, unlooked for and unexpected, broke on her face in the darkness.

What she wanted more than anything was to stay here with Barry until morning and then wake him up by climbing on top and . . .

That had been good. That had been so good. It wasn't supposed to be that good, the first time, was it?

The first time was, she had heard from reliable sources, usually a mortifying damp squib.

Oh God. Has he been with other girls? Is that why . . .

She cut off that train of thought.

Stop, she told herself sharply. *Stop doing that. Stop thinking of ways to make yourself miserable. Fuck's sake. He's an ag student. 'Course he knew what he was doing. Animal husbandry. Basically the same skills.*

She would have to get up. She had work in around five hours. Five hours to get back to Dublin, shower, get changed . . .

She'd get up.

She would get up.

Any second.

She'd get up now.

She was going to get up.

She had to get up. Her job at Mrs. Pygott's newsagent's wasn't exactly a golden ladder but it paid well enough, and jobs were scarce in Dublin and only getting scarcer. If she was going to get married she'd need—

A thought suddenly struck her.

Barry hadn't actually asked her to marry him. He hadn't said the words. She'd just told him "Yes." Had he actually even been going to propose?

Of course he was. He'd taken the ring out of his pocket to . . .

No. He'd never actually given her the ring. He'd lost his nerve and put it back in his pocket.

Ah well, she had at least *seen* the ring . . .

No. No, she hadn't. She had seen a box that she had assumed contained a ring.

Oh Jesus. Tell me I didn't just trade my virginity for a fucking watch.

She kicked Barry in the thigh to wake him up. It was like kicking a shank of mutton.

He jolted awake with a grunt.

"Oi," she whispered to him, half angry and half joking. "Where's my ring, ya bollocks?"

It took a few seconds for the words to reach his brain.

"Fuck!" he cursed thickly. "Did I not . . ."

"No, you didn't."

"Sorry, Tain," he mumbled, and reached over to where his discarded trousers lay curled on the floor.

He worked the chunky blue box out of his trouser pocket.

Realizing that it was too dark for her to see, she got out of bed and found a small study lamp that had been set on a desk by the wall.

"Watch your eyes," she whispered as the bulb flared white-hot.

The light revealed him stretching out to reach his trousers, half in and half out of the bed, like God reaching for Adam.

It was the first time she had ever seen his naked body. All she had seen during their lovemaking was flashes of skin, shapes in the corner of her eye. Here he was, revealed at last.

He looked up at her, shielding his face against the harsh light with his hand.

She took a moment to appreciate every inch of him, the million freckles that covered his shoulders and arms and legs. The hard contours of his forearms and shoulders, the little pockets of fat around his stomach. The great orange bush of pubic hair that crowned a cock that was, even flaccid, an impressive thing to see in the wild.

He was looking back at her and, without a hint of self-consciousness, she turned the lamplight on herself, slowly letting it play over her body, showing him everything in turn.

And for a few moments they stayed that way, gazing at each other in mutual awe and wonder.

Finally, she put the lamp down, angled so that it shone toward the bed, and got back under the covers with him.

"So," he said, presenting her with the blue velvet ring box, "here it is."

He's nervous, she thought. *He doesn't think I'll like it.*

She took a deep breath and opened the box.

The ring was not what she had expected and her first sensation was an instant swell of dislike.

It was clearly not a new ring, but some old family heirloom that had been sold on. It was far, far too large for her, and would have to be significantly resized if it was ever going to fit on her slender ring finger. It was thick and bulky, and seemed altogether too ostentatious for her. But as she studied it, she found herself warming to it. The jewel was a deep blue sapphire, held in place by the silver band that, on closer inspection, was cast in the shape of a woman combing her hair, with her long tresses flowing back until they became a flock of crows in flight. The detail was breathtaking. And the more she gazed at the ring, the more dislike turned to appreciation, and then to love. Perhaps it was not a ring that Etain Larkin would wear. But she had done a lot of things in the last day that Etain Larkin would not have done. Perhaps it was time to become someone else. She slipped it on her finger and held her hand up to her face to admire.

"Fuck. It's too big. I knew it," Barry sighed.

She shook her head.

"Doesn't matter," she said. "I can get it resized."

"Do you like it?" he asked tentatively.

"I love it," she told him. And, to her surprise, she meant it.

He helped her find her clothes and tried to convince her to stay but she was adamant. Mairéad, who had been banished into darkness by the light and joy of the last few hours, had returned to her throne in Etain's always turbulent mind.

There were storms on the horizon. There would be a reckoning over the car and an even greater one over the engagement. If she had to admit that she was now unemployed on top of everything . . . no. Two apocalypses were more than enough to be getting on with.

She kissed him again, told him to go back to sleep, and promised to call him when she had a chance.

He protested, but only so much. He was absolutely exhausted.

The living room was dark, and the floor was a maze of sleeping, rumbling bodies. She picked her way carefully through them, trying not to disturb the sleepers. Someone must have been awake because she heard a voice tsking at her from the sofa and the whispered word "slut."

She blushed in the darkness. They knew. Everyone knew. They'd probably been listening at the door.

She couldn't be sure if the whisperer was mocking her or congratulating her, but she didn't like it either way. She reached the other side of the room and opened the door to the kitchen.

She almost let out a scream.

Kate was sitting at the table, a steaming cup of tea in hand, perfectly framed in a circle of light. She looked immaculate, makeup and hair both faultless, and she was not dressed for bed.

She gave her sister a knowing half smile.

Have you really been waiting for me this whole time? Etain wondered.

"Leaving?" Kate asked.

"I have to. I told you that," Etain replied.

Kate rolled her eyes.

"You should have woken me," Etain said.

"I think we both know I shouldn't have," Kate replied. "I was not going in there for love nor money."

Etain blushed again. Kate saw she was uncomfortable and her voice softened.

"Etain," she said, "are you going to let me see it or do I have to beg?"

It took her a second to realize what her sister meant. She held out her hand.

Kate stood up and examined the ring with a practiced eye.

"It's . . . it's a very 'Barry Mallen' ring," she said at last.

Etain nodded. She wasn't wrong.

"I love it," she said simply.

"I know you do," said Kate with a smile. And then suddenly she was hugging her, which took her completely by surprise.

They were not a hugging family.

She stiffened unconsciously and then relaxed.

Kate held her close and whispered in her ear.

"I love you. I am so happy for you."

"Thanks, Kate," she whispered back.

"I love him, too," she said. "He is so good for you."

"He thinks you think he's an eejit."

"He is an eejit," she laughed. "He's a great big eejit. But he's full of love. And that's what matters. And he'll get you out of the dragon's den."

Etain wondered if that had been Kate's plan all along. If arranging for Etain to come here so that Barry could propose had been motivated, like seemingly everything else Kate did, out of a desire to spite Mairéad?

Kate and Mairéad were as different as two people could be, except in one respect. They both held their grudges like misers held their gold, close to the chest and never to be traded or given away.

They talked for around twenty minutes, with Kate peppering her with questions that she had not even given a moment's thought to. Cork or Dublin? Bridesmaids? Dresses? Honeymoon? Kate was downright giddy for once in her life. Etain was just exhausted. The euphoria had worn off, the long midnight drive home was now looming unavoidably ahead of her. Kate tried to talk her out of it, told her to call in sick, but she couldn't risk it.

Kate walked her to the door and as Etain was going out she reached her hand into a small marble font of holy water that hung on the jamb, to bless her sister before her long journey. Her fingers came out green with algae and Etain darted to avoid being touched with them.

"Probably should clean that out," Kate said ruefully.

They wished each other a last goodnight, and Kate closed the door.

Etain's fingers were shaking with tiredness as she unlocked the door of the car. Inside, a damp chill had settled on the seats. She sat in the car for a few moments, thinking on all the ways that this was a very bad idea. She gripped the steering wheel and the huge ring on her finger clinked against it like a loose tooth.

She smacked her face a few times to wake herself up and started the engine.

The car growled to life and she set off down through the dripping, clicking dirt track, thick with thorns and brambles that clawed the car's hide as she pushed through. The high beams from the car turned the bushes on either side into a buzzing static of edges and shadows. The light passing over them raised up faces and eyes and teeth, shapes constantly rising out of chaos and falling away.

The daylight had civilized the path somewhat; now it was wilderness. Pure jungle.

And then she was out, out through the brambles and on the open road, floating on an endless sea of black. There was no starlight. No moon. Rain clouds hung overhead, black and heavy as rotten fruit. The car was a flat spark of light, a tiny, shining cell, drifting down the crooked little veins of the island.

How was it even possible to get home on a road like this?

The road would surely go on forever.

Like any city-dweller newly alone in the dark countryside, Etain realized that she suddenly believed in ghosts.

She felt certain that if she were to turn her head to look out the window, she would see an awful, shambling mob of famine specters keeping pace with the car, skin hanging from their translucent bones, driven on by a hunger so fierce even death could not quiet it.

And so she kept her eyes on the road ahead. To raise her spirits she pretended she was Jacques Cousteau in a tiny submarine, floating a few feet off the bottom of the ocean. The headlights cut through the blackness, peeling back the night to reveal its secrets.

Moths with bodies as big as babies' thumbs floundered in light-addled ecstasy.

A bat glided by, stately in its horror.

A stoat, like black ink, slipped over a drystone wall, something in its mouth still twitching, still bleeding. Off to be torn apart in darkness.

She drove on.

She tried turning on some music to keep herself awake. The radio hissed and slurred like it was drunk and mumbled something that might have been a few bars of "Bright Eyes" before slipping into static.

She left the static on, hoping it would be better than silence.

How long had she been driving?

She should have turned by now.

There should have been a turn.

Where was she?

The static was not having the desired effect. She was being lulled. Hypnotized.

She was so tired.

The road was endless. The darkness, absolute.

Suddenly, a raindrop splattered on the windshield so large and heavy that it jolted her out of her reverie.

Then came another, and another. And suddenly the lit road ahead was a milky haze as a solid curtain of rain fell on the Earth like a reckoning.

This was not rain to water and replenish. This was rain sent in fury, to wash away the Earth and all its sin. This was a storm for the ages.

She was dimly aware that there was something wrong. She was too tired. The rain was too heavy. She was almost certainly lost. She should stop. Sleep. Wait until morning.

But it was easier to keep driving.

She drove on.

She was not herself. She felt drugged. Anaesthetized.

The static of the radio, the endless drumbeat of the storm on the roof of the car, and the flash of raindrops, long and gray as nails before her eyes, had altered her consciousness.

She had been drugged by exhaustion. Overdosed on static. She was high on rain.

The ring on her finger, so loose at the start of her journey, was tight now.

That couldn't be right. Her finger hadn't grown bigger. The ring could not have shrunk. And yet she could feel it biting into her flesh and bone like a rat.

How was that possible?

That wasn't right at all.

And yet, it seemed like such a silly thing to worry over. A ring couldn't suddenly shrink. But, what if it did? What difference did that make? It was at once impossible, and utterly trivial.

She was too tired to care.

And then, with a suddenness that can only happen in a nightmare, two shapes appeared on the road before her. She slammed on the brakes and the car screeched to a stop so violent that she banged her head against the steering wheel.

The world burned in stars and she heard a woman screaming far, far away.

She sounds so frightened. Someone should help her, Etain thought dimly to herself.

It's you, she realized at last. *You're the woman who's screaming.*

And yet, she couldn't make herself stop.

In the center of the road was a dog.

A tiny wire terrier, even smaller with its fur plastered to its scrawny carcass by the rain.

It was staring at the car, its golden eyes impossibly large, looking like they were going to pop out of their sockets. With every bark he flashed tiny, fish-white teeth, and his lower jaw was slightly misaligned, which gave the bark a hideous, slantwise shape.

Finally, realizing that the car was no threat, he returned to what he had been doing before Etain had slammed on the brakes.

The second shape had not moved. It lay half in and half out of the column of light cast by Etain's headlamps. The face was only barely visible. Etain thought she could make out the outlines of a thick beard before realizing her mistake. The dog had succeeded in peeling the face partially off the corpse, and a bundle of skin and flesh was rumpled in folds at the chin.

All that she could see clearly was the left arm. The hand was white as chalk, and the sleeve was of a checked blazer, such as a farmer might wear.

The dog had returned to its work, and was standing on the body's chest, tugging at the man's face.

She was filled with a sudden, intense hatred. Not just for the dog, but for the whole sickening scene.

She wanted to run the car over both of them, to crush them out of existence, out of her sight, out of her memory.

But as suddenly as it came, the thought was dispelled by intense pity. That poor man. His poor family.

What a way to die. What an end to come to.

The rational thing to do, she considered, would be to drive on and stop as soon as she came to a house, and call the Gardaí.

She rubbed her ring finger. It was aching slightly.

But it would not be right, she found herself thinking, to leave the body out here for that filthy animal to devour. It was not right. It was not right. Indecent.

She should take it with her. She should carry the corpse . . .

NO.

There was room in the back seat. There was plenty of room in the back seat.

She started the car and . . .

She turned off the engine.

There is plenty of room in the back seat. Scare the dog away and carry it to the car, Etain. Carry it to the car, Etain. It's not right to leave it there. It's not right. Think of his family. Think of his friends. Put your friend in the back.

NO.

She started the car.

She shut off the engine.

She sat in the car. Perfectly still. She watched the dog eat the man's face like it was playing with a dishcloth.

Her finger felt like it was being squeezed white.

She opened the door.

Within seconds of stepping out of the car her clothes and hair had drunk up as much rain as they could and now rivulets of water were pouring down her skin and running in streams down her fingers and pooling in her shoes. The rain was so cold she could feel her muscles clenching in protest and she had to force herself to walk toward the hideous mound lying in front of her. The dog, sensing that its meal was about to be disturbed, leapt off the chest of the corpse and marched stridently toward her, hackles raised, teeth bared, a long devil's beard of blood-drenched fur hanging from its lower jaw.

It barked hatefully at her, a high, spiteful, screeching yelp.

Etain had never liked dogs, not even big, friendly dogs.

"You have trouble trusting anything that loves you unconditionally," Kate had once said, which was no less cruel for being true.

But she had always hated and feared small dogs. There had been a Jack Russell on her road that had traumatized her twice a day for eight years on the walk to and from school, throwing itself at the garden gate as she had run past.

They must breed them to hate, she thought to herself.

The dog was still barking at her, barking so fast it was forgetting to breathe and making itself hoarse with rage. It barked like it was broken, like some spring inside it had snapped.

With a mixture of loathing and pity, Etain reached down and picked up a stone.

The dog flinched at the motion but held its ground.

"Go on!" she yelled at him, her voice soft and edgeless against the hissing of the rain.

The dog stopped barking and started to snarl, bending its legs as if preparing to spring at her.

She let fly with the stone and it struck him on the bridge of the nose. The animal spun around in fear and panic and then resumed its barking, but even higher pitched now, frenzied, terrified.

She bent down and picked up another stone. Heavier this time, more jagged. She let loose again and it bounced off his back.

That was enough. The dog wailed miserably and ran off into the night.

She was now alone with the dead man.

He did not look to be a heavy man, but he was tall and gangly. She stood silently in the lashing rain, trying to work out the best way to carry him to the car.

Most important, she would have to do it in a way that did not involve seeing his face or, rather, the place on his body where his face had been. That would break her nerve, she knew.

Taking a deep breath, she plunged. She dug her hands deeply into the armpits and pulled him up off the road and hoisted him up on her back, his legs sticking out in front of her, his arms and head hanging drunkenly over her shoulder.

A river of rainwater and, she could only assume, blood and particles of flesh from the open wound that had been his face went cascading down her back.

He felt like the weight of the world.

She staggered back to the car, carrying her cross inch by tortured inch. Every nerve screamed and every muscle seemed on the point of raveling. The ring now felt like it had eaten through the flesh of her finger and welded itself onto the bone.

She reached the car door and let her burden drop heavily to the ground. The body slumped upright against the driver's door and she saw the face, plainly enough. She flinched away and wept. She wept in fear, she wept from exhaustion, and she wept from pain.

Her fingers now numb from cold and exertion, she clumsily hooked the passenger door open and steeled herself. Now would come the hardest part.

She had to look at the face as she hoisted the body into the back seat of the car.

She gripped the heels of his worn brown leather shoes and bent his legs so that he would fit on the narrow seat. The knees popped like cracking eggs.

She slammed the door shut and laid her head against the roof of the car, breathing deeply and trying to find a moment's calm.

Then she heard it. Low and insistent under the constant sibilance of the rainfall against the road; growling.

She turned and there, standing defiant in the harsh headlamps, was the dog.

It was, if anything, even scrawnier and more waterlogged, but by sheer force of rage the hairs on its back stood upward as it growled so ferociously its whole body seemed to tremble.

It stared at her, pure hatred in its golden eyes.

Etain's feelings toward the dog had not been mellowed by her ordeal. Now, as she searched for a stone, it was only for want of a brick. She would quite happily kill this dog, and sleep soundly every night after.

A shadow moved behind the dog.

It stepped into the light.

It was not a wolf, it could not be a wolf.

The last wolf in Ireland had been killed in 1786. In Carlow.

What a useful time to remember that little nugget of school trivia, she thought to herself bitterly.

The thing in front of her must simply be a farmer's dog. A mastiff or something similar.

It was impossible to believe that the tiny, growling thing in front of her and this monster could be of the same species.

The larger animal stared at her, placidly, almost bored.

And then suddenly, its face contorted. The ears flattened, the muzzle separated, a fire was lit behind the eyes, and it seemed the creature's face was all angles and teeth. The growl that emerged from the beast was like a pneumatic drill; it shook her to her bones.

And now there were more of them. Dogs emerging from the shadows at all sides. Border collies and terriers. Spaniels and hounds. All advancing, hackles raised, teeth bared. There were dozens of them.

It must be a dream, she thought. *Only a dream. I am not here.*

And, as in a dream, her limbs moved of their own volition. As the great wolf-beast arched its back and leapt forward, her hand shot out for the handle of the car door, pulled it open, and slammed it into the creature's face. She flung herself into the driver's seat and yanked the door closed behind her.

There was a second's calm, and then the car window became a portrait of mad yellow eyes, fangs, and teeth as the hound leapt at the door, trying to batter its way through. It was inches away from her face and she could almost feel its teeth meeting in her neck. She screamed as a shape lunged at her from out of the corner of her eye—the fucking awful little terrier had leapt onto the hood and was screaming at her through the windshield. Not barking, *screaming.* The car was shaking and she could hear the clicking of claws over the roof. They had surrounded the car, swarming over it like a pack of jackals devouring a carcass.

She told herself that she was safe. The car was metal and glass, they were only flesh and bone. They couldn't break through.

The terrier smashed its skull against the windshield, leaving a spiderweb of small white cracks against which blood ran before being washed away by the torrential rain.

Something snapped in Etain, some trance was broken. She turned the key in the ignition, slammed her foot on the accelerator, and screamed in defiance and hate and terror.

The wheels spun on the rain-slick tarmac and then the car lurched forward.

She heard the shrieking, hollering of dogs and the sound of bones snapping like wet bamboo. The car rolled over bodies and she could feel them bursting and pulping through the accelerator.

In the rearview mirror, she could see, just over the hump of the corpse's gut, a frenzied swarm of canine bodies chasing after the car like a black river of eyes and fur and glinting teeth.

At last they broke off pursuit and she watched as they gradually shrank into a tiny, irregular, hateful shape in the distance.

She drove on.

She was dimly aware of the pain in her finger, but now almost all sensation had drained away.

She felt eerily calm. Dead calm.

The only sound now was the low hum of the engine and gentle thrum of rain on the roof and windshield.

A voice from the back seat quietly told her to keep driving.

She nodded gently, as if asleep.

She drove on.

The farmhouse was sick.

Everywhere it showed signs of decay and rot. The timber of the roof was shot through with woodworm, the mortar between the old red brick crumbled at the touch. Cracks in the windows had been mended with masking tape. It had originally been a pauper's cottage from before the Famine, a tiny two-room hovel. Over the decades it had been enlarged with cheap and indifferently executed extensions, expanding its borders outward into the thick, lush greenery that surrounded it. The low forms of life, weeds and vermin, had worked assiduously to reverse this encroachment and the house now seemed to teeter on collapse, held up by a few steel braces and the will of its owners.

Feidhlim Lowney stood in the kitchen of the farmhouse and stared out the window. He watched as the torrential rain slowly filled up a steel bucket in the front yard that his wife used to feed the chickens.

He waited as the bubbling lip of water rose higher and higher, and yet the cathartic moment where it finally overflowed never came.

He felt trapped in this moment.

He would always be standing here by the window, waiting for the bucket to overflow.

Waiting for the guest who must be made welcome.

The kitchen was bathed in the light from a fluorescent strip that was at once too harsh to look at and too weak to fully alleviate the moist, jungle-like gloom of the kitchen.

His wife, Bernadette, sat rigidly at the kitchen table, playing solitaire.

She always played solitaire.

She had not said a word to him all day. He wondered if she hated him for what was going to happen. Or perhaps she was simply indifferent to him.

He realized with a pang of regret that if they were a different kind of couple, he might know these things. He might know if the stony silence, broken only by the plastic kiss of the cards being laid on the shiny PVC tablecloth, was indicative of hatred or resentment or simply a lack of anything to say on the part of his wife. But they were not that kind of couple. Bernadette's emotions were simply a language he had never had the ear to learn.

He gazed out again at the flooding farmyard. In the window he could see his reflection, a man who looked less like a farmer than an itinerant preacher. His beard was long and scraggly, the color of wet ash. His face was gaunt to the point of emaciation, and his eyes had the mad look of a man who has been touched by God or the bottle. He made people nervous, Feidhlim knew. But he was neither a mystic nor a drunk.

Feidhlim Lowney was, at heart, as pragmatic and coldly rational as any animal caught in a trap.

Since he had inherited the farm thirteen years ago from his mother he had been stalked. By debt, by bad weather, by waves of disease and still-births that had afflicted his livestock with a merciless, clockwork regularity. And by the hatred of his neighbors, who had ostracized his family in the last century for some long-forgotten sin by his great-grandfather. It didn't matter that neither Feidhlim nor his neighbors could remember the details of his great-grandfather's transgression. Memory was ephemeral. Hatred was a rock.

Tonight's transaction was not a choice, he told himself. He was not choosing to take this terrible risk.

An animal in a trap does not *choose* to gnaw its own leg off.

It does it because it has no choice left.

And if he was not doing it of his own free will, then it could not be sin.

The lights of a car appeared at the gate, hazy and fractured in the pouring rain.

In the farmyard, the bucket overflowed.

* * *

The knock on the door was quiet and languid. It was not the rapid staccato of someone seeking entry in the pouring rain, it sounded like a tree branch striking the glass at random. There was no rhythm to it.

Feidhlim felt sweat forming on his brow, a sick dryness in his mouth, and a white-hot burning in his stomach. He suddenly realized he was not ready for what was coming through that door. *Why am I doing this?* he asked himself.

Bernadette shuffled the cards and lit a cigarette.

She wasn't afraid, he realized. She had no fear at all.

She adjusted the large silver band on her left hand and idly tapped the dead gray crown of her cigarette into the ashtray.

"You'd better answer that," she said, as if addressing the smoldering ash.

When he had been a young man living in Birmingham in the '50s, homesick and lonely, Feidhlim had lost his virginity to a prostitute. She had been a Scottish woman, much older than him and bitterly unhappy in her work, and the whole experience had been as distressing and miserable an ushering into sexual awakening as could be imagined.

The memory that stuck with him of that night was of waiting in the dimly lit hallway of her flat in Druid's Heath, trying to work up the courage to knock on her door.

He remembered the fear, a terrible acid-tasting panic that felt as if it was seeping from his stomach into every vein and artery, fizzing his senses and making his thoughts unmoored and skittish.

An overwhelming dread, a sensation that he was about to cross some terrible threshold.

As he stepped into his own hallway, far, far away from Druid's Heath, and saw a figure looming through the frosted glass, he felt that same fear returning now.

Far stronger now, and older, and cruel with age.

You are about to do a terrible thing, he told himself.

The Lowneys had been on the land long enough to know that there were ways to arrange transactions. But what Feidhlim had in mind was far beyond anything his ancestors would ever have dared. He had driven as far as the outskirts of Dublin and left notes wedged in electricity pylons. He had stayed awake in the kitchen until the pale hours tuning his radio to the far edges of the band, listening for whispered offers in the static. Until at last, he had received the call from the Man in Dublin. He did not know his name, of course, and never would.

He then had to tell Bernadette what the terms of the deal were and was both stunned and horrified when she had agreed. He had expected . . . what had he expected?

He had expected her to hit him. And then stalk out of the house never to return.

She had simply stared at him across the kitchen table, given a sigh of barely concealed contempt, and said: "When?"

"Sometime in the winter," he had mumbled in response.

She nodded, as if that did not disrupt her schedule.

Things had moved fast then.

The next night they had knelt in front of the television and professed fealty to the Station.

The rings had arrived in the post in blank envelopes, delivered by someone who was seen by no one. Large silver things, bulky and intricately detailed. They both wore them now, at all times.

Symbols of allegiance. Badges of ownership.

All this had occurred without speaking with another human being face-to-face.

Now there was someone outside the door. It was about to become real in a way that it hadn't been before. He wondered what kind of person could do this.

Someone like you?

Not like me, he thought. *I'm not doing this by choice.*

He took a sharp breath and pulled the door open.

He did not know what he had expected. It was not the thin, shivering, bespectacled girl, barely out of her teens, who stood swaying unevenly in his doorway, on the very brink of collapse. Her long brown hair was plastered to her face and her glasses were fogged to the point that she must be almost blind.

"He's . . ." she said, her teeth chattering as she spoke, ". . . he's . . . he's . . . in the back. Please help."

Her legs gave out from under her and he caught her. Gently, he laid her down on her back on the hall carpet. He looked at her, unsure of what to do.

Grimly, he noted the silver ring on her finger, a crimson snail trail of blood seeping from where it met her skin.

What was her story, he wondered. How did she come to be entangled in tonight's work?

And what to do with her?

The Groom was the priority, certainly. But it would be much harder to bring him into the house with the girl lying there.

Carefully, gingerly, he turned her over on her back, took hold of her by her oxters, and slowly dragged her through the kitchen.

Bernadette did not even look up, but continued laying down cards as her husband struggled to manhandle an unconscious twenty-two-year-old woman into their spare bedroom.

He laid her on top of the duvet. She was so still he had to lean over and put his ear over her mouth to catch her faint, rasping breath.

Her clothes were soaked through. Should he . . . change her? Put her in pajamas?

He shut that line of thought down, thoroughly and forcefully. *No. Let Bernadette deal with her. You have enough on your plate.*

The fear of what was going to happen now, and what had yet to be done, returned like an old wound.

He took a deep breath, and walked out through the kitchen, past his wife who only had eyes for the Jack of Hearts, out the hall and into the gnashing teeth of the storm.

She had left the driver's door open. He reached in and unlocked the rear passenger door. The weak light from the open hall door unveiled the back seat for him and he was heartily sick.

Jesus Christ. He had been warned that this would be an ugly business, but obviously not enough.

He was a farmer, and had been for most of his life. And it was not a line of work for anyone with a weak stomach. He had seen eyeless sheep picked at by crows, men gored by bulls and trampled by cattle. He had seen calves emerging screaming into the world twisted like rope, ready to begin three-second lives of agony.

But the thing in the back of the girl's car, the violence that had been visited upon it, the dull *gleam* of light on the naked skull . . .

He was sick again, the bile hitting the ground and instantly being swept away by the torrential downpour.

He turned his face upward, as if hoping the deluge would wash him clean. He closed his eyes and took a deep breath. He took every ounce of hatred and anger and resentment and terror inside him and mustered it all into the act of grabbing the loathsome thing by the lapels of its shirt and dragging it, stinking and dripping, out of the back seat, through the front door, slowly, slowly up the hallway.

Bernadette did, for once, briefly look up as Feidhlim came backward through the kitchen door, snarling like an animal with the effort, swabbing a thick trail of muck and rainwater and blood behind him as he dragged the carcass into their bedroom.

He flung it furiously down at the end of the bed and reemerged into the kitchen.

Without a word he went to the sink and began washing his hands. He could have sworn he heard a brief, sharp exhalation of amusement and mockery from his wife as he washed them. His ring finger was starting to ache. He felt like he was driving with an empty tank of petrol. He was still moving forward, but on borrowed time only. Any second now, he was going to grind to a halt as the reality of what was about to happen became concrete in his mind.

He knew, intellectually, that this was It.

But there is knowing, and there is understanding.

He sat down at the table across from her, unable to meet her gaze.

There was a silence so thick, you could hear the paper clinging to the walls.

Bernadette casually lit another cigarette.

"Who's your one?" she said, indicating the guest room.

"Dunno," he mumbled. "One of theirs. She has the . . ."

He gestured to the ring on his finger.

"She's young," his wife noted.

"Yeah," said Feidhlim. "She is, yeah."

Bernadette simply stared at him, as if there was more to be said.

"So?" he said.

"So," she said. "Seems a bit of a waste."

There was a long silence.

"A waste," he said at last.

"What are we getting?" she inquired.

It took him a few moments to realize what she was asking.

"A new Packo. Fifty Moiled. No sickness for the next five years. And some money to fix up the house . . ."

She took a drag from her cigarette.

"What about that field?" she asked.

She'd lost him.

"What field?" he said.

"That field you were talking about, the other day. Dan Hegarty's."

The "other day" had been almost three months ago. He'd wistfully mentioned to her what he could do with Dan Hegarty's field if he had the money. But he might as well have been talking about his plans for a lunar colony. Hegarty was selling to no one, and if he had been, Feidhlim was broke, and even if he wasn't, Hegarty would salt the field before he'd sell it to a Lowney. The Jews and Arabs could hold a grudge well enough, but compared to the Lowneys and Hegartys they were rank amateurs.

"Ask him," she said. "Ask him for the field. Two instead of one."

He had thought that dragging the body from the car had been terrifying. But the casual way she said those words. Hearing that? Now *there* was fear. There was fear that washed the nerves to their tips.

"Ask him," she said again. It was more than a command. It was an ultimatum. Do it, or it's all off.

She would suffer anything, but not alone.

The Groom had arrived and was lying on the Lowneys' marriage bed, his lipless mouth grinning at the ceiling.

It was time to call the Man in Dublin.

Feidhlim's finger trembled as he tried to find the right numbers in the dial. Once he'd entered the last digit, there was a silence that felt too long before the dialing tone began its low, metallic song. Part of him hoped that there would be no answer, even as he realized that the terror and uncertainty that would bring would be far worse.

Without instruction, this night might never end.

The tone was cut off cleanly and a heavy, jagged breath billowed up from the earpiece.

"What time do you call this?" said a voice.

The voice had a Dublin accent as thick as tar, deep as a well filled with old plastic bags and empty cans. It sounded like cigarette smoke and varnish and stout the color of old rivers. Phlegm and gravel.

Feidhlim realized he had forgotten what he was supposed to say.

The voice repeated the question.

"What time do you call this?"

In a panicky white flash, Feidhlim remembered.

"Six nine," he said. "No, shite! Nine six. Sorry. Nine six."

There was an exhalation at the other end of the line, the kind of weary sigh given by an old professional who has been forced to work with a bumbling amateur.

"Fine. You clear what you have to do, yeah?"

Feidhlim nodded.

"Yeah. We know, yeah."

"You sound jittery."

Feidhlim said nothing. Denial would sound false, admission would be weakness. So he said nothing.

"Just think about your lovely cows," said the voice, not even bothering to mask its mockery.

Fuck you, Feidhlim thought savagely.

He sensed movement behind him and twisted around like a startled rabbit.

Bernadette stood silhouetted in the light from the kitchen, watching him silently. He could feel her gaze on his forehead.

"There's something else," Feidhlim muttered.

"Oh?"

"The driver. She's a girl. Young, like."

"Is that right?"

"Yeah."

"Where's she now?"

"In the guest room."

"Awake?"

"No. No, she's dead to the world."

"Leave her. She'll wander off in the morning. Won't remember a thing."

"But . . ." Feidhlim tried to piece together a sentence. ". . . Well, we were thinking, what about her as well?"

There was a long pause.

"Ahhhh," said the Man in Dublin. The tone was warm and friendly, and Feidhlim was not fooled for so much as a second. *"Two for the price of one, you mean?"*

"No," said Feidhlim, finding a little steel. "Two for the price of two. We'd want more. There's a field . . ."

"Of course there's a fucking field," the Man in Dublin growled, as if to himself.

Feidhlim pressed on.

"What do you think? We can do it. With the girl, too. But you'd have to clear it with them. I'd need your word, that we'd get the field . . ."

"Oh, you're very fucking clever, aren't you?" the Man in Dublin said in a tone that could cut inches off a man. *"Very fucking clever. Do you know who else was fucking clever? He's lying on your bed right now. Trust me, try being stupid. It'll suit you and you'll live longer. Don't try to be fucking clever, don't get greedy, and do what you're fucking told. Cunt."*

There was a crack, and the line went dead.

Humiliated, he struggled to meet his wife's gaze.

"He says no," Feidhlim mumbled.

Bernadette calmly pulled on her cigarette. Her face was briefly illuminated, but nothing was revealed. There was no expression.

"Ask them," she said simply.

He shook his head vehemently. A line had to be drawn.

"I can't do that," he said.

"Why not?" she whispered.

Because even the thought of it makes me want to take a knife to my wrist, he thought.

Instead, he asked.

"Why? Why does she have to do it?"

"Why do I?" she asked him. "Why do you only care if *she* has to?"

"We agreed to this," he said. "We made a choice."

"No, we didn't," she replied. "We never had a choice. Losing the farm is not a choice. Wandering the road is not a choice. Dying poor and cold and hungry is not a choice. I'm never doing this again, Feidhlim. So we are getting everything we can."

The television sat innocently on a dresser at the end of their bed. It was a small, fat, black-and-white set that he had bought secondhand in the pub eight years ago.

Feidhlim stood staring at it in a cold sweat.

Turning it on meant turning his back on the corpse on the bed. That was fine.

Better to turn his back to the corpse than to the television.

Feidhlim knelt down in front of the screen and pressed the On switch.

He briefly considered saying a prayer, and then dismissed the idea as ludicrous.

Like putting on sunscreen before stepping into a furnace.

He pressed the switch and the screen was suddenly aflame with white static.

Behind him, he heard the faintest rustle of sheets. A mere twitch in cotton.

He ignored it and focused all his attention on the screen.

He reached for the dial and turned it eight notches to the left.

Now he had to wait.

The white visual noise now seemed, if it was possible, even more chaotic than before. He recalled something he'd learned from a Dane he'd once worked with on a building site.

In Denmark, they call the static "myrekrig," he remembered. *A war of ants.*

The static was swarming, eating at the edges of the screen, dissolving and bleeding into the air.

He couldn't say how long the figure had been standing there, watching him.

It was in the corner of the screen, a little cluster of ants. He could vaguely make out a head, and shoulders. But it was like looking at a copy of a copy of an old photograph of a ghost in mist. Several removes from something obscured that might not even be there in the first place.

But it was there. Feidhlim knew it was there.

"We're almost ready to begin," he whispered.

The figure nodded, languidly, like a monarch listening to a minor piece of court gossip.

Feidhlim remembered the warning of the Man in Dublin, but pressed on.

"I want Dan Hegarty's field," he said.

The figure in the corner of the television suddenly froze and its outlines became horribly sharp.

Feidhlim shut his eyes to keep the image out.

"For the girl." He whined in pain. "Dan Hegarty's field for the girl too."

He opened his eyes. The figure in the corner had once again half melted away into the furious *myrekrig,* the never-ending war of ants that had raged since the dawn of time.

It nodded.

Feidhlim awoke on the floor of his bedroom in a cold sweat and with a feeling of disease in his skin. The corpse still lay on his bed.

The television was still on, showing nothing in particular.

He let out a long, shuddering breath like a death rattle.

Now, the worst began.

I have never felt so good in my life, Etain thought to herself.

She was lying in bed under clean, dry sheets. The farmer's wife (for he must be a farmer, and she must be his wife) had showered her and dressed her in soft white pajamas. She had tucked her into bed and laid a cool, gentle hand on her brow to make sure she wasn't feverish. And then she had closed the door, leaving her in a silence as soft and restful as the blankets and the pajamas and the pleasant numbness that had spread from her ring finger to the rest of her body.

Everything is fine. Everything is fine.

Idly, she glanced around the room. The wallpaper was white with blue flecks. There was a sturdy wooden dresser at the end of the bed, and a tiny faded portrait of some saint or other watched over the room with the indifferent gaze of a bored guard on traffic patrol. It was clean and warm and featureless. She leaned back on the pillow and gave a deep, relieved sigh.

Her mind felt curiously abandoned. Normally she was a walking cacophony of worries and reminders and inner recriminations. A song her mother had taught her early on that she had never been able to get out of her head. But now, there was only peace.

To her left, a small window looked out onto the farmyard. She dimly remembered being carried in.

It had been raining then, and the window had been a black square shaking with the relentless patter of the downpour. Now the clouds had parted and the farmyard stood sculpted in tarnished silver from the light of a great, shining, waxing gibbous moon.

What a beautiful moon. So bright. I see the moon and the moon sees me. God bless the moon. And God bless me.

The old lullaby swum gently in her head, round and round. She smiled.

A brief, fleeting, and thoroughly unwelcome thought flashed through her mind, telling her to take the ring off.

It died, quickly, silently, and un-mourned.

She couldn't take the ring off. She was getting married. And besides, it fit perfectly now. It fit perfectly. It was perfect. Everything was perfect.

She dozed, and awoke to hear a sound coming from the next room. It was not a loud sound, and her first impulse was simply to ignore it and drift back into a warm, soft, dreamless sleep. But, although quiet, there was something about the sound that cut into the fugue. It was a harsh, metallic sound. High pitched and coppery. Rhythmic.

She remembered Barry on top of her and halfway through her on the old settle bed in her aunt's house, the springs complaining loudly in their high-pitched voices.

It was the sound of bed springs, she could hear now. And once she had realized that, she could hear another sound, lower and deeper, lurking below the screech of the springs.

A woman's voice, breathing harshly. Grunting, hard and angry. The sound of someone pushing themselves through tough, unpleasant work.

The farmer wants a wife. The farmer wants a wife. Eee-eye-eee-eye the farmer wants a wife.

She lay there in bed, innocently listening to the sounds of the farmer and his wife making love through the thin walls.

Once, perhaps, she would have been embarrassed and ashamed. But she was a mature woman of the world, now. There was something reassuring about it.

Nothing wrong with it. Most natural thing in the world.

It had been an awful night. But everything had turned out all right in the end. Briefly, very briefly, she wondered what had happened to that poor man she had found on the road. The farmer and his wife must have called someone to take the body away. An ambulance, maybe. Or the Gardaí. Whatever. It had been taken care of. It was over. She was warm and safe. Everything was fine.

She turned her head and gazed out the window at the farmyard, bathed in the light of the bone-white moon.

The farmer stood in the farmyard, black as coal against the moonlight, smoking a cigarette and staring at nothing.

She was dimly aware that there was something wrong about that. But the thought could not find its way in, and ran off.

Through the wall, only silence now.

The house was still.

Etain slept.

She awoke, or rather half woke, in total darkness.

The curtains had been pulled, and the room was now pitch black.

Something was moving at the foot of the bed. She thought that she could make out the shadow of a man moving some large weight near the back wall. The floorboards were creaking quietly and she could hear heavy breathing.

Etain was not afraid. This was not her room, after all. If there was someone here in the dead of night, they surely had a right to be there.

Everything was fine.

Something was . . . lain down. There was silence. And then footsteps. The creak of the door. The footsteps returned, heavy again, laden down.

The shape in the darkness set his weight down on the dresser at the end of the bed. Simply from the way it rested on the dresser's surface, the sound of glass and plastic and an indescribable whisper from inactive electronics, she knew that it was a television set. There was something about a television that just sounded different when it was moved. It was a different kind of weight.

She heard the metallic scrape of the teeth of the plug biting into the socket and then a click.

Suddenly the room was bathed in white light as the television became a white-hot sun in the center of the room.

She instinctively closed her eyes against the glare but before she did she saw the farmer standing beside the television and staring at her, his hand still resting on the dial.

There was a second man, lying at the foot of the bed.

His face was too far out of the light of the television to be seen. He was wearing a checked flannel blazer and old brown shoes. His hands were large and the nails filthy.

She felt that she should know this person, and that it was strange that he was lying at the foot of her bed. But she couldn't think why.

Without a word, the farmer turned and left her, closing the door firmly behind him.

There was nothing showing on the screen, just a waterfall of never-ending static.

The screen was too bright, and the noise of the static was harsh and irritating. The happy warmth that had settled on her was now evaporating and the pain in her ring finger was back. She felt queasy and angry. She didn't want to be here anymore. She had almost reached the point of getting out of bed and trying to find her clothes when the roar of the static suddenly ceased. In its place came something more than silence.

If the television had simply fallen silent, there would have been other noises to replace it. The creaks and tiny shudders of an old house. The secret midnight whispers of the countryside. Her own breath and heartbeat.

But the static fell away and suddenly there was nothing. A void of sound. A deafness upon the universe.

There was a stirring at the foot of the bed but she did not care. Her eyes were on the screen, locked.

On the screen was a room.

She knew that room. It was reassuringly familiar. A room that she had spent many an afternoon of her childhood watching. Bare white walls, and the only things of note in the room were a long black box and a red door.

Puckeen *shouldn't be on this late,* she thought to herself. *It's for little children.*

Noiselessly, onscreen, the red door opened. The image was in black-and-white of course, but she had seen the show enough times in color to know that the door was red. A brilliant, fiery red. In a program that had always seemed strangely averse to color for a children's show, the Magic Red Door had always stood out.

A man dressed in a Pierrot costume stepped through the door.

He might have been the same man who Etain had seen instructing young Tom Pygott on the mysteries of the square a thousand years ago. Or he might have been someone completely different. His face seemed almost designed to thwart memory. There were no distinguishing features at all. His face was as bland and soft as snow, with nothing for the mind to hook on to. He walked closer and closer to the screen and peered out.

Etain realized that he was looking at her. When he saw her, he raised his hand and gave a half-hearted little wave and a smile that was a slight raising of the ends of the mouth and absolutely nothing more.

Satisfied, he turned and walked toward the box.

Standing beside it, he leaned over and knocked twice on the lid.

Knock. Knock.

She heard the knocks. But not with her ears. She felt them against the inside of her skull.

He briskly turned and made for the Magic Red Door. He opened it and was gone.

There was a perfect stillness.

And then, with the awful slowness of a landslide, the top of the box began to stir.

Puckeen is coming out of his box, she told herself as if it was a joke.

But Puckeen never comes out of his box.

. . .

I would like very much to go home.

She was suddenly very, very aware that she could not move.

She had not been able to move for some time now but it had not been a problem before.

She wanted to move before she saw what came out of the box.

The box was open and it was rising. Before she had even seen the first inch of the tip of a horn she could feel her blood boiling in her head, rivulets pouring out of her nose, and a taste of rancid chicken on her tongue . . .

A sharp bite on her finger and suddenly everything was fine again everything was fine.

As if on a string she jerked her head away from the television to where the Groom now stood beside her bed, bathed in the white light from the screen.

He gazed down upon her with lidless eyes, and he smiled so ecstatically at her for there were no lips to mask his joy.

He looked magnificent.

SEPTEMBER 1999

The Belfield campus of University College Dublin had been built in the late '60s and early '70s, evidently as an ode to the beauty and grace of the concrete cinderblock. Every structure was huge and gray and weirdly shaped, and new arrivals to the university felt like they had landed on a world built for creatures very different from themselves. But it was a sunny day, the grass around the lake was green and perfect for sitting with a book, and the lake was filled with ducks and geese who enjoyed human company as long as it came with a free crust of bread.

For Betty Fitzpatrick, it was all perfect and she wouldn't have changed an inch of it.

After registering for her courses she made her way down to the freshers' tent, a massive white marquee where the university's societies had set up their stalls to entice, cajole, and hook the next generation of members. Like a woman shopping hungry, she spent far too much, and by lunchtime she had joined the Literary and Historical Society, SciFi Soc, GameSoc, FilmSoc, LitSoc, the Chess Club, the Gay Society, the UCD chapter of Amnesty International, An Cumann Gaelach, and (seemingly by accident) the Formula 1 Society. At last, laden down with plastic bags full of the T-shirts, gewgaws, and welcoming tat she had been gifted she tried to find the exit and escape the sweltering tent.

"Hey, can I talk to you for a second?" she heard a voice behind her say.

"Sorry," Betty said, "I don't really want to join any—"

"No, no, listen," the voice insisted.

Betty turned and suddenly she found that she was very interested in what this person had to say.

Her hair was jet black and shaved into a tight buzz cut. Her eyes were green and a little hard, her nose was delicate, and as for her lips, there was nothing to be said of them other than that they were painted black, and that they were flawless.

"Oh, you joined Amnesty," the girl said casually, gesturing to a yellow T-shirt poking out of one of Betty's bags. "Good for you, that's awesome. Look, I need you to do me a favor. See that bitch?"

The girl gestured behind her to where a large, bored-looking brunette in her twenties was sitting at a table under a sign that said UCD DRAMA SOCIETY and leafing through a magazine.

"Yeah, that bitch," said the girl.

Betty was pretty certain that the woman in question was in earshot, but she did not seem to notice in the slightest.

"She's been riding my arse all day about getting people to join because she's running for auditor this year and she's gone mad with power. Don't worry, I'm not trying to get you to join. But could you just talk to me for like two minutes so she thinks that I am and will get off my fucking case?"

Betty had not been listening. She did not have terribly well-developed gaydar but what little she did have was currently chiming merrily. It might just have been wishful thinking.

She did a scan.

Hair: Good sign.

Jewelry: Ambiguous.

Makeup: Bad sign.

Dress: Bad sign.

Doc Martens: Very good sign.

Result: Inconclusive. Further testing necessary.

"Join what?" Betty asked. "The drama society?"

The girl rolled her eyes.

"Don't ever call it that. Dramsoc. It's always Dramsoc. Don't join. It's a cult."

As it happened, Betty had heard of Dramsoc, even before coming to UCD. The college's drama society was quite famous, and many well-known Irish actors had made their bones there.

"Plus . . ." the girl continued, "everyone hates us because they think we're cliquey. We're not. We're just a bunch of people with a shared obsession who spend all our time locked in a basement together."

"People can be so unfair," said Betty.

"They *can*," the girl said, and her eyes flashed appreciatively at finding someone on her wavelength.

Everything about you is so beautiful in a million different ways. Every time you speak and move I see something new that takes my breath away.

"I mean, it's not all bad," the girl conceded. "It's the most active student drama society in Europe, we put on two shows every week. If you're at all interested in acting you absolutely should join. But you're not, so . . . could you just nod? Just so she thinks . . . yeah, thanks . . . love your outfit by the way, this is gorgeous . . ."

She casually laid a hand on the sleeve of Betty's top, which made Betty say:

"What about writers? Do you . . . need writers?"

The girl looked at her with newfound interest, respect, and (Betty was certain) a hint of attraction.

"You write, madam?"

"I . . . yeah, I . . ."

I write Star Trek *fan fiction and short stories. Very short stories. As in, unfinished,* Betty thought.

"Not for stage," she said. "But y'know, I've been thinking about it."

"Well then maybe you *should* join," the girl mused. "We have a new writing festival every year. It's a great way to get your stuff out there in front of an audience. You just have to be willing to join a cult."

"Why is it a cult?" Betty asked.

"Because it'll suck up every spare minute you have, you won't go to your lectures, you'll spend all your time rehearsing or acting or hanging around in the LGs with the rest of us losers. It'll eat you alive. Your whole life just becomes theater and drama."

"Aren't those the same thing?" Betty asked innocently.

"Oh, sweetie," the black lips said, and the words sounded wonderful coming from them.

That clinched it.

"How do I join?" Betty asked.

The girl with the buzz cut looked at her, surprised.

"Oh. Okay. Gemma?"

The large brunette, as if on cue, folded up her magazine and pushed a clipboard toward her. Betty put down her name, student number, mobile number, and email address, and Gemma took her two-pound membership fee and gave her a card.

"Welcome to Dramsoc," she said, as if pronouncing a sentence.

"Deadly," said the buzz-cut girl. "Come down to the LGs when you get a chance. We'll be putting up notices for auditions soon . . ."

She began rattling off dates for auditions for the Freshers' Play, which was not the same as the Freshers' Project, which in turn was not the same as the Freshers' Co-Op . . .

Betty could feel herself getting light-headed. She'd missed breakfast and the air inside the tent was starting to taste of students.

"I'll see you around," she said to the buzz-cut girl, who gave her a smile and a wave goodbye.

Betty turned to leave, stopped, and walked back to the Dramsoc table. The girl looked up at her curiously.

"You were trying to get me to join the whole time, weren't you?" Betty said quietly.

The buzz-cut girl exchanged a slightly pitying glance with Gemma and explained patiently:

"We do two plays a week. You get good at acting."

"So," said Betty, "you don't really like my outfit?"

Suddenly very serious, the buzz-cut girl stood up and took both of Betty's hands in hers.

"Bad acting is lying," she said. "Good acting is telling the truth."

Betty blushed and looked away awkwardly.

"You look a little overwhelmed," the buzz-cut girl said. "Do you want to meet up for coffee later?"

That would be the greatest thing that has ever happened to anyone ever.

"Sure," said Betty. "I'd like that."

"Cool. Meet you in Hilpers in the arts block at one?"

Betty spent around twenty minutes searching the ground floor of the John Henry Newman Building for a place called Hilpers. The closest she could find was a small café at the front entrance called Finnegan's Break. She could see the stairway heading down to the lower ground level ("the LGs" that the buzz-cut girl had mentioned) and wondered if Hilpers might be down there, although she'd never heard of a café in a basement. She was about to leave when she ran into the buzz-cut girl, who looked at her in surprise and a little disappointment.

"Shit, I'm not late, am I?" she asked. "Were you going?"

"Oh, I was just looking for Hilpers," said Betty.

"You're in Hilpers," said the buzz-cut girl with a smile.

"But the sign says . . ."

"They tried to change the name," said the buzz-cut girl, with the stony, contemptuous anger of a Tutsi woman recalling the depredations of her Hutu neighbors. "We refuse to indulge them."

They found a table near the window and the girl spotted Betty the cost of a cup of tea after she realized that she'd spent all her money on memberships.

"So, do you do a lot of acting?" Betty asked.

The girl shrugged.

"Yeah, I get cast a bit. Not as much as I'd like. The whole society's on this massive Mamet kick, which means zero good parts for women. I mean, at least when it was Beckett you might get to play a mouth on a wall or an old lady in a bin. That's one of the reasons I wanted you to join, Jesus, we need some women writers, y'know?"

Betty nodded, hoping to disguise that she only knew Beckett by name, and didn't know Mamet at all.

"So what's your course?"

"Arts. English, philosophy, and psychology."

"Cool. Yeah, most of Dramsoc's in arts, you'll fit right in."

"How about you?"

"Television production."

"Oh, you want to be, like, a TV actor?"

The girl snorted.

"Fuck no. No, I want to be a producer. I want to be a showrunner. It's why I joined Dramsoc. Directing a stage show isn't exactly like running a TV set but it's about as close as you're going to get if you're looking for hands-on experience. You know, music, lighting cues, rigging, ordering people around?"

"Have you directed any plays?" Betty asked.

"No," the girl admitted. "Haven't found the right script yet. And it's only my second year. Committee doesn't really like freshers directing. I'm definitely going to try my hand this year though."

I will write you a script. Just you wait.

"So you want to work in TV? Like *Glenroe* or . . ."

"Children's TV," the girl said without a moment's hesitation.

"Really?"

"What?"

"You don't seem . . ."

"What?"

"Nothing. Sorry."

Children's television, for Betty at least, conjured images of *Puckeen* and *Sooty and Sweep*. Safe. Motherly. Painfully dull. Utterly square.

"So how about you?" said the girl.

"Oh, well . . ." Betty mumbled.

"Three things about yourself."

"What?"

"It's a trick we use to break the ice when we start rehearsal. Tell me three things about yourself in the order they come to you."

"My mind's gone blank."

"One."

"I . . . live in Harold's Cross . . ."

"Two."

"I'm a big science fiction fan."

"Three."

"I really want a tattoo but I keep chickening out."

"Only live once. Three."

"I already gave you three!"

"You gave me two and an address, one was boring, give me another."

Betty took a deep breath.

"I'm gay," she said.

"Uh-huh," said the girl, as if she had just mentioned the weather. Then she noticed Betty's expression.

"Oh. Oh shit, I'm the first person you've told that to, amn't I?"

Betty nodded.

"Yeah. I mean . . . yeah. I'm pretty sure the guy at the Gay Soc table got it by inference but . . . yeah. You're the first person I actually said it to. With words."

Of course, there were others who knew. Síofra Ní Caomhánach, for instance, who had asked her behind the bike sheds in her last year of school. They had kissed for three of the most wonderful seconds of Betty's life, before Síofra had roughly flung her back onto the pebbledash wall and run off hollering: "She is! She is! Total lezzer!"

It had been, if nothing else, a memorable first kiss.

The girl breathed out slowly.

"Give me the line again," she said.

"It's fine."

"No, it's not. Tell me again."

Betty took another breath. Weirdly, it was almost as hard the second time.

"I'm gay," she said.

The girl put her hand on Betty's.

"That's wonderful," she said, with quiet sincerity. "I am so happy for you. And I feel incredibly proud and grateful that you felt you could share that with me."

"Thank you," said Betty.

"Closer to what you were hoping for?"

"You pretty much nailed it, yeah."

Oh please, please be gay. Or bi. I can work with bi.

"Can I ask you something?" said the girl.

"Sure."

"When did you know?"

"When I was fifteen. Roxanne Dawson."

"Who?"

"She's an actress," said Betty. "In *Star Trek*."

"Ah," said the girl. "Not really a sci-fi fan."

Oof. Break my heart, why don't you?

"And you were sure? Like, was it a sudden . . ."

"Oh yeah," said Betty. "Not a doubt."

"Huh," said the girl quietly to herself.

Betty felt hope stirring cautiously within her.

"Why? Are you . . ."

"Me?" said the girl with a snort. "Fuck. You want to know what I am?"

She took a large silver pound coin from her purse and spun it on the table. Betty watched it spinning elegantly between a teaspoon and the sugar bowl, the harp and stag dancing round and round each other.

"That's me. Just spinning around, wondering what side I'm going to land on," said the girl. "I have no fucking clue what I am. It's like, I see a cute guy and I'm like 'yeah, okay' and I see a cute girl and I'm like 'yeah, okay.' But never really any better than 'okay,' y'know? It's like, I'm settling for guys and girls while I'm waiting for something better to come along."

The coin had now rolled onto its side and was hula-hooping on the table. The girl placed her hand on it and put it back in her purse.

Betty noticed that she hadn't bothered to check whether it had come up stag or harp.

They chatted for a long time, until the girl said that she should probably head back to the freshers' tent. They said goodbye at the entrance to Hilpers, and she made Betty promise that she'd come down to the LGs to audition for the first crop of plays.

"It was great meeting you . . . Shit, I never asked you your name," said the girl.

"Betty Fitzpatrick."

"Betty?"

"What?"

"Nothing. You just don't look like a Betty."

Betty chose to take that as a compliment.

"How about you?"

"Oh, I look like a Sinead," said the girl, pointing to her hair.

Betty groaned and the girl stuck out her tongue, cheekily. It was pierced.

Oh Jesus Christ, come on.

Pushing some rather ribald thoughts aside, Betty asked again.

"What's your name, smartarse?"

The girl smiled.

"Ashling Mallen," she said softly. "Call me Ash. That's an order."

And with that she turned and headed down the steps to the LGs, and was gone.

Oh, I'm going to fall for you, Betty thought to herself wearily. *Fuck. I'm already in the air, plummeting down the side of the building.*

NOVEMBER 1979

On the night of Saturday the third of November, Feidhlim Lowney was hit by a sudden and jagged certainty that both women were dead and that he would soon join them. He had been staring at the two doors, the one leading to his bedroom and the other to the guest room, for three days, waiting for someone to emerge.

When the realization came that he was the only living thing in the house, he sat hunched on the sofa, cradling his knees in a cold sweat and weeping. He gave a long, anguished scream, a howl of fear and grief loud enough to shake the house's sodden, half-rotted timbers.

The doors did not open.

He awoke at noon to the sound of a knocking on the door.

He shambled, barely awake, down the hall and threw the door open with the force of someone not wholly in control of their body.

A tiny, elderly woman flinched at the suddenness of the opening, and at the gaunt figure with heavy, bloodshot eyes, face pale as death, and the hair of a wild man.

"Good morning, Feidhlim," she said, recovering her composure with a bright little smile.

"Good morning, Rita," he lied.

"New car?"

"What?" Feidhlim grunted. "No?"

He craned his head out to see where she was looking.

The girl's tiny blue car sat innocently in his driveway. He cursed inwardly at his own stupidity. How the hell was he going to get rid of that? At least the old woman hadn't gotten close enough to the car to peer inside, and see the great black grin of filth and blood on the back seat.

"Oh, no . . ." he mumbled. "We had a guest. That's her car."

"Oh, a guest," the elder said brightly. She was the kind of old woman who could find entertainment in the most banal little bits of information.

"That's right," Feidhlim said.

The old woman nodded, as if expecting more data.

"She's just . . . family," he said.

"Oh, yours or Bernadette's?" she asked.

"I don't know," he snapped irritably.

Fool. Bloody fool. Why don't you just fucking confess now?

"I mean," he said, desperately trying to limit the damage, "niece. She's Bernadette's niece."

Bernadette had no brothers or sisters. And he was sure Rita knew that.

An unmistakable cloud of confusion and suspicion passed over her face.

But when she spoke, she was all sunshine.

"Well, I brought you the missalette, Feidhlim," she said brightly.

She was holding out a thin booklet printed on orange paper. It took a few seconds for him to realize what it was.

Rita Hall, seventy-nine, attended Mass every morning in the local church. On Sundays she kept a mental tally of the entire congregation. If there was an absence, she took it upon herself to personally deliver the day's missalette to the home of the errant congregant so that they could see for themselves what they had been missing out on. Feidhlim had always found it an insufferable habit, but had never said so. Rita was one of the few of his neighbors who he was on good enough terms with to borrow milk or sugar, and he couldn't risk offending her.

"Thanks, Rita," he mumbled, and reached to take it.

Her gaze fell on the ring and her eyes widened. She tried to mask it and keep her face neutral but with a sickening lurch in his stomach he realized that she knew what it was. Somehow, she knew.

Without a word he snatched the missalette from her and shut the door. Before it closed, he saw her face through the vanishing gap and saw her mask slip, to be replaced with horror, disgust, and an almost feral look of loathing.

Traitor!

Panicking now, he flattened himself against the wall and peered through the blinds to see if she was still outside. She was hurrying down the path toward the main road, the jerky little gait of an elderly woman who would be sprinting if only age and rheumatism would allow it.

And then she was gone.

He took a deep breath and tried to calm himself.

She doesn't know. She can't know. I only imagined it.

No, I didn't.

All right. Well, maybe she knows. But so what? What can she do? Who can she tell?

It was only afterward that he realized that she had not turned right at the gate, which she would have if she had been going home. Rita Hall had turned left, back the way she came.

Back toward the church.

He slept well that night. It was not that his fears had been alleviated. It was that they had become so immovable and solid in his mind that he no longer had the nervous energy that required hope to feed it. He was a dead man. He was worse than a dead man.

Death, he now had no doubt, would not be the end of his terrors but merely the prelude.

And so he slept.

At around six o'clock on the morning of November fifth, the door to the Lowneys' bedroom opened.

Bernadette Lowney walked into the living room, dressed in her blue nightgown and slippers.

She paused a moment to look down at Feidhlim, sound asleep on the sofa, and then went into the kitchen.

Despite not having eaten for almost a week, she did not feel hungry. She picked up her pack of cigarettes and lighter where she had left them on the kitchen table and walked out into the pale blue morning.

With a lit cigarette clamped in her right hand she made the walk down to the hill on the far end of the Lowneys' farm, where one could get a good view of Dan Hegarty's field.

It looked so small from this distance. Terribly small for the price.

But Bernadette refused to allow herself the luxury of regret.

Before she had become a Lowney, she had been a Keane, an old Connemara family well used to scraping a living off bare rock. Nor were they strangers to making deals of flesh and land with Na Daoine Maithe, the Good People, a name utterly wrong in every particular.

Her family were survivors. They did what needed to be done.

She pulled on her cigarette and watched the smoke rise in the periwinkle murk of the early-morning mist.

Her thoughts turned to the girl.

She wondered how Feidhlim had gotten rid of her.

Father Jim Fitt was a man of many qualities. He was quiet, conscientious, took simple joy in the satisfaction of a job well done, and had no moral scruples whatsoever, or even a belief in the existence of good and evil.

This did not make him a good priest, or a good man, but it did make him ideally suited to his work for the Diocese.

In appearance, he was almost comically unthreatening. He was not actually fat, as such, but his face was soft and jowly. His eyes peered out at the world from behind horn-rimmed glasses with lenses nearly half an inch thick and his voice was almost childishly high. Although still in his thirties, he had the posture and gait of a much older man, and his lank brown hair was shot through with premature gray.

Amongst the other priests of the Diocese, it was known that he had family in Cavan, a mother and two brothers, his father having abandoned the family twenty-two years previous, never to be seen again.

Other details of his past were known only to certain of the most senior members of the Diocese, and were not discussed.

Father Fitt's soul was a subject of much whispered speculation amongst the priests of the Diocese, as it was generally agreed that he did not possess one. It was not the sort of thing you would notice sitting next to him at a bus stop or in a taxi. He did not (usually) inspire chills or feelings of creeping terror by his mere presence. It was simply that, the more time you spent with him, the more you became aware of an absence. Small talk with Father Fitt left you with the feeling that you were holding a dialogue with a tape recording that simply happened to neatly align with your conversation.

The words made sense, but the machine did not care.

Around fifteen fathers worked in the Diocese's office on Henrietta

Street, a small Georgian house two doors down from the archway that led to King's Inn.

Other residents on the street were aware that the church owned the property, as they could scarcely miss the steady traffic of black-garbed figures coming and going every day like a line of somber ants. But the older, more observant neighbors had some time ago realized that it was never the same priests for very long. Whatever work was being done behind that fading Georgian façade, it had a more than healthy rate of turnover. And it was true, very few of the fathers who were sent to work for the Diocese lasted more than half a year before returning to their parishes, now very different men.

Father Fitt had been there for eight years.

It was this strange durability that made him so vital to the Diocese's work, despite the fact that he was no more loved than the black mold that caked much of the building's walls. Father So-and-So might plead to return to his parish, but Father Fitt remained. Father Such-and-Such might have a breakdown and be quietly shipped off to Saint Pat's while Father Fitt was in the dining hall eating corn flakes. Father You Know Yourself might return to visit the family farm and end the weekend in the barn with a shotgun. Father Fitt would be in Henrietta Street, blandly feigning sorrow, come Monday morning.

It was for this reason that, when the time came for the reverend fathers of the Diocese to be sent out into the world, it was Father Fitt who drove them.

It was early morning on the fifth of November when Father Fitt left Dublin for Wexford with two of the reverend fathers of the Diocese in the back seat. He had been instructed, in the usual manner, to deliver his charges to a certain homestead in Scarnagh, a tiny hamlet in County Wexford.

For one to be sent out was unusual enough, a rare and drastic measure.

Two was unprecedented.

The fact that Father Fitt did not, even for a moment, speculate as to what was going on in Scarnagh that could justify such a show of force was one of the reasons why he was so perfect for his role.

He drove conscientiously, never once breaching the speed limit. He drove like a man in an instructional video, utterly without error.

Behind him, he would occasionally hear a rustling like a snake moving under silk sheets. But for most of the journey, the passengers remained as still as the hands on a broken clock.

It was a bleak morning, with a suffocating gray overcast sky and an indolent drizzle splattering on the windshield. The Wexford countryside looked flat and ugly in the gloom.

In the distance, Father Fitt could see a splash of bright yellow, stark and livid. As he drove close, the yellow coalesced into the figure of a young guard in a high-vis jacket calmly gesturing for him to come to a stop.

There was a stirring in the back seat. Father Fitt briefly glanced in the rearview mirror, to remind his passengers to be on their best behavior.

He calmly brought the car to a smooth stop and rolled down the window.

The guard came up to the side of the car, half bowed, and gave a respectful smile when he saw the collar. He was young. Late twenties. And there was an alertness and intelligence in his eyes that warned Father Fitt to be cautious.

The Department and the Diocese were in a period of alliance at present, but it was so hard to know who to trust these days.

And mistakes could always be made.

"Hello, Garda," he said, all bland courtesy. "Is everything in order?"

"Sorry to stop you, Father," the guard replied. "We're looking for a young woman, we believe she went missing somewhere in the area."

"How terrible," said Father Fitt. "Terrible" was a good word. It showed you cared.

"Could I ask you to take a look at this photograph, please?" the guard asked, and passed it through the window.

Father Fitt glanced at the image of a pale young woman in her twenties with long brown hair, a large, toothy grin, and unmistakably sad blue eyes. It looked like it had been taken at a house party. She was holding a bottle of beer in one hand, and someone's arm was draped over her shoulder. He realized that he had seen her face before, this exact picture in fact, on the front page of most of the newspapers in the city for the last few days, before she had been driven off by the Iranian hostage crisis.

Father Fitt did not read newspapers as, with rare exceptions, they belonged to the Station or were English (which, of course, was worse). But from the headlines he had gleaned that this young woman had gone missing and that her fiancé was suspected of foul play. As he held up the photograph he sensed a . . . what? A tensing. From the back seat.

That was odd.

He passed the photograph back to the young guard.

"I'm sorry, I haven't seen her," he said.

The guard thanked him and then passed him a photograph of an old Ford Cortina, bright blue. Had he seen this car on the road? Father Fitt had not, and said as much.

He could sense a restlessness coming from the back seat. It would be best to move on quickly. Mentally, he willed the young guard to wave him on.

"And may I ask where you're headed, Father?" the guard asked.

"We're just driving toward Enniscorthy," Father Fitt said, which was not a lie.

"I." Not "we."

The guard had not looked at the back seat. This was because the reverend fathers did not wish him to see them and part of the young guard's mind wished very dearly for the same thing. As long as Father Fitt had not drawn attention to his passengers, the guard was perfectly happy to ignore them. But he had said "we." And the guard had suddenly realized that Father Fitt was not alone in the car.

Fitt saw the young guard's eyes glance to the back seat and rest upon what sat there like a fly landing on a lit bulb. *"There now,"* said Father Fitt, laying his hand on the guard's shoulder as he vomited the last of his breakfast onto the side of the road.

His stomach void, he still retched for another three minutes until at last his body steadied. He squatted, taking desperate, gulping drafts of the morning air, while rivers of sweat and spit and snot dripped from his flushed pink face.

"Oh Jesus . . ." he wheezed. "Oh Jesus. Sorry, Father."

"Oh, that's all right," said Father Fitt. *"He'll forgive you."*

"I . . . I don't know . . . what . . ."

"A dose of food poisoning, I suspect," said Father Fitt. *"Or a bug. It's the time of year."*

The guard nodded, utterly drained and barely even able to talk.

"Well. I'm afraid I must be off. I'd take a day to recuperate, if I were you."

The guard nodded in thanks, and watched as Father Fitt drove off down the empty road.

The farther the car went into the distance the more the awful nausea in his stomach began to relax and melt away. But the terrible feeling of dread remained.

As he stood trembling by the side of the road, and tried to re-build in his mind what had just happened, he found only jagged edges and blankness. He felt like his mind had been cut open, and left to bleed to death by the side of the road.

Feidhlim awoke from a dream of black trees, rustling feathers, and cold sweat.

He got wearily to his feet and pulled on his clothes, shoes, and socks. He did not notice that the bedroom door behind him was open. Only three-quarters awake, he shuffled into the kitchen. He had slept deeply, and he was now hungry. Bacon and eggs. No better thing.

He put the pan on the hob, took the box of matches and lit one, and then twisted the knob to release the gas.

The phone rang.

Suddenly, the languid, doomed calm that had settled over him vanished. The ringing of the phone meant hope. And hope meant desperation.

Without thinking, Feidhlim doused the match, crossed the kitchen floor, and snatched up the handset.

"Hello?" he whispered, pleadingly, into the phone.

All he could hear was static.

"Hello?!" he sobbed.

Please. Please help me.

And then, a word. Or a scream in the shape of a word. Not a human voice. Static rose to a terrible volume and formed a single screeched command.

RUN.

Feidhlim Lowney had never known fear until this moment. Everything before now had been pale imitation. At last, in the final few minutes, he felt the true, shining thing. Fear so pure and bright that it annihilated the being called Feidhlim Lowney, and left mere instinct behind.

He ran to the bedroom and stood, agape, staring at the empty bed.

Where is she where is she where is she . . .

Bernadette was gone. That was all there was to it. He couldn't waste time. Instead he ran into the next room.

The first thing he saw was the television, its screen a dead, still gray.

In the bed, Etain sat staring at the blank television and did not turn to look at him as he burst into the room.

He might have noticed the long streak of white that now ran through her hair. He might have noticed that she looked a good ten years older. But he was not in a frame of mind for noticing. He picked up her unresisting body and slung her over his shoulder and ran out of the room, almost tripping over a pair of brown shoes and a checked blazer that had been strewn carelessly at the foot of the bed.

Etain's memories would resume at this point.

This was her second birth, this moment.

Feidhlim Lowney's bony shoulder digging into her stomach, her own hair forming a thick, impenetrable veil across her eyes. Cold morning air on her bare skin, the rough gravel path winding beneath her like a gray python.

Beneath her, Feidhlim Lowney was wheezing and whining in pain, like a horse being run to death.

He stumbled and almost fell, and the sudden jerk caused her hair to fly back. She caught a glimpse of the farmhouse, back up the hill, clinging like a damp scab on the landscape. She saw motion. A black car, pulling up to the side of the house.

Father Fitt applied the handbrake and studied the farmhouse. He could feel a terrible rising anticipation in the back seat of the car. The whole vehicle seemed to be vibrating with the desperate, frantic energy of a trapped animal. He stepped out of the car and took hold of the handle of the rear passenger door and pulled it open.

The reverend fathers emerged with the speed of dogs on the hunt.

Their shape was roughly human in terms of the number of limbs and the presence of a head and torso. But the movement and arrangement of the joints was closer to the arachnid. They moved across the ground too quickly, with the hideous suddenness of lizards.

The faces were as if the most awful, hateful old men in the world, poisoned close to death with spite, had had their visages taken and then smudged by a giant thumb. There were no necks, simply impossibly long strands of black tar that tethered the bodies to heads that seemed to float weightlessly in the air.

One worked its way noiselessly through the letterbox of the front door, the second slipped around the side of the house like a shadow.

Father Fitt sat on the trunk of the car and lit a cigarette.

As Bernadette entered the kitchen door she was almost overpowered by the stench of butane.

Feidhlim, you fucking eejit, she thought to herself as she pulled the collar of her nightgown up to her mouth and staggered toward the cooker, trying to shut off the gas before it overpowered her.

Just as she touched the knob she sensed motion to her left and turned to see one of the reverend fathers skittering noiselessly over the ceiling, bearing down on her with the speed of a nightmare.

Bernadette Lowney did not scream, and she did not run.

She was not her husband. She had a mind that, even on the wild outskirts of terror, still worked with a cold efficiency.

Ah well, she thought. *We gambled. We lost.*

And she reached for the cigarette lighter in her pocket.

Outside the house, Father Fitt sprang to his feet as the explosion shattered the cheap single-glazed windows and a thick plume of smoke arose from the far side of the house, followed by the crackling roar of an inferno.

Cautiously, Fitt approached the front door, and peered into the house through the shattered windows. The kitchen and most of the hallway were aflame, the burning wallpaper creating a tunnel of fire through which he could just about make out the charred body of a woman lying on the kitchen floor and the reverend father squatting over her, eating her stomach.

The creature went about its work with stolid diligence, utterly indifferent to the blaze around it. Fitt, for his part, could already feel his face beginning to blister and burn, and he turned back to the car. He took a deep breath of cold air, and saw a flash of color far down the hill.

Feidhlim Lowney had been staggering down the path with the girl on his back when he heard his home and wife explode.

In shock, he spun around to see a fireball blossoming over the farmhouse before inertia pulled him down and he and his burden went toppling into a ditch by the side of the path.

His ankle twisted and his knees bleeding, he pulled himself out and looked around for the girl.

She was lying on her back in the ditch, a bruise forming on her forehead. Her eyes were staring up at the sky, and her breath was hoarse and wheezing, as if any second she was about to scream.

Leave her, he thought to himself. *You've done enough, save yourself.*

He turned to look up at his house. There was a man standing on the hill beside the burning husk of his home, looking down at him. He was dressed all in black.

The second of the reverend fathers had returned from its reconnoiter of the farmhouse. Father Fitt gestured to the tiny figure that had emerged from the ditch.

The reverend father took off and the figure began to sprint.

With a wan smile, Father Fitt gave the tiny figure a blessing with his right hand, which still held the lit cigarette.

The crucifix of blue smoke hung in the air as Father Fitt watched the last moments of Feidhlim Lowney.

Feidhlim did not truly see the thing that had come beetling down the hill toward him. He simply saw a darkish blur, like a stabbing knife, and then his body took over.

He was running so fast down the road now that it felt like his arms and legs were no longer connected and were just a loose cluster of particles flying around each other.

He was dimly aware that he could hear barking and snarling.

From his vantage point, Father Fitt watched as a pack of dogs, a great motley, snarling, furious mix of breeds and sizes, appeared where the reverend father had roughly been mere seconds earlier.

Etain, near comatose with shock and hunger, listened as forty pairs of clawed feet clicked past the ditch, mere inches from her head. She closed her eyes, and hoped to wake up.

Feidhlim Lowney felt lightning strike his leg and fell to the ground. A second bolt came as another dog bit into his leg, and then a third, and then teeth fell on his body like a rainstorm.

He felt two muzzles biting into his shoulders and pulling him back up the path. He tried to beat them off but his hands flashed before his eyes, trailing blood and streamers of skin and muscle. The pack had broken in two and some of the dogs were dragging something heavy and dark down the road.

He was dimly aware that it was his legs and lower torso.

A great Alsatian stood on his chest.

It opened its maw a million miles wide and swallowed the world. Etain listened.

She lay as still as bone and let the sound of Feidhlim Lowney's death wash over her.

She heard him screaming and tearing and cracking open and spilling.

She listened to the snarls and howls of the dogs, and then the contented wetness of their feasting.

She listened to all of it, as if it was a gentle half-remembered song from childhood, lilting over the gravel lip of the ditch.

She knew the farmer was dead and had suffered greatly. And the happiness she felt at this knowledge left a numbness in its wake.

A smile, long and wide and twisted, snaked upon her pale features and then vanished, as if it had heard footsteps.

Something moved overhead. It might have been dogs. It might not have been dogs.

There was a silence, the kind that lets you hear worms stirring in the earth. She could hear something burning and crackling far away and the baritone hum of an old car driving off in the distance.

She watched her hand, trembling uncontrollably, as it reached for the edge of the ditch.

Am I standing now? she asked herself. *I must be standing now.*

She swayed like a flag in the wind as she padded barefoot down the gravel path.

Where is he? she thought to herself. There was no carcass. No bones. Not so much as a drop of blood on the path.

She stumbled on. She came to a gate leading to the main road, behind which was parked an old, filthy white jeep.

Must have been running for this. My car was parked beside the house, but he probably didn't know where my keys were.

She was thin enough to slip through the bars of the gate, which was fortunate, as she did not have the strength to either open it or climb over it.

Her staggering, broken progress continued out onto the main road, small stones and the occasional dull chunk of glass digging coarsely into her bare feet.

She walked for years. Until, far ahead, she saw a flash of yellow.

The young guard turned and saw her. She saw three distinct waves of amazement pass over his young, beautiful face.

The first, as he saw this specter, this emaciated woman walking barefoot toward him on a country road wearing nothing but a filthy pair of pajamas.

The second, as he recognized her face.

The third as he realized that he had just found Etain Larkin and was about to become a national hero. He broke into a sprint and raced toward her.

And it was only in that moment, as she saw the guard coming for her and realized that it was all finally over, that Etain finally allowed herself to collapse to the ground and scream her voice away into the sky.

NOVEMBER 1999

Betty's first term in UCD passed in a mad rush of stress, drink-ing too much, eating too little, insecurity, and anxiety that would years later, somehow, bake and cool in her memory as happiness.

Ashling Mallen's predictions came true in short order and within a month, Betty had indeed been eaten alive by Dramsoc. She spent her days rehearsing, auditioning, going to see shows, and bitching about the society's Byzantine politics.

But Betty had also made a prediction, and it had also come true.

She was in love with Ashling.

They had both been cast in the Freshers' Co-Op, traditionally a show with a large cast of both first years and more experienced members, a way for the society to more closely knit its newest acquisitions into its fabric. This year the play was *Romeo and Juliet*. Of course, no student drama society worthy of the name would ever do anything as gauche as setting the play in Renaissance Verona. Therefore, Dramsoc's 1999 production of *Romeo and Juliet* was set in Dublin in the 1980s during the height of the heroin epidemic.

"Why?" was not a question to be asked, for Dramsoc lived by the Shavian principle of dreaming of things that never were, and asking "Why not?" (and sometimes not even asking that).

Another, somewhat more logical deviation from theatrical tra-dition had been made to accommodate the demographics of the society. Dramsoc was in majority female, and so the decision was made that all the Capulet roles, regardless of gender as per the script, would be played by female actors. Similarly, all the Mon-tagues would be male.

Betty was cast as Samson, a small Capulet part who had the first line of the play. Betty's only experience of the story was the film directed by Baz Luhrmann, which had barely featured Samson at all. She soon realized why in the first table read.

"True; and therefore women, being the . . . weaker vessels, are ever thrust to the wall: therefore I will push Montague's men from the wall . . . and thrust his maids to the wall."

Oh, terrific, Betty thought. *I'm playing a rapist.*

There was an awkward silence around the table. Someone piped up from the back.

"What maids, love? They're all blokes."

Dramsoc productions did not have the luxury of time. By the end of the first week she was expected to be off book. By the middle of the second they were in dress rehearsals. It would have been a punishing routine for a small, intimate two-hander. For a massive three-hour show with dozens of actors, elaborate sets, and hundreds of props it was collective, rolling hysteria. Everyone was stressed, everyone was panicked, and everyone feared that the production would be a massive catastrophic failure while secretly knowing in their heart of hearts that the gods of theater would not abandon them and that it would all be fine on the night. The fear was part of the experience, after all.

For Betty, the moment of revelation came during their first costumed rehearsal of the very first scene of the play.

As Betty and her fellow "Capulettes" drew their weapons and prepared to battle the "Mentagues" she heard a voice roaring behind her, savagely rolling its Rs, purring with menace.

"What, art thou drawn amongst these heartless hinds?"

And there was Ashling, or rather, there was Tybalt wearing the body of Ashling.

A switchblade elegantly held at the throat of the world, eyes burning green with joyous fury, a pearl-white shark's smile on her perfect face.

And, oh yes, a period-accurate black leather jacket.

I get it, thought Betty. *I get why people love Shakespeare.*

But that was not the scene that stayed with Betty for years; long, long decades after the show had finished and was just a dim half-remembered memory.

The play's director, Simon Tierney, a slight, quiet-spoken redhead with professorial glasses and an aura of latent, manic energy, had come to the production with one iron-clad conviction:

During the Capulets' Ball, the entire cast would dance to U2's "With or Without You," fully choreographed, from the beginning of the song right through to the end.

He was easygoing, reasonable, and quick to compromise on any other aspect of the production, but on this he could not be moved. No matter how often it was explained to him that time was at a premium, that the show was already too long, or that Bono was a pox. On this, he would not compromise.

For that, Betty would always owe him a debt she could never repay.

Like all bit players dreaming of better things, Betty and Ashling had worked out their own backstory for their characters. Samson, Betty had decided, simply acted coarse and lecherous to mask his true feelings for Tybalt. Tybalt had saved Samson's life during a brutal midnight brawl with the Montagues, and afterward the two had had a single, sweltering, passionate night together.

"Samson completely loves Tybalt. Tybalt likes him but doesn't do relationships" was how Ashling described it, unaware that she was casually stabbing Betty in the chest. In their own surreptitious play, running secretly under the skin of Shakespeare's work, the Capulet Ball was the moment that Tybalt realized that he loved Samson, and extended a hand to him, offering him a dance.

The memory that would always stay with Betty from that time was of gazing at Ashling from across the dance floor. First came the drum, gentle but insistent. The slow, beautiful, melancholy guitar.

"See the stone set in your eyes, see the thorn twist in your side . . ."

Ashling's hand reaching out to her. Come. Dance with me.

And then, as one, the whole cast began to dance. A surreal, hypnotic ballet. The sight of the whole cast dancing together, perfectly in sync, reaching for the sky, pushing each other away and pulling each other back. Simon Tierney had been right. But for

Betty, there was only ever two of them onstage, only two in the whole universe.

There was her, and there was Ashling, those beautiful green eyes glittering in the twilight blue of the darkened stage.

There was the dark, heavy smell of the leather jacket, the silvery sweat on her neck, the pain in her muscles as she was hoisted from the earth by Ashling's strong, wiry arms, and the ecstasy of that weightless second, as if the spotlights were holding her in midair.

Then the giddy, butterfly-in-the-stomach roll down as Ashling returned her to the Earth, a half smile playing on her perfect lips as she mouthed the words to her.

I can't live.
With or without you.

NOVEMBER 1979

Barry had been expecting a call from Etain the day after the party, and had been waiting by the phone in the house for most of the morning as Kate and Keano rather pointedly cleaned the room around him. When she didn't call, he reasoned that she must have simply been too exhausted after the drive back and a full day's work. So, he headed back to Cork to tell his family the good news.

By the evening of November 2, he finally broke and tried to call her. He knew well enough not to try calling her at home, so he looked up the number for Maude Pygott's Newsagent in the 01 Yellow Pages and tried to reach her at work. Maude, with a faint but detectable hint of worry in her voice, told Barry that Etain had not been in to work either today or yesterday, and had not called to say why.

Barry would always remember that moment, a sensation of liquid nitrogen being dropped into his stomach.

Now very worried, he broke an iron-clad rule and called Etain's mother.

It took three attempts to finally get an answer and when he did, there was only silence on the other end. Mairéad Larkin did not give a greeting, or ask him why he was calling. She simply picked up the receiver and waited for him to speak.

Trying to keep the panic out of his voice, Barry had asked her if Etain had come home on the first.

No answer.

Not this fucking shite again, he thought. *Not now.*

"Mrs. Larkin," he said, as calmly and respectfully as he could muster, "I'm very worried about her. Can you please just tell me if she made it home safe?"

He heard a rustle on the other end of the line, but not a word.

"Can you just tell me if she's there. Please. Please tell me she made it home safely. Mrs. Larkin, please, I'm begging you. I know you don't like me and I'm sorry. But . . . on Wednesday I asked Etain to marry me. And she said yes. And that means you and I are going to be family."

Even as he said the words, he could feel he was making a terrible mistake. He did not know if there was a right way to break the news to Mairéad, but he felt in his bones that this was the worst of the wrong ways.

"So I'm going to ask you one more time," he said, his voice cracking. "Did she come home? Is she there? Is she safe?"

For a second he thought he heard an intake of breath, as if she was about to speak.

No. Nothing but silence. He might as well have screamed into a grave.

The line went dead.

Barry almost broke the handset and swore so loudly that his mother, Anne, came running into the kitchen. She saw her son hunched at the kitchen table, hands clenched in his hair, tears of frustration running down his face.

She gave him a hug and told him it would be all right.

"She's had a falling-out with her mother and hasn't had time to call, love," she said. "That's all it is. She'll call in the morning. I know she will. You're getting yourself worked up over nothing."

Finally, Barry gave way to his mother's entreaties and went to bed.

The next morning, he was woken by his father, who told him that there were two sergeants at the door who wished to speak to him.

They took him down to Bantry Garda Station and questioned him for five hours.

When had he last seen Etain Larkin?

In the early morning of November 1 when she had left for Dublin.

Did she talk to anyone else at the party?

Not that he saw, and certainly not for any length of time.

How long had they been a couple?

A little more than a year.

What had they discussed the night of the party?

He had proposed to her and she had accepted.

Did they have a fight?

A fight? No. Absolutely not.

The Gardaí had heard there had been an argument between them, would he care to shed any light on that?

An argument? No. Nothing like that.

Now why would someone think they'd been fighting?

Maybe they had overheard . . .

Overheard what?

After she said yes, they had made love.

Why hadn't he mentioned that before, the Gardaí wanted to know?

Because, Barry explained, he had not felt it was any of their fucking business.

The Gardaí proceeded to frankly and comprehensively disabuse him of that notion.

Finally they released him and told him not to leave Cork.

On the car ride back from the police station he had suddenly felt a terrible premonition that Etain was dead.

He went home, wordlessly ate the dinner his mother put in front of him, and then went to bed.

As he tried to sleep he saw Etain in his mind's eye, her face bloodied, and lying on the side of the road.

In Dublin, the *Evening Herald* was breaking the story of Etain's disappearance and Barry's arrest.

By the next morning, it would be the front page of most of the major Irish newspapers.

While Barry Mallen lay in bed in a near catatonic depression, his father was already taking charge of the situation. Tadhg Mallen was a much-loved figure in the community. He was known to be a good father and loving husband, a devout Catholic, and a loyal friend. Everyone had time for him.

Like his son, Tadhg was a big-hearted bear of a man. Unlike Barry, however, Tadhg had never been called an eejit in his life, and for good reason. A voracious reader, he had a savvy far beyond what might have been expected for a man who'd never completed secondary education. When the first media reports began to appear, Tadhg immediately saw that his son was being fitted for the noose, and put in a call to a friend who lived in Dublin who knew a man who knew a man who knew an editor at the *Irish Press*. The *Press* was a Fianna Fáil paper, its readership primarily rural and more conservative-leaning than the rest of the Dublin rags. It had also been sharply critical in its coverage of the Garda Síochána and Tadhg astutely reasoned that if there was any paper where a decent farmer's son who had been victimized by the police might find a sympathetic hearing, it was the *Press*.

After a few phone calls, Tadhg had arranged an exclusive interview for his son with Patricia Skelton herself, whose only stipulation was that she be allowed to interview him in person.

Tadhg Mallen had never been called an eejit, and never would be.

Patricia Skelton arrived in Bantry like a character from an American soap opera, hair and makeup impeccable, and wearing "the suit."

The suit, a pink Chanel number, had been a tactic at first. When starting out as a young political correspondent, Skelton had taken to wearing pink in order to lull interviewees into a false sense of security. Nowadays, her reputation firmly established, the suit tended to have the opposite effect and in government circles she had earned the nicknames "the Pink Barracuda" and "the Tooth Fairy." The latter came from a political cartoon by Martyn Turner depicting her adorned with pink wings and a tiara, gruesomely extracting the truth from the mouth of Minister for Justice Patrick Cooney with a pair of pliers. Skelton had gotten it signed by the artist, framed it, and put it on her desk.

The interview was conducted in the kitchen of the Mallens' farmhouse.

Barry sat slumped across from Patricia, red-eyed, ashen-faced, with the posture of a sack of potatoes.

Patricia felt exhausted just looking at him. As she set up her tape recorder on the kitchen table she glanced briefly around the room.

Tadhg stood away from them, leaning with his back to the kitchen sink, his face unreadable.

One of the other Mallen boys, Tomás, mirrored his father against the stove, the pair of them forming a set of parentheses around the table.

Tomás looked like someone had taken Barry and tried to make him more convenient for travel. He had his brother's eyes, hair, and complexion. But he was a good half a foot shorter than Barry, and lean as barbed wire. His body language was knotted and hostile, his expression one of cold rage.

Oh, you don't like me, do you, boy? Patricia mused to herself. She didn't take it personally. Nothing could make an entire family view the press as a curse on humanity as quickly as being in the news. Tadhg Mallen had obviously brought her here to push back on the narrative that was forming, but Tomás was visibly unhappy. As far as he was concerned, she was the enemy.

And maybe I am, Patricia thought to herself. *Let's get a look at you, Barry Mallen. Saint or sinner?*

The boy, the man rather, sitting across the table reminded her of a neglected and abused dog. Unable to meet her gaze. Listless. Heavy with misery.

Which of the three Gs is this? Patricia asked herself. *Grief, guilt, or guile?*

She leaned forward and pressed Play and Record on the cassette player.

Without so much as a preamble, she began.

"It's Monday, fifth of November, 1979. And everyone wants to know, where is Etain Larkin?"

Barry did not look up.

"Hm?" Patricia asked.

"Was that a question?" Barry asked wearily.

"It was an opening," she replied. "Where do you think she might be?"

He shuddered.

"I don't know," he whispered. "I don't . . . Christ . . ."

Tomás stood and looked like he might be about to escort his brother from the room.

Tadhg glanced at him. Tomás leaned back on the stove.

"Why would you think I'd know?" he asked.

Patricia tilted her head curiously.

"You were the last one to see her a—"

She cut herself off but the first syllable hung in the air like a moment of realization. *Ah.*

But Barry was shaking his head.

"No. No, I wasn't. Kate spoke to her before she left the house."

"Who's Kate?"

"Etain's sister."

"The one who was throwing the party?"

"Yeah. She arranged the whole thing. I told her I wanted to propose to Etain. She arranged the whole thing."

"And she spoke to Etain? When?"

"As she was leaving the house. After we'd . . ."

He blushed awkwardly and glanced sheepishly in the direction of his father.

Patricia felt a pang of sympathy. *Poor kid,* she thought. *Catholic guilt on top of everything else.*

A thought struck her.

"Barry," she said. "Have the guards spoken to Kate Larkin? Do you know?"

Barry nodded. "Yeah. They took a statement."

"And she confirmed that she saw her sister Etain alive and well before she left the house in Duncannon?"

"Yeah."

"And that she wasn't upset or . . ."

"No! No, she said she was happy. That she showed her the ring and that she was happy, like . . ."

Patricia was scribbling in her notebook: *talk to Kate Larkin ASAP.*

All right, what the fuck is going on here? Patricia thought to herself.

Girl goes missing, and the boyfriend is the last person to see her alive, fine. Suspect. Obviously.

But if Kate Larkin was the last person to see her sister and could corroborate Barry's story then there was no logical reason to think that he was a suspect in her disappearance.

So why are we all talking about Barry Mallen like he's the second coming of Geoffrey Evans?

Why are the guards still looking at him? Why does no one seem to know that Kate Larkin spoke to her sister?

She made a mental list of journalists to call as soon as she was able to get to the phone.

Who's feeding us this narrative? she wondered. *The guards? Or someone else?*

"What about this fight you and Etain . . ." Patricia began.

Tomás exploded on the stove like a pot who'd been left to boil too long.

"For fuck's sake, there wasn't any fucking fight! You lot keep saying it, it's a load of shite!"

"Tomás," said Tadhg. One word, and his son was silent.

"Is that true, Barry?" said Patricia. "You and Etain didn't have a fight?"

"No," Barry whispered. "We didn't."

"Not even an argument? A minor tiff? Something . . ."

"I swear to almighty God," said Barry, looking her straight in the eye. "We didn't say a single cross word to each other. Not the whole night."

All right, Mr. Mallen, I believe you. Turn off the puppy-dog eyes before I start to weep.

Patricia cleared her throat, wondering how best to phrase her next question.

"Barry?" she asked. "Do you have any enemies?"

It felt like such a ridiculous question.

"What?" he asked, not sure he had heard her right.

"What I mean is . . . if I was to say, *hypothetically, you understand,* that it's starting to feel like someone is feeding a false narrative to the Gardaí. Or the press. Or both. Someone who clearly does not have your best interests at heart. Or Etain's. Someone who doesn't care that the Gardaí are focusing so much attention on you when (to me at least), you clearly don't look like a viable suspect. If, *hypothetically,* I were to say that . . . who is the first person you think of? Does anyone spring to mind?"

Barry Mallen stared at her for a few moments. It was like she had spoken to him in a foreign language he barely understood, and he was slowly translating her question in his mind.

"No," he said at last.

Ah. So that's what Barry Mallen looks like when he lies.

She cast an eye around the room. Tadhg was inscrutable, just as before. But Tomás was an anthill, squirming with the desire to say something. He was now looking at her almost pleadingly, like a bright pupil in a crowded classroom. *Pick me. Pick me.*

"How about you?" she asked him. "Can you think of anyone?"

"Tomás," Tadhg said gently, with just a hair of iron. *"Ná bí ag insint scéalta."**

Ach is breá liom scéalta,[†] Patricia thought, but said nothing. If they saw fit to converse in front of her in Irish because they assumed a Dubliner wouldn't understand, she certainly wasn't going to stop them.

But Tomás said nothing.

A silence fell on the kitchen, until Patricia could hear the murmur of the fridge behind her.

Patricia Skelton knew silences. This was a very specific, very Irish kind of silence. The silence of a family closing ranks.

Suddenly, all four looked up as they heard screaming.

"BARRY!" A woman's voice came from the hallway. "BARRY!"

Anne Mallen exploded into the kitchen. Wild-eyed and almost hyperventilating, she shouted:

"THEY FOUND HER, LOVE! ETAIN! OH GOD, THEY FOUND HER!"

A stunned silence.

"Where!?" Barry said, leaping to his feet.

"On the side of a road in Wexford . . ." Anne replied. She stopped as she saw her son turn white as a marble gravestone and begin to totter.

Tadhg and Tomás ran to him and grabbed a shoulder each to support him.

Anne realized what she had said.

She put both hands on her son's face and tearfully kissed him and said, "Alive! Alive, love! She's alive! Sorry, love! Oh Jesus, I'm sorry, I

---

* "Don't be telling stories."

† "But I love stories."

didn't mean . . . She's alive, Barry! She's alive! Oh God, I'm so sorry, I didn't mean to frighten you, love! I didn't mean to frighten you . . ."

For all her fearsome reputation and vivid taste in fashion, Patricia was perfectly capable of blending into the background and allowing herself to be forgotten. She did not ask if she could accompany Barry and his family as they piled into the car to begin the long journey to Wexford General Hospital, she simply sat in the back seat as quietly and unobtrusively as possible, observing for posterity.

A crowd of around six or seven journalists was in the hospital lobby by the time the Mallens arrived, and a young doctor with obvious stage fright was quietly stammering to them that Miss Larkin was suffering from severe malnutrition and dehydration but was responding well to treatment and was in good spirits.

"Good spirits," as Patricia knew from professional experience, was meaningless. She had heard the description applied to a man who'd been sitting in a hospital bed bursting his stitches laughing at an episode of *Porridge,* and a woman on a ventilator who was practically comatose. She wondered where on the spectrum Etain Larkin would fall.

The doctor was telling the journalists that under no circumstances would they be allowed up to the ward to interview Etain. As the Mallens and Patricia were escorted past them by hospital staff, Patricia saw recognition play across the faces of some of the Dublin journos. She took a perverse satisfaction in watching a wordless drama play on their expressions.

Fuck, is that the Skelton wagon?
Are they letting her up?
Do they think she's one of the family?
Oh, fuck no, I'm going to say something!
Wait, do I really want to grass on the Tooth Fairy?
. . .
Best say nothing, sure.

When they reached the ward, a young woman in her twenties ran out into the corridor and embraced Barry in a fierce, bone-cracking hug. Barry's mother then embraced her gently and they began to talk in hushed tones.

Patricia held back, partially out of respect and partially because it was a scene better observed than listened to. She studied the newcomer carefully. Dark haired, sharp-eyed. A looker. Already wiping the tears from her eyes and carefully reassembling her composure.

She heard the name "Kate."

So, Kate Larkin of *talk to Kate Larkin ASAP* fame.

She took a half step to the right, just enough to give her line of sight into the ward.

A uniformed guard was sitting at the end of a bed, casually leafing through a magazine. The subject of his diligent watch lay prone, staring up at the ceiling. Her long hair, brown but for a single streak of white, was fanned out over the white pillow, and a drip was feeding sugar water into her left arm. Patricia was reminded of any one of a dozen paintings of Ophelia drifting down a reed-choked river.

Her clothes spread wide, and mermaid-like awhile they bore her up.

On her left hand was a ring. The engagement band that Barry had given her. There it was, true enough. Silver, with an intricate engraved design.

It looked oddly big and ugly on her tiny hand, which lay resting on her chest as motionless as a dead bird.

She looked about as still as any human being Patricia had ever seen, and her eyes gazed upward like beads of pale blue glass.

Oh, hon. What happened to you?

And then . . .

And then . . .

The head shifted on the pillow and suddenly Etain Larkin's eyes were locked with hers.

Patricia Skelton did not know what this woman had experienced.

But in that gaze she caught the shadow of it, and it chilled her to her marrow.

And then the great bulk of Barry Mallen broke the line of fire and he had practically thrown himself on Etain, casting his great arms around her and sobbing and calling out her name like a lamentation. She embraced him back, weakly, but with everything she had.

Her hands moved up and down his back, testing. Making sure it was really him.

She whispered something in his ear and he shook his head. He held her in silence.

They stayed like that for what felt like hours, gently rocking back and forth.

The guard put down his magazine, stepped outside, and closed the door to give them some privacy.

MAY 2000–FEBRUARY 2001

By the end of first year, it was clear that Betty was in trouble.
Thanks to Dramsoc she had fallen so far behind in her studying and missed so many lectures that she had barely scraped a pass in the end-of-year exams. She had done quite well in English, but had botched psychology and the less said about philosophy, the better.

This left her with a serious problem. Going into second year, arts students were required to drop one of their three subjects and focus on the remaining two. Betty would have preferred to ditch philosophy, which had become unendurable to her ever since they'd left the Greeks behind and succumbed to the cold, joyless, existential embrace of the Germans. But psychology only allowed the top 10 percent of the class to continue on to second year and Betty had been lucky to be in the top half. This left her facing another two years of philosophy, which had, appropriately enough, left her questioning the point of existence. It was Gemma who had come to her rescue, telling her that the college offered two-year courses that could be started in second year. With the end-of-term deadline rushing toward her like an oncoming train, she had hurriedly filled out her application form and elected, almost at random, to study Irish folklore.

The UCD Department of Irish Folklore had been part of the university since the 1970s, but its origins went back much further.

It had begun as a small volunteer organization in the '20s, the Folklore of Ireland Society (An Cumann le Béaloideas Éireann) headed by Séamus Ó Duilearga, with a mission as noble as it was apparently futile: to catalog and record the entirety of Ireland's oral tradition of native song and story before it vanished forever.

Armed with a bulky Ediphone recorder, or sometimes just a pen and pad, Ó Duilearga's collectors ventured forth into the nooks and crannies of the map like prospectors looking for gold. Rarely were they disappointed. It was true that some towns and villages wanted nothing to do with them, but a man who wants to listen is seldom in want of a welcome.

The society's work was rewarded when, in the 1930s, it was officially reconstituted as the Irish Folklore Commission under the aegis of the government of Éamon De Valera. In the '40s, at De Valera's behest, the commission had traveled to the Isle of Man to record some of the last living speakers of Manx, recordings that would later prove vital to the language's revival in the late twentieth century.

Then, in the 1970s, the commission and its entire collection of manuscripts, photographs, artifacts, and audio recordings had been relocated to Belfield, to begin their new life as the UCD Department of Irish Folklore.

Betty learned all of this in the introductory lecture given by Anna, a tall, thin, blond sound archivist with a kind, maternal smile and palpable and infectious enthusiasm for the work of the department.

If she was honest with herself, Betty had plumped for Irish folklore because she thought it would be easy, essentially a slightly more scholarly version of the myths and fairy tales she had been taught in primary school. "The Children of Lir," "The Salmon of Knowledge," "Setanta and the Hound," and the like. The mythological tales were indeed a subject of study in her first year, but she was quickly disabused of the notion that the course would be easy. "Folklore," as she soon learned, was not simply stories. It was, in essence, any information that was passed along verbally. Stories and songs, yes. But also vernacular architecture, superstitions, folk cures, fairy lore, recipes, marriage customs, and on and on. There were curses to be learned, such as the infamous Malacht Cromail: *May you carry your child until its twentieth year,* which Betty vowed to work into casual conversation at every opportunity.

The subject was vast, and the workload was heavy. And while many of the lectures were fascinating and deeply engaging, others were less so.

During one two-hour marathon on the techniques used by the Folklore Commission to catalog different spade types used in the west of Ireland, Betty had experienced boredom so profound that she entered a meditative state and (she would swear years afterward) had an actual out-of-body experience.

She had not yet written her play. She had a few short sketches put on, but anything larger than that drowned in white after a few lines. She had decided, more out of desperation than anything, to base a play on Irish folklore, and had vaguely settled on something about changelings.

The department's specialist in fairy lore was Professor Ó hÓgáin, a silver-haired, blue-eyed man with a face built for smiling and a theatrical flair. Although, as he had told his class in their very first lecture, the term "fairy lore" was *verboten*.

"We shall not use the word '*sí*,'" he told his students in their first lecture. "We shall not refer to them as *síogaí* or (God forbid!) fairies. For the sake of politeness (and our own safety) we shall use the terms Na Daoine Maithe or Na Daoine Uaisle.* For, as we shall see, when dealing with these gentlemen we must at all times be seen to be respectful. Or else."

He paused as an appreciative chuckle ran through the small classroom.

"Who are they? Some accounts say they are the Tuatha De Danann, the old gods of Ireland, who retreated beneath the earth when they lost the country to the Gaels and now peek out jealously at us from every bush and hill. Later, with the arrival of Christianity, they were seen as fallen angels who refused to take sides during Lucifer's rebellion and were cast down by God Almighty to Ireland, as a slightly milder alternative to damnation. But who are they really?"

He took a piece of chalk and began to scratch large, blocky words down the left side of the blackboard. CERTAINTY. SAFETY. ORDER.

Then, on the other side, he wrote three corresponding words. MYSTERY. TRAGEDY. CHAOS.

Then he drew a line vertically between the two columns and then tapped it with a knuckle.

----

* "The Noble People."

"*É seo*,"* he said. "They are the dividing line between the known and the unknown. The face we put on the forces beyond our control. Disease. Misfortune. Loss. Death. Take the changelings. A changeling story often begins with a once-healthy baby suddenly becoming weak, pale, unhealthy. Failing to thrive. The parents discover that their true child has been taken by Na Daoine Maithe and replaced with this pitiful doppelgänger. The changeling is exposed and sent back to the otherworld, and the true child is returned. Now, this category of tale is one of the most widely distributed, found in every county, south and north. Why?"

He looked out over the classroom. A dozen or so students. No hands in the air.

He sighed.

"What if I told you that for most of the last two centuries, the rate of infant mortality in this country was one in ten? That is the purpose of Na Daoine Maithe. The awful and arbitrary cruelty of life, reduced to something that can be bargained with, reasoned, or outwitted. A face, put upon that which cannot be faced."

After one lecture she finally worked up the courage and approached him awkwardly.

"Yes, Betty?" he said, pleasantly surprised, as she had scarcely said a word in class since beginning the course.

"I was just wondering," she said. "Are there any stories where the changeling *doesn't* get found out?"

"No," he said. Not even a moment's hesitation.

"Oh," she said. In her experience, professors did not give one-word answers, and she wasn't quite sure how to react.

"A changeling story where the changeling is never discovered would be like a version of Cinderella where she never goes to the ball," the professor explained. "The revelation of the infant's true nature is the entire purpose of the story."

"But, aren't there stories where the changeling grows up? Or is it always a baby?"

He furrowed his brow.

---

* "This."

"Ah . . . well, that's a little different," he muttered. "You mean a story where a changeling is only revealed in adulthood?"

She nodded.

He thought for a moment and stuck his tongue in his cheek.

"I'm not sure," he admitted at last. "Why?"

"It's, well, I'm trying to write a play. And she, the main character, she discovers that she's not who she thought she was . . ."

"Ah well, if it's your own work you can write whatever you like!" he said with a chuckle. "Every writer who draws on these tales puts his or her own spin on it."

"I know," she said. "But still, I'd like to be accurate. If I could."

He nodded and thought again.

"Well, well. An adult changeling. Oh, I know! Eilis!"

"Eilis?" Betty asked, confused, as Professor Ó hÓgáin sat down at his desk and began looking through his drawers.

"Eilis Mulcahy, one of our informants. Wonderful woman."

"Informant" was the department's term for individuals who had been interviewed for the folklore archive. To Betty's ears, it made the department's work sound like an ongoing murder investigation.

"Lives just outside of Clifden. Hundred and three, if you can believe it. I've interviewed her eight or nine times now and I seem to recall she had a story that was something like what you're looking for."

"Great!" said Betty. "Is it in the archive?"

"It is!" he said merrily.

"Will you give me the reference number?" she asked.

"I will not!" he said, with the exact same tone.

"Oh," she said. "Why not?"

"Because you are going to go and interview her yourself," he said. "You still need to conduct an interview, correct?"

Betty nodded. One of her assignments this term was to arrange an interview with an informant and to record and transcribe the result in accordance with the department's guidelines.

"Well, there you are," he said. "Two birds with one stone. She lives with her granddaughter. Give her a call and see if Eilis is willing to talk to you. Get it straight from the horse's mouth."

"So, Gemma," Ashling said. "Be honest. What do you think of my pussy?"

"Darling, I thought you'd never ask," Gemma deadpanned, not bothering to look up from her magazine.

"Hi, guys," said Betty, arriving in the Dramsoc foyer. "Gemma, can I ask you a question?"

"You may," said Gemma.

"Heya, love," said Ashling from the top of a ladder, where her head was still lodged in the hood of the nine-foot-tall papier-mâché vulva that had been constructed over the theater entrance.

"Holy shit, Ash," breathed Betty in a voice filled with both wonder and terror, "that looks *amazing*."

"Dunnit though?" said Ashling proudly, arranging the fabric labial folds like a florist perfecting a wedding bouquet.

"I think it's a little crooked," said Gemma.

"Oh, like yours is perfectly fucking symmetrical," Ashling snapped irritably.

"It is," Gemma replied. "Famously so."

Ashling looked like she was about to tell Gemma what she could do with her perfectly symmetrical pussy when Eugene Hill, dressed as Pozzo from *Waiting for Godot,* glanced out of the theater and accidentally jostled the ladder. Ashling shrieked as she almost lost her balance and nearly achieved penetration.

Eugene grabbed the ladder to steady it.

"Shit, sorry, Ash!" he called. "You okay?"

"Yup," she wheezed, clinging to the ladder and breathing deeply. "All good."

Eugene looked up admiringly at her handiwork, and his eyes fell on the Gaelic football that had been covered in pink papier-mâché and placed under the hood as a clitoris.

"Found it!" he called, pointing at it proudly.

"Very funny, Euge," Ashling said.

"You're the first person to make that joke," Gemma informed him.

Chuckling to himself, he passed through the moveable wall into LG2, which served as the society's rehearsal space, costume storage, prop storage, set workshop, and fire hazard.

"What did you want to ask me?" Gemma asked.

Betty started. By raising her arms to stop herself from falling, Ashling had pulled up the hem of her top, revealing a pierced belly button and a small fairy tattoo just left of the navel, and Betty had suddenly found it very hard to focus on anything else.

"Oh right. Gemma," said Betty. "Where's Clifden?"

Gemma put her magazine down and glared at her.

"Betty, just because I'm from Tipp doesn't mean I'm familiar with every bog-hole in the country. I'm not your culchie whisperer. It's in Galway," she added grudgingly.

"Galway?" said Betty. "Fuck."

"Why?" Ashling asked, from overhead.

"Because I need to get there tomorrow. And I don't drive."

"What's in Clifden?"

"A one-hundred-and-three-year-old woman who I have to interview about fairies. Apparently."

"Sounds awesome. I'll drive you," said Ashling.

"You will not," said Gemma sharply.

"Says who?" said Ashling.

"It's like an eight-hour round trip. You'll be gone all day and the show goes up on Thursday."

"So what? 'Gemma' here," she said, proudly patting the gigantic pudenda, "is finished apart from the hair."

Gemma's aunt, a hairdresser, had very kindly offered to gift the Dramsoc production of Eve Ensler's *The Vagina Monologues* two full rubbish bags of human hair, sufficient to adorn the colossal cunt.

Gemma frowned.

"You named it after me?" she said quietly.

"I did," said Ashling.

"Why, pray tell?"

"Guess."

"You don't have time to go to Clifden," Gemma insisted, refusing to take the bait. "We need to rehearse. We *desperately* need to rehearse. We're going on Thursday and some of our vaginas aren't even off book."

Ashling closed her eyes and a string of rapid, but perfectly enunciated logorrhea flowed forth:

"*You cannot love a vagina unless you love hair many people do not love hair my first and only husband hated hair he said it was cluttered and dirty he made me shave my vagina it looked puffy and exposed and like a little girl this excited him . . .*"

"All right, all right, *fine*," Gemma grumbled irritably. "You're off book. I get it."

"Pick you up tomorrow, Betty? Say nine?"

Betty, an Irishwoman to her core, feebly protested that she couldn't ask Ashling to go to the trouble. But the idea of spending eight hours uninterrupted with Ashling, just the two of them talking in a small car while Connemara drifted by in all its stark, windswept beauty . . .

It made her feel a little high, just thinking about it.

The strange, silly, fantastical part of her brain had imagined Ashling pulling up to her door in a bright red whatever-the-car-from-*Ferris-Bueller's-Day-Off*-was, pulling down her sunglasses, and purring, "Hey, babe."

The car turned out to be a weather-beaten, six-year-old black Nissan Micra with a floor so dirty that when Betty stepped inside it felt like walking on gravel.

Ashling was not wearing glasses, as it was a miserable, rainy February morning and the sun had evidently taken one look at the scene and gone back to bed in disgust.

She gave Betty a smile.

"Hey, babe," she said.

Every trace of disappointment, blown away like dust.

The drive seemed to take minutes. They chatted about everything; friends, enemies, family (or at least, Betty's family). They sang along to the radio. They sang Disney. They sang Alanis. They sang Oasis. They sang the Beatles, the Stones, the Who.

Betty started to realize that she had never before known someone who she felt so totally at ease with.

"Don't take this the wrong way, Ash," she said. "I feel like I could trust you with a murder confession."

"Really?"

"Yeah. Like, I literally feel like I could tell you where I hid the body."

"Right back at ya, girl."

"Thanks."

"Back garden, under the pepper tree."

"What?"

"God, you're easy . . ."

* * *

They stopped at a petrol station in Galway City and Betty insisted on paying while Ashling went to the bathroom.

As she stepped into the service station to pay she passed a rack of Valentine's Day cards and then backtracked and stopped.

Oh fuck. Should I? Should I really?

Absurdly, she began to blush as she perused the cards on display. She could feel the cashier's eyes on her.

Yes, yes, the fat girl is buying a Valentine's Day card, hilarious.

She saw one that looked quite nice, reached out, picked it up, realized that it was actually the most vile card she had ever seen, and put it back.

She could almost smell her forehead singeing from where the cashier was staring at her.

Christ. This feels like buying porn.

Realizing that Ashling would be back in the car within minutes, she grabbed a card almost at random.

It was a simple pink affair with a large red love heart and, in curly elaborate font, the words "Your Parents Are Going to Hate Me."

Great. Cute. Funny. Plausibly deniable. Not a real valentine, it was just a joke! A funny, funny joke! Ha ha ha ha.

She brought the card to the till and paid for the petrol and the card. She also bought a packet of crisps and some mints to show that that had been her real intent and the card was just a casual afterthought.

I think I'm going crazy, she thought to herself as she sat in the passenger seat, the card carefully stashed in her back pocket.

Ireland hardens as it goes west.

The soil becomes bare and rocky.

The roads become small and winding.

Miles lengthen.

Time slows. In fact, there are fields and mountains where it has never moved at all.

This is Connemara. Not a county, not a province. A place that existed before counties, before provinces.

A land. A stillness.

As they left the soft tissue of the Midlands and hit the hard bone of the West, they became silent. It was a landscape that demanded silence. Gray mountains drifted by in monarchical solemnity.

Sheep gazed out at them from over drystone walls older than the Great Pyramid of Giza.

They drove on.

Their destination was a large redbrick farmhouse on a hill that gave the impression of being a mansion through sheer force of personality. It was the only house for miles around, and as they stepped out of the car a cold wind rushed up to greet them across the huge, stark, rocky field that surrounded the house in all directions.

A woman named Maggie answered the door; pink-faced and friendly, and with a hearty Connemara accent as thick as cheddar.

"Come in come in come in," she barked jovially, leading them into the red-tiled kitchen.

"I'll see if Eilis is up for visitors. Granny!" she barked, ascending the stairs like a boulder reversing up a mountain.

Ashling's eyes widened and she glanced at Betty and mouthed the word "Granny?"

Maggie must have been fifty, at least.

Betty nodded.

They were shown into a darkened room, where a woman lay in bed.

Betty had never known another human being to be so still, and for a moment felt sure the old woman was dead. But then she shifted, like a pile of leaves disturbed by some hidden animal buried beneath.

"Granny, this is . . . what're your names, loves?" her granddaughter said.

"Betty."

"Ashling."

"This is BETTY and ASHLING, Granny," she boomed, and Betty felt a sudden irrational fear that she was speaking loud enough to stop the old woman's heart.

"They're from the college, Granny. Do you want to tell them one of your stories? Sit down there and give her a minute."

She gestured to a chair and a stool beside the bed and Betty and Ashling slowly and quietly sat down beside the crone, like two women who'd seen a rabbit and were afraid it would bolt.

The granddaughter left them and Betty took out her Dicta-phone while Ashling stared at the old woman in mute amazement. One hundred and three years. She did not simply seem like an old woman. She seemed something different entirely. Changed by over a century of increments into something other. When she stared at her with those milky white eyes, Ashling had to repress a shudder. It was unkind, she knew, but the old woman reminded her of nothing more than a great lizard; ancient, still, and utterly alien.

"Hello, Eilis," said Betty, in the voice of someone trying to project confidence while being painfully aware that she's wasting everyone's time. "I was wondering if we could talk about changelings?"

Eilis was staring at Ashling in quiet fascination, but she slowly twisted her neck to look at Betty.

"Professor Ó hÓgáin said you knew a story about a changeling? Usually it's a baby, isn't it?"

Eilis nodded.

"But he said you knew about one who wasn't a baby? One who grew up?"

"He was a priest," Eilis said.

Her voice was so faint and raspy it sounded like she was coming through over an old wireless.

"A priest?" said Betty. "Could you tell me the story?"

"There was a young man," Eilis began, without preamble. "A scholar, he was. He was far from home, wandering the roads at night. Lost, he was. And who does he see on the road but a great, black goat. And he says to himself, 'If I follow that goat, he'll lead me to whatever farm he came from and I can seek my shelter for the night.' And didn't he follow the goat over miles and miles. But then the goat up and vanished and what does he see on the road but a dead man. And of course, he couldn't leave the poor man there. So doesn't the scholar take the dead man on his shoulders, and begin to walk on, hoping he can find somewhere to give the man a good Christian burial."

Betty nodded.

"The dead man began to talk to him," the old woman said.

There was something distinctly unsettling about the way she said that. She didn't seem to be telling a story at all, but recounting some banal tragedy that had happened a long time ago.

"He told the young scholar that if he did what he told him, there'd be great money in it for him. And of course the scholar, well, he was a poor man. So he said he would. He said he'd do whatever he asked. They walked and walked and they came to a house. And the scholar said, 'Shall we rest here?' And the dead man said, 'No, because in that house they are saying the rosary, and I cannot enter.' They walked on. And they came to another house. And the scholar said, 'Shall we rest here?' And the dead man said, 'No, there's a cross laid over the door. I cannot enter there.'

"Then they came to another house, and they could hear a man and his wife arguing. Shouting and cursing and all sorts. And the dead man said, 'We'll stay here. We'll stay here,' he said.

"And the scholar and the dead man had to share a bed, which the scholar did not care for at all. But when he woke the dead man was gone, and he could hear sounds coming from the farmer's bedroom. He could hear the wife."

"He could hear the wife?" Betty repeated, not sure what she meant.

"That's right. He could hear her with the dead man."

It took a few seconds for the hideous penny to drop.

"You mean they were . . . she was?"

"*Ag bualadh craiceann,*"* Eilis said, and gave a hideous skull's grin.

Betty felt her stomach turn. There was a line between pleasantly scary and grotesque and upsetting, and Eilis had lightly stepped over it and grinned at her while she did it.

"He woke again in the night and the dead man was back in the bed with him and oh, he was very boastful. He was telling the scholar that he'd done his job and that the woman was going to bear him a son who'd be a priest. But that everyone the priest ever blessed would belong to him. Well, the scholar had heard enough, and he ran from the house that very night. But he couldn't forget what he'd heard. And many years later he returned to that village. And he goes into the church and who does he see but the young man who's back from the seminary and about to say Mass for the first time. And when he goes to sprinkle the holy water on them all didn't the scholar leap up and say, 'Stop!'?

"The priest was in shock, truly, and didn't know what to do or say, or who this fellow was at all. But the scholar took him aside and told

---

* "Beating skin."

him everything. And the priest of course didn't believe him at first. But when he asked his mother she collapsed in tears and admitted the whole thing. So what was he to do? The priest went to Rome and spoke to the Holy Father, saying how he was in thrall to the Devil. And the Holy Father said he could not be a priest anymore. 'Oh, Father,' said the priest. 'Is there no way? Am I damned, then?'

"And the Holy Father said, 'There is only one remedy that I know of.'"

What Betty thought was a dramatic pause stretched on and on and on. Betty looked up. The old woman was staring at Ashling. Betty could not read any expression on her features. Her face was too old, too slack, too wrinkled. She was like a book whose text had faded away into inscrutability.

"What did he say?" Ashling asked the old woman. It was the first time she had spoken since they had set foot in this room.

Eilis stared back at Ashling. Betty suddenly felt as if she had walked into the middle of an old family feud. It felt like there was unfinished business between these two, who had never met.

The kind of resentment that lurks beneath still waters, deep, dark, and silent, like an alligator.

The old woman smiled. A contemptuous, sneering smile. A distant cousin to a snarl.

"I don't remember," she said simply.

That was all Betty could get out of her. She simply repeated that the story had vanished from her mind without a trace. Betty had no choice but to stop the recording, thank Eilis for her valuable (if only for the scarcity of what remained) time, and hope that a recording of a story with only a beginning and middle would be enough to pass her assignment.

She went downstairs and used the bathroom. When she emerged, Maggie was in the kitchen feeding vegetables into an old blender that wailed loud enough to rattle teeth.

"Where's Ashling?" she asked, having to shout over the noise.

She realized that she had not actually seen Ashling since she emerged from Eilis's room. The stairway had been too narrow to even turn; she had simply assumed Ashling had followed her out.

"She's in with Granny now, getting her story," Maggie yelled over the din.

"What?" Betty asked, confused.

"SHE SAID YOU WERE DONE AND SHE JUST NEEDED TO GET HERS," Maggie roared, thinking that Betty had been unable to hear her.

Betty looked at her in mute confusion. Had Ashling lied to Maggie, pretending to be a folklore student? Or had Maggie simply misunderstood? And, regardless, why was Ashling still up there? What had she to discuss with the ancient woman?

She decided not to say anything and went out to the car to check that the Dictaphone had managed to collect Eilis's whispers.

The sky had become leaden and overcast, and the afternoon light was already starting to gray. Tides of wind washed against the back window as she sat in the passenger seat and listened.

. . . A scholar, he was. He was far from home, wandering the roads at night. Lost, he was. And who does he see on the road but a great, black goat . . .

There was movement in the rearview mirror. Something stirred on the bone-white dry stone wall that encircled the house.

Betty looked up. The Dictaphone slipped from her fingers and Eilis Mulcahy continued whispering her tale from the car floor.

There was a child on the wall.

She was standing, staring at her with the palest blue eyes Betty had ever seen. They seemed to glow in the wintery gloom.

Her hair, light brown and filthy, was caked in dried mud and hung still by her cheeks, even in the howling wind.

Her head seemed unnaturally round. Her cheeks had collapsed and her mouth hung permanently open, like a broken bird's beak, as if she did not have the strength to hold her jaw up. Her teeth lay naked and exposed where the gums had receded. Nothing was left of the arms and legs but bone, and the modesty of skin.

Betty stared at the child in the mirror. But only in the mirror.

She could not bring herself to turn around, and make her real.

For the child could not be real.

She was barefoot, and wearing a filthy dress that hung on her like a towel on a clotheshorse. Around her head and shoulders was a woolen shawl, far too big for her. It was a bright, arterial red, and seemed to blaze against the dull, pale brown of her dress and the sickly white of her complexion.

The child looked like she'd been winnowed. Pared down until nothing was left but bone and hunger.

She stood there on the wall, impossibly real. Horrifically, atrociously present.

Betty had stopped breathing without realizing it. Suddenly she gasped, and as if she had been waiting for the moment, the child vanished.

Betty sprung out of the car and ran for the wall without even understanding why.

Wouldn't anyone? she asked herself. *Would you just go back to the world being normal after that? Wouldn't anyone run?*

She leaped over the wall and found herself in a huge field. She ran, without knowing where she was going. She told herself she had seen the child go this way, even though she hadn't. She was running on pure instinct.

She ran through the field, along the drystone wall, until she came to a certain patch of grass and screamed and gasped and keeled over.

She was, she knew with utter certainty, going to die. All life had leached out of her. She did not have the strength to so much as move her head. The only thoughts she could form were . . .

I am going to die

. . . and . . .

Why, why am I going to die?

Had she been poisoned? Was this a stroke? Had some long-dormant genetic bomb suddenly gone off and blown her to kingdom come?

There were tears running down her face but she was not crying. She did not have the strength to cry. The tears were simply bleeding out of her.

She felt hands grabbing her under her armpits, lifting her off the grass, and turning her over on her back.

That was it.

The sensation was gone. She gave a delayed scream of pain and panic and tried to sit up but those hands held her down. A face was sharpening in her vision. A beautiful face. Ashling.

"Betty!" Ashling mouthed and a few centuries later the words arrived, booming like church bells heard underwater. BETTY.

"I'm okay . . ." she wheezed. She sat up. Her head was swimming and she suddenly realized what the sensation she had felt was.

Hunger.

A hunger more intense than she had ever felt before in her life. A hunger that likely no one still living had ever felt. Because if you felt it, you would soon no longer be living.

Ashling watched in shock and disbelief as Betty reached for her coat pocket and took out the mints and the packet of crisps she had bought at the petrol station and devoured them, practically eating the wrappers in her haste.

But she said nothing, kneeling on the grass beside her until she was ready to talk.

Betty breathed deeply and gave a great shuddering moan.

"Oh fuck . . ." she breathed. "Oh fuck . . ."

"Betty," said Ashling gently. "What the hell was that?"

Betty laughed bitterly and gestured for Ashling to help her to her feet.

Ashling shepherded her back to the car and helped her get inside.

"So?" Ashling asked.

Betty shook her head.

"Not here," she said. "I need to get out of here. I don't want to be here anymore."

Ashling had already started the car before she finished the sentence.

"Do you need a hospital?" Ashling asked after they had been driving for some time.

Betty shook her head. A thought occurred to her.

"How did you know I was there?" she asked.

Ashling looked a little embarrassed.

"I saw you from the upstairs window. I saw you keel over in the field. I thought you were dead."

Betty felt guilty enough that she didn't ask why Ashling had been in Eilis Mulcahy's room in the first place, or why she had lied to Maggie.

Maybe that's why she said it, an unpleasant thought interjected. But she brushed it aside.

"Are you okay, Betty?" Ashling persisted.

Betty nodded.

"Come on. Tell me what happened. Please."

"You're going to say I'm crazy," Betty mumbled.

"I'll say it now. You're crazy. There? Was that so bad? Come on, tell me," Ashling said.

Betty gave a hoarse laugh and braced herself.

"Okay. Do you know what hungry grass is?"

"No."

"It's . . . in folklore, it's a patch of grass where someone died. During the Famine. And if you step on it, you feel what they felt. Right before they . . . yeah."

No need to talk about the girl. This is enough to be getting on with.

Ashling said nothing for a few seconds.

"What did you feel?" she said.

"Like . . . like I was dying. But too slowly," said Betty. "I . . . I've never felt . . ."

Her eyes began to well up.

She could have gone back to the house. That's what they always did in the stories. She would have gone back and asked Maggie, "Tell me, what happened in that field?" and Maggie would go very pale and very quiet and say, "Oh, during the Great Hunger there was a girl . . ."

But she hadn't needed to.

There was no mystery.

She had stepped on the place where the girl had fallen. Where her reed-thin legs had finally surrendered. Where she had lain crumpled on the grass in agony, waiting at last for release.

She felt the car slowing and before she knew what was happening Ashling's arms were around her, holding her tight.

"I believe you" was all she said.

Ashling had wanted to leave her home but Betty had insisted that they go back to the college. She wanted to upload her recording onto the archive computer and then be *done*. The thought of misplacing or accidentally erasing the recording and then having to go *back* . . .

No.

Ashling gave her a comforting squeeze on the shoulder as they parted ways.

After leaving the recording safely in the Folklore Department, she sat in Hilpers with a cup of tea and stared blankly at the wall.

Ironically enough, she did not feel hungry, and doubted she ever would again.

Out of habit more than anything else, she ambled down the stairs to Dramsoc and stopped when she heard angry yelling coming from below. There were two voices.

Ashling was shouting, and Gemma was talking at the exact same volume she always did, but slower (which was her version of shouting).

"We don't have time," Gemma repeated.

"I can get the hair! I can fucking drive there myself!"

"No. I need you here. We've already lost a day."

"Gemma, we *can't* have a shaved cunt over the entrance for V week, that goes against the whole . . . My entire monologue is called 'Hair is there for a reason.'"

"No, it's about how it's fine to shave or not shave as long as it's your decision . . ."

"It's *your* decision!" said Ashling angrily.

"Fine," said Gemma coldly. "Find the fifty-foot-tall papier-mâché woman with the detachable fanny and ask her if it's okay."

"No, look. I'm going to be up onstage talking about how body hair is a beautiful and natural thing after the audience have walked through this fucking bald Playboy bunny cooch! We'll look like a bunch of hypocrites."

"Ash, it's really not that big a deal."

"No, Gem. It's not a big deal *to you*," said Ashling, eyes flashing. "Because this is just something to put on the CV for you. This is just one more body on your path to power."

She turned, and stormed out of the theater.

"See you at rehearsals," Gemma called after her.

"You might," Ashling replied from the corridor.

"I will. Or there'll be *another* body on my path to power," Gemma informed her.

Betty descended nervously down the stairs, like the first miner back in the pit after a tunnel collapse.

"Everything okay?"

"Yeah," said Gemma. "My aunt wasn't able to bring the hair. So we won't have a hairy cunt and now I've destroyed feminism forever. You free to do some postering?"

As it happened, Betty wanted nothing more than to go home,

crawl into bed, and forget every mad, bad thing that had happened to her today, but it was an unspoken Dramsoc rule that you never turned down a request to help poster for a show.

"Sure," she said.

Gemma could see the concern in her face.

"Ash will be fine," she said. "Trust me. She'll get over it."

She moved out of the way for Kev Power, who had just entered the theater dressed in white robes with a fake white beard, fishnet stockings, and red high heels.

"Found it," he said, without even bothering to look up at the clitoris.

"Very funny, Kev," Betty said.

"You're the first person to make that joke," Gemma told him.

After he'd gone, Betty glanced at Gemma and mouthed the word "What?"

"He's playing Godot," Gemma told her.

"But . . ." said Betty, very confused, "Godot never actually appears . . ."

"Oh, they are taking some fucking liberties, that shower," said Gemma darkly.

Betty followed Gemma down the corridor to the Dramsoc office.

The committee was not in session and the room was empty of people and full of just about everything else.

Gemma surveyed the office like a young Julius Caesar gazing upon the Capitoline Hill for the first time, and her eyes finally lighted on the auditor's chair at the top of the table. She had run for auditor unsuccessfully twice already, and was planning on making a third and final attempt this year.

"God, I want this so bad I can taste it," she murmured, gesturing to the office.

Between the poor ventilation, the smell of body odor, the ancient and historically significant remains of a pizza on the table, and the undeniable scent of a small carton of milk trapped and helpless somewhere beneath a landslide of books, clothes, and rubbish, Betty was certain she *could* already taste it.

Gemma went to the filing cabinet (which was rather suspiciously located right beside the shredder) and removed a large stack of black-and-white posters advertising *The Vagina Monologues* with an image far more genteel and refined than either Gemma or Ashling had wanted.

Posters for shows always suffered attrition as other societies tore them down or postered over them in the fiercely competitive struggle for advertising space on campus. But *The Vagina Monologues* had seen a particularly aggressive war against their advertising, with dozens of posters being torn down mere hours after being posted. It was so systematic that Gemma had started to half suspect the college itself was behind it.

She gestured for Betty to pass her bag over to take the posters and noticed that she was looking distractedly at the large pink cardboard box in the center of the table.

"Are you going to put a card in?" she asked.

Betty sighed and, from her coat pocket, took out the card that she'd bought in the service station.

It looked so cheap and silly now. Valentine's cards were for crushes. What she felt for Ashling now was love. It was, she knew, not a particularly healthy kind of love. She loved Ashling because Ashling had cared for her, looked after her, held her, saved her when she most desperately needed her. It was the kind of love wounded soldiers felt for their nurses. It was the love you felt for a fireman carrying you out of a blazing building. Not exactly the foundation for a lasting relationship.

Oh, well. I'll just forget about it, then.

"No," she said at last. "Bad idea."

"Can I see?" Gemma asked.

Betty handed it to her with a shrug.

"I haven't written anything yet."

Gemma frowned as she looked at the card.

"It's stupid, isn't it?" Betty asked.

"Why?"

"I don't know if she even . . ."

"What?"

"Visits the island of Lesbos," said Betty, and then paused to commit the memory of saying that to the part of her brain that would wake her up randomly in the middle of the night to cringe for saying it until the day she died.

"I'm pretty sure she lives there," said Gemma. "Apart from that brief trip she took in first year to the Isle of Man."

This was news to Betty.

"And . . . how was that trip?"

"From what she's told me it was nicer than she expected, she enjoyed her time there, but it wasn't exactly life-changing and she probably won't go back. But Douglas was really nice."

Betty was now thoroughly confused.

"Douglas. Her boyfriend in first year was called Douglas," Gemma explained. "Studying law. Really nice guy. Also figuring some stuff out. Honestly, I say go for it. But not with this card."

"Why not?" Betty asked.

Gemma traced her finger under the text on the front of the card.

Your Parents Are Going to Hate Me

Betty didn't get it. "So?"

"Oh . . . shit. You don't know, do you?" Gemma said quietly.

Betty looked at her blankly.

Gemma hissed awkwardly.

"Ash's dad is dead. And she *does not* get on with her mother. So I would leave any mention of parents out of Valentine's Day cards. I mean, in general. But specifically if you're writing one for Ash."

"Shit," said Betty. "I never knew that. How old was she when he . . ."

"Eight or nine," said Gemma. "I think. I don't know. I don't go there. That whole neighborhood is bad news."

"Oh" was all Betty said.

She felt ashamed that she hadn't known that, that she had never bothered to ask Ashling about her family. And she felt ashamed that Ashling had apparently never felt like she could tell her.

Fuck it. It was a bad idea. It had always been a bad idea.

She took the Valentine's Day card, and fed it to the shredder.

It was already dark when Betty left the Belfield campus on her bus home. The overcast February sky hung ominously over Donnybrook like a billion tons of dull gray iron and a lazy half-hearted rain had started to spatter on the bus window.

She wondered whose idea it had been to have Valentine's Day in the middle of the bleakest, most depressing month of the year.

She was still in shock from her encounter in Clifden. But something about the yellow streetlamps going past soothed her nerves. They were so ordinary, and so very urban. The city was safe and rational. Outside its borders, she now knew, you could trust nothing.

Not even your own eyes or body.

Arriving home, she opened the front door only to find that something was blocking it, and had to squeeze through a gap around a foot wide. Inside, she saw the culprit. The hallway was crammed with cardboard boxes, each one containing around six rolls of glossy red wrapping paper.

"Mam?" she called. "Hi and what the fuck?"

"Oh, hi, love," her mother said, poking her head into the hall and vanishing just as quickly.

"What's all this?" Betty asked, setting down her bag and stretching to work the kinks out of her back.

"Oh, they were using it to decorate the office for Valentine's Day and they had a few rolls left over. I said I'd take them. Save us having to buy wrapping paper at Christmas."

Great idea. Never mind that Christmas is ten months away and we have nowhere to store all this.

There was a time when she would have made that very point to her mother, but she was tired, she was miserable, she was cold, and there was a shower upstairs ready and waiting to wash her troubles away.

In the bathroom, she undressed and paused before stepping into the shower to look at her naked body in the mirror. She stared at her crotch and the large, wild bushel of coarse, curly red hair that covered it.

Hair is there for a reason, she thought. *In this instance, the reason being I can't be arsed to do anything with it. It would be like tidying the garden shed. What's the point, it's not like I'm going to have visitors there.*

But now that she'd noticed it, she realized that it bothered her. She took a small pair of scissors from the bathroom cabinet and began to trim around the edges. She quickly realized that she was in over her head and that trying to keep both sides even was resulting in more and more hair being cut. After around five minutes she looked at the sorry results in the mirror and snorted in exasperation.

A new monologue: my vagina looks like it got its hair cut in the Barbers' College.

Taking some toilet paper, she began to gather up the glossy red hairs that had formed drifts on the bathroom tiles.

She stopped.

She stared.

An idea started to run naked through the streets of her mind, waving its arms and loudly yelling for her attention.

From experience she knew that ideas like that were either very good or very bad and she would only know which after it was already too late.

She threw on her clothes and ran downstairs.

"Mam!" she called.

"Yes, love?"

"I need to go back to college, I'll be late home!"

"What about dinner?"

"Save me some!"

"Will you not wait—"

"Sorry, can't! Mam, can I take one of these boxes? Or two?"

"Sure, I suppose . . ."

The door slammed before she could finish the sentence.

Betty was already staggering toward the bus stop, two boxes of shiny red wrapping paper stacked precariously in her arms.

"Oh my *God.*"

"Are they serious?"

"I think it's great. It's a strong statement. It's in your face."

"If you had that in your face, you'd suffocate."

"I dunno. I mean, the show's not really about the *vaginas,* is it?"

"Eh, no. It absolutely is."

"Technically it's a vulva, not a vagina."

A collective groan went up from the women waiting outside the theater to be let in for rehearsals.

"Oh my God, Leanne, nobody cares," said Louise Malpas ("Reclaiming Cunt").

"Plus, you're wrong," said Gemma, coming down the stairs at a brisk pace. "Sorry I'm late."

The cast of *The Vagina Monologues* tutted disapprovingly at their director.

"All right, fuck off, I'm not that sorry," Gemma said.

"How am I wrong?" asked Leanne Riordan ("My Angry Vagina").

"You go through it to enter the theater. That makes it a passageway, which makes it a vagina as well as—"

Gemma stopped as she parted the crowd and saw the object under discussion.

"Huh . . ." she said. Glancing over her shoulder, she saw Betty watching from the lockers, trying to look as unobtrusive as possible.

Gemma gave a little smile and then turned to the cast.

"Who are we missing?" she asked. "Is Ash here?"

"Yup," said Ashling Mallen ("Hair") sullenly, coming through the door from the Dramsoc office.

"All right, everyone," said Gemma loudly. "A round of applause, please, for Ash and her amazing vagina slash vulva."

Ashling stared daggers at Gemma as the applause rose, crescendoed, and faded away.

Then, as the cast began to file into the theater, she saw it for the first time.

She grabbed Gemma by the arm.

"Did you do this?" she whispered.

Gemma said nothing but gestured with her chin to Betty, who was still behind the lockers trying to pretend that she wasn't watching, and failing rather adorably.

Gemma followed the cast into the theater and Ashling was left alone, staring up at the massive vulva over the entrance to the theater, which was now adorned with what looked like a thick coat of glossy red hair.

When she had pictured this moment, Betty had imagined swaggering over to Ashling, putting an arm over her shoulder, and saying something irresistibly sexy.

Instead, she found herself shuffling awkwardly and standing beside her in tense silence.

Ashling did not seem happy. She looked like a five-year-old who'd been told of the death of a grandparent. Numb incomprehension.

"You did this?" she said at last, her eyes never wavering from it.

Betty nodded.

"How?"

"Well . . ." Betty began. "My mam had loads of this spare red wrapping paper and I was in the . . . I just got this idea . . . so, I came back here with the paper and I ran the sheets through the shredder in the office. And then I found the glue gun and just . . . yeah."

She trailed off as she realized Ashling was staring at her.

"Wrapping paper?" said Ashling.

"Yup," said Betty.

"That . . ." Ashling began, ". . . was really, really fucking clever. Why the fuck didn't I think of it?"

"Well, you didn't have time anyway . . ."

"I was going to use *fucking actual hair*. It would have been gross and it would have smelled and probably been a fire hazard and I would have been covered in glue and other people's hair. And it would have looked *awful*. Why the fuck didn't I think of this?!"

A ball of stress that had been building and building in Betty's stomach suddenly burst and she felt a wave of relief.

She likes it. She likes my giant hairy vagina. Oh thank God.

"Betty, how long did this take you?" Ashling asked.

"Just a few hours," Betty lied.

She had almost been locked in the building by security and had missed the last bus. She had had to get a taxi home and then wake her mother to pay for it and then endure a noticeably chilly breakfast the next morning.

"You must have been here most of the night," Ashling said, shaking her head.

"I think you might have saved my life yesterday," said Betty. "And this was really important to you. So it was important to me. Y'know. By osmosis."

Osmosis? What the fuck are you talking about?

"Okay," said Ashling. "Okay. So. This is probably the single sweetest thing that anyone has ever done for me. And I don't know what to do with that. I'm not good with affection. I don't know how to properly thank you for this. I don't know how."

"You don't have to," Betty blurted out. "I wasn't trying to . . . You don't owe me anything. Seriously. Nothing. I don't want you to feel that you do. I would never want you to fee—"

She stopped because Ashling had put a finger on her lower lip.

Who has fingers that soft? It's like a little bunny's paw in a wee satin glove.

Ashling gazed at her. Her eyes were the color of mossy stone on the bed of a lake.

"I am here. And I am listening. What. Do. You. Want?"

Betty's mouth felt very dry.

"You want to go for coffee?" she asked.

Ashling smiled.

"We go for coffee all the time."

"No. We go and sit in the same place and drink coffee. I mean, go for coffee."

The smile remained.

"You know what? I would really like that."

A voice called from inside the theater.

"Ash, get your monologue in here!"

"Go," said Betty. "I'm coming to the show, I'll see you after."

"Okay," said Ashling. She turned and began to walk through the giant papier-mâché vagina. She stopped, and Betty heard her mutter "Ah fuck it" under her breath.

Suddenly she had turned around, pulled Betty to her, and all at once there was a hand in her hair, a tongue in her mouth, and joy in every last cell of her body.

The kiss was long, and playful and tender and wonderful. And it only ended when she had a sudden thought that made her burst out laughing.

"What?" Ashling asked, her hands cradling her face, and her forehead pressed against hers. "What's so funny?"

"I was just thinking, this will be the weirdest fucking story to tell people . . ." And Betty didn't even get to finish as Ashling burst out laughing herself.

Betty realized she had never heard her laugh. It was a deliciously filthy cackle, and she loved the sound of it.

They kissed again and Betty's eyes glanced up at the papier-mâché clitoris that hung over them like mistletoe.

Found it, she thought.

PS: *(inaudible over background noise) . . . ah, got it. Got it. There it is. It's recording now.*

CPF: *Is it not very loud here? Do you want to go somewhere quieter?*

PS: *Here should be fine. It's the thirteenth of May, 1999, and I am here in the White Horse Pub in West London with . . .*

CPF: *Cian Flynn. Call me Keano.*

PS: *Thank you very much for agreeing to talk to me.*

CPF: *Sure. Sure. Happy to. What do you want to know?*

PS: *So, as I said before, I've been investigating Scarnagh since . . . well, since Scarnagh. Since just after Etain Larkin's disappearance . . .*

CPF: *Well then, can I ask* you *a question?*

PS: *Sure, go ahead.*

CPF: *Do you think they're connected?*

PS: *Do I think what's connected?*

CPF: *Everything that came after. With Barry and the . . . (inaudible)*

PS: *(inaudible) . . . know. I don't think so. I certainly don't think he had anything to do with it. I mean, you knew Barry, didn't you?*

CPF: *Oh yeah. Lovely bloke. But that's what they always say, isn't it?*

PS: *Do they?*

CPF: *Yeah. Like "Oh, he always seemed like such a nice guy" when he was actually . . .*

PS: *Actually what?*

CPF: *Nothing. Nothing. I don't think Barry did anything.*

PS: *Keano, do you remember very early on, right after Etain went missing, there was all this talk in the press about a fight?*

CPF: *At the party. Yeah.*

PS: *There was one?*

CPF: *No, I mean I remember people talking about it. I was there the whole night. I never heard anything. They went into the back room together and they didn't come out again . . . Etain left in the middle of the night and Barry came out in the morning. I mean, they might have had a fight when they were alone together . . .*

PS: *But then they'd be the only two who'd know about it. Barry, Etain, maybe Kate. But all three said there was no fight.*

CPF: *Yeah.*

PS: *So where does the story of the fight come from? Who tells the Gardaí that Etain and Barry had a fight and poisons the first few days of the investigation?*

CPF: *(inaudible)*

PS: *I've tried. She's hard to get in touch with. Why?*

CPF: *I think she knew.*

PS: What makes you say that?

CPF: Kate. Right before we broke up. Before she moved to London. She said, "Etain knows who shopped Barry." She wouldn't tell me who. Then I asked her if she thought she was right.

PS: And what did she say?

CPF: She didn't say anything. She just looked at me like . . .

PS: Like . . . "No"?

CPF: Like "Yeah." Like "Absolutely fucking 'yeah.'"

Transcript of call recorded May 13, 1999
File "Skelton. P. #109817"
Archive of the Department of Policy Oversight

MAY 1981

Breakup. I'd bet good money she's here to break some poor *fellah's heart.*

Brendan Flanagan, publican by trade, observer of the human animal by inclination, stood behind the bar idly cleaning a glass and studying the young woman seated at the far end of the pub. She was sitting alone, a half-pint of Guinness in front of her that she'd apparently purchased purely because it matched her outfit for all the interest she seemed to have in drinking it.

She was, to put it bluntly, only gorgeous.

Long black hair, and the dark, almost Italian-looking features of many Dublin women. That, coupled with her tense expression and her hawk-like surveillance of the entrance, was what had Brendan convinced that he was about to witness some hapless sod getting his marching orders.

She was not a regular, and not the kind of patron who would ever become a regular. Brendan Flanagan prided himself on running a reputable establishment, but he was under no illusions that this was the kind of pub that highly eligible young women would flock to. Flanagan's was an Old Man Pub, and would be until the breaking of the Seventh Seal.

Just off Kildare Street, it had been the watering hole of weary civil servants of the most unglamorous sort for twenty years now.

She's meeting him here to give him the boot because she's not planning on ever setting foot here again, Brendan said to himself. He made a mental note to stand the intended victim a pint on the house after surgery had concluded.

As if on cue, a large freckle-faced young man in his twenties with an untidy heap of ginger hair flustered through the front door of the pub.

Him? Brendan thought to himself as the dark-haired beauty rose from her seat with a sad-looking smile and embraced the newcomer warmly. *Ah, fair's fair. You can do better, love.*

"Hi, Kate," said Barry, kissing his sister-in-law on the cheek. "You're looking well."

"You too," she said, and she meant it. He'd been working in the Department of Agriculture for almost a year now and it seemed to have done him good. He was a bit more confident. Sure of himself. He also looked fairly exhausted, but that was only to be expected under the circumstances. He asked her if she wanted anything from the bar and, when she declined, left the table and returned with a pint which had been poured for him with a look of kind, paternal sympathy from the barman.

He sat across from her, and they waited to see who would speak first.

"So . . ." he said.

"Are you . . ." she asked.

Silence.

"How are you doing?" he asked softly.

Kate shrugged.

"Good," she said. "Better than I expected. A lot better than I expected. Funerals are like that though. Is that just me? I sort of like them. Is that weird?"

"No," he said. "Not a bit. I know exactly what you mean."

He sighed wearily.

"I'm sorry we weren't there . . ."

She reached out and put her hand on his and looked him dead in the eye.

"No," she said firmly, an absolute command. "Don't say that. Neither of you owed her that. Especially not Etain, but not you either."

He didn't get that, she could see it in his face. Guilt, but also confusion. That was not how his family did things. Larkins and Mallens. Different species.

She knew without asking that he had wanted to go to the funeral, and that it was Etain who had refused.

Kate herself had very nearly done the same thing, and God knew she had less reason than her sister.

But in the end, whether out of guilt or a lingering sense of filial obligation or perhaps just a need to bear witness, she had attended the funeral and stood in Glasnevin Cemetery as the remains of Mairéad Larkin were returned to the earth.

As Kate had watched the gravediggers work, every shovelful of soil laid on the coffin had felt like it was being scooped off her own chest.

As the mother was buried, the daughter was exhumed.

She had felt liberated, and had enjoyed the rest of the day, catching up with relatives and friends of the family that she had not spoken to for many years.

It was only in the days and weeks afterward that old memories had started to align themselves in ominous shapes. She had not been sleeping well, and a feeling of dread had begun to thicken and blacken in her mind.

"We should have at least been here to help with the arrangements," said Barry.

"Honestly, I hardly did anything," Kate replied.

That was true. Mairéad had been very active in the local chapter of the Legion of Mary. They had taken on the task of arranging the funeral. Kate had been left to make a few phone calls to the rest of the family while occasionally answering questions as to what her mother would have liked in terms of floral arrangements. This had largely been guesswork, as Kate could not recall her mother ever speaking favorably of flowers.

Or anything else, for that matter, she thought to herself.

Enough. She's gone. If you can't think of anything nice, stop thinking about her. Just leave her be, for fuck's sake.

In fact, since the funeral, Kate had found herself grappling with a new and alien emotion toward her mother.

Pity.

At the afters, held in the parish hall, a tiny silver-haired man in his sixties had tapped her theatrically on the shoulder. She had turned to look at him and he gave her a wink and a broad smile full of devilment and declared in a Dublin accent as thick as leather: "Ah, is it little Katie?"

It had taken her a few seconds to remember Francis Corcoran. She recalled him dressing up as Santa Claus many years ago at a family Christmas party. Four-year-old Etain had run screaming but Kate had held her nerve and got a coloring book, some crayons, and that same wink.

"Uncle Fran," she said warmly, and gave him a hug.

It was like hugging a child, he was so small, and she felt him wince slightly from the pressure of her arms.

Of course. They're all like that, aren't they? All the Corcorans. Small and fragile as china cups.

Mairéad Larkin (née Corcoran) had been born in the early '20s in a tenement in Rialto. She had been the sixth of eleven children, eight of whom had lived to adulthood. There were three left now.

Fran gestured to where his two sisters, Rita and Teresa, shuffled up and down the buffet table looking for a sandwich that hadn't been defiled with mayonnaise. They both looked shockingly like her mother, Rita particularly.

So that's what Ma would look like if she had ever smiled, Kate had thought. None of the three Corcorans, not Fran, not Rita, and not Teresa, were taller than five foot three.

Stunted growth. Brittle bones.

A childhood spent starving would do that.

A cold, terrible realization hit Kate. That's why she was such a snob. That's why she drove Etain to tears trying to crush that accent out of her.

Mairéad had grown up in one of the most impoverished neighborhoods in one of the poorest cities in Western Europe. But she had finished school. Gotten a job as a secretary. She had met Kate's father, who came from a quite well-off middle-class background. For Mairéad, it must have been like marrying into the aristocracy.

Was she a snob?

How could she *not* be obsessed with class, with status, with sounding like you belonged where you knew you didn't? For her, learning to speak like she'd been raised in a home with running water had not been a matter of pride. It had been a matter of survival, and escape.

And in that moment Kate did feel pity for her mother.

Mairéad had not escaped. Not in the end. Poverty and starvation might not have left their mark on her voice, but they had cursed her bones. She had suffered from osteoporosis all her life. In the end, it had killed her.

"Elaine couldn't make it?" Fran asked.

"Etain," she corrected. "No. She's abroad."

It was the same lie she'd used every time someone had asked her about her sister's whereabouts.

Abroad. In the People's Republic of Cork.

Barry took a slurp from his pint and then gave a long, leonine yawn. He hadn't had a good night's sleep for the better part of a year. Probably longer.

"How are the girls?" she asked.

Barry smiled tiredly. "Niamh is as good as gold. Sleeps like a log. Eats everything you put in front of her. Ashling . . . Mam says God gave us Niamh to apologize for Ashling."

The expression on Kate's face was not what he had been hoping for.

"It's just a joke," he reassured her.

Kate was funny about Ashling, he remembered.

"Ashling's fine," he said. "She's feeding better at least. The doctor was very happy with her on the last checkup. Said she's starting to put on weight, thank God."

"And Etain?" Kate asked.

Barry thought for a few seconds.

"Good. I think. I think she's good. Moving back up to Dublin helped her a lot. She seems more . . . settled in herself? You know? I hate to say it, but I think Mairéad's passing, God rest her . . ."

"Lifted a weight?"

"Yeah."

He frowned, troubled by the thought.

You don't say? Kate thought miserably.

"She's still not . . . she's still not back to where she used to be," he admitted. "And I don't expect her to be. I don't expect her to just get over Scarnagh."

Scarnagh.

Like "Watergate" or "Weimar," it was not simply the name of a place. For Barry and Kate it was a one-word summation of an entire universe of dates and events and people. "Scarnagh" was the farmstead where Etain had been taken. It was the disappearance itself. It was the media circus that had followed. It was Etain's severing of all ties with Mairéad. It was the fact that Feidhlim Lowney's body had never been discovered and that he was presumably still out there somewhere. And more than what was known, "Scarnagh" was the name of the unknown. Why had Etain been taken? What had Lowney wanted with her? How had the farmhouse gone up in flames, by arson or accident? Were the charred remains found in the kitchen really Bernadette Lowney, or someone else?

Scarnagh was the sensation of waking up at five in the morning in a cold sweat.

Scarnagh was wondering who had told the guards there had been a fight between Etain and Barry.

Scarnagh was the pregnancy.

In April 2014, a meme was posted on the r/Scarnaghaffair Reddit page. It depicted a middle-aged African American woman seated in front of a computer, with an expression of exasperation and weary despair on her face.

The caption read: THE MOMENT YOU REALIZE YOU ASKED ETAIN LARKIN TO REMEMBER YOUR PASSWORD FOR YOU.

It was as good an illustration as any as to the frustrated, sometimes even hostile, attitude with which the r/Scarnaghaffair community viewed the victim at the heart of the mystery.

One post, entitled "Why Etain Larkin is just the worst," acted out an imaginary conversation with her:

"Why did you drive to Scarnagh?"

"Don't 'member."

"What did Lowney do to you?"

"Don't 'member."

"How did the fire start?"

"Don't 'member."

"Kitchen bones. Any thoughts?"

"Don't 'member."

"Care to shed some light on how you got out of the house before it went boom?"

"Don't 'member."

"BITCH, I SWEAR TO GOD . . ."

Occasionally, a commenter would remind the thread that Etain had suffered massive trauma as well as severe dehydration and malnutrition, and that it was entirely to be expected that she would be unwilling or unable to remember what had happened. Whereupon, the commenter would be asked to refrain from being a white-knighting cuck and the conversation would return to how frustrating it was that Etain Larkin couldn't seem to remember a single, solitary thing about her captivity in the Lowneys' farmhouse.

But that was not entirely true.

There was one point on which Etain Larkin was absolutely, unequivocally certain:

Feidhlim Lowney had not raped her.

That question, already lurking in the background, had suddenly lurched into a new and terrible prominence with the discovery that she was pregnant.

They had returned to the Mallens' homestead after visiting the doctor (Etain had flatly refused to return home to Mairéad's house and was living in the Mallens' spare bedroom until after the wedding).

The silence as they had sat together in the kitchen had seemed to go on forever. Finally, he had croaked, "Did—"

"No," she cut across him. "He never touched me. It's yours."

"That's not . . ." he began helplessly.

What? What had he meant? What had he been trying to say?

It's all right? It doesn't matter? I don't care?

It wasn't all right. It mattered. He cared.

But what to say? What to say.

What do you want to do?

How can I help?

I'll fix this?

I'll make it right?

He had no way forward. He had no words.

She had put her hand on his. Gently rubbed it with her thumb and then fixed him with a stare that he could feel on the back of his skull.

Her pale blue eyes seemed to be casting light.

"He never touched me," she repeated. "It's yours."

Those were the words.

The tone said: *and that is the last time we will ever discuss this.*

She wasn't lying. He knew that.

She absolutely believed it.

The question was whether she believed it because it was true, or because she needed it to be.

In time, Barry had put it out of his mind.

Barry and Etain had slept together right before her disappearance.

She had become pregnant.

As a theory it was simple, elegant, and perfectly plausible.

Barry believed it, because he had no reason not to.

He loved his children, both of them.

That was all that mattered.

He reached into the pocket of his jacket and pulled out a battered, worn leather wallet. He opened the wallet to show her the picture that he kept there: himself, Etain, and the twins seated on a faded red living room couch.

The twins were around six months old. Barry, grinning proudly, was seated on the left, Niamh balanced on his knee. Blond as a daffodil and giving a smile to the camera worthy of a baby on a Calvita box, the platonic ideal of infant bonhomie.

On the right, Etain, managing a watery smile that could not quite mask the tiredness that was plain on her face. In her arms, tiny Ashling, sleeping uneasily and with a look of discomfort on her scrunched, sallow features.

The contrast, Barry and Niamh on one side, Etain and Ashling on the other, gave the impression of a picture starting strong before slumping at the finish line.

Kate instinctively knew that they had had to wait until Ashling was asleep before even attempting to take the photograph.

Poor dote, thought Kate, looking at the picture of her youngest niece. She felt a surge of protectiveness.

Ashling, born struggling into the world. Too small. Unwilling to take the breast. Sleepless. Restless. While Niamh slept like a winter hedgehog, Etain and Barry took shifts through the long ragged nights with howling Ashling in their arms, trying to rock her into thin and precious silence.

When she had come to visit Etain in the hospital the first time, Etain had silently passed Ashling to Kate to hold. The tiny girl had cried weakly and Kate had cooed down at her.

"Hush now, love. It's okay. Auntie Kate's here. It'll be okay."

The child furrowed her brow but had stopped crying and looked up cautiously at the stranger looking down at her.

Then she had gripped Kate's finger and held on to it tightly, like someone finding a friend in a hostile foreign land.

Kate loved both her nieces, but Ashling had a special place in her heart. She loved Ashling in the same way she had always loved Etain. And for the same reason.

I love them because they deserve to be loved. And because I know their mothers don't.

Where did these awful, cruel thoughts come from, Kate wondered.

Is it the whole human race that's awful, or just me? Which is worse?

She'd been having a lot of bad thoughts recently. She'd been pulling them up like weeds every hour of every day for weeks.

She was starting to lose the fight. She was starting to succumb to sheer exhaustion, trying not to think the things that she was thinking.

Barry now came to the business at hand. He reached into his jacket pocket and took out a new white envelope that was already crumpled.

Barry had that effect on paper. Nothing stayed pristine in his company.

If Barry Mallen had been charged with bringing the stone tablets down from Mount Sinai, Kate thought, *they would have been creased by the time he reached the bottom.*

He passed it over to her with a look of awkward shyness.

"Thanks," she said, and put it in her handbag.

"Don't you want to take a look?" he asked, surprised.

She shook her head. "Not here," she said.

He nodded, understanding.

"Barry . . ." And she suddenly reached out and took his hand.

He looked at her in surprise and not a little concern.

"What's wrong?" he asked.

She desperately tried to think of the right way to ask the question.

"Barry," she said again. "When Etain found out. About Mam. How was she? How did she take it?"

"Well . . . you tell me?" Barry answered.

Fuck.

"She was with you?" he said.

Fuck. Fuck. Fuck. No. Fuck.

Kate closed her eyes and said, "Yeah. 'Course. I meant . . . when she got home. When you saw her? I meant . . . Fuck, I don't know what I meant, forget it. It's fine."

She pulled away and he looked at her with concern and a trace of distrust. Suspicion was not something she could ever remember seeing on his face. It didn't suit him.

The morning her mother died, she had been having a quiet coffee in the kitchen when the phone had rung. She had answered it and been pleasantly surprised to hear Barry on the other end.

"Kate! Guess what!" he had said, sounding like a ten-year-old boy whose parents had got him an Atari.

"Go on?"

"I got the job!"

"Ah, Barry, I'm delighted for you!" she'd said, and she had been.

Barry, Etain, and the twins had been staying with the Mallens while Barry had looked for work in the midst of the worst recession in the nation's history. He'd come up to Dublin a few weeks prior to apply for an entry-level position in the Department of Agriculture. She'd met up with him for coffee afterward and he'd been convinced that he'd made a hames of the interview. Happily, it seemed he'd been wrong.

"I'm starting next month!"

"So, how's that going to work?" she asked. "Are you all coming up to Dublin or . . ."

He gave a sigh.

"I dunno, like," he said. "Probably just have to find somewhere cheap in Dublin to rent until I can save up enough to put a deposit down for a house. Go back to Cork on the weekends, like."

There was a touch of dread in his voice.

Ah. Etain is not exactly thrilled with you leaving her with the kids for five days out of every week, is she?

Reading between the lines, she knew that things were becoming a little *tense* between Etain and her mother-in-law, Anne. Only to be expected. The house was overcrowded and no one was getting any sleep thanks to Ashling. Kate didn't know how they had managed to avoid bloodshed for this long.

"Do you have anywhere in mind?" she asked.

"One or two places."

"Well, worse comes to worst there's room here," she said, and felt a sudden pang of irrational social anxiety.

Is that allowed? Asking your brother-in-law to live with you? Is that weird?

Barry apparently didn't think so.

"Kate, honestly, that'd be fantastic! Hopefully it'd just be for a few months."

"Yeah, no bother."

And then he said it.

"Hey, is Etain there?"

She answered the question before she even really fully understood it.

"Eh . . . no?" she'd said.

Barry had not caught the confusion.

"Ah, no worries," he said. "If she's lying in, don't wake her. Will you just tell her to give me a call when she's free?"

Kate had felt a sudden spark of panic.

Does Barry think Etain is staying with me?

Why?

Oh God. Oh God, tell me she's not missing again.

They never caught him. Lowney. They never caught—

No. If Barry thinks she's here she must have lied and told him that she's staying with me.

And she did that because . . .

From the other end of the line she heard a baby crying and Barry swearing.

"Shite. Sorry, Kate, duty calls. Bye."

"Bye, Barry," she murmured as he hung up.

She stared at the phone, wondering if she should call him back.

Where was Etain? Why was she lying to Barry?

Is she . . . holy shit, is she having an affair?

She promptly dismissed the idea as ludicrous. Etain would never do that to Barry. Perhaps more to the point, Kate doubted she *could* do that. Etain was spending her days in a house, in a field, in a state of constant nervous exhaustion. How could she even have the *energy* for an affair?

And who with? Where was she finding the time to mingle with eligible single men in between looking after two babies?

She decided that it was simply a misunderstanding on Barry's part. Etain was visiting someone else. Another Kate maybe. Wasn't there a Kate or a Katie or a Kathleen that Etain had been friends with in college? Kates were everywhere. They were a plague. It was fine.

It was fine.

She had finished her coffee and gone into town to buy a new outfit for a job interview. She was flying to London the next month for an opening in an ad agency. As she left Cleary's with the suit folded under one arm, she headed north up O'Connell Street. When she reached the entrance to the Savoy Cinema her shoe got stuck on some chewing gum and she almost tripped, dropping the suit.

Cursing under her breath, she bent down to pick it up.

There was a padlocked bike in front of her and, through the spokes of the front wheel, she saw a figure moving down the other side of O'Connell Street.

It was Etain.

Her sister was heading south in the direction of O'Connell Bridge.

Years afterward, Kate would try to remember the expression her sister had worn in that moment. Sometimes she remembered seeing regret. Sometimes triumph. Sometimes joy.

But the truth was, Etain had no expression at all. She simply had the blank, neutral look of a young woman in town on an errand.

It was a face for getting the milk.

Kate stood up and almost waved and shouted to her, but Etain was already too far away and the road was busy and loud. So Kate simply watched her until she had melted away into the crowd.

So she was in Dublin, after all, she mused to herself.

She was a little hurt that Etain hadn't called her to let her know she'd be in town.

It was early too. She must have spent the night in Dublin. Who could she have stayed with?

Farther up the road, a bus pulled out and continued on its route down toward the Liffey, a 19A.

If Etain had gotten off that bus, there was only one place she could have come from.

She hoped that she was wrong.

Tell me you didn't go to make peace with Mam, Tain. She's out of your life now. And good riddance.

* * *

"Look . . ." said Barry, glancing at his watch. "I told Etain I'd be home by . . ."

"Go, go, go . . ." she said with a sad smile.

He stood up and gave her a peck on the cheek.

"Need a lift?" he asked.

"Nah," she said. "I'm fine. You go on."

She watched him go and then stared blankly into her drink.

"Cheer up, love," the barman called. "Plenty more fish."

She laughed, and was about to correct him before realizing she didn't have the energy.

"Yeah," she just said. "Yeah."

The ladies' restroom was empty at first glance but she could hear labored breathing coming from the furthest stall, and the woolly snap of toilet paper being torn.

Kate sat in the middle stall and let her head sink almost to her knees.

She couldn't have told him. She was glad that she hadn't.

But the weight of this thing. The weight of it.

She leaned back and gazed up at the bird's nest of graffiti that covered the back of the toilet door. Between the tangle of names, crude jokes, and declarations of eternal fealty to U2, a song lyric jumped out at her. She vaguely remembered hearing the song a few years back, a republican ballad about the suspicious death of an IRA man in British custody:

HUMPTY DUMPTY WAS PUSHED

After the funeral she had gone home.

Back to the dragon's den.

She had stood on the porch, her old key clenched in her hand, praying that it wouldn't fit.

Please tell me she changed the locks.

The key slipped in as smooth as a scalpel and the front door swung open.

She stepped into the hallway and the smell of childhood and

anger and resentment hit her, disguised as the scent of varnish and kitchen spices and bathroom soap.

The house was exactly as she remembered it, as she knew it would be.

Mairéad did not allow things to change.

Not even the locks on the doors.

For decency's sake, she stood over the spot in the hall where her mother had lain after falling down the entire flight of stairs.

Mairéad had lost her balance on the landing and come crashing down the stairwell, breaking like an egg on every step.

She had rolled to the bottom, both arms and five ribs broken, her hip in pieces.

It had taken her half a day to die.

Kate had never thought of herself as someone who was afraid of dying. But she knew now that was because she had always assumed she would die in her sleep, in a warm bed.

There was death, and there was death.

She thought of her mother lying right where she was now standing. Croaking in pain. Unable to even crawl to the phone to call an ambulance. Twitching in agony like a half-crushed fly.

Alone.

Utterly alone.

Ah, Mam . . .

Blinking away the tears, she mounted the steps until she stood upon the landing.

Not so much as a picture on the wall changed. Not a mote of dust in the wrong sunbeam.

Everything exactly as she remembered it.

The door to her old room at the end of the landing. Then Mairéad's. Then Etain's, beside the stairwell.

She pushed the door to her sister's room open.

It was, as she knew it would be, absolutely immaculate.

Even after both her daughters had fled the cave, Mairéad had kept their bedrooms in showroom condition. Everything dusted. Beds made. Carpet hoovered. Windows cleaned.

Like a child who prefers to play with the box more than the toy that came in it, Mairéad had lavished more care and attention on the spaces where her daughters had slept than on the daughters themselves.

There was only one thing out of place. A tiny flaw that most wouldn't even see as a flaw at all. The pillow was not quite perfectly parallel with the rest of the bed. Less than an inch. Less than half an inch.

Just slightly askew.

As if someone had rested their head on it and lain perfectly still.

And waited.

And waited.

Until they heard footsteps coming up the landing.

Past the door.

Toward the stairwell.

She was brought back from her reverie by the creak of a pulled chain and the watery belch of the toilet being flushed at the far end of the restroom.

From her pocket she took the crumpled envelope that Barry had given her. She knew what it contained but she opened it regardless. There, as expected, was a check for close to fifteen thousand pounds.

Her cut.

With Mairéad's death, the house went to her daughters, according to the terms of Maeliosa Larkin's will.

And just like that, all problems evaporated.

Barry, Etain, and the girls could move into the family home.

Barry could now take the job in Dublin without spending months or even years saving up to put a deposit on a house.

Etain was back in Dublin, the city she had grown up in, in a house with room to spare to raise the girls.

Niamh and Ashling could attend the same school their mother had gone to, only a few minutes' walk down the road.

And they had taken out a loan to pay Kate her share of the value of the house, enough money to move to London and actually start some kind of life.

Oh hip hip hooray, Kate thought bitterly to herself.

Isn't it all so fucking neat.

Two weeks later, after Barry had gone to work, Etain was standing in the kitchen, looking out into the garden at her least favorite tree.

It was a large pepper tree that dominated the back half of the garden. As a child, her mother's preferred punishment when she had misbehaved had been to make her go and stand under it and think about what she had done. She could have drawn every knot and gnarl of the old tree's bark from memory, if she had to. Cutting the tree down had been one of the first things on her plan of action when they had moved back to Dublin, but there never seemed to be time to make the arrangements. A few gardeners had been contacted, but they weren't interested in the work. She had gently needled Barry about it, but couldn't get him to treat it as a priority, which (to him, at least) it wasn't. And so the tree remained where it was, a stubborn, intractable monument to past miseries.

No matter. It was a beautiful day, and not even the sight of her old nemesis gently swaying in the spring breeze could dent her good spirits.

The twins were both in their high chairs, Niamh chortling and enthusiastically conducting an orchestra only she could see while Ashling regarded the apple slices in front of her with dour suspicion.

Etain heard the letterbox burp and went to the front door to find a letter with a British postmark on her doormat. She took it back into the kitchen and opened it.

The letter, brief to the point of terseness, informed Etain that Kate had moved to London and did not wish to be contacted. She said that she had deposited the money into a bank account with details as to how it could be accessed. The money was ultimately to be gifted to Niamh and Ashling when they turned eighteen, but before that it was to pay for the birthdays, first holy communions, and confirmations that Kate would not be around to see.

Etain had a sudden moment of inspiration. She could put the twins in the buggy and take them for a walk in the botanical gardens. It would be heavenly.

She glanced back at the letter.

Kate asked Etain not to let Barry know she was returning the money, because Barry would ask questions which neither she nor Etain wanted to answer.

She wished her sister well, and hoped that she was happy at last.

Etain folded the letter and put it in her pocket. She picked up the bowl of Weetabix in hot milk that she'd left cooling on the counter and gave a big smile to Niamh, who responded with an open-mouthed, three-toothed grin and a gurgle of pure joy.

"Yes, Babba," she said to Niamh, as she slowly spoon-fed her eldest daughter. "We're very happy, aren't we? Yes! Yes we are!"

From her high chair on the other side of the table, Ashling watched in silence.

Then, she gave a low keen and dropped her apple slice on the floor, hoping that her mother would look at her.

DH: Hello?
PS: Hello, is this . . .
(Loud barking)
DH: Sorry! Sorry! Hang on there now (barking continues). Shut up, will ya!
PS: Hello?
DH: Sorry about that. The dogs saw someone go past, there.
PS: Oh, right. I'm sorry, is this Mr. Dan Hegarty?
DH: Speaking?
PS: Hello, my name is Patricia Skelton . . .
DH: Oh fuck . . .
PS: I'm sorry?
DH: I don't want to talk to you, all right? I've got nothing to say about that cunt Lowney, I barely knew the man.
PS: What about Rita Hall?
DH: Rita Hall?
PS: She was your neighbor. And Lowney's.
DH: Rita . . . she's dead, isn't she?
PS: No, Mr. Hegarty. She's not. She's in a rest home in Enniscorthy. I've just come from there.
DH: Rita Hall. Jaysus. How is she?
PS: Well, honestly she's not all there . . .
DH: Away with the fairies?
PS: Yeah. Yeah. But, she said something that I thought was very interesting . . .
DH: Jesus Christ, she must be ninety-odd, would you not leave the woman alone . . .
PS: She said, "He took the ring."
DH: . . .
PS: "He took the ring. He deserved everything he got because he took the ring."
DH: . . .
PS: Does that mean anything to you, Mr. Hegarty?

DH: No. It doesn't mean anything to me. I don't know anything about any ring.

PS: What about him getting what he deserved?

DH: He did. Lowney was a cunt. All the Lowneys were cunts. Not a good one in the whole fucking clan. He got exactly what was coming to him.

PS: And what was that, Mr. Hegarty?

DH: What do you mean?

PS: Feidhlim Lowney disappeared ten years ago. No one knows what happened to him.

DH: . . .

PS: Unless you know different?

DH: I don't know anything.

PS: You don't know he's dead?

DH: No.

PS: Have you seen him around? Did he ever come back to the house, Mr. Hegarty?

DH: No.

PS: What about his wife?

DH: . . . What the fuck did you just say to me?

PS: Have you seen his wife, Mr. Hegarty?

DH: WHAT THE FUCK DID YOU JUST SAY TO ME?!

(Dogs bark furiously in the background)

DH: SHUT THE FUCK UP!

(Sounds of shouting, barking, loud impact, dogs whining)

DH: YOU LISTEN TO ME, CUNT! DON'T FUCKING CALL ME AGAIN! DON'T YOU DARE FUCKING CALL ME AGAIN! AND IF YOU EVER SHOW YOUR FACE AROUND MY FARM I'LL SET THE FUCKING DOGS ON YOU! YEAH?!

CALL ENDS

Transcript of call recorded January 12, 1990
File "Skelton. P. #109817"
Archive of the Department of Policy Oversight

APRIL 2001

"You guys look great," Sarah Clancy yelled over the sound of the music.

"What?" Betty said, leaning in with a hand cupped to her ear. Between the noise of the crowd, Destiny's Child belting "Survivor," Sarah's strong Wexford accent, and the fact that they'd both had quite a lot to drink, the conversation was tough sledding.

"I said yiz look great!" she said.

"Oh, thanks!" roared Betty. "Ash has been teaching me how to do makeup 'cos I was terrible."

"You weren't terrible," Ashling bellowed. "You just needed a little direction."

"Like what?"

"Like 'put on some makeup.'"

"No," said Sarah, interrupting. "I mean you guys look great together. You're a beautiful couple and I'm . . . I'm really happy for yiz . . ."

Betty and Ashling both made "aw" noises but Sarah pushed on.

"I mean it," she slurred. "I mean it. You're both beautiful and it makes me happy to see you happy, so there you are now . . ."

She trailed off and they gave her a hug.

It was that kind of night.

"And you!" Sarah said, taking Ashling's face in her hands and squeezing her cheeks until she looked like a gerbil. "You are going to be a fucking *badass* production manager."

She released her and Ashling smiled modestly and said, "Thanks. It was really close, though."

"Yeah," said Betty. "You won by a cunt hair."

"Fuck off," said Ashling, exploding with laughter, and elbowed her gently in the ribs.

It was true enough. While Ashling had built and designed many excellent sets over the past year, it was well known that it was her

V Week masterpiece (with Betty's assistance) that had won her a place on the committee.

"And how's herself?" Sarah asked.

Ashling sighed.

"Gemma's . . . y'know, it's hard."

"It is," said Sarah, nodding sympathetically.

Gemma had lost her third bid for the position of auditor, and had made no secret of the fact that she would not be running again. Next year would be her last in college, and she would be focusing on exams.

"She'll be fine," said Ashling. "She just needs some time."

"Yeah," said Sarah. "Right, so I actually wanted to talk to you about something. Next year I want to do the *Rocky Horror Picture Show* and I was thinking, could we actually build a working lift onstage—"

"Hang on a minute," Ashling interrupted her, and took a vibrating phone out of her pocket.

She looked at the display and her good humor evaporated.

"Sorry," she said to Betty and Sarah. "I just have to take this, I'll be back in a minute."

Liar, Betty thought glumly.

It was the end of the second trimester, and they'd been dating for two months. It was a casual, breezy, low-stakes kind of affair. They didn't spend their days planning their future together. They went for coffee and bitched about friends and tutors. They got drunk at house parties and made out. They snuck into dark, empty lecture halls and kissed and petted and groped, moving softly and gently in the shadows.

They enjoyed each other. They had fun. Growing up could come later.

They did not discuss family.

Betty had not yet come out to her parents.

She was 90 percent sure they would both be supportive, but who steps on a mine that "only" has a one in ten chance of going off?

As for Ashling, Betty had taken Gemma's advice to heart and never once raised the subject of either of Ashling's parents with her.

To hear Ashling and Betty talk, you'd think both of them had sprung fully formed from a cabbage patch.

But every so often while they were out together, Ashling would get a phone call. Her face would fall, the fire in her would be doused, and she would go somewhere private to take it.

Ten, twenty, thirty minutes later she would return, and good luck getting a two-syllable word out of her for the rest of the day.

Betty was half-seriously considering taking the phone when Ashling wasn't looking and putting it under someone's tires.

She found her on the stairwell beside the door to the ladies', knees pulled up almost to her chin. The phone lay on the step beside her, like an empty smoking gun.

Betty sat down. Ashling looked up. She had not been crying. She looked like she didn't have the energy.

"Hey."

"Heya."

"Oh wow," said Ashling. "You *do* look good tonight."

"Thanks," Betty replied with a sad smile. She was wearing eye shadow for the first time this decade.

"Okay," she said. "I'm really sorry, Ash."

"Why?" said Ashling, suddenly looking very worried.

"Because I haven't been a very good girlfriend. Gemma once told me that if I wanted to be with you I should just never mention your mam. And I've really, really, *really* loved being with you. Like, you're fucking amazing. And I didn't want to lose that. So I haven't asked you about what's going on with you and her. And I should have. Because this isn't normal. So. Two questions. What's going on with you and your mam and are you going to break up with me?"

Ashling threw her head back and laughed and then sighed wearily.

"Well, can I answer the second question first?"

"You can."

"No. You eejit."

"Oh, thank Christ," Betty breathed.

"Eejit," Ashling whispered again, and kissed her hand.

"And the first question?" Betty pressed.

They listened to the ocean-rumble of the packed bar on the other side of the wall.

Ashling turned to look at her. There were tears in her eyes, at last.

"Betty," she whispered. "I can't go home tonight. Can I please come home with you?"

Betty's mind raced.

I . . . no. I can't. We can't.

My parents don't know I'm gay, and there are ways you're supposed to let people know these things. Just bringing your girlfriend back to sleep in your bed isn't one of them.

This is a terrible, terrible idea.

"Sure," she said. "Sure, no problem."

"Really?" Ashling said, but the look of relief on her face told Betty that there was no way she could back out now. "I'm not, it's not . . ."

"It's fine," said Betty firmly. "It's fine. We'll figure it out. Promise."

They stayed out late that night and by 3 A.M. they were shambling down Nassau Street in a clump of eight or nine Dramsoccers, croaking a medley of songs from *South Park* and trying to flag down any taxi brave or foolish enough to risk them.

Betty was drunk, but not nearly as drunk as she should have been given her intake during the night.

A constant electric shiver of fear and anticipation ran through her, sharply cutting through the fog of the alcohol. In the back seat of the taxi beside her, Ashling had lain a head on her shoulder.

Betty stroked her tight, bristly hair and watched as Ashling's long, silver earrings shimmered in the darkness of the taxi, catching yellow beams from the passing streetlamps.

As she rifled through her dresser to find a pair of pajamas for Ashling, Betty mentally rehearsed what she would say to her parents in the morning.

Mam, Dad, this is my friend Ashling. We were out last night and she realized she didn't have her key and her mam's away and there was no one in the house to let her in sooooo I said she could crash here for the night and I could have gotten the guest room ready but that would have meant changing the sheets and we were both really tired so we just shared a bed like two average straight women would absolutely do in this situation. Nothing suspicious. Just two straight gal pals sleeping in the same bed. These aren't the lesbians you're looking for, move along.

She felt some relief.

It was fine. It would be fine.

"So pajama-wise we have ducks and we have . . ."

She turned to see Ashling sitting on her bed, wearing her earrings.

Exclusively.

". . . sunflowers," she finished. Somehow.

"Mmmmm . . . not really a pajama kinda girl," Ashling mused aloud.

"I . . . think we have a nightgown?" Betty stammered, trying very hard not to stare at Ashling's tiny, chestnut-brown nipples or the way her body curved in and out like an angel's violin.

Ashling stood up and casually turned around, taking in the room.

"This room is really you," she said. "I love it."

"Yeah," said Betty awkwardly.

"Are you going to put your hands on me, or what?"

Betty dropped the pajamas like they had caught fire and hurried over to her.

Cautiously, as if she was afraid she would break her, she placed her hands on Ashling's naked shoulders and kissed her gently.

"Oh babe, you're cold."

"So do something about it, dummy."

"Okay."

She kissed her again. Deeper. Happier.

"Tell me you need me," Ashling whispered.

"I love you," Betty whispered back, and meant it to her bones.

Ashling shook her head as if trying to ward away a wasp.

"No. No. Tell me you need me. Tell me you need me."

"I need you, Ash," Betty whispered.

She felt cold, slender fingers working her belt.

"I need you," she said again as Ashling kissed and bit her neck.

"I need you!" she yelped as Ashling pushed her onto the bed, her jeans gathered around her ankles, her plump, pale thighs exposed to the air.

"I need you," she croaked hoarsely as she felt something hard and small and warm and smooth glance over her clitoris and realized it was Ashling's tongue stud.

"I . . . need . . . you . . ." she growled as she felt the first, the second, the third finger and a pleasure so fierce it brushed gently against pain.

* * *

Afterward, Betty lay awake in bed and Ashling lay asleep on her chest, as still and heavy as a layer of turf.

Betty kissed her sleeping lover on the forehead and swore a silent oath.

I will always protect you. I will always love you.

It was a foolish thing to think. They'd been together two months.

Fuck it, thought Betty. *I know what I know.*

Something woke her up at around six o'clock in the morning. Some motion or movement.

Half-asleep, she opened her eyes just in time to see Ashling's naked buttocks vanishing through the door and walking down the upstairs landing.

She should have reacted much quicker to the realization that her girlfriend had decided to take a morning stroll through her parents' home completely naked, but she was half-asleep, hungover, and the sheer shock of what she was seeing was so immense that it took a good three seconds to filter from her eyes to her brain.

When the shoe finally dropped she uttered a hoarse, phlegmy "FUCK!" and tumbled out of bed.

She raced after Ashling and reached her just as she was about to turn down the stairs.

She could hear movement from her parents' room, someone's feet hitting the floor and bedsprings exhaling.

Like a mother suddenly gifted the strength to lift a burning car to free her trapped child, Betty found it within her to hoist her naked girlfriend over her shoulder, sprint with her down the corridor, and slam her bedroom door behind her mere seconds before her father emerged sleepily from his bedroom.

"Oi! No slamming doors, it's six in the morning!" he groused.

"Sorry, Dad," she called through the door.

She waited until she heard the bathroom door close and then rounded on Ashling.

"What the fuck are you doing!?" she whispered, her voice squeaking with the strain.

Ashling was standing in the center of the room, naked as the day she was born and swaying slightly.

Her eyes were open, but they weren't focused on anything.

She muttered something incoherent, that Betty thought might have been "Leave."

"Ash?" said Betty. "Are you . . . are you asleep?"

She leaned in closer and waved a hand in front of Ashling's face.

Ashling's eyes suddenly focused on Betty and she woke up with a scream which made Betty scream in turn.

And then her stomach turned to lead as she heard her father's voice from behind the door.

"Betty? Is there someone in there with you?"

"Oh, no more tea, Pauline, thanks, this is grand," said Ashling, smiling sweetly at Betty's mother over the breakfast table.

"You're sure?" said Pauline Fitzpatrick, still holding the teapot.

"Oh, go on then. Cheers," Ashling said as she held out the mug. "And thank you so much for putting me up last night, I can't believe I lost my key, I am *such* an eejit."

Across the table from her, Betty watched Ashling charm her parents with a mixture of pride, relief, and the faint unease of realizing that her girlfriend could lie as easily as she could breathe.

"Did you ever see those little plastic rocks in Woodie's?" Betty's father asked amiably while he crunched a slice of toast.

"Plastic rocks?" Ashling asked, apparently intrigued and anxious to know more.

"Yeah, they look completely real but they have a little slot you can put a spare key in. You leave them in the garden in case you ever get locked out."

"That is a great idea, I might stop in at Woodie's over the weekend," Ashling said.

Ambrose Fitzpatrick, satisfied that he had made a contribution to the good of the world, nodded and returned to leafing through the *Irish Times* and giving his full attention to the opinion page, where Fintan O'Toole was dying on the cross for the nation's sins.

"I just can't believe Betty didn't offer you the spare room," Pauline said pointedly.

"It was too late to make the room up, Ma," Betty retorted. "I didn't want to wake anyone."

"Well, it can't have been comfortable?" Pauline said with concern. "Your bed's very narrow, Betty. Isn't it very narrow, Ambrose?"

"It is an incredibly narrow bed," Ambrose agreed.

"We were grand," said Betty.

"Yeah, absolutely," said Ashling.

"It was fine."

"It was great! Ow."

"Sorry, Ash, I think I might have accidentally kicked you. I think I kicked you there."

"Yeah. You did."

"Did I? Sorry."

It was Saturday, so after breakfast they watched TV in the living room.

This is nice, thought Betty. *Nice and domestic.*

Ashling's phone began to buzz and Betty's heart sank. But to her surprise, Ashling's face lit up when she saw the name onscreen, and she headed out into the hallway with the phone to her ear, saying, "Hey, you! When did you get in?"

Betty tried not to eavesdrop but she could hear Ashling talking happily on the phone and heard her give out the Fitzpatricks' address.

She came back into the room and said: "I'm gonna have to bounce, hon. I have a lift picking me up in around twenty minutes."

"Oh," said Betty, disappointed. "Is everything okay?"

"Everything's great," Ashling assured her, but offered nothing more.

Twenty minutes came and went, seemingly in a heartbeat.

They heard the honk of a car outside. Ashling planted a chaste and easily explicable kiss on Betty's cheek, called goodbye to Ambrose and Pauline, and headed out the front door to where the familiar black Nissan Micra was parked outside.

She seemed happy and at ease and Betty could practically feel her melting away into intangibility.

You're escaping. You're running. You're free. This isn't a lift, it's a getaway.

Betty followed her out into the cool white morning and tried to get a glimpse of the person in the car. A person who, she saw, was trying to get a glimpse of her.

She felt a surge of relief when she saw them. The irrational, paranoid part of her brain had been expecting some beautiful, cool, better girlfriend that Ashling had called to take her away from this humdrum existence.

The woman in the car was indeed beautiful, and might very well have been cool. But, Betty thought, she could only be Ashling's mother. The slightly hard green eyes, the sallow complexion, the dark hair.

This was Ashling in her forties, and wearing them magnificently.

Ashling gave Betty a last wave, got into the car, and pecked the driver affectionately on the cheek, which struck Betty as very odd given what little she knew of their relationship.

Not how I pictured you, Mrs. Mallen, Betty thought.

The car drove off, and Betty felt a sudden surge of sadness that hit as hard as nausea.

She went upstairs and sat on the toilet, and stared at her pale, exhausted-looking features in the bathroom mirror.

"Hey, Ash," she murmured to her own reflection.

"So . . . we need to talk about all the things we need to talk about. Let's see. We need to talk about the fact that we had sex for the first time. We need to talk about the fact that the sheets are still warm and you're already gone. What else? We need to talk about whatever the fuck is going on with you and your mother."

She felt tears stinging her eyes, took a deep breath, and fought them off.

"We . . . we need to talk about the fact that you used sex to get out of having to tell me what the fuck is going on with you and your mother. We need to talk about the fact that you and her actually seem to get on fine? From what I saw? Assuming that woman was your mother, which I don't even fucking know. And we need to talk about that. Sleepwalking. We need to talk about the sleepwalking."

She stood up, pulled up her tracksuit bottoms, and leaned on the sink, staring deep into her own eyes.

"We need to talk about the fact that I told you I loved you and you blew right past that. And maybe it was too soon. But if it was . . . yeah. Got it in one. We need to talk about that."

She began to wash her hands.

"We need to talk about how you can just lie so easily," she said. "Because I'm not saying it's not a useful skill for us right now, but it's also fucking terrifying how you can just turn it on."

The tears came back, and now they were angry and in force.

"We need . . . to talk . . ." she hissed, trying her hardest to keep her voice from cracking. "About how I am so fucking in love with every last fucking inch of you but when I look at us I just see red flags and flashing warning lights as far as the eye can see. And we need to talk about the fact that I am such a coward I am not going to tell you any of this because I'm already too scared to lose you."

With an angry slap, she knocked off the running water.

"Okay," she said to her reflection. "Good talk."

As they drove through the quiet Saturday streets, the dark-haired woman glanced over to the passenger seat, where Ashling was gazing out the window with a strangely stern expression.

"So," she said, carefully breaking the silence. "You want to tell me about last night?"

Ashling gave her a look of surprise and disgust.

"Christ, Kate, you want details?"

Kate Larkin rolled her eyes at her niece.

"Not about . . . what was her name?"

Ashling grimaced and looked away.

"Betty," she grunted.

"Betty?"

"What?"

"Nothing. It's just a very straight name."

"And you're an expert?"

"Darling, I live in Camden."

Ashling had no answer to that, and so gave none.

"She seems lovely," Kate offered. "Of course, if you'd introduced us I might . . ."

"Yeah, that's not going to happen," said Ashling shortly. "I'm ending it."

"Oh. Right," said Kate, trying to keep the tone of disapproval out of her voice, and failing.

"'Oh right' what?" Ashling said tersely.

"Nothing," said Kate. "Just seems a bit rough on her to just . . . what do you kids call it? Pump and dump?"

Ashling looked at her aunt with an expression of horror bordering on nausea.

"We most certainly do *not* call it that!"

"No?"

"No! Because that's *disgusting.*"

"I've definitely heard it in London."

"Well, fucking keep it in London. Jesus!"

"Well, whatever you call it, it's no way to treat anyone."

"It's not like that."

"Oh, it's not?"

"No, Kate, it's not! I just . . . remember Douglas? Remember him? I just want to end it before we get to that point. Because I didn't actually enjoy that, am I crazy?"

"Okay, okay," said Kate soothingly. "Sorry."

They drove up Mobhí Road, so heavily lined with trees that the bright morning became a cool green twilight. They came to a stop at a red light.

A young woman shepherded two small children across the road. The older child, a girl, bobbed beside her mother with a strange, one-legged canter while the younger boy, barely walking, gripped her hand and howled with glee as his mother whooshed him over the concrete lip to the safety of the pavement.

"She called me last night," Ashling whispered. "She'd gotten into something."

Kate did not have to ask who "she" was. The tone with which the word had been said was as clear an identification as could be asked for.

"Got into what?" Kate asked.

Ashling shrugged.

"Gin? Port? A bottle of liquified hate? I dunno. Whatever it was, she got her money's worth."

Kate cursed.

"Christ, where did she hide it?"

"I don't know."

"Don't you check?"

"Yeah! Yeah, Kate, I do!" Ashling flared. "Every fucking day! I check every fucking day but sometimes I actually have to leave the house!"

The car behind them informed them that the light had gone green with a brisk, spirited honking.

"Yes, thank you, arsehole," Kate said, smiling sweetly into the rearview mirror and continuing through the lights.

134	NEIL SHARPSON

"Sorry," said Kate. "It's not your fault. I shouldn't have said that. It is absolutely not your fault."

"Well, she begs to differ."

"Well, fuck her," said Kate bluntly.

Ashling gave a snort of laughter, but there was a small sob wrapped in it.

"What was she on about?" Kate asked.

"Oh, the usual," said Ashling airily. "'Where is she? Where is she? Give her back, you bitch. Give her back. Haven't you taken enough from me?' But no, you're right. I should definitely bring Betty back home to meet her."

Kate shook her head. "God, if only your father was still here."

Ashling groaned.

"Kate, look, I know we all worship at the altar of Saint Barry around here but I don't think Mr. Super-Duper Catholic would have been cool with me and I definitely don't think he would have been cool with my girlfriend."

Kate bit back the urge to say something she would have deeply regretted afterward and simply said softly: "He might have surprised you."

"Yeah, well, he made sure he wouldn't get the chance, didn't he?"

Oh, you are on thin ice now, you little hoor, thin fucking ice, Kate thought.

As they pulled into the driveway, she swallowed her anger and said firmly:

"Look, Ashling, you can't just put your life on hold and blow up every chance for happiness that comes your way. Etain isn't going anywhere, so you need to find a way to—"

"Sorry, are you Kate Larkin?" Ashling said, furious. "Didn't you just leave home and cut your mother out of your life? Aren't you the one who fucked off to London and might as well have been dead for the last twenty years? That Kate Larkin? Aren't you going to be back in London this time next week? Why are you the only one who gets to make people go away?"

"That was different!"

"Oh, I'm sure it was!" Ashling hissed. "But you do not get to swan back in here, try and fix my life, and then swan back out again. I don't want your advice. You're not my mother, you just think you are."

And with that, Ashling flung open the door before the car had even stopped, causing Kate to swear and jam on the brakes as Ashling stormed out.

"Too fucking right," Kate growled under her breath as she watched Ashling vanish into the house. "If I'd birthed a brat like you I'd be fucking mortified."

JULY 2001–JANUARY 2002

Over the summer, Betty finally wrote her play.

She sat down one evening in front of her PC with a sense of weary dread, hoping that she would be able to string together a few lines that wouldn't fill her with disgust.

By 4 A.M., she had written two acts, and only crushing tiredness compelled her not to write any more. For the first time in her life, Betty had experienced true creative inspiration. She felt as if the play already existed, heavy and solid, buried beneath a layer of the finest sand and only needing her to come and gently blow the grains away.

The next night, the fever held and she discovered, to her shock, that she had completed an entire draft. She typed the words "THE END" and gasped as something she didn't even realize had been holding her let go. Then she tapped and tapped, up and up, taking in the length of the thing she had brought into the world.

Once she'd finished the play, she knew she'd have to show it to Ashling. To ensure the script got the best reception possible she waited for a weekend when she knew her parents would be out of the house and invited Ashling over.

They ordered pizza, watched a half dozen episodes of *Family Guy* on DVD, and then went upstairs where Betty used every trick, talent, and tactic at her disposal to get Ashling to the point where she was physically unable to come any more.

At last, as they lay together in an afterglow as soft as a quilt, Ashling leafed through the printed script with one hand. Betty lay on her chest, listening to the rustling of the pages and the steadying boom of Ashling's heartbeat. She could feel her lover's hand in her hair, stroking gently so as not to catch the strands in the rings on her fingers. The smell of her sweat was harsh and acrid and yet it was working on Betty like opium. She felt at once asleep and awake, either dreaming with the vividness of real life, or so happy and rested that consciousness felt like slumber.

And then she felt the script being lain down on her naked back and a kiss planted on her forehead and the gently whispered words "you fucking genius."

The world's first staging of *The Girl on the Wall* by Betty Fitzpatrick did not have an untroubled production. Worse, they would be the first show onstage after the Christmas break, which would mean having to arrange rehearsals off campus. As an original script with a first-time director, they were given a less-prestigious lunchtime slot. And worst of all, the evening show running the same week as them would be a production of Carol Churchill's *Top Girls,* directed by Sarah Clancy (she having abandoned her plans for *The Rocky Horror* for the time being). *Top Girls* had fourteen female characters and every actress in the society was gunning hard for a chance at a role that did not involve saying some variation on "What's wrong, dear?" every five minutes until the curtain came down.

This left Ashling and Betty with an unprecedented problem with casting their play: there were not enough women.

After the last day of auditions Betty turned to Ashling, whose despondent expression matched her own.

"Are you going to make me say it?" Betty asked at last.

"No," said Ashling glumly. "We're going to have to cast ourselves."

"Yup."

"Christ, they are going to eat us alive."

"Yup," said Betty glumly.

By the end of the week *The Girl on the Wall* had become the center of a nexus of swirling anti-hype. The issue of nepotism and unfair casting was always ebbing and flowing in Dramsoc, and there was always one play in every semester that would, rightly or wrongly, be held up as a totem for everything that was wrong with the society. This term, the play where a lesbian couple had held auditions and

then simply cast *themselves* in the roles of the two leads rankled a
great many people. The few female actors who *had* auditioned for
them and been passed over quickly caught the slight and were sure
to let anyone who would listen know that the play was a preachy,
weird mess that would prove to be an absolute garbage fire when it
was finally staged. Two narratives quickly took shape: the first was
that Betty and Ashling were narcissistic divas who could have cast
other people in their vanity project but chose not to out of sheer
damnable hubris *and* that they had had no choice but to cast themselves because the play was so terrible that no one else was willing
to act in it. The fact that these two narratives were contradictory did
not impede them in the slightest, and they worked together most
amicably.

As was often the case in theater, *The Girl on the Wall* had needed
to fail before it could succeed. By the time word of mouth had fil-
tered through the society that the play was not the train wreck that
had been expected, there were only two nights left in which to see
it. Scarcity created demand, and suddenly the show was the hottest
ticket of the season.

The two packed houses on Thursday and Friday night had crack-
led with the energy of a crowd that knew that they were a privileged
few.

Within the space of a few days, the play had gone from pariah to
legend. The fact that the vast majority of the society had never had a
chance to see it only made the legend more seductive.

Betty would leave a part of herself in those final moments of the Friday performance. A bookmark of the soul, a memory she would
keep by her bedside or under her pillow. Always within easy reach.

The theater, dark and hot as a midnight greenhouse.

The audience rapt and silent as birds of prey.

She improvised one last line. As the light faded, and before the applause washed over them like an Atlantic torrent, roaring and foaming, she had leaned in and whispered in Ashling's ear: *"I love you."*

There was no answer. But she felt Ashling melt against her. Leaning her head against her shoulder, letting her, for a precious moment, take the weight.

And that was answer enough, for now.

The house lights flickered on, their harsh white glare sterilizing the last traces of magic from the stage. Ashling had set to work striking the set and Betty had gone and sat in the dark of LG2 and tried to work through the massive backlog of emotion she was feeling. There was a huge store of joy and relief. Pride. Exhaustion.

Disappointment that it was over. But she was unable to make much headway with any of them and instead sat there feeling oddly numb.

She heard Ashling shouting instructions to some of the stage-hands and tracked her voice moving past the thin partition and out to the front of house where it stopped and then resumed speaking with a new tone. Surprise. Happiness.

Betty stood up, still wearing her costume dress, and curiously made her way out to the front of house.

"I thought you weren't going to be able to make it?" Ashling said.

"Something fell through at work. I thought I'd surprise you," said Kate. "Oh, and here's the woman of the hour!"

Betty emerged from LG2 and Ashling spun around like she'd been caught in bed with a suitcase of cocaine and the entire lineup of Atomic Kitten.

Betty froze. *Oh shit. It's her mother.*

Over the past few months, Betty had finally begun to pry a few details about Ashling's home life.

She knew that Ashling's mother had a drinking problem, and that when she got drunk she would call Ashling and remind her that she had destroyed her life. When she was sober, things were better, but when you had said that you had said everything.

Betty could not square all that with the beautiful, poised woman who stood in front of her now, smiling and shaking her hand warmly.

"You must be so, so proud," said Kate. "What a gorgeous piece of writing."

"Th-thank you," Betty stammered, blushing.

"And not just the writing, of course," Kate continued. "The acting! You were both so good! I was in tears! I swear to God, I was in actual tears."

Betty shook her head modestly and looked away.

Ashling had been wonderful. She herself had been . . . fine. Betty the writer had had to adapt to the limitations of Betty the actor. Kate continued with the review.

"I mean, I was stunned. It was better, I'd say, than ninety percent of the plays I see in London. I mean that. It looked like a professional production. The sets, the costumes—this is *gorgeous,*" she said, taking the sleeve of Betty's dress in a way that felt perturbingly familiar.

"Thank you," said Betty, and, feeling that after all these compliments she should return some, she said, "I love what *you're* wearing."

"Okay, stop flirting with my aunt, you," Ashling groaned.

The scales fell from Betty's eyes.

"Oh! You're Ashling's . . . Sorry, I thought . . ."

She left the sentence beached and flapping feebly on the sand.

Kate broke the silence with a theatrical clap.

"Thank you, Betty. Thank you for proving my point. This is getting absolutely fucking ridiculous. You two have been together how long? Six months? More? Betty, what are you doing on Sunday evening?"

"Oh, I—" Betty began.

"We're doing—" Ashling cut across.

"No, you're not," said Kate firmly. "Betty, you are coming over to our place Sunday week for dinner so that we can all get to know you. I will take care of everything."

"Kate, we are not—" Ashling said.

"I. Will take care. Of *everything,*" Kate said in a voice that made it clear that the conversation was now over.

"I'd love to," said Betty, not looking at Ashling, who was glaring at her hard enough to leave a scar on her cheek.

"Fantastic," said Kate. "We look forward to seeing you, Betty."

I really like you and wish you were my girlfriend's mother, Betty thought to herself. *And that is a really weird thing to think.*

"Okay, well, I'm going to get changed," said Betty. "See you in the Forum?"

"Yup," said Ashling sullenly, as Betty vanished, a noticeable spring in her step.

"I didn't do anything," Kate said. "You brought this on yourself."

"Sunday dinner?" said Ashling. "Really?"

"Really," said Kate firmly.

"Sure. Why not?" said Ashling bitterly. "Come over. Have dinner. Meet the family. Morticia, Fester, and the little fucking . . . hand . . . yoke . . ."

"Thing."

"What?"

"Never mind. Bloody kids," said Kate.

"So. This is where you live?" Betty said, standing expectantly outside the porch door.

She had straightened her hair and was wearing it down and the change was so drastic that Ashling hadn't recognized her when she had opened the door.

"Yeah," said Ashling stiffly. "This is where I live."

"It's gorgeous," said Betty. "I mean, from the outside."

Don't judge a book by its cover, Ashling thought.

"Sooooo . . . should I use the servants' entrance?" Betty asked.

Ashling suddenly realized that she was not simply standing in the way, but was resting both arms on the doorframe, blocking the entrance to her home like a goalie.

"Sorry," she muttered. "Sorry, c'mon in."

The hallway was quite dark, but cozy and inviting. Kate had lit candles on the hall table.

"Oh, this is for you . . ." Betty said, presenting Ashling with an off-license bag containing a nice, modest Chilean red.

A look of horror suddenly blanched her features.

"Which . . . I shouldn't have brought because of your . . . Ash, I'm sorry, I didn't think!"

Without a word, Ashling took the alcohol and shoved it, bag and all, into a cupboard under the stairs, behind the vacuum cleaner.

"Ash, I am so sorry . . ." Betty whispered, but Ashling just gestured to her to stop talking about it.

She nodded miserably and, shoulders slumped, followed Ashling into the living room. The sliding doors had been pushed back, creating a single space of the living and dining rooms.

"Hello, Betty!" Kate called cheerily from the kitchen, her words rafting in on the scent of roast beef, potatoes, and buttered carrots.

"Hi, Kate! That smells gorgeous!" Betty said, wandering into the kitchen to find someone who would actually be happy to see her.

Kate flashed her the slightly harried smile of a woman who had started one part of the cooking too early and another part too late and was trying desperately to get the two ends to meet in the middle.

"Can I help?" Betty asked.

Kate waved her away.

"Stop, stop, stop. You sit down. It'll be ready in a few minutes."

Glumly, Betty went back to the living room and sat down on the sofa.

She wondered where Ashling had gone to.

For want of anything better to do, her eyes scanned the room and fell on a silver-framed picture on the mantelpiece. It was a picture of a man in his late twenties, well-built with a shock of ginger hair and an open, kind face. He was crouched beside a tree that Betty could see still stood in the back garden of Ashling's home. In his arms he held a child, a little girl of five years of age who was laughing riotously at the camera as her father tickled her belly.

The sheer sunny happiness that burst forth from the picture made Betty smile without thinking. The child did not resemble Ashling in the slightest, but Betty felt like she knew her nonetheless.

She stood up and wandered around the room, taking in the other pictures. She soon noticed a common theme: the little girl was in all of them.

There was one of her standing in front of the doorway of a church, angelic in a snow-white communion dress, delicate golden ringlets falling on her shoulders as she held her hands together reverentially and gazed at the camera with a look of saintly piety. Greatly amused, Betty picked up the picture to look at it more closely.

She heard something stirring behind her and turned to see Ashling standing stiffly in the doorway.

"You never told me you used to be blond," she said with a smile.

Ashling did not return the smile.

"That's not me" was all she said.

Behind her, a woman entered the room. She was an inch shorter than Betty and gazed blankly at her from behind thick, square glasses that reminded Betty of old television sets. At first, Betty thought that this must be Ashling's grandmother or an elderly aunt. Her hair was as dry and unkempt as summer hay and almost entirely gray. Her posture was stooped and she had the manner of a woman deep in her years, almost slipped below the surface.

And yet, as she stepped closer to Betty and stood mere inches away from her, silently appraising, Betty realized that she was not that old after all.

Something had indeed aged this woman, but it was not time.

The woman reached out and took ahold of the frame in Betty's hand and yanked it out of her grip without a word. She put it back in its place on the mantelpiece with the delicacy of a farmer placing a chick in an incubator and then went into the dining room and sat down at the table without so much as an acknowledgment that she was not the only woman in the entire world.

Betty could practically feel Ashling's glare singeing the back of her head.

She understood that by picking up the picture she had broken some terrible taboo. She just couldn't understand what it was.

The food finally arrived and Betty had complimented Kate on the meal at least three times before Kate realized that nobody else at the table was making conversation.

"So what are your plans for the play?" Kate asked brightly.

"Oh, well. Nothing really," said Betty, caught off guard. "The run's over."

"But it can't end there?" Kate insisted. "Have you thought about sending it to the Abbey?"

Betty almost laughed. It was a good play, but she didn't think it was quite ready for the national theater.

"What play is this?" said a voice.

All eyes turned to the end of the table. Etain had not looked up from her beef, which she was tearing from the gristle with angry little slices. Betty experienced a jolt of panic when, for a split second, she thought Etain had sliced through her own finger with the carving knife. She then realized that the wound was old, and that Etain must have lost her ring finger on her left hand many years ago.

"Betty wrote a play," Kate explained to Etain. "And Ashling acted in it. It was wonderful."

"My invitation must have gotten lost in the post," Etain mused aloud. Her accent was slightly odd, Betty thought. A definite hard, Dublin edge, to be sure. But also a kind of regal sonorousness.

The queen of the Northside, Betty thought to herself.

"You wouldn't have liked it," Ashling said dully.

There was silence for a few moments. Etain put down her knife and fork as if suddenly realizing something.

"Who's 'Betty'?" she declared.

"Um . . . I am," said Betty, nervously raising her hand like a pupil.

"And who are you?" Etain asked, peering skeptically at her through her spectacles.

"I'm . . . well . . ." She looked desperately at Ashling.

"She's my girlfriend," said Ashling, meeting the gaze of no one at the table.

Etain looked deeply confused by this.

"Is Ashling gay?" she said at last, to Kate, with the vaguely disinterested tone of someone walking in on an episode of a soap opera that she is several weeks behind on.

"Yes," said Kate.

"No," said Ashling.

There was a stunned silence.

Betty stared at Ashling, dumbfounded, like she'd just thrown the gravy boat at her.

Ashling glared at Betty, and said coldly, "I told you this. First day we met."

"Well, yeah," said Betty, her temper rising, "but there have been *developments since then.*"

"Look, I'd love to give a detailed explanation of my sexuality but it's not really appropriate dinner table conversation, is it?" Ashling replied.

"Fuck it, we're all here," said Kate, spreading her hands. "It'll save you time."

Ashling rolled her eyes and took a deep breath.

"Fine," she said to Betty. "I'm not really attracted to men *or* women. I just get attracted to certain people sometimes. Actually just you. You're the first person I've ever had a real . . . y'know. I've never felt the way I feel about you with anyone else. So I don't think I'm gay or straight. I think I'm just . . . Beterosexual."

Betty laughed and Ashling kissed her hand gently.

"Okay," Betty whispered. "I can live with that."

"Cool."

"I'm gay though."

"I know."

"I am *super* gay."

"I know. My crack team of investigators uncovered your terrible secret."

"Or to put it another way . . ." Etain said, ". . . she's 'less-bian' and you're 'more-bian'?"

Kate and Ashling both stared at Etain as if she'd grown a second head. And then suddenly they burst out laughing. Betty joined in, but she couldn't help feeling that their laughter was more out of relief than the quality of the joke. She had actually thought it quite funny, but she had a fatal weakness for puns.

Etain chuckled quietly, and tucked in to her potatoes. A satisfied, more easy silence settled on the table and they finished their meal.

Betty felt the iron spring in her stomach begin to slowly uncoil.

Maybe she had survived the ordeal after all.

Again, she wondered who the blond-haired girl was in all those pictures.

She had a sudden, troubling realization.

Never mind who the blond girl is. Why isn't Ashling in a single one?

After dinner, Etain politely made her excuses and told the party that she was going to bed. Betty could practically hear the muscles in Ashling's frame unlocking once Etain vanished behind the dining room door. Kate began to put away the dishes and shooed away any attempts to assist, so Ashling and Betty retired to the living room, pulled the sliding doors over, and cuddled anxiously on the sofa.

"That wasn't bad, right?" Betty whispered.

". . . no," said Ashling.

Betty heard the hesitation, and it spoke louder than the word.

"You did good," Ashling reassured her, and kissed her on the forehead.

Betty's eyes returned again to the silver-framed picture on the mantelpiece.

"So . . ." she said. "That's your dad?"

Beneath her, she felt Ashling tightening up again.

"Yeah," Ashling breathed. "Yeah, that's Barry."

"And the little girl . . ."

"Who do you think she is, Betty?" Ashling whispered sadly.

Betty suddenly realized just what kind of story she had begun to read.

"You never mentioned you had a sister."

"I don't," said Ashling simply. "Now."

"Ah, love . . . I'm so sorry."

"It's fine. It's fine."

"No . . ."

"It's long enough ago that I can pretend it's fine."

"How old were you?"

"Eight. We were both eight years old. Twins."

"What happened?"

Ashling gave an exaggerated shrug.

"Well, that's the question, innit? Someone picked her up after school and they just . . . poof. Gone. Vanished."

She said it airily, but her body was a thorn tree.

"Jesus. Ash, I don't know what to say."

"Yeah."

There was a quiet, tentative knock on the door. Kate poked her head in, like a soldier cautiously scouting an area for enemy snipers.

"Cuppa tea?" she asked.

Ashling and Betty both nodded.

With a hot mug of tea in hand, Betty mused, *what can the Irishwoman not face?*

A good cuppa made the world safe and normal again. It brought you back to reality, and made the horrors of life seem like fiction. Unpleasant, but fundamentally unreal and unable to inflict true pain.

Ashling had been left ajar. She was not fully open, by any means. But light was streaming in from the next room at last.

She told Betty about her sister, Niamh, who had wanted to be a vet so badly that she once turned the entire back garden into a field hospital for every toy animal in the house, which subsequently got drenched in a downpour. She showed her a picture of Etain solemnly drying a row of twenty-four stuffed animals with a hair dryer at the kitchen table while the golden-haired cherub looked on. On the back of the photograph someone had written, in a sloppy, masculine hand, *Brave Survivors of the Great Hospital Flooding of '86!*

Betty caught a glimpse of a single chubby arm and a lock of

jet-black curly hair on the very edge of the frame, the tiniest fraction of Ashling that had been allowed into the picture.

She wanted to ask why there were no pictures of Ashling but she didn't want to interrupt. Ashling, it seemed, had wanted to tell Betty about Niamh for a long time and Betty could not bring herself to break her flow.

But the more Ashling talked about Niamh's disappearance, the more Betty began to feel a queasy sense of déjà vu. She remembered the feeling of recognition when she had first laid eyes on that picture of Niamh. And the more details Ashling gave her, the more Betty realized that she had heard this story before.

Yes. Yes!

There *had* been a little girl who had gone missing in Glasnevin in '89, hadn't there? Even as a child, she had seen pictures of her on the news and in her parents' morning newspapers. There had been a talk given by the principal in the assembly hall. Garda Pat had come into the class to warn them about not talking to strangers. It had been a big story, hadn't it? National news.

Wait a minute. Didn't they find the guy who did it? Hadn't it been . . .

Ashling stopped. Betty's face had suddenly gone very pale.

"What?" she asked.

Betty shook her head, trying desperately not to show the memory that had risen in her mind like a blister.

Ashling sighed and took a deep swig from her mug before placing it down on the coffee table with an air of finality.

"You want to know if my dad did it."

Betty shook her head vigorously. She was not at *all* sure that she did.

"I don't think he did," said Ashling. "And maybe I'm a fool. But I don't believe the man I remember could have done that."

Which no one has ever said about any murderer, Betty unwillingly found herself thinking, but she would not have said that out loud under torture.

"Plus. It doesn't make sense. Who abducts their own child? I mean, if he wanted to rape her they live in the same house. Why go through—"

She stopped. The sudden look of horror on Betty's face as she had casually mused about the logistics of her father raping her sister had brought her up short.

"Sorry," Ashling said. "Sorry. I forget that this is not normal stuff to be talking about. But no. I don't think he did it. He had an alibi, and I think the witnesses just saw someone who looked like him."

Betty was disappointed to hear the little modulation in the tone of her voice. A subtle little corkscrew that Betty had learned was a tell for when Ashling was lying.

Well, if she's lying, she's lying to herself. And I can't really blame her.

Betty was quite willing to let the conversation end there and move on to something more pleasant but Ashling was not done yet.

"I mean . . . I'm not sure. I can't say for certain. Maybe he did, I dunno."

"What makes you say that?" Betty asked.

"How he died," Ashling answered. "That's what . . . I mean, what the fuck was he doing in Youghal? He just . . . he just takes a few days off work, drives down to Cork. Doesn't visit any of his family down there. Just goes to Youghal, books a hotel room, and kills himself. Doesn't leave a note, doesn't . . . What was that? Guilt? Or . . . he just couldn't live without her anymore. Even though I was still here . . ."

The words had become thick and heavy now.

Betty held her until she was still again.

"I'm sorry, love," she whispered. "I am so sorry for what you've been through."

Ashling wiped her eyes and pulled herself upright again.

"So. Yeah," she croaked. "I don't know. I go back and forth. He did it. He didn't. He was a good man. He was a monster. Sometimes I believe both at once."

"What about your mam?" Betty asked.

"Hm?"

"Well, she was married to him. She'd know him better than anyone. Does she blame him?"

Ashling actually laughed and cast a rueful glance around the room.

"Nah. Isn't that obvious? She blames me."

Betty's taxi arrived at 1 A.M. and waited patiently outside the house while they kissed tenderly in the hall.

"Tonight was good," Betty said, nodding to herself in the dark. She kissed Ashling again.

"Yeah," said Ashling, smiling sadly.

"And tomorrow will be better," Betty said.

Ashling said nothing. She had already decided to end it.

"I love you," Ashling told Betty, and she meant it.

"I need you," Betty replied.

Happy as only the innocent can be, Betty kissed her one last time and left the house.

Ashling closed the door behind her.

Kate had already gone to bed, so Ashling felt safe crying quietly for a few moments.

Then, she repaired herself, putting her expression back together and gathering up her scattered thoughts and emotions and replacing them seamlessly within her.

Progress, she congratulated herself dully. *You never let anyone get that far. But that's as far as anyone goes. Betty will leave in the end; sent away crying, or running away screaming. There are no other options.*

She turned to mount the stairs and stopped dead. The door to the cupboard under the stairs was ajar. Swearing hotly, Ashling reached inside in the darkness, desperately hoping to feel the cool kiss of the glass bottle. It was gone.

Ashling slammed the door shut and cursed until she had run out of swear words.

In a reverie in the back seat of the taxi Betty was suddenly jolted by a bark of "Jaysus!" from the taxi driver. As they passed Ashling's house, Betty stared in dumbfounded horror at the sight that went by.

Etain, wearing the yellow light of a nearby streetlamp and not a stitch else, sat casually on the wall of the Mallens' garden.

She saw Betty's shocked face in the window of the taxi as they drove past.

Half smiling, she raised her hand, in which she held a bottle of Chilean red wine.

She saluted Betty, like Dionysius thanking a worshiper for their libation, and then proceeded to neck the bottle.

The image of her girlfriend's mother, drinking wine stark naked by the light of a lamppost, faded in the rearview mirror, but not from Betty's mind, where it would remain until she died.

They have the same nipples, she found herself utterly unable to not think.

"Christ. Wouldn't you know you were on the Northside?" the taxi driver asked, chuckling to himself.

❖

The morning after the dinner, Betty had gotten a text from Ashling telling her to meet her at the lake after her morning English lecture. She had thought they would go get coffee. She knew Ashling would probably have a lot to say about the previous night but she had been looking forward to that. She had wanted to look after Ashling. To comfort her. To assure her that everything was fine. To thank her for finally, *finally* letting her into her inner life.

She had waited by the side of the lake, shivering in the library block's massive, brutalist shadow. Ashling had arrived at last, wearing no makeup, and with a purple woolen beanie pulled tight over her scalp.

When she spoke her voice was hoarse, like she'd spent the night in a smoky nightclub.

Maybe she was sick.

"Hey . . ." she'd croaked.

"Hey, are you—"

"I think we're over. Sorry. I'm really sorry."

Betty didn't hear anything after that. There were words in the air but they were just sounds, flat and ugly. Syllables with no meaning. Cacophony, not music.

Ashling finally shrugged miserably, and trudged away, leaving Betty by the side of the lake, hollowed out like an orange rind.

She drifted numbly up the lakeside and made her way back to Dramsoc front of house. She heard footsteps running toward her but didn't look up and so was taken completely by surprise when Gemma enveloped her in a crushing bear hug, kissed her cheek, and yelled, "Well done, hon!"

Gemma took her shoulders and wheeled her around until she was facing the noticeboard. There, pinned to the board, was a large hand-drawn poster from the Dramsoc committee. She saw "ISDA" and suddenly remembered that today was the day the Dramsoc committee were announcing the society's entrants for the Irish Student Drama Awards, which would be held in Limerick in March.

She read the titles:

THE PRIME OF MISS JEAN BRODIE by Muriel Spark
BLUE REMEMBERED HILLS by Dennis Potter
BATMAN THE MUSICAL by Tony Cogivan
THE GIRL ON THE WALL by Betty Fitzpatrick

"Oh Christ," said Betty. "Fuck, no."

Gemma looked at her in shock.

"Look, I know it's in Limerick but it's still a fantastic opportunity . . ."

Betty shook her head.

I should be running up and down the halls.

I should be whooping with joy.

I should be calling Ashling and telling her that our play is going to be seen by people from all over the country.

This could be the start of something amazing. This could be the beginning of my career as a writer. This could be what kicks it all off.

"I can't go," she said.

"Eh, fuck that," said Gemma. "You absolutely can."

"I can't."

"Why not?"

"Because I was just dumped by the director and the lead actor in the same day," said Betty.

Gemma seemed to visibly deflate.

"Ah, love . . ." she moaned.

"Yeah," said Betty. There didn't seem to be anything else to say.

"Right, come on," said Gemma, hooking her arm in hers and marching her toward the stairs.

"Where are we going?"

"George's Street. Laser Video. Tesco. We're stocking up on crap movies and ice cream and then heading back to your place."

"Ugh. That's so cliché."

"So's penicillin for pneumonia. Take the damn cure."

* * *

The "cure" consisted of several tubs of Ben & Jerry's, *Lost and Delirious* (Betty's choice), *The Wedding Singer* (Gemma's choice), and *Blow Dry* (by joint affirmation), and by the end Betty felt as if the knife in her had had its edges blunted somewhat.

She leaned her head back over the headrest of the couch and focused on the ceiling to give her eyes a break from the screen.

"Look, you'll be fine," said Gemma. "Plenty more fish in the sea."

"Yeah, but most of the fish are straight," Betty said glumly. "There's like five lesbian fish in the whole ocean and I've already eaten one."

Gemma burst out laughing and Betty joined in with a melancholy chuckle.

"Ah, you'll be grand," said Gemma.

"What about Ashling?" Betty asked.

"What about her?" Gemma asked.

"Shouldn't you be trying to kill her with ice cream and Adam Sandler? She's your best friend?"

Gemma looked at her in surprise.

"Betty, *you're* my best friend," she said, as if that was obvious.

Betty furrowed her brow.

"You've known her for years," said Betty. "You told me once she was your best friend."

"No, I said I was *her* best friend," said Gemma. "I like Ashling. She's great craic. But in all the time I've known her I haven't been in her house once."

"Trust me, you're not missing anything," Betty muttered darkly.

She felt a sharp pang of sympathy and anger and mortification by proxy when she remembered that night in Ashling's house. The tensing of Ashling's body whenever her mother spoke. The terrible family history she had imparted.

She has suffered so much.

But pity instantly turned to acid.

Fuck her.

FEBRUARY 2002

There was a fox in the garden, tearing at the body of a magpie.
Ashling watched him through the kitchen window, faintly mesmerized. The garden was almost totally black, and with the kitchen light on she never would have seen him had the snow-white chest and wingtips of the bird not caught her attention as the fox shook it, a checkered flag waving at her in the darkness.

Big fucker, she thought to herself. *Snatch a baby out of a pram, that one.*

As if he had heard the insult, the animal glanced up at her with a switchblade snap, his eyes glowing green as they caught the light from the kitchen before burying his snout in a bloody cavity he had gored in the bird's back.

As she watched with grim fascination, Ashling reached into her pocket and took out her mobile phone.

She scrolled through her list of contacts looking for Betty's number before realizing that she'd deleted it immediately after the breakup. She knew her own weaknesses, and had not wanted to risk succumbing to temptation.

Last thing either of us needs is to fall into some fucking awful on-again-off-again spiral, Ashling thought. She knew from hard, lived experience that the only good breakups were clean ones.

But she needed the number now, so she looked through her outward calls, found the one number that outnumbered all the others by six to one, and pressed the Dial button.

The line was answered after only two rings and Ashling winced in pity.

Oof. C'mon, hon. Play it cool.

"Hello?"

There was Betty's voice. Amazing how many emotions could be packed into two syllables. There was a definite haughty anger. A distinct undertone of guilt and sorrow. And a sharp grace note of hope.

"Hey. It's me," said Ashling.

"Oh," said the voice at the other end.

Ashling waited for more, but more never came, so she pressed on.

"Right. So," said Ashling gingerly, picking her way through the minefield, "I just wanted to call to tell you congratulations on ISDA."

She could hear a hiss of pain on the other end of the line.

"I'm really happy for you. You deserve it. And it's going to be a fantastic show."

Betty gave a hollow, bitter laugh. "Yeah, well. It's not going to happen now. Gemma's not going to do it. And I don't blame her."

It had been a classic case of petty Dramsoc bullshit. Betty had asked Gemma to take over as director of the show and Gemma had been sorely tempted. After the humiliation of her third failed run for auditor, taking a show to ISDA represented a way for Gemma to go out on a high. But she would only do it with Ashling's blessing, which Betty had assured her they had. When Ashling had walked down the stairs to find auditions to replace her as the lead in full swing with Gemma, the new director, overseeing them, it had led to a three-way screaming match between her, Betty, and Gemma in front of several dozen auditionees who hadn't realized just what kind of drama they had signed up for.

It had been rough.

"Gemma will do it," said Ashling simply.

"How do you know that?" Betty asked.

"Because I called her up and said I wanted her to do it. And that you guys will be fantastic. Whoever you end up casting."

Another silence. When she spoke again, Betty appeared to be having trouble forming words.

"Why . . ." She cleared her throat and tried again. "Why did you do that?"

Ashling opened her mouth to say:

Because I love you so much that not being with you feels like a slow, aching sickness. Because I can't stop thinking of stupid little things like how your cheeks get so cold on winter days that my lips get slightly numb when I kiss you. Or how your hair gets caught in my rings when I stroke your head. Or how every so often the light will hit you just right and you will be so beautiful that you will leave me speechless.

Because you changed the shape of the world and made it fit me for a little while. Because I could never be good enough for you but I could do this, at least.

What she said was:

"'Cos, y'know, it's a good play. Deserves to be seen. Oh Jesus!"

"What?" Betty yelped at the end of the line.

"Sorry," said Ashling.

The fox had pulled something wet and wriggling from the cavity in the back of the butchered magpie. The fox's frenzied tugging caused the bird's carcass to flap its wings like a macabre puppet.

"Sorry, there's a fox in the garden. He's eating a magpie. Blood everywhere. It's like Vietnam out there."

"Aww, I love foxes. So cute."

As she said the word "cute," the fox flashed brilliant teeth and tore a chunk loose and swallowed it with obvious relish, the dark red blood dripping plentifully down its muzzle and chest.

"Yeah," said Ashling. "Cute."

They spoke for a little while more. It hurt. But it was good pain. The pain of something healing.

"All right . . ." said Ashling, and she mentally cycled through all possible candidates for the second word . . . *love, hon, babe, doll, Betty, you, buddy, pal,* and so on and so on.

She tested each one, like she was appraising gemstones:

This one, too affectionate. This one, too cold. This one, almost mocking. This one, too truthful.

". . . hon. Break a leg."

"Thanks," was Betty's husky reply.

She heard an intake of breath on the other line, a cracking in the air, a dam about to break.

She hung up.

End it there.

In the garden, the fox was snapping bones. She could hear them through the glass of the window, like boots stepping on dry twigs.

Making herself a cup of coffee, she left the grim spectacle in the kitchen and took the steaming mug up to her bedroom, being careful to avoid the squeaky floorboard at the foot of the stairs. It had been there for as long as she could remember; step on it and it would whine loud enough to be heard in the next room. Many a time she had been grassed on by that floorboard when sneaking into the house in the wee small hours, drunk and reeking of cigarette smoke and teenage rebellion. Her mother had told her, when she was very little, that someone was buried under that floorboard, and stepping there made their ghost cry out in pain. Etain had told lots of stories like that.

Whose ghost it was had always gone unmentioned.

She sat down at her PC, took a swig from her coffee, and stared at the nearly blank screen and the beginnings of what she believed would be the most important letter she would ever write. Three words stood defiantly at the top of the letter, challenging her to continue.

Dear Mr. Land

Ashling took a deep breath, and began to type.

Dear Mr. Land,
I hope this letter finds you well. My name is Ashling Mallen and I'm currently completing the final year of my BA in Film and Television Production at UCD. I also have significant hands-on experience in television production, having interned with your colleague Mr. Michael McCormack (reference attached) last summer.
    I understand that you are currently interviewing for a production assistant and I need this job . . .

Ashling stopped, and slapped the Backspace key as if it had misbehaved.

    . . . and I would be very interested in applying for this role. My skills include . . .

She expended a paragraph on extolling her own skills, assets, and virtues, which felt like rolling a cheese grater over her soul. She was halfway down the page now and with a flush of panic she realized that she would not hire the person who wrote this letter. She changed tack.

I consider children's programming to be the most important and necessary function any national broadcaster can perform.

Jesus, she thought to herself. *You're supposed to be a good actor. Is this the best you can do?*

Puckeen is a program that has always had a very deep, personal significance to me. It was a formative experience of my childhood.

She halted suddenly. She felt as if someone had just told a dead-baby joke at a christening. She had thoroughly shocked herself. She carried on.

My sister and I . . .

Again, she pulled up short, but this sentence was obstinate. It refused to remain unwritten.

My sister and I would watch every day after school. We especially loved the Magic Door and watching Puckeen coming out of his box. We always used to watch the box, waiting for the lid to move. That was our favorite part.

I saw the box once.

We were on a school trip, my sister and I. They showed us around the studio. Then a big fat man pulled a name out of a hat and said that one of us would be allowed to go and look in Puckeen's box. But he called out two names. Mine and my sister's. He said that we could both look. He said that was very special, and had never happened before.

My sister went first. She looked inside but she said there was nothing there.

She was lying, wasn't she?

Were you the fat man?

I've looked up pictures of you but I can't be sure. It was dark. I couldn't see your face.

I remember your hands. You had very big hands. You had a silver ring on one of them.

I thought it was strange because it looked like a woman's ring.

I can't remember why I thought that.

I thought you were scary and nice.

You were both at once and I didn't know things could be scary and nice at the same time.

Then I heard your voice and I thought to myself, "Oh. He's something scary pretending to be something nice. He's something that's very good at pretending."

My mother keeps asking me where my sister is.

She thinks it's my fault. She thinks I *lost* her.

I want to find her again but I've run out of places to look.

I think she's in the box.

If you give me this job will you let me look in the box?

Let me look in the box. I'll give you everything.

I will give you me.

She slammed her finger on the Backspace key and burned the entire letter white.

She took a deep, deep breath.

She began to type.

Dear Mr. Land

After writing and printing off the letter she went down to the kitchen and rooted around in a drawer for a book of stamps. The stamps were a few years old and still in punts. Rather than waste time trying to mentally convert them into euro, she simply slapped a row of stamps on the envelope in the hope that it would be enough to get the letter to Donnybrook. The stamps were all pictures of Irish wildlife; squirrels, rabbits, and a fox. On a whim, she looked through the book again until she found a magpie. It was only worth a penny, but she affixed it next to the fox. Maybe the penny would make the difference. Or, if nothing else, ensure that the fox did not go hungry.

Her mother did not look up from the television when Ashling entered the living room and placed a mug of tea beside her.

Etain was watching the news, the volume turned down so low that it was little more than a gentle, soporific cattle-low in the background. The green and blue light from the screen caught the cigarette smoke around her head, and her wild, dry stack of gray hair.

She smoked with her left hand, the cigarette clenched between index and middle finger, which made the gap between middle and little finger seem even more yawning.

Ashling sat down in an armchair by the window and proceeded to mentally rewrite the letter she had already sent.

"Jaysus," said Etain, as if she had always been there. "Do you think I'll get a turnout like that when I go?"

Ashling started and looked at the screen.

Princess Margaret, Countess of Snowdon, had died six days earlier. But her funeral had been a quiet, relatively unostentatious affair. The news media, understanding their audience, had taken her passing as an opportunity to show a montage of other, more visually spectacular royal funerals from years past.

Diana, the beloved golden child, had edged out Margaret, the overlooked sister.

Etain and Ashling watched the people lining the streets three deep and standing in dutiful silence as the royal casket wound its way to Westminster Abbey. Ashling wondered if Kate was somewhere down there, head bowed in respectful silence. *Taking the soup, Kate Larkin. For shame.*

"They say a million turned out," Ashling said.

"Don't think I could get a million?" Etain asked.

She said it playfully. A bit of banter. *Where is this coming from?* Ashling wondered.

"Maybe," she answered. "People actually like the royals, though."

"Me arse," said Etain, dragging extravagantly on her cigarette. "My mother got a great turnout and she was an awful hoor."

It was a strange thing to realize, but Ashling had never heard her maternal grandmother mentioned by Etain. Kate, occasionally, would let something slip through the cracks. But Etain was a wall.

When she thought of the word "grandmother," Ashling instantly pictured Granny Mallen with her glossy red cheeks and round face like a baby's. She remembered the smell of flour and cooking grease, and thick red arms gathering her up and holding her until the pain from a scraped knee had burned its way out. Anne had died three years ago, with a heart full of love but not built to last.

But on the other side of the family tree, perched like a black crow, was a void.

"Did I ever meet her?" Ashling asked. She knew only that Mairéad Larkin had died when she, Ashling, had been very young.

Etain grunted and shook her head.

This was her house, Ashling thought. *How much of it is still hers? How much of the furniture belonged to her? Which pictures did she hang? How many of the walls still have her paint and paper?*

Kate had once described how, if you had displeased her, her mother would simply erase your existence. She had a way with silences that could make you feel like you were not really there, simply a ghost observing the mortal world passing around you. And in a moment of dull revelation she saw it, descending down the years from Mairéad to Etain to herself at the very bottom. A legacy of absence. A river of nothing.

"What's Betty up to?" Etain asked.

Ashling tried to remember the last time her mother had asked her a question about her personal life, and came up empty.

"I . . . we're not together anymore, Ma."

"Oh," said Etain. "That's a pity. I liked her."

Fooled me, thought Ashling. *Damn sure you fooled Betty, too.*

"How did that happen?" Etain asked disinterestedly.

"I broke up with her."

"Why?"

"Because if I hadn't she would have wanted us to live together. I can't leave you alone and I didn't want her moving in here."

"Why's that?"

"Because I knew she wouldn't be happy here."

"She would be the first," Etain admitted.

She would, wouldn't she? First in years.

"Do you hate me, Ma?" she asked.

"I do," said Etain.

Ashling burst out laughing.

She couldn't help it. The casual way it had been said. The utter, total lack of hesitation. The perfect, if unwitting, comic timing of it.

You had to laugh.

You had to laugh.

Even Etain gave a husky chuckle.

"I did try," she said wearily. "I tried to love you. But you weren't made for loving, Ashling. You didn't come from love. Not like . . ."

She left the name unspoken, hanging in the air like a dagger.

"I did try," Etain repeated. "It never came easy to me. Love. And now everyone I ever gave my love to is dead. Or took it and ran. I don't have any left for you, see? I gave it all away."

Ashling had stopped laughing now. Now she was feeling it. But Etain carried on.

"Aren't we done now? Aren't we done now, Ashling? Go back. Just go back to where you came from."

Ashling closed her eyes and waited until the tide receded. She thought of her letter, lying in the iron belly of the old green post box on the corner.

"I'm working on it," she whispered.

They sat alone in silence.

On the screen, George VI was being wheeled before Buckingham Palace like a grocer's stall, flanked by guards with black bearskin caps.

"Why do they wear those stupid hats?" Etain asked.

"I don't know, Ma."

"What?"

"I don't know why they wear the stupid hats."

Weeks passed with the speed of a prison sentence.

She was beginning to realize that she had misjudged how badly she would take the breakup.

She had lost her appetite and her face had become sharp and drawn.

When the time came for her usual buzz cut, she decided on a nihilistic whim to shave clean to the scalp. But instead of looking edgy or cool, she just looked like she was in the middle of a brutal course of chemotherapy.

She was staying out of Dramsoc. She told herself it was because she was in her final year and needed to study. One day she had walked past the reception desk, just over the stairwell leading down to the LGs, and she heard Betty's laugh, a filthy, goofy cackle, rising up from below, and suddenly she was lost in heady memories of curly red hair and soft freckly shoulders and teeth gently biting on her lower lip . . .

She had started sobbing and slumped on the desk with such force that the receptionist, a young Nigerian man with kind eyes, had run over to ask her if she needed help. Clearly he had thought that whatever was wrong with her was finally about to kill her.

"Go to Limerick," Kate said.

Ashling said nothing and simply continued staring out the kitchen window.

But silences did not work on Kate. Kate had been trained by experts in the art.

"Go. To. Limerick," said Kate firmly.

"You just want us to get back together," said Ashling.

"I do want that," said Kate, nodding. "I want you to get back together because you love each other and there will be enough people trying to make life miserable for you without you doing it to yourself because you think you don't deserve to be happy. But that's not why I'm telling you to go."

"Oh, it's not?"

"No, it's not. I'm telling you to go and see the play because if you miss it you'll regret it for the rest of your life."

"Fuck off."

"And you know I'm right because you're already regretting it and it hasn't even happened yet. Go to Limerick."

"You're like a shark, you know that? If you ever stopped interfering in my life you'd drop dead."

Kate sighed and rubbed the bridge of her nose wearily.

"Let me ask you this: Do you want Betty out of your life completely? Literally never see her again?"

She didn't need to hear the answer. The pain in Ashling's eyes at the very idea spoke loudly enough.

"You want to still be friends with her, right? You want to still be there for her in some way?"

Ashling nodded.

"Then you might as well start now. Go and be a good friend. Support her. Go. To. Limerick. Fuckface."

Ashling snorted with laughter, despite herself. Well. She had to go now, didn't she?

"Fine," she said sullenly. "I'll go to stupid fucking Limerick."

"Good," said her aunt primly.

They spent a few minutes in silence, watching some sparrows dancing on the bird table.

"You didn't even mention my hair," said Ashling.

"I prefer not to speak ill of the dead," said Kate.

"Thanks."

"Was that you I saw on that autopsy table in Roswell?"

"Fuck off."

She tried to read on the journey down to Limerick but the motion of the bus and the weird stale-meat-and-coffee smell endemic to the Bus Éireann fleet soon had her stomach in knots. So she put the book aside and huddled against the window, watching the gray fade to green.

She felt like she was going into battle, and she didn't even know what the war was about.

Why am I here? Why am I doing this? What's the plan? Why do I listen to Kate?

Above all, she did not want to hurt Betty.

Betty had been through enough.

She took too long getting ready, agonizing over whether to wear makeup or not and what signals that might or might not send, and so arrived too late to see the show.

She slumped off to a nearby café and suffered through the worst cup of tea she had ever had in her life while trying and failing to compose a text message to Betty apologizing for missing the play.

After a while she gave up and contented herself with finding patterns in the stains on the wall. She made the tea last as long as she could while the girl behind the counter eyed her with increasing suspicion, clearly suspecting her of being a junkie.

Bitch, you wish this place was classy enough to attract junkies, Ashling thought as loudly as she could, and glared back at the girl so that she at least caught the gist.

She returned after the curtain had gone down to find the stage being swept clean by the theater staff and no sign of the cast or crew of *The*

Girl on the Wall. Ashling almost gave up there and then but something in her forced her on. She got the name of the club they had gone to, promising herself that if she was turned away at the door she could just go back to the hostel and sleep.

Her heart sank once she reached the club, a black concrete cube called Blue Tito's that she was certain she had seen on the front page of a newspaper more than once, accompanied by a headline that began with the word "GRUESOME" . . .

There were bouncers, but it seemed that the only criteria being applied to those queuing to get in was that they be bipedal, and even that seemed more like a loose guideline.

She could tell she was at the right place, as she could see young first-year Dramsoccers, recognizable by face if not by name, hanging around outside in the smoking area. A slim Greek boy had his arms around someone with short brown hair and beautiful eyes. Ashling couldn't tell if it was a boy or a girl that the Greek kissed tenderly in the shadows, and clearly neither of them cared.

She suddenly felt very lonely indeed.

And she realized that she should be wearing makeup.

She did not want the blast of heat and noise. She did not want the darkness, the crushing bodies, the strobe lighting, the techno music beating her eardrums raw. The club spread out in front of her like a landfill of refuse to be picked through. She pushed her way across the dance floor looking desperately for a familiar face.

A hand fell on her shoulder and she spun around to see Gemma giving her a huge, open-mouthed grin as she mimed the words "You made it!" over the pounding beat.

Behind her Ashling could see almost a dozen Dramsoc women, some waving and gesturing for her to join them. She leaned in and yelled in Gemma's ear: "WHERE'S BETTY?!"

Without a word, Gemma pointed upward.

Ashling followed with her glance and saw a figure on the balcony overlooking the dance floor. Short, with long red curly hair.

Ashling strode forward, pushing her way through the dancers, and then suddenly stopped.

She could see Betty more clearly now. She was talking with Alicia

Ní Ghráinne, the actor who had replaced her. They were laughing together. Betty actually looked happy.

Ashling felt the floor crack beneath her.

What am I doing here? What the fuck am I doing here?

Too late. Betty glanced down and their eyes met.

Betty looked like she'd been struck. She stared at Ashling. Tentatively she raised a hand. To wave hello, Ashling knew. But she looked like a child raising her hand to ask a question.

Panicked, Ashling broke off eye contact and turned away, but not quick enough to avoid the look of pain and betrayal in Betty's face.

Ashling cursed herself savagely. This had been the worst idea she had ever had in her life and when she got home she would change the locks and make sure that Kate Larkin never darkened her door again.

And then she heard it.

The awful techno music suddenly ended and Ashling heard a familiar, never unwelcome beat.

The drums, gentle but insistent. A slow, beautiful, melancholy guitar.

Years later, Betty would still refuse to believe that it had been a coincidence.

She would always believe that Ashling had requested the song. But Ashling would shake her head and insist that it had been pure chance.

Standing on the dance floor Ashling felt a great calm come over her. She turned and looked right up into Betty's face.

Smiled.

Extended an arm.

An unspoken invitation.

Come.

Dance with me.

Betty did not even think. There was no time to get to the stairs; Bono, the pox, was about to start singing any second now. She simply grabbed hold of an iron beam and slid down to ground level like a fireman.

Ashling and Betty faced each other on the dance floor.

What happened next would enter the folklore of the city of Limerick and be told to friends and family and later children and even grandchildren, none of whom would ever believe a word of it.

After all, that was the night that "With or Without You" had started playing and two women in the club had launched into a perfectly choreographed dance number.

They had then been joined by around twenty or thirty other women, all Dubliners, who somehow had the whole dance routine perfectly memorized and proceeded to perform it in its entirety for the stunned patrons.

After the song had ended, the DJ had not put on another and simply let the stunned silence breathe.

Like a great beast, the entire club had seemed to inhale.

And then they roared. Whoops of mighty approval. Feet stamping. Hands applauding. The Dramsoc women, true to the ways of their tribe, linked arms and bowed gratefully, mile-wide grins on their flushed and glistening faces.

And behind them, in the center of the storm; perfect calm.

Betty had her arms around Ashling and was holding her so tightly that she must be nestled deep between her lungs and heart.

They kissed until the pain had gone away.

Betty placed her lips on Ashling's ear and whispered.

"We are never doing that again."

Ashling nodded, the tears running freely.

She had failed.

She had not been strong enough.

And the joy was so fierce it burned.

NOVEMBER 1989

Ruairí Finucane snorted in irritation and held up a picture beside his face.

It was a cartoon, quite skillfully drawn, of a man with a wide grin and a black, bushy mustache.

"What the hell is this, I ask you?" he barked.

Patricia Skelton, seated across the desk from her editor in his cramped office, furrowed her brow and took the drawing from him.

"He definitely looks familiar," she said.

"Would you believe it if I told you that's supposed to be Albert Reynolds?" Ruairí said contemptuously.

Patricia guffawed. The cartoon depicted a person who was white and male, but that was where any resemblance to the current minister for finance began and ended.

Ruairí, a large, red-faced, harried-looking man with a brown comb-over, spread his hands as if to say, "Do you see the nonsense I have to deal with?"

Patricia liked Ruairí quite a bit. He was one of the few people at the *Dublin Herald* who had not seemed to be intimidated by her reputation when she came to work for the paper, and they had soon formed a good rapport.

"Sure I could draw you a better Albert Reynolds," said Patricia. "Here, give me a pen and paper."

Ruairí watched with an impressed expression as she began to draw. She had always been good at art.

"Not bad. Not bad at all," he said, regarding her handiwork. "Nose is a bit long. Want a job?"

He was only half joking. The paper's political cartoonist of thirty years was moving on to pastures new and Ruairí had put out an open call for artists, asking them to submit caricatures of Albert Reynolds as an audition piece.

"Sorry," said Patricia. "Content in my current role."

"Speaking of. What did he say?"

"Off the record, he confirmed every word of it," Patricia said. "The payments. Quashing the DUI. All of it."

"And will he go *on* the record?"

"He will not."

"Why not?"

"Because he says that if he does the taoiseach will rip out his arse-hole and feed it to him."

"Pah!" said Ruairí contemptuously. "Is he a man or a mouse?"

The current government had been in power for less than three years and already the amount of corruption and double-dealing had reached such a level that Ruairí liked to joke that soon they would need to publish the *Herald* in hardback volumes. But simply saying there was corruption was one thing. Getting someone in government to attest on the record was something else entirely.

"So we're fucked?" Ruairí inquired.

"We might not be entirely fucked," Patricia replied. "There's Johnny Logue in Wexford."

John Logue, the eighty-two-year-old Fianna Fáil deputy of the Model County, had held his seat since the late '50s and had announced that he would not be running in the next general election, whenever that might be. It was well known that he had little love for the leader of his party, and Patricia was willing to bet that he would be quite happy to toss a couple of lit matches over his shoulder on his way out.

Ruairí, however, looked dubious.

"Ah, Logue's a party man to his core. He won't grass."

"You never know. Old men like to have their egos stroked, Ruairí, someone as clever and handsome as you doesn't need to be told that. If I frame it as giving him a chance to show his party how far they've strayed from their ideals . . ."

"'I didn't leave Fianna Fáil, Fianna Fáil left me'?" Ruairí suggested mischievously.

Patricia smiled. "Something like that."

"Look who went native," he said with a grin.

Patricia had spent most of the previous year in the United States, covering the presidential campaign of George Bush to succeed his boss, Ronald Reagan, to the presidency.

"I was thinking of driving down to Wexford and hiding in a bin and pouncing on him as he goes past," she said. "Not call ahead, just show up and see if he'll sit down for an interview."

Ruairí still looked dubious, but nodded his assent, evidently convinced that it was at least worth the price of petrol to try.

She rose to leave and headed for the door and had a moment of epiphany. She spun around and took the cartoon off his desk and showed it to him.

"It's *Burt* Reynolds, you plonker!" she crowed. "He's after drawing you *Burt* Reynolds."

"What?" Ruairí spluttered, putting on his glasses and re-examining the cartoon. "Who's he, again?"

"*Deliverance.*"

"Diddled by the hillbillies?"

"Went over the waterfall in the canoe."

"I'd walked out before then. Me heart couldn't take it. Oh wait, I know him. Wasn't he in that thing with Dolly Parton and the hoors?"

"That's him."

"Well, Jaysus, that's not bad at all, is it?"

"It's not. I'd give him a call, Ruairí. Where's he from?"

"Scotland, I think. Sure, that explains it. How is someone from Scotland supposed to know who Albert Reynolds is?"

Or care? Patricia thought glumly to herself as she walked back to her desk. She knew she was turning into a stereotype, the woman who'd been to America and now thought she was too good for the auld sod. But there it was. The political beat in Ireland just didn't have the same feeling of significance that she'd gotten covering the battle for the most potent office in the world. Irish politics seemed unchanging, tawdry, mediocre, and futile in comparison.

How you gonna keep them down at the Fine Gael Ard Fheis, after they've seen DC?

When she got back to her desk there was something waiting for her, an issue of the *Dublin Herald* from a few months ago with a sticky note saying, *Sorry I missed you, Luce.*

She had requested the issue from the archive, as she had wanted to cross-check her own research with an article on Johnny Logue's relationship with the taoiseach, but all thoughts on the matter evaporated the very second she saw the front page.

The headline read: LITTLE NIAMH: GARDAÍ APPEAL FOR WITNESSES.

Beneath it was a photograph of a smiling blond girl of seven or eight years of age being held by her mother, a slim woman with sad eyes and graying, light brown hair. Dollymount Strand stretched off into infinity behind them.

Patricia's eyes shot up to the date on the masthead: May 10, 1989.

She did a mental calculation; just over six and a half months ago. She had still been in America then, working as the Washington correspondent of the *Irish Press*. A few weeks later, the *Press* had dropped her like a desperate balloonist trying to remain financially airborne and she'd been snapped up by the *Herald* and returned home. No wonder she hadn't heard. To be absolutely sure, she scanned the article for the child's name.

Niamh Mallen.

Ruairí looked up in surprise to see Patricia come through his door again. She stood in the center of the room, as if unsure how to begin. He waited patiently.

"Ruairí," she began. "Does the name Etain Larkin mean anything to you?"

He folded his arms and stared at the ceiling as if the cracks in the plaster might yield an answer.

"Etain Larkin . . . Etain Larkin . . . how do I know that name?"

"Nineteen seventy-nine. Scarnagh."

"Bombing or shooting?"

"No, neither. You have to remember. It was one of the biggest stories of the year."

"Really? Bigger than the pope, was she?"

"Ah, you remember. Young girl, in her twenties. Goes to a party in Duncannon. Gets engaged to her boyfriend. Leaves the party in the middle of the night. Doesn't make it home. They were searching for her for days."

Sudden realization spread over Ruairí's face.

"Oh wait, I remember, yeah, yeah. You wrote a lot on it, didn't you? For the *Press*?"

She nodded.

"It was the boyfriend, wasn't it?"

She shook her head vehemently.

"It *wasn't* the boyfriend, no," he corrected himself. "Because they found her. That's right. And she couldn't remember . . . yes, yes. I remember now. Big mystery."

"And now there's another one," said Patricia darkly, sliding the newspaper over to him and tapping a pink fingernail on the face of the woman in the picture. "Because that is Etain Larkin."

"You're pulling my leg," said Ruairí, peering at the picture through his glasses.

"I am not touching your leg," Patricia replied.

"Jaysus, don't some families have all the luck?" he murmured sadly.

Patricia suddenly realized that she knew nothing about Niamh's disappearance other than what was in the article, which apparently had been written only a week or two after her vanishing.

"What happened?" Patricia asked.

"Oh, of course. You were gone for all of it," Ruairí replied.

"Did they ever find her?" she asked quietly.

"No. No. They never did. She was taken from the playground after school, if memory serves. No one really saw who took her but . . . oh, there was some suspicion that the father might have done it, that's right . . ."

Patricia felt a sudden sickening jolt in her stomach. Niamh *Mallen*. Which of course meant that the father was . . .

"Barry Mallen?" she asked.

"I don't remember his name," said Ruairí. "It might well have been."

"Why did they suspect him?"

"Oh, a few witnesses testified to seeing a man matching his description with a child matching hers driving away from the school. Very insubstantial. He had an alibi. He was at work at the time, his colleagues attested to it. Nothing proven."

Patricia wished she could take more solace in that.

In the aftermath of Scarnagh she had defended Barry's innocence many times, as it had seemed to her to be incontrovertible. The Mallens had even invited her to Barry and Etain's wedding to show their gratitude. She had almost gone, too, if only to see the story reach a happy ending. But she had declined, ultimately. It would have been unprofessional.

And, as it happened, it had not been the end of the story after all.

She had believed in Barry Mallen's innocence. But how unlucky could one man be?

A thought suddenly occurred to her.

"Ruairí, you didn't know?"

"Know what?"

"That Niamh Mallen's mother had also been abducted herself ten years ago? That her father was a suspect in another disappearance?"

He shrugged and shook his head.

I can't be the first person to make this connection, Patricia thought to herself. *This case is months old. Somebody has to have realized this. Etain Larkin's disappearance was front-page news. Unless the entirety of Irish journalism has been replaced with toddlers, somebody is old enough to remember this. It's only been ten years.*

"I'm going to look into this," she said.

"Why?" said Ruairí.

"It's me job," she said, surprised.

"You cover politics. Not crime."

"I'm Patricia Skelton," she said, without a hint of pretense. "I'll cover the bloody Rose of Tralee if the mood takes me."

"Pat," he said wearily. "Leave them alone."

"Who?" she said. She could not understand why he was pushing back on this.

"The family," he said. "The Mallens. Leave them be. They've suffered enough. Leave the family alone."

Ah, there was the word. "Family." It was an old Irish word.

It meant: "Do nothing. Challenge nothing. Change nothing."

Ireland was a rocky garden, dig a few inches deep and you found stone; solid and impassable. And carved into its face, as like as not; the word FAMILY.

She slumped back into her chair, despondent and angry and sick to her stomach.

She had fought for Barry Mallen. Defended him. Guarded his reputation with her own.

The idea that he might have been a monster all along filled her with an existential dread. It was the kind of thing that could negate your entire existence. She would forever be Barry Mallen's stooge. A dupe. An unwitting accessory to the murder (and God knew what else) of a child.

Anything else she had ever done, anything she had achieved: meaningless.

She tried to dig herself out.

Calm down. The evidence against him was . . . nothing. There was no evidence. A few people thought they saw someone like him, it could have been any—

How could she have been so stupid?

It could have been one very specific person.

The next question that came to her was so important she actually said it aloud:

"What did Feidhlim Lowney look like?"

They had never caught him. And the only remains in the house had been the bones of a woman presumed to be Bernadette Lowney. His motives, to this day, were unknown. And, looking back, Patricia could not remember ever seeing a photograph of the man.

He could look like anything at all.

He could, for example, be a tall, well-built man with ginger hair.

She snatched up the phone and called the archive.

"Hi, Luce?"

"How's it going, Pat, did you get that paper I left for you?"

"I did, you're a star. C'mere to me, can you dig up a photograph?"

"Ah, sorry, we're all locked up down here and I'm on me way out. Is it urgent? Sure, give me the details and I'll get it up to you tomorrow."

"Okay, thanks. It's a man called Feidhlim Lowney, he was involved in an abduction back in seventy-nine . . ."

She gave as many details as she could and then hung up. Ruairí had told her not to investigate Barry Mallen, but he had said nothing about exonerating him.

There you go again, she thought to herself. *So quick to assume he's innocent.*

The next day she drove down to Enniscorthy and waited patiently in the reception of John Logue's constituency clinic for almost an hour and a half for the clerical officer to tell her whether he could take time from doing the work of the people to speak to her.

"Sorry, it looks like he's not going to have an opening today," said the young woman at the desk with as decent a simulacrum of regret as could be expected on a civil service salary.

Then, apparently thinking the conversation had reached a natural and organic conclusion, she lifted the earpiece of her phone and began to dial.

"Sorry," said Patricia. "You did tell him my name? Patricia *Skelton*?"

The girl looked at her skeptically, as if she could not understand what possible difference that could make.

"I did, yes," she said curtly.

Bloody typical. You leave the country for a few months and your name no longer strikes terror in all who hear it.

"Well, you know what . . ." she began.

But suddenly she realized she had nothing to give.

There was a time when she would have dug her heels in, told this young get that she would not be moving an inch from the premises until she had Johnny Logue served to her on a silver platter with an apple in his mouth . . .

". . . that's absolutely fine. Tell Johnny I was asking for him. Bye now."

As she walked out into the cold November morning she wondered if she should take a holiday. Recharge her batteries. Get the fire back.

But she knew she was fooling herself.

She wasn't tired. She just didn't care anymore.

Maybe Logue would have gone on the record. Maybe she would have returned to Ruairí with a shiny new arrow to shoot at the taoiseach's chest.

And he would dance out of the way like he always did and buy another island.

She stopped for petrol at a tiny service station on the road back to Dublin, seeing as she was still on the *Herald*'s shilling.

She filled the tank to the brim and entered the shop to settle. On a whim, she went to the newspaper rack at the back of the shop to see if they had today's issue of the *Herald*, which put her in the perfect position to spy Barry Mallen as he exited the restroom and ambled up to the counter to pay.

She stared at him, dumbfounded. She almost called out to him before stifling herself. Instead, she watched him pay for his petrol in complete silence, hoping desperately that he would not turn around.

After he left, she briskly walked to the counter, paid her own bill, and walked back onto the forecourt. She could see Barry behind the row of pumps, his back to her, getting into a blue family sedan. He was alone. As nonchalantly as she could, she got into her own car and, not entirely sure what she was doing, began to follow him from a distance as he pulled out of the service station.

Despite nineteen years in investigative journalism, Patricia had never actually "tailed" anyone before.

Why are you doing this? she asked herself as she followed Barry's car off the main road and down a narrow and winding boreen. *Why are you pursuing this man?*

It wasn't that running into Barry Mallen was that remarkable. It was a tiny country of less than four million people. You constantly ran into people you knew in unexpected places.

But she did not need to consult the OSI map stashed in her glove compartment to know that there was only one place that Barry Mallen could be going.

He's going to Scarnagh. Fuck me. Why is he going to Scarnagh?

Had he and Lowney been working together? Had he been in on it all along?

What even was "it"?

She kept her distance, close enough to keep his car in sight, not so close that he might see her face in the rearview mirror.

It began to rain, a heavy, blotchy, wintery downpour, and suddenly she was keeping the wipers on full speed just to keep a shred of visibility.

In front of her, Barry's car became a cloud of blue particles that suddenly flared bright red. He had stopped, along with Patricia's heart. Squinting through the windshield she saw what had happened. Slow, listing, black-and-white shapes filled the road in front of Barry's car.

A farmer was driving cattle across the road into a neighboring field.

As she watched, Barry stepped out of his car and she saw him talking with the farmer. He nodded and then turned and walked back.

But he did not stop at his own car.

With a feeling of dread she watched as the dark shape grew larger and larger in the windshield.

She had forgotten just how big he was.

The inside of the car grew darker as he stopped outside her door window.

A knuckle the size of a small walnut rapped politely against the glass.

Taking a deep breath, she rolled the window down.

He did not look angry, or surprised. Just weary. Disappointed.

"Hello, Miss Skelton," he said softly.

For a mad moment, she considered doing the whole "Barry Mallen, is that you?!" rigmarole but she decided it was beneath her dignity and his. So she simply gave him a sad, apologetic smile.

"Hi, Barry," she whispered.

He sighed.

"Your man says he'll be a few minutes," he said, gesturing to the farmer in the distance.

"That's a lot of cows," she noted, feeling stupid as soon as she said it.

"Aye, it's a good herd." He nodded, like a man who knew what he was talking about.

He turned back to look at her.

"He'll have them off the road in a tick. Then we can move on."

She noted how he said "we," as if they were traveling together.

Without another word he turned and walked back toward his car.

"Where are we going?" she called after him, shouting to be heard over the downpour.

"I think you know," he called back, and she heard bitterness and anger in his voice for the first time.

The rain had cleared but, if anything, that made the scene even bleaker.

A rainstorm had a bit of wild vitality to it. But now with only a lethargic drizzle overhead, the charred remains of Feidhlim Lowney's home, jutting out of the weeds like a lower jaw full of rotten teeth, seemed unbearably morose.

They stood together, in what had once been the Lowneys' hallway.

The massive man, and the tiny woman dressed in pink.

She felt a great urge to take his hand, or squeeze his shoulder. Something comforting.

And she was still not convinced that he hadn't brought her here to kill her.

Why come, then? she asked herself.

Because I had to know.

"How long were you following me?" he asked her eventually.

"Just from the Esso," she said.

He looked at her, quizzically.

She spread her hands apologetically.

"I was on my way back from Enniscorthy. Saw you getting petrol. Curiosity got the better of me."

He gave a disbelieving laugh and shook his head.

"Fuck's sake. I thought you must have tailed me from Dublin, or something."

"Sorry. I don't know what came over me. I just . . . I knew you had to be coming here. And I had to know why."

He nodded.

"Why are we here, Barry?" she asked quietly.

She could see tears welling in his eyes and his voice, when he spoke, was weak.

"You . . . em . . . you know about . . ."

"I heard." She nodded her head. "I am so, so sorry, Barry. I can't imagine what you and Etain are going through."

"Thank you" was all he said.

She hated giving condolences. It always felt like adding to someone's suffering, not taking away. Forcing them to acknowledge you. To thank you for the gift of useless, meaningless words.

She looked around the ruins of the farmhouse. What had not been burned had been demolished, and what could not be demolished had been left for the weeds that swarmed hungrily over the rubble.

"Surprised no one bought the land," she said.

Barry grunted, as if to say that he was not. But he did not elaborate.

"What are we looking for?" she asked.

He sighed wearily.

"I dunno," he admitted. "Etain . . . Etain's been . . . not right. Since Niamh was taken."

"I can imagine," said Patricia. She couldn't. But it seemed like the right thing to say.

"She's been talking about this place," Barry went on. "She hadn't mentioned it in years, we never really discussed it but . . . she seemed convinced that the two things . . . you know, the two disappearances . . . I dunno . . ."

"What exactly did she say, Barry?" Patricia asked. She could tell that he was dancing around something. Trying to get past something that was in the way without touching it.

He shook his head dismissively.

"Doesn't matter," he said. "Mad stuff."

Patricia looked at him disbelievingly.

"I don't think it's mad at all," she said. "In fact, one of the first things I thought when I heard about Niamh's disappearance was that Feidhlim Lowney might be behind it."

She saw the look he gave her when she said "one of the first things." She remembered that he was now a decade older than the boy she had first met in Tadhg Mallen's kitchen.

He had struck her then as being a nice lad, but totally oblivious.

Age and fatherhood appeared to have sharpened him quite a bit. This was a cannier Barry Mallen. She could see more of his father in him, now.

"It was the first thing we thought of too," he said.

"Did you tell the guards?"

"'Course we did."

"What did they say?"

"They said they've been looking for Feidhlim Lowney for ten years and haven't seen a hair of the man in all that time. Useless fuckers, the lot of them."

"So you came here to look for him?" Patricia asked.

Barry looked around the ruin.

"I dunno," he said softly. "I guess I just wanted to see it for myself. See where he took her. Try make it real in my head. D'you ever feel like you can't trust anything anyone says? Like you're living in a little room and people are talking to you through the letterbox and they're telling you about . . . everything. Everything that's outside. The sun and the wind and the stars in the sky. But you don't really know if any of it's true. It could all be lies."

"What do you mean? You think . . . Etain wasn't really . . ."

"No," he said, raising his hand to stop her. "That's not what I mean. It's not what I'm thinking. It's what I'm feeling. Like I can't trust anything anymore except what's in front of my eyes or in my hands. Maybe not even that. I just needed to come here. See it for myself."

After a few minutes she started to get cold.

She left him standing in what had once been the kitchen and walked to her car to get her scarf out of the back seat.

There was a sudden gust of bone-chilling November wind that caught the tail of the scarf and blew it over her eyes. She pulled it away, and then saw him.

He was standing on a hill, on the other side of what had once been the Lowneys' farmyard. He was standing with his back to her, looking down the hill. He was tall and thin as a whip, dressed like a farmer.

He had hair the color of wet ash.

She walked toward him, stumbling awkwardly over the uneven ground.

"Hello!" she called.

He did not seem to hear her.

"Hello!" she called again. "I'm sorry, do you live around here?"

He did not turn to face her but his head inclined slightly. She caught a glimpse of a wiry, unkempt beard.

She stood beside him, shoulder to shoulder.

He seemed to be looking down at a field behind a row of blackly naked rowan trees at the foot of the hill.

"My name's Patricia," she said. "I'm a writer with the *Dublin Herald*. Would you mind if I asked you a few questions?"

His head gave a twitch that might have been assent.

"It's a lovely view," she said, trying to stir a little conversation. "Just out for a walk?"

"Do you see her?" he asked her.

His voice was so soft that she wasn't sure she had heard him. He sounded like a man talking in his sleep, murmuring the name of a long-lost love.

"Who?" she asked.

He raised a rail-thin arm and pointed downward to the line of trees.

"My wife," he whispered. "My wife is in that field."

She looked where he was pointing.

At first, all she could see was the trees, their bark slick and ebony from the rain. Then she caught a flicker of motion. A wisp of blue amongst the black.

"Oh yes," she murmured. "I see her."

The man threw back his head and screamed, screamed down the hill, screamed so loudly that Patricia threw her hands to her ears to protect them.

It was a voice of a man burning and cursing those who had set fire to him.

It struck the ear like lightning.

It left scorch marks in the air.

The same words, over and over again.

Will you not look at me!?

Will you not look at me!?

Will you not look at me!?

Will you not look at me!?

Patricia stumbled and almost tripped in shock.

Without another word she raced back to the car and felt for the keys in her pocket. She felt certain that the man, drunk or mad certainly, was about to do something terrible.

No one could speak with that much hatred and rage in their voice and not do *something* to extirpate it. A rage like that would not be content with mere words.

She could still hear him screaming, vomiting his bile down the hill.

And then, as sudden as a trap, silence.

She turned and looked.

The crest of the hill was naked as a skull. He was gone.

She breathed a sigh of relief before realizing that he had run down the hill. She wondered what he would do when he reached the woman, his wife.

She called for Barry but he was too far away, or he was ignoring her.

Cursing all men everywhere and until the end of time, she ran to the hill and looked down it.

The forest of rowan trees was graveyard still. She could not see the man, or his wife.

All was silent.

Relieved and unsettled in equal measure, she walked back to the car.

She tried to remember what she knew of the Scarnagh case and remembered that the path that led down away from the house termi-nated in a gate that opened onto the main road where the Gardaí had found Etain. And here was the ditch that Etain had said she had wo-ken up in. Patricia followed the ditch down the hill, and stopped dead.

In her time Patricia had frequently had cause to visit places where terrible and bloody acts of violence had occurred. She had once stood in the ruins of a home in Belfast that had been torched by loy-alist paramilitaries, burning a family of five to death. She was not a religious woman but had nonetheless felt a deep spiritual revulsion when she had stepped into that space, one that she felt certain she would have felt even had she not known its grisly history.

And, for whatever reason, she felt the same awful wrongness now. A sense that the gravel beneath her feet had been the site of some appalling transgression.

Something was glinting dully at her in the mud, like a long-dead star in a smog-filled sky.

She reached down and picked it up.

"What's that?"

She started and looked up to see Barry Mallen ambling down the hill toward her like a boulder.

She was about to ask him if he was deaf, and if not, why the hell he had not come running when he heard a maniac screaming at her, but it didn't seem to matter now.

She held up the tiny object in her hand.

"Look familiar?" she asked.

He stared at it, dumbfounded, and took it without a word.

"Am I right in thinking that's Etain's ring?" she asked.

He shook his head.

"Etain is wearing her ring. She had it on her when I left her in Dublin."

"You're sure?"

He nodded.

"Where did you find this?" he asked her.

She pointed to her feet.

"It was buried in the mud. Could have been here for years."

He was turning it over and over in his hand. Feeling every line and crevice.

"It's the same ring . . ." he whispered to himself. "It's the same fucking ring. Why did he have the same ring?"

Patricia guessed that by "he," Barry meant Feidhlim Lowney. She was about to correct him that they had no way of knowing that the ring had belonged to Lowney, but then again, he had lived here for decades and it looked like no one had been on the property since the Gardaí had concluded their investigation. It was not certain that the ring belonged to him or his wife, but it was far more likely than not.

But even if it did, what of it?

"Maybe it's just a very common ring?"

He glared at her defensively. Ah. Perhaps not the most sensitive thing to say about the engagement ring he had bought his fiancée.

"Have you ever seen anyone else with one of these?" he challenged her.

Now that he mentioned it, she never had. If they were truly rare then maybe that was the connection? Maybe . . . maybe Lowney had gotten his ring from the same place? Maybe that was how he and Barry had first crossed paths? It was a slender reed, but perhaps it would hold.

"Where did you get it, Barry?" she asked. "Etain's, I mean?"

The wind picked up and it began to rain again. They took shelter in Patricia's car.

"It was a jeweler's in Youghal," he told her over the sound of the rain's drumbeat on the windshield. "I was just going past and I saw it in the window and I just . . . I knew I had to buy it. I had to give it to Etain. I felt like the rest of my life was just hinging on that moment, like."

"Really?" she said, trying not to sound incredulous. It was such an ungainly, ugly thing, she thought.

"Yeah."

"Did you see any other rings like it in the shop?" she asked.

He sighed. "C'mon now, it was ten years ago."

"Do you think that jeweler's is still open?"

"You want to drive to Youghal?" he asked.

She shrugged.

"I don't have any plans. Do you?"

He smiled sadly.

"All right. Why not?"

She regretted that they had two cars.

Youghal was almost three hours away and it would have been the perfect opportunity to get more information about Niamh's disappearance.

She also got the impression that he desperately needed someone to talk to.

By the time they drove into Youghal, the evening Angelus was lowing solemnly over the city and it was already night to all intents and purposes.

Like any seaside town, Youghal was at its best in summer in bright sunshine. Here, in the dying gasp of the year with a bone-chilling wind blowing in from the sea, the hamlet seemed unbearably grim.

"We should figure out where we're staying first," said Patricia, trying to keep her teeth from chattering.

Barry wanted to begin searching for the jeweler's immediately but Patricia pointed out that it would probably be closed by now, so they would be better off booking rooms in a hotel and continuing the search in the morning. He saw the sense of it and they made their way up the steps of the Florence Newton Hotel and rang the bell.

Patricia left Barry to book his room and cast an eye around the lobby. It seemed a pleasant enough place. There was a cozy little bar with a roaring fire off to the side, complete with comfortable private nooks with little tables and stools. The perfect place, in short, to buy a man a drink and take down everything he said with a notepad.

The clerk had arrived at the desk and was taking Barry's details.

"Two single rooms?" he asked, glancing from Barry to Patricia.

Patricia felt a small flare of irritation. There was around fifteen years between her and Barry, but she felt certain that if their ages had been reversed, the clerk would absolutely have assumed that they wanted a double.

She wasn't entirely sure if her annoyance was righteous feminist indignation or simple vanity.

What? Just because I'm in my forties I couldn't get a Barry Mallen?

She dismissed the thought. The man was married and emotionally vulnerable and possibly a child murderer. All excellent reasons not to pursue that line of thinking an inch further.

Ah, but I don't really think he did it anymore, do I?

She didn't. Once again Barry Mallen had convinced her of his innocence simply by being . . . Barry Mallen. There was a guileless innocence to his whole manner that made it impossible to distrust him.

And wouldn't that be a useful trait for a killer? she mused.

After they had booked their rooms, they trudged back out into the chill night as Barry Mallen tried to retrace his steps from ten years ago, Patricia struggling to keep up with his great strides.

Making their way down the narrow cobbled streets, they suddenly came to a stop and Barry cursed under his breath.

Patricia looked around his shoulder and saw the issue.

The jeweler's was indeed closed. In fact, it was so closed that it was now a bookshop and looked like it had been for several years.

Barry swore again.

"Well, that's it," he said glumly.

"Ah, Barry," she chided him. "You wouldn't last in journalism, you know that? C'mon."

There was a pub beside the bookshop and Patricia noted the date of establishment over the door as 1952. Shops and cafés were like mayflies, but pubs were trees.

She pushed through the door and made her way to the bar, her companion following unsurely after her. Behind the bar was a girl of around eighteen with long brown hair. Patricia gave her a winning smile and said:

"Excuse me, love, used there to be a jeweler's next door, do you remember?"

The girl frowned.

"Oh Jesus, I dunno," she said, in a lilting Cork accent. "It's always been the bookshop since I've been here. Hang on. HANNAH!"

She called over her shoulder and a woman in her late sixties with an impressive mustache of bristly white hair came bustling out of the kitchen, drying her red hands with a dishcloth.

"Sorry to bother you," Patricia said. "We're looking for a jeweler's who used to be next door to you, here. What was the name, Barry?"

"Oh fuck," said Barry, then glanced abashedly at the girl, who smiled shyly at him. "Sorry. It was . . . Colper . . . Coughran . . . C something . . ."

Hannah nodded impatiently. "Cotter. Martin Cotter was his name."

Barry's face lit up.

"Cotter! That was it."

"He's dead," said Hannah bluntly, who apparently did not believe in sugar-coating bad news.

"Dead?" Patricia repeated blankly.

"Yeah," said Hannah, wiping the bar. "Yeah, yeah, yeah. He died . . . seven years ago now. Cancer."

Patricia could hear Barry deflating beside her. She was about to suggest they head back to the hotel but then the young bargirl piped up curiously.

"Wait? Cotter the jeweler? Isn't he on De Valera Street?"

"No," said Hannah with a touch of irritation. "That's his brother. The two of them ran the shop together. Joe Cotter moved the shop to De Valera Street after Martin died."

Patricia and Barry glanced at each other.

"Could you . . ." Patricia began.

"She'll give you directions," Hannah said with a jerk of her thumb at the young girl as she returned to the kitchen, tossing the dishcloth rakishly over her shoulder.

The shop had seemed to be hiding from them.

After two passes up and down De Valera Street they found it, a doorway at the foot of a flight of stairs, wedged at the side of a chemist's that was closed and shuttered.

In the dim yellow light from a streetlamp, Patricia could just about make out the words J. COTTER, JEWELER & WATCHMAKER over the doorway, painted in flaking gold lettering on a red, equally flaking background.

In one of the windows over the chemist she thought she could see a dim light, but the stairs themselves climbed into perfect darkness.

Barry went first, the shoulders of his coat creating a thin, uneasy whine as they rubbed against the vinyl wallpaper, the stairs creaking lazily under his bulk.

At the top of the stairs there was a thin door with the name of the shop once again painted indifferently on the glass. Barry pushed through.

A bell jangled.

They found themselves standing in a tiny room. Displays of rings and brooches and jewelry of all kinds glinted ephemerally in the gloom. The only light was from a small lamp set upon a desk where a tiny man sat on a stool, utterly focused on the jeweled necklace laid in front of him. He was cleaning it methodically, moving from one gem to the next like a small guppy cleaning the teeth of an eel. He seemed to be of an age where the years were now haphazardly piling their gifts on top of him. He could have been in his eighties or nineties or past the century. The wrinkles were too numerous to be read. White noise on the skin.

He did not look up as they entered.

"Excuse me?" said Patricia. "Are you open?"

"*A strange question,*" he said, and his voice was a high, reedy whisper. "*For you stand within.*"

He glanced up at them. His eyes, Patricia was sure, were there somewhere. But they were so deeply sunken into his head that the light from the lamp could not find them. He looked unsettlingly like an eyeless skull.

"*How may I be of service?*" he whined amicably.

Barry stepped forward with the natural care of a large man in a cramped space full of fragile, valuable things.

"A few years ago I bought a ring from your brother."

"*Ah,*" said the old man, placing a hand theatrically on his thin chest. "*Poor Martin. May God rest him and keep him.*"

Patricia could not think why, but she found the jeweler's expression of remorse over the death of his brother to be palpably insincere.

"I was wondering," Barry pressed on, "if you could please take a look at it."

"*Is it in need of repair?*"

"No. I just . . ."

"We were wondering if you could tell us if there was any significance to this ring," Patricia interjected. "If there was something special about it?"

The old man gave a smile that was . . . Patricia did not know the word.

"*Well, I am sure the young gentleman could tell me more about the significance of the ring than I could. For what significance do these tokens have but what we give to them?*"

"Please," said Barry. "Could you please take a look at it?"

The old man shrugged, which made Patricia think of a praying mantis. He extended a hand of long, elegant fingers and took the ring from Barry.

He held it under the lamp.

Patricia wondered if Barry noticed the sudden, almost imperceptible stiffening of the old man's body before he seemed to relax and launch into what sounded like a well-rehearsed spiel.

"*Ohhhhh yes, yes, yes. Fáinne an Mór-Ríoghan. It's a Morrigan ring.*"

"What's that?" Barry asked.

"Morrigan was . . . the goddess of war?" Patricia asked, a half-remembered school lesson coming back to her.

The old man smiled. "*That was indeed one of her portfolios. However, she was also a goddess of fertility, land, and sovereignty. Goddess of political power, and the methods of its acquisition and retention, as it were. This one is, let me see . . . ah, yes, Badbh . . .*"

"Bov?" Barry repeated.

"*Well, you see, she was a triple-goddess. Three aspects to her,*" the jeweler explained. "*The sisters Badbh, Macha, and Neimhann (or Anand depending on who you ask). Each one represented one of the three pillars of the ancient Irish world. Badbh represented the fili.*"

"The poets?" Patricia asked.

"*Bards.*" The jeweler nodded. "*Keepers of song and story in the time before the written word. Very influential. Very powerful. Even the kings feared them, for they could destroy a reputation with a satirical verse or slanderous tale. Your ancestors, you might say?*"

He was looking at Patricia. She felt a shiver of unease.

"I'm sorry?" she asked coldly.

"*Are you not Patricia Skelton?*" he asked innocently.

"How do you know that?" she asked him.

Try and keep the panic out of your voice there, Pat. You're scaring Barry.

"*My dear lady, you are a very well-known and respected journalist. Why should I not know you? I read the papers.*"

He was mocking her. And yet, what could she say?

Barry did not seem to care.

"What about the ring?" he asked.

"*Ah yes, they were very popular in the late nineteenth century. The Celtic Revival and so on. They would come in three varieties. This one here, you see, is a Badbh ring. Silver. You also had Macha rings, in gold. And Neimhann rings in bronze. It was a tradition to give one to a young man or woman embarking on a new career. The Badbh rings were usually given to people entering into higher education or, say, a young woman becoming a schoolteacher. Anything to do with the written word, really. She represents the bards, you see. The Badbh. Macha*

was the goddess of the king, so Macha rings were given to those enter-
ing the civil service."

"And the bronze rings?"

"Neimhann. Neimhann represented the druids. The priestly class.
Naturally, the Neimhann rings were given to those beginning a life in
the church."

"That's a bit weird, isn't it?" Patricia asked. "You're going off
to become a priest, so they give you a ring with a Celtic goddess
on it?"

"Ah, but this is Ireland," said the jeweler softly. *"There's more of the*
pagan in us than we might like to admit, isn't that right?"

Barry gestured to the ring.

"Would they be rare?"

The old man pursed his lips noncommittally.

"As I say, they were very common at the time. But I haven't seen one
in many years."

"Would it be valuable?" Patricia asked.

The old man sighed, as if that was a vexed question.

"Not in and of itself. But if you had someone trying to complete a
collection you might be able to negotiate a decent price. If you wish to
leave it with me, I could make inquiries . . ."

His hand had closed on the ring and was halfway to his pocket.

Barry extended his hand.

"Please give it back," he said.

The old man froze, and, with seeming reluctance, returned the
ring to him.

"Now I think of it . . ." the old man said. *"I am sure I could find*
someone willing to pay handsomely . . ."

"Can you recall selling a ring like this to anyone? Have you yourself ever sold a Morrigan ring?" Barry asked, and if the old man
thought it sounded like an accusation he did not show it.

The jeweler looked at him serenely.

"Oh, I'm sure one or two have passed through here."

"Who did you sell them to?" Barry asked, almost a whisper.

"I simply could not recall," the old man said.

He said it slowly, deliberately. As if he was enjoying every syllable.

Barry looked at him in impotent rage and for a second Patricia
felt sure he was going to strike the old man dead with a single blow.

Then, without a word, he turned and made for the door. Patricia
followed him.

Then they heard the old man speak, in that same mocking, toying tone.

"Do you know it has occurred to me just this very moment in time that I can recall in perfect detail a gentleman who was looking for just. Such. A. Ring."

Patricia and Barry froze and turned to look at him.

The old man continued his monologue, seemingly oblivious to his audience.

"Yes, yes. A gentleman paid a visit to the shop, quite anxious to obtain a Badbh ring. He said that he had lost his almost a decade prior. And was quite desperate to find a new one."

He turned to look at them. Patricia could finally see his eyes. They glittered at her, like those of a snake. Cold and green and knowing no emotion but hunger.

"Is that right?" Barry growled.

"Indeed yes," the old man replied. *"Would you like me to contact him on your behalf?"*

"Why don't you just give us his number," Barry said, struggling to keep the rage out of his voice. "And we'll call him ourselves?"

"Oh no, oh no," said the old man, tutting sorrowfully. *"I would have to consult my files to find the man's number. But if you leave me details as to where you might be found, I can pass on the information. He seemed very anxious to acquire this ring. I would not be surprised if he paid you a visit tonight."*

Patricia watched Barry approach the desk and scribble out the details of the hotel on a yellow pad, tear off the page, and hand it to the old man with a look that showed him an inch away from murder.

It was only when they had vanished down the steps and reached the end of the road that Barry rounded on her and exploded.

"Did you hear him?! Did you hear that cunt?!"

"I know, I heard . . ."

"That fucker knows something! He knows something, I'm going back—"

"No, you're not!" Patricia barked at him, and placed both hands on his chest.

For a second she thought he was going to swing at her, but instead he spun around and kicked a bin hard enough that it left a dent in the side. Patricia could sense windows twitching overhead and guessed that whispered conversations were occurring in bedrooms up and down the street as to whether to call the guards.

"Barry," she said consolingly. "He knew who you were. He reads the papers, he recognized you. He's just toying with you because he's a sadistic old . . . If you go back there and hit him you will kill that man and you will go to jail. And I think your family have been through enough already, don't you?"

He leaned against the wall and buried his face in his hands.

"Fuck," he breathed. "What am I doing? What the fuck am I doing here?"

"Come on," she said, linking his arm and pulling him gently off the wall. "Come on. Back to the hotel. I'll buy you a drink."

She ended up buying him several.

As they sat in the back of the hotel bar she let him take her through the history of the family Mallen in the years since they'd last spoken. She didn't take any notes. It didn't feel right.

"I'm going mad," he told her hoarsely. "I mean it. Losing her is just . . . do you have kids?"

"No," she said. "I can't imagine, Barry."

"Do you want to hear something awful?" He leaned in close. "Sometimes I wish that they'd just call me up and say, 'Mr. Mallen, we've found her, she's . . .'"

He couldn't say the word.

"Christ forgive me," he went on. "But at least then it'd be over. It's this . . . this fucking purgatory of not knowing."

He took her through the disappearance but there really was nothing to tell.

Niamh Mallen had been beloved by everyone. Her parents, her sister, her teachers, her schoolmates. A sweet, happy, funny child. A ray of sunshine. She had loved drawing with crayons and playing camogie and she had had dreams of being a veterinarian. And one day, just before leaving work, Barry had received a frantic call from Etain telling him that Niamh had not come home from school.

There had been two eyewitnesses who claimed to have seen a blond eight-year-old girl being driven away from the school in the opposite direction from the Mallens' house by a man who roughly matched Barry's description.

"It was fucking happening again. It was all fucking happening again," he sobbed, like a man being carved with a drill.

But the car they described was not one that Barry had ever owned, and besides, he had the testimony of six work colleagues to count on. Barry was quickly dropped as a suspect.

But no one was picked up in his place. The case was cold. For the second time, someone in Barry Mallen's life had vanished without explanation. And this time, there was no happy ending. The child was gone.

"We're all in pieces," he said numbly. "Etain is . . . it's broken her. My parents too. Poor little Ashling . . ." He trailed off.

"Ashling?"

"My daughter," he said. "They were twins. Quiet little dote. Good as gold. She just doesn't know what's happening. Couldn't stand leaving her there with . . . what with everything's going on."

He had changed course there, Patricia noted. What had he been going to say?

"What about Kate? How's she holding up?" Patricia asked.

She remembered Kate Larkin well. She had interviewed her a few times in the aftermath of Etain's return. They had got on like a house on fire.

Barry's face darkened.

"I haven't spoken to Kate in years," he said sourly.

"Oh," said Patricia, surprised. "Falling-out?"

"Not with me!" he said exasperatedly. "She just upped stakes and moved to London and we never heard from her again."

Patricia stared at him in surprise. That did not sound at all like Kate.

"When was this?" she asked.

"Shortly after her ma's death," Barry said.

"Ah. Were they close?"

"Like fuck."

Ah yes. She remembered Mairéad Larkin now. Only by reputation, of course. She had not had the pleasure.

"Well. Maybe she just needed a fresh start."

"Didn't leave us a number or an address. Just cut us out of her life."

All right, thought Patricia. *That's not on.*

"That's very odd," she mused.

"Between you and me," said Barry conspiratorially, "I think there was a falling-out between the sisters."

"Over what?"

"Not a clue. Bloody Larkins. They're a curse," he said bitterly, and downed the last of his cider.

They talked for hours. She told him about America and how she hadn't really found her footing since coming back. He said he'd always dreamed of seeing California but life had had other ideas.

"Jew vaholler lag?" he said, and for a moment she thought he was speaking German.

Her brain reshaped the words correctly to "Do you have a hollow leg?"

She cackled. He was roughly twice her size and yet she was matching him pint for pint.

"Civil servants," she snorted. "Bunch of lightweights."

"That'sh not true," he protested. "Flann O'Brien was a civil servant."

"He was a writer who pretended to be a civil servant," she countered triumphantly. "He was one of us, tribe of Badbh."

As soon as she said it, she regretted it. His face became flushed, and not with booze.

"That bastard knows!" he hissed to her. "He knows where my girl is . . ."

"No."

"He does!"

She gripped his hand tightly.

"He doesn't, Barry. I'm sorry. He was just being cruel."

And yet, she wasn't entirely sure she believed it. She felt quite sure that the old man knew who Barry was, and that he could indeed have simply gleaned that from reading the papers. But what was it that he had said? A man who lost his ring almost a decade ago?

He had to have meant Feidhlim Lowney. Which meant he had to know the connection between Lowney and the ring, even if only to lie about it. Maybe he had been telling the truth. Maybe Feidhlim Lowney was even now making his way to the hotel, desperate to get his ring back. His . . . cheap, ugly ring that had value only to a rabid collector and that he would risk his freedom to come out of ten years of hiding to acquire? No. It was ridiculous.

She was brought out of her reverie by the realization that Barry was kissing her hand.

Gently but firmly she pulled it away. His eyes seemed to regain focus and he sat up.

"Sorry," he mumbled. "I'm really sorry. I wasn't thinking. Christ, I'm pissed."

She shook her head. There had been nothing lecherous about it. He had simply been trying to show affection and his booze-addled brain had given him a bum steer.

"It's fine," she told him. "Forget it."

"I should go to bed," he slurred. "I'm really sorry, Patricia. I'll go. I'll go. I have to call Etain anyway. Let her know where I am."

He struggled to his feet and staggered rather unsteadily to the door and was gone.

She felt like she should follow him to make sure he got to his room safely but he had been so mortified that she felt it kinder to give him some space.

Poor kid, she thought to herself.

Feck off, he's not a kid anymore. He's a grown man with a wife and two—

She winced.

Poor kid.

That was it, wasn't it? To her, he was still that distraught young man sitting in Tadhg Mallen's kitchen, staring into space, desperately in need of an ally.

She heard the clink of a glass and realized that she was not alone in the pub anymore.

Peering over her shoulder she saw a priest sitting by the window.

He was in his forties, with a bland jowly face and gray hair occasionally shot through with dark brown. His glasses were thick to the point of being comical. He was as unimpressive-looking a man as Patricia had ever laid eyes on.

Patricia had met plenty of priests in her life, enough to know that you could not judge a dog by its collar. Some of them were among the most intelligent and erudite men she had ever met, and some of them were utter dullards. Some of them were pleasant, some foul. She had known some who were saints, and others who were monsters.

But she had never met one like the father sitting by the window, and she knew that instantly.

It was the ring. She had been looking for it, without looking for it.

A bronze ring of Neimhann on his finger. She might have seen a million of them before, she realized, and simply never noticed, as she had not known to look for it. But there it was, on his hand as he raised his glass of sherry to his lips.

That was when he saw her looking at him, and met her gaze.

It felt like falling down a well into icy water. No. Not water. Simply cold. Sheer, icy nothingness. There was nothing in the man.

She averted her gaze, an instinctive defensive gesture as much as anything else.

She suddenly felt very queasy. She staggered miserably out into the lobby and found the ladies' restroom.

A short time later she emerged, still feeling minutes from death but slightly more sober.

She leaned against the reception desk and waited for the world to stop turning.

The priest was still in the bar, calmly writing a letter while taking occasional sips from his sherry.

Barry showered until he could feel the effects of gravity again and walked a little more steadily into the bedroom.

He checked the time on his watch and swore. He picked up the phone and dialed a Dublin number. It was answered almost immediately.

"Where the *fuck* have you been?!" a woman's voice hissed at the other end.

"I'm sorry," he said, slurring slightly.

"You said you'd call."

"I know. I know. I just . . . lost track of time."

"Jesus Christ, are you drunk?"

"No," he said honestly. "I am absolutely langers."

He expected an entirely deserved torrent of abuse. Instead, when she spoke again there was genuine fear in her voice.

"Barry, are you okay?"

What a question.

"No, Tain. No, I'm not. Are you?"

"Where are you?" she asked. "Do you need me to come and get you?"

"I'm fine," he said. "I'm in Youghal. I'm in a hotel. The . . . what's it . . . the Florence Newton."

"Youghal? What are you doing in Cork?"

"It doesn't matter," he murmured. "I had a bit of a funny turn. Just needed to get out of the house."

"All right, look," she said. "I know things have been awful. But you can't do that. You can't go disappearing on me . . ."

"I know."

"Not right now!"

"I know. I know. Tain, I'm sorry. I don't know what to say."

"You were looking for her, weren't you?"

He lay back on the bed.

"Yeah. I went to Scarnagh."

At the name, there was a long pause at the other end.

"How was it?" she said at last.

"It's a fucking kip," he said.

"Yeah, see why I left?" she said.

He burst out laughing. She joined in.

"I love you," he said.

"I love you too, ya big eejit," she said. "Why did you go to Scarnagh, Barry?"

He felt what he was about to say needed a preface.

"That stuff you said about Niamh and Ashling—"

"Barry, I told you, I was drunk, I wasn't thinking—"

"I know. I think it just got in my head and I needed to see the place for myself."

"And?"

"And . . . nothing. It's just a pile of rubble. It's nothing. It's nowhere."

"Come home," she said.

"I will. First thing tomorrow. Tain?"

"What?"

He sat up again. "Do you still have that ring?"

"What ring?"

"The ring. Your engagement ring."

"Yeah?" she said, a very subtle note of fear rising in her voice. "Why?"

He was about to tell her the chain of events that had brought him to Youghal but he stopped.

Don't send her down this rabbit hole. You're halfway down your-self.

"It's just . . ." he said. "Sometimes I think you'd have been better off if I'd never given it to you. Sometimes I think I've brought you nothing but pain."

He heard a tiny sob on the end of the line, but when she spoke again she was coldly furious.

"Now you listen here. You never, ever say that again to me. I love you. None of this. None of it. Scarnagh or Niamh going missing, *none of it* changes that. The good will always outweigh the bad. Million to one. D'you hear me?"

"I do," he said, smiling through the tears.

"Do you?"

"I hear you. And you're right."

"I am *always* right, Mr. Mallen. You'd think you'd know that by now."

He nodded.

"How's Ashling?" he asked.

"She's fine," Etain answered. He winced. The tone told him everything. They'd been fighting again. Sometimes it seemed like they never stopped, and had been having one long argument since Ashling had learned to talk.

"She's asleep," Etain said. "Want me to wake her?"

He desperately wanted to hear his daughter's voice again but he knew that listening to her father drunkenly sobbing on the other end of a telephone at one o'clock in the morning would be formative in the wrong kind of way.

"No," he said. "Leave her be."

Knock knock.

Two gentle taps on the door.

Barry looked up.

"Who's this?" he murmured.

"Who's who?" Etain asked.

Phone still in hand, Barry walked to the door and looked through the peephole.

He saw two large-rimmed lenses suspended by a pudgy nose over a snow-white collar.

"It's a priest," he said, scarcely more edified than he had been before.

"I'll see you tomorrow, love," he whispered, and went to hang up.

He thought he heard her say "Barry, wait . . ." but it was too late. The headset was down.

Knock knock.

Barry opened the door and gave a deferential nod to the black-clad man outside.

"Good evening, Father," he said, speaking slowly to keep his words clear.

"My apologies for the lateness of the hour," said the priest gently. *"Am I correct in thinking that you are Mr. Barry Mallen?"*

Barry felt gravity increasing. Whenever strangers knew his name, it was never a good omen.

"Yes," he said.

The priest nodded sympathetically.

He leaned in and whispered somewhat conspiratorially.

"Would we be able to speak inside, Mr. Mallen?"

Barry nodded wearily. He might well be in need of spiritual succor, but right now that was secondary to the need for sleep. But he stepped aside and allowed the priest to enter his room.

"Please, sit down," said the priest, gesturing to a chair.

Barry did, and felt a terrible apprehension. Priests were like doctors and guards. When they asked you to sit down, it was a preamble to the world breaking apart.

The father turned his back to him and filled the kettle in the back of the room with water and turned it on. Barry could not quite see what he was doing, but after a few moments he smelled freshly made coffee.

"I think you need this," the priest said over his shoulder.

"You know who I am?" Barry said.

"I do."

"Are you here to tell me everything's going to be all right?"

"I am not. Drink this."

Barry shook his head.

"Drink," the priest said.

Barry accepted it. It tasted good. Rich and sweet. He noticed dully that the priest was wearing gloves indoors, which seemed odd.

The priest sat opposite him on the bed. Barry realized that he was supposed to say something.

"It finally hit home to me that she's dead," he said. "Something switched in my head. Something went from 'searching' to 'mourning,' like milk going sour. She's gone and I . . . I can't shake this feeling that it's my fault. That I was just blundering through life like a bull in a china shop and I did something terrible and I don't even know what it is and I'm paying for it now. I'm not doing well, Father. I don't know how I can . . . I mean, I was always taught that suicide is a sin and I believe that. It's a terrible thing to do to those you leave behind. But I'm running out of reasons not to . . ."

He stopped. The priest had raised his hand.

"Mr. Mallen. That is not why I'm here."

Barry felt like he'd been hit in the chest with a sledgehammer. The look of total, banal indifference on the priest's face was chilling.

"I am of course aware of your daughter's disappearance. Terrible case. But I am here on a different matter."

"Oh?" was all Barry could say.

"Yes," said the priest. *"I'm here for the ring."*

There was a sudden, knife-keen silence.

Barry lunged for the priest. Or rather, he tried.

His arms hung by his sides, dead and cold as the limbs of a corpse. He couldn't move. The numbness was spreading to his legs. He rolled off the chair and lay on his side, staring in terrified awe at the wastepaper basket in the corner.

"What . . . was in the coffee . . ." he said, the words tumbling out like the soggy, unformed utterances of a toddler.

"This," said the priest, and he dimly felt his big, dead fingers being folded over a small plastic container. The priest was wearing gloves, and that did not seem so odd now.

Suddenly the phone rang.

Etain. Etain was calling back to see if he was all right.

Something was foaming in his stomach, and climbing up his throat looking for a way out.

The chimes of the phone sounded like bells ringing madly in a cathedral tower. They seemed to be swinging, and he felt himself swinging along with them. The floor was sliding under him, like a red-and-brown serpent trying to shake him off its back.

The priest calmly walked over to the phone and with a single, savage tug he tore the cable from the distribution box on the wall. The phone fell silent.

"Please . . . please . . ." Barry begged as his mouth and nose filled with liquid that smelled of bile and rancid chicken. "Please tell my wife . . ."

"That would be rather problematic for me, no?" the priest replied

mildly. *"Fear not, she shall be in no doubt as to the particulars of the matter."*

He laid a piece of paper on the nightstand, folded so that it formed a neat little tent, plainly visible to anyone who entered the room.

My suicide note, Barry thought bitterly.

His vision was fading into dark greens and browns now. A black shape loomed over him and he could barely feel something rooting furtively in his pockets.

In that moment Barry Mallen understood that death was tangible.

He could feel it settling upon him like snow or sheaves of falling paper.

And yet the weight of it was inexorable.

He knew at last that the soul was a tiny, fragile thing, and could be crushed by the fall of a feather.

He was dying in a room with a priest, but there would be no last rites to give meaning to his passing.

He ended the matter in chaos.

Father Fitt stood up and regarded the silver ring carefully in the dim light. Something, a distant cousin of satisfaction perhaps, played upon his impassive features. Without a glance at the mound on the carpet, he placed the ring carefully in his pocket and left.

She had been half dressed for bed when her phone rang.

"Hello?" she said, trying to keep her words sharp and defined.

"Miss Skelton?" said a young wavering female voice at the other end. "This is Nuala at reception. You . . . you arrived with Mr. Mallen, didn't you?"

"Yes, that's right?" she answered.

Jesus, love, calm down, you sound like you're about to burst into tears.

"I . . . just . . . sorry, I didn't know what else to do. There's a gentleman on the line, he wants to talk to Mr. Mallen but he's not picking up . . ."

I'm not surprised. The amount he had, it'd take Fat Man and Little Boy going off on either side of him to wake him up, Patricia thought.

"The gentleman is being . . . he's *very* insistent that he talk to Mr. Mallen, do you think you could?"

Ah. The "gentleman" is no such thing. The "gentleman" is scream-ing abuse at you, isn't he? Well, let's see how he handles me.

"Put him through to me, love," said Patricia primly. "I'll handle it."

"Thank you . . . thank you," the girl repeated, and Patricia could actually hear a sob bubbling in her throat.

The line went silent.

"Hello?" said Patricia.

"Who the fuck are you?"

Dublin accent. Deep and thick as molasses. It was a voice that knocked you over, held you down, and made you listen to it. Bris-tling with anger and contempt. She unsheathed her haughtiest Fox-rock accent and prepared to do battle.

"I think the question is 'who are you?' And . . ."

"Shut your fucking mouth and listen to me, you bitch. I need to talk to Mallen. Now."

"I'm hanging up."

"Do it and he's a dead man."

"Are you threatening him?"

"Like fuck, I am. I'm trying to save the bastard. There's someone after him. Tell him to watch out. Tell him to watch his fucking back."

Patricia was frantically pulling her notepad and pen out of her bag.

"Who? Who's trying to kill him?" she said thickly, the phone wedged between her cheek and shoulder.

"A priest. Tell him to look out for a priest," said the voice, and hung up.

Patricia instantly dropped the pad and pen and dialed the num-ber for Barry's room. It rang three times and suddenly cut out mid ring. She got up and got dressed, becoming more and more frantic with every item of clothing she put on.

She opened her door and had to stifle a shriek as she saw him, the priest, making his way down the stairway, his bald spot staring un-blinking at her as he trotted neatly down to the lobby.

She glanced to the end of the hall where Barry's room was (the receptionist had been able to give them rooms on the same floor, though not adjacent).

She ran to his door and began to knock. No answer.

She knocked again.

No answer.

She called his name.

She began to hammer.

She called his name again.

She could hear angry stirring in the room beside his and on the other side of the hall but nothing from Barry's room.

She ran to the reception desk, looking all the while for the priest, but the bar was closed and there was no sign of him. She rang for the night clerk and, when she finally appeared, implored her to open the door to Barry's room.

The room, when they finally opened it, disgorged a vile and greasy bubble of odor. Coffee, vomit, alcohol, piss, and fear. Barry Mallen lay on his stomach, large white eyes glinting like bone in the light of the doorway.

She fell to her knees and began shaking him, calling his name. Nuala, the clerk, stared dumbstruck and unblinking.

"Call an ambulance!" she screamed. "For fuck's sake!"

She started and leaped for the room phone and stopped when she saw that it had been pulled from the wall.

"Reception!" Patricia barked.

She nodded and ran out the door.

Patricia stared at the body.

She saw the empty pill bottle in his hands.

She had been with him for most of the day, so unless he had brought it with him to Scarnagh, it was not his.

But perhaps that's why he had gone to Scarnagh in the first place? To end it all? Had he come with her to Youghal with the pills in his pocket, maybe hoping she could find a reason for him to keep living? Had she simply delayed the inevitable?

But she remembered the priest vanishing down the stairway like a stage devil through a trapdoor.

She looked around the room for any trace that the cleric might have left.

There, beside the bed, a piece of paper stood to attention, as if begging to be read.

She could hear footsteps out in the hall, either the clerk running back or a curious hotel guest wanting to see what all the commotion was about.

She realized that what she was about to do was a serious crime, and one that would instantly end her career if it was ever uncovered.

But she did not hesitate for a second.

She snatched the paper from the table and stuffed it into her pocket.

In that moment she was sure of nothing but this: the piece of paper was the same one that she had seen in the priest's hands in the hotel bar. And whatever words it now contained, Barry Mallen had not written them.

She gave a statement to the Gardaí after Barry's body had been removed to the local hospital. She had been expecting a grueling and traumatic interrogation but they seemed content with her answers. Too content, if she was honest.

She told them, twice, about the phone call. The abusive man with the Dublin accent who had ordered her to warn Barry Mallen.

They said they'd look into it.

She told them about the priest. She begged them to look for the priest.

They said they would.

Once safely back in Dublin, she took the note out and read three lines before destroying it in disgust. It was a confession of the murder of Niamh Mallen, at once laden down with performative and extravagant declarations of guilt and remorse, coupled with despicably lurid and sordid descriptions of her desecration and murder.

She knew that the note was her best, most tangible proof that someone had murdered Barry Mallen and framed him for the death of his daughter. And she knew that if she ever approached the Gardaí with this evidence she would destroy her own career and possibly be jailed, and the Barry Mallen depicted in the "suicide note" would live forever in infamy. The Gardaí would be only too happy to take the note at its word and close the case.

So it burned.

* * *

Finally, exhausted, hungover, sick, and despondent, she at last returned to the *Herald*'s office and tried to think of a plausible explanation for her absence to give Ruairí.

Picking through the memos and notes of missed calls on her desk, Patricia found a stiff cardboard envelope with a note that read, *Only picture in the archive, Luce.*

Patricia broke the seal.

Sitting in his office, Ruairí looked up in shock as he heard a yell of "FUCK!" so loud he almost spilled his coffee.

"Would you excuse me a moment?" he said to the young Scotsman sitting in a chair opposite him and awkwardly nudged his way past him to the door. He opened it just in time to watch his star political reporter storming out with tears in her eyes and a look on her face that left him in no doubt that she was done for the day. Several other hacks were watching her go curiously. Ruairí walked over to Patricia's desk and picked up a photograph that she had evidently dropped.

It was an enlarged photocopy of a picture of a man drinking in the back of a pub, a man Ruairí did not recognize.

He had a thin, emaciated face, a scraggly beard, and hair the color of wet ash.

JANUARY 1990

It was the week after New Year's when Kate Larkin closed up shop and walked down toward Camden Lock, striding briskly to stop the cold getting its teeth in her.

It was on the old iron bridge that she saw a familiar face.

Cian Proinsias Flynn, who would always be "Keano" to his friends (and, indeed, to everyone else), stopped when he saw her, and she watched as several emotions competed for real estate on his face.

She imagined that her own face was much the same.

They had broken up just after Etain and Barry's wedding and it had not been particularly amicable. To be honest, if she'd run into him in Dublin she would have pretended she hadn't seen him.

But they were two Irish in London, and that meant something, so she stopped and asked him how he was. He smiled gratefully, and she could tell at once that he was not doing well.

The last she had heard of him, he had got married to some girl from Lucan and she was sure she had heard rumors of children. But here was Keano alone in London, dressed casually on a weekday and clearly not eating well. Kate took a mental inventory of all the good times that she and Keano had had together and decided that they were worth a coffee, and she took him to a bistro around the corner.

He devoured a sandwich and gave her the story, most of which she had already deduced. The girl from Lucan had taken a punt on him and had hoped that her investment would mature. It hadn't. They had stayed together for one last Christmas for the boys (four and two), and then she had given him his marching orders.

Kate listened with a mixture of sympathy and the relief of someone who has dodged a bullet, and asked him what he was doing in London.

"I have some mates over here who said they might be able to get me some work." He shrugged, not sounding particularly hopeful.

He took a swig from his coffee. "Really sorry about Barry, by the way. Fuckin' shockin.'"

She had nodded in agreement twice before she actually realized what he had said.

"Which Barry?" she asked. "Barry *Mallen*?"

He looked at her in surprise.

"Yeah? 'Course?"

She stared at him, and her eyes seemed to get larger in her head.

"Jesus. You know, don't you?"

"Know what? What happened?"

Keano looked like he wanted to be anywhere else.

"Kate . . . I'm sorry, Barry's dead."

She seemed to jolt with the words. He did not know what he expected her to say but it was not this:

"What did she do?"

Keano didn't know what he could possibly say to that. He didn't even know who "she" was.

Kate suddenly seemed to realize what she had said and tried to cover.

"I mean . . . I mean . . . what happened? How did he die?"

Why did I open my big fucking mouth? he thought to himself furiously. *And why is she only learning this from me?*

"I don't . . . really . . . know all the details . . ."

"Keano. Tell me. Just tell me, please."

She was crying now. Properly weeping. There were three large men, builders maybe, drinking coffee at the other end of the café.

"Oi!" one called. "Is he bovvering you, love?"

"FUCK OFF!" she snarled at him and turned back to Keano.

"Keano . . ."

"Kate . . . he . . . he killed himself. Pills, they said."

She shook her head defiantly.

"No. No. You heard wrong. Different Barry."

"Kate . . ."

"He would never do that to Etain and the girls . . ."

"Well, after what happened with Niamh they say . . ."

He watched the color drain from her face and Keano suddenly wished that the plane that had taken him to London had gone down in the Irish Sea.

Oh no. No, no, no, you know that. You have to know that. It was months ago. Someone has to have told you by now.

"What happened to Niamh, Keano?"

Now, more than anything, he felt angry. He should not be in this position. This was not his fault.

"Keano," she whispered. "What happened to Niamh?"

Irish news, at least concerning events south of the border, rarely had opportunity to penetrate the consciousness of the typical Londoner. Irish in the city looking to keep abreast of events at home had to put the legwork in, either finding one of the few shops that carried Irish newspapers, or calling home on a regular basis. Kate, the bitter exile, had done neither and was now paying the price.

As she booked the next flight back to Dublin she felt guilt like she had never known before settling in her stomach like swallowed shards of broken glass.

She had thought that she was doing the right thing by cutting Etain out of her life. Clearly she had been lethally, catastrophically wrong.

She had abandoned her family, and they had paid the most terrible price imaginable.

She did not blame herself for Niamh's disappearance, but she blamed herself for Barry's death.

Her guilt was such that when she was selected for a "random" security check while waiting in line at the airport, she almost assumed that the police knew what she had done.

Relax, she thought to herself. *They just think you're a Provo. They don't know you're a murderer.*

The thing that struck her after arriving in the city of her birth for the first time in almost a decade was the air. She had been expecting the usual winter smog, and as the bus from the airport made its way through the dense suburbs of North Dublin she was surprised to see that there was no silvery-gray pall of coal and turf smoke hanging over the roofs like a great, filthy spiderweb.

It was around four o'clock when she finally arrived.

The house where she had been raised looked smaller and tamer now. She had precious few happy memories of this place, none since her father had died if she was honest. And yet, she felt something like happiness to see that door again. Or perhaps happiness was the wrong word.

Satisfaction. The contented pride of looking at an old scar and remembering something that had tried to kill you and failed.

There was a car in the driveway that she did not recognize so she assumed that there was someone home, but the house had an unmistakable air of stillness about it. The windows stared at her, dark and blank. She took a deep breath and rang the bell.

She thought she could hear a tinny chime coming through the door, but no one answered.

She tried knocking. No one came.

Kate had considered calling from the airport to make sure Etain was home but she hadn't been able to bring herself to. This was a reunion that had to be done face-to-face. Now, however, it seemed like that would have been wiser.

With a sudden flash of panic, she realized she wasn't even sure that Etain still lived here.

She tried knocking for another ten minutes before finally giving up. It was time for a change of plan. First things first was to find a place to stay. She remembered that the Skylon Hotel in Drumcondra was only a short walk away. She could check herself in and then maybe try and call the Mallens in Cork and see if they knew where Etain—

The scream came from deep within the house and yet it was so loud, so horrendously raw and full of rage and pain, that she heard it plainly through brick, mortar, wood, and glass.

Kate felt the blood draining from her face and froze as she tried to think what to do. She was about to start rooting around in the front garden for a rock to break a window when she remembered the visit she had paid to this very house after Mairéad's funeral and the old key that still stubbornly clung to her keyring after all these years.

Mairéad never changed the locks. Maybe Etain didn't either?

Panicked and swearing, she took her handbag and dumped the contents roughly onto the tiled floor of the porch, shattering a makeup mirror and sending Tic-Tacs skittering like hailstones. Her keys fell out with a weighty clank and she snatched them up, found the right one, and jammed it into the lock and turned.

* * *

The house had changed at last, Mairéad Larkin's reign of stasis broken in the end.

The smell of the house was different, for one. There were still the low notes of wood varnish from the banisters, but the kitchen smelled different now. Different ingredients, different recipes. She could see the faded marks where murals of vivid crayon had been graffitied onto the walls by small hands, something that filled Kate with a burst of joy even as she ran through the house to find the source of the scream.

She stopped dead in the living room.

There were shards of glass all over the floor and, in the corner, the television stared at her like a blinded cyclops, a large jagged black hole in the center of the screen.

What happened here? Kate thought, her thoughts blackening with dread. *Were they robbed? Was there a fight? A kidnapping? Where is Etain? Where is Ashling?*

Stepping carefully to avoid the glass, she crossed into the kitchen and almost screamed.

Her mother was kneeling in the garden with her back to her, rocking herself softly. Through the window Kate could hear her moaning or singing or weeping. It was impossible to be sure which. Her voice was a river, flowing this way and that between pain and grief and pure, ecstatic joy. Kate felt sudden relief as she realized that she was looking at Etain, not her mother walking the Earth again.

Christ, she looks so old, Kate thought.

Etain was kneeling on the grass in front of the garden shed, the open door swinging gently in the breeze.

Her hair was now completely gray, almost white, and looked stark as a dandelion seedhead against the heavy, leaden winter clouds.

Never taking her eyes off her sister, Kate walked to the kitchen door and entered the back garden.

There was light drizzle starting, and the clouds were threatening rain.

Etain did not look up as she approached, though she must have heard her.

"Etain?" she called. "It's me."

Etain raised her head but did not look around.

"Hello, stranger," she said.

Her voice was controlled and tight as a drum, as if she was speaking through immense pain.

"I heard. I heard about everything," Kate said. "Etain, I'm so sorry, love."

"Oh, *everyone's* sorry," Etain said in a huge breath, like she was breathing through labor. "Everyone is sooooo sorry."

"What are you doing out here?" Kate asked.

"A bit of . . . trimming . . ." Etain wheezed.

For the first time, Kate noticed the large pair of secateurs lying on the long grass by Etain's hip. She recognized them as belonging to Mairéad. They were almost a meter long, with enough bite to decapitate a young sapling or a sturdy rosebush. The old iron was black and slick and wet with grease . . .

That was not grease.

"Oh, JESUS, JESUS CHRIST!" Kate screamed as she caught a glimpse, a mere frame of Etain's hand and the giant crimson spider of blood gushing between the fingers that she was clamping over the severed stump of her left ring finger.

Her neck jerked her head away, refusing to let her see anymore.

"Oh God, where is it?"

"Where's what?" Etain asked, still breathing deeply to numb the pain.

"Your finger! Your finger! We have to get it on ice!"

"Oh, I threw it . . . over there somewhere . . ."

Without releasing her grip she made a two-handed gesture to the dark hedges at the back of the garden. Thin trails of blood whipped the grass.

Kate swore, knowing full well that she might spend an hour searching for the severed digit in the undergrowth and still not find it.

"What did you do? Fuck, Etain, what did you do to yourself?"

At the word "yourself" Etain gave a grim, satisfied smile.

"They're gone now," she whispered happily. "Yes, yes, they're gone now."

Fuck shit fuck shit fuck shit she's crazy she's fucking crazy.

"Kate?" Etain wheezed.

"What? What do you need me to do?" Kate pleaded, kneeling down beside her on the grass.

"I think I'm about to pass out," Etain said calmly. "Be a love and call me an ambulance."

She had indeed fainted from shock by the time the ambulance had arrived and the nurse had stanched the bleeding. She was lain on a stretcher and wheeled out through the front door to the driveway where the ambulance was parked.

The nurse held the back door of the ambulance open for Kate and she was about to climb in when a sudden thought hit her.

Where is Ashling?

"Go on ahead, I'll follow on!" she called to the driver, and the ambulance sped off, lights flashing and siren wolf-whistling loudly down the avenue.

She ran upstairs, gently calling her niece's name and hoping that she wouldn't be too terrified by this strange, wild-eyed woman with blood on her hands wandering the house.

The two children's rooms were empty, as was Etain and Barry's. She even checked under the beds to make sure.

She checked the bathroom. Nobody.

She walked back downstairs, unconsciously avoiding the spot where she knew her mother had breathed her last, agonized gasp.

Where was she? Did she have some after-school lessons? Was she at a friend's house?

She realized that she didn't know anything about Ashling at all. Her interests. What she looked like. If she were to call the police and tell them that she was missing, what could she say? What description could she give?

"Ashling?" she called softly.

There was no answer.

But, from behind the door of the downstairs bathroom, something stirred.

Kate realized that this was now the one room in the house that she had not checked. She tried to open the door but it was locked tight.

As soon as she turned the handle she heard a tiny yelp of fear from the other side and then a smack, as if someone had slapped a hand over their own mouth.

She took her hand off the handle and placed her ear against the door.

"Ashling?" she said, trying to sound as calm and reassuring as possible. "Is that you in there, love?"

Silence.

"Are you okay? Are you hurt?"

Silence.

"I'm your auntie Kate. I'm your mam's sister. Who lives in London, yeah? Did your mam ever talk about me?"

Still nothing. Just when she was starting to wonder if she had been hearing things, a tiny, hoarse voice that sounded like it had been crying for hours spoke up.

"I'm not s'posed to talk to strangers," it mumbled apologetically.

The child most likely did not intend that to feel like a knife to the gut, but it did.

Yup. That's me. A stranger to my own niece.

She put that aside.

"Well, you know what, that makes you a very, very clever young lady. So I'll tell you what. Do you know the 'once for yes, twice for no' game? I'll ask you a question and you knock once if the answer is yes and twice for no, okay? And that way you don't actually have to talk to me."

There was a silence, and then a tiny, velvet knock on the door.

"Okay," said Kate. "Are you hurt? Are you injured?"

Two knocks.

"Do you want to come out?"

One knock.

"Can you come out?"

Knock knock.

"Is the door locked?"

Knock.

"Did Etain lock you in there?"

Knock.

"Is the key in there with you?"

Knock knock.

"Do you know where she put the key?"

Knock knock.

Kate swore under her breath.

"All right, love, can you hang on there and I'll go look for it?"

Knock.

* * *

After a few minutes of searching, she gave up. Etain could have hidden the key in any one of a million places in the house. It could be in her pocket and speeding its way to the Mater Hospital at this very moment. She might have swallowed it. She might have flushed it down the upstairs toilet. She might have flung it away in the garden with her finger.

She would most likely never find the key.

But she still had to get into the bathroom.

In the garden, the door of the shed banged in the wind as if trying to attract her attention.

"Ashling, love, I'm going to need you to stand back as far as you can, okay?"

"Okay," was the tiny, whispered response.

Kate gripped the ax tightly in her hand, raised it above her head, and resisted the urge to yell, "HERE'S JOHNNY!"

The ax broke through the wood like aero board. Another few swings and she had cut the ornate brass lock out of the door. It swung open.

Inside, a nine-year-old girl who looked closer to seven sat on the toilet, her knees pulled up to her chin.

Kate stared in shock. The child's hair was jet black and curly, not straight like her own. But in the face, the nose, the large green eyes, for Kate it was like looking at an old picture of herself brought to life.

She was wearing the uniform of the local school, unchanged from the days Kate had worn one just like it, and she was trembling so violently that the toilet seat vibrated against the porcelain lip of the commode, making a sound like chattering teeth.

Kate caught a glimpse of herself in the bathroom mirror, hair wild and unkempt, eyes exhausted and staring, and a large ax gripped in her bloodstained hands. She dropped the ax and knelt down.

"Hello," she said, trying to keep her voice as calm as possible even as she struggled to recover her breath. "Well. That was an adventure, now, wasn't it?"

The child simply stared at the blood on her hands.

Kate went to the sink and began to wash them clean.

"It's nothing to worry about, love. Your mammy just had a bit of an accident. It's fine. There now, see? All gone."

She held up her hands, clean palms out. She didn't show her the fingernails, with black, dried blood still caked underneath. The child continued to stare. Kate wondered if she was in shock. *What can I do? What does this child need?*

"Here," she said. "Are you hungry?"

The girl nodded vigorously.

"All right, well. I don't know how you do it now but when I was growing up in this house we never ate dinner in our school uniform. So why don't you go upstairs and change and I'll fix you up something nice, okay?"

She was not concerned about the child getting food on her school uniform.

She just needed a few minutes to clean up the broken glass in the living room, and the blood in the kitchen from where she had sat with Etain, desperately waiting for the ambulance to arrive.

It seemed Etain had not done a shop recently, and Kate could find nothing in the fridge to cook. She eventually found a press full of canned goods and heated up a tin of Heinz Haunted House, which Ashling devoured hungrily with a dinner spoon and then asked for more.

Kate realized that she did not know how long Ashling had been locked in the bathroom. Maybe she'd been there for hours. *Jesus. Maybe she was in there for days?*

"So . . ." said Kate delicately. "Do you know why your mammy locked you in the bathroom, hon?"

The girl glanced at her nervously.

"You're not in trouble," Kate said soothingly. "Whatever it was . . . you didn't deserve that. She shouldn't have done that."

The child frowned. The idea that her mother could be in the wrong was clearly troubling on a deep, theological level.

"I was bold," Ashling said simply.

"Well," said Kate, leaning in conspiratorially, "I used to be pretty bold too. In fact, I don't think you were that bold at all. I bet you, if you tell me, I'll be really bored."

She made an exaggerated face of complete tedium and Ashling actually laughed.

I'm not bad at this, Kate thought to herself wistfully. *I could have been a good aunt. To both of them.*

But Ashling still did not want to tell her.

"Why don't you just whisper it?" Kate asked her, and tilted her ear toward her.

Ashling bit her lip indecisively and then, hesitantly, leaned in and whispered three words.

"I saw Niamh."

It took a split second for the meaning to hit her and then Kate grabbed Ashling by the shoulders.

"Where? Where did you see her?!"

Ashling screamed hysterically and tried desperately to pull away and Kate suddenly realized what she had done.

Ashling must have told Etain. Kate did not know what Etain had said or done, but the child was screaming at the thought that it would happen again.

Like a woman throwing herself on a hand grenade she embraced the panicking child and held her close until, at last, she became calm again.

"It's okay . . ." she whispered to her, stroking her hair. "I promise, I will never, ever, ever hurt you. Not as long as I live. Okay?"

She felt Ashling's chin rubbing up and down on her shoulder.

Kate released her gently and stood up.

"But it's really important that you tell me where you saw Niamh. Do you understand?"

The child said nothing. She simply stared up at Kate with those dark green eyes, as if assessing her trustworthiness.

Then, without a word, she took Kate by the hand. Kate was sure she was going to lead her out of the house, maybe to the schoolyard a few minutes down the road.

But instead, Ashling towed her gently into the living room.

She raised a tiny hand with a finger outstretched and pointed to the television set.

A little ashamed, she turned to look at Kate.

"I broke it," she whispered. "I was trying to let her out."

The television was broken, but the record player still worked. They sat on the couch, Ashling curled up with her head resting on Kate's thigh, and her aunt stroked her hair gently.

They listened to "Fast Car" by Tracy Chapman. Kate asked her if she liked it.

Ashling nodded, but said that she couldn't tell if it was a sad song or a happy one.

"It's a song about being trapped," Kate told her. "Which means it's also a song about escaping. Like a glass that's half empty and half full at the same time."

Ashling said nothing, and they listened in silence.

Kate glanced at the clock. She had called the hospital and been told that someone would call later that night to tell her how Etain was doing.

"What time do you normally go to bed?" she asked Ashling.

Ashling gave a noncommittal shrug.

"Okay, well, we'll wait until the end of the album and then it's time to sleep, okay?"

"Okay."

"And then in the morning we'll go into the hospital to see your mam, yeah?"

Ashling said something, a tiny whisper so low that it got lost in the folds of Kate's skirt.

"What did you say, love?"

"Are you my mother?" the child whispered.

Kate's hand stopped stroking her hair.

"No, love. You know who your mother is."

"She said I'm not really hers," Ashling murmured. "She said I shouldn't be here. I thought you might be . . ."

For a brief second, Kate bitterly regretted calling the ambulance.

"Well . . . I don't know why she said that, love," said Kate. "That was an awful thing to say. But it's not true. I was there when you were born. And you were so, so beautiful."

And even then, she remembered, Etain had not wanted the second child. She would always hold Niamh, and let Barry or Kate or Anne or someone else hold Ashling. It had been whatever the opposite of imprinting was.

"Are you sure?" the child asked.

"I'm sure," she replied.

"Can I pretend?" Ashling asked.

Kate did not answer, but kissed her gently on the forehead and hugged her close.

September 27, 2002
Whiskey is the key to the basement.

It unlocks everything below the surface.

I've been trying to explain to Doctor Doom that I'm not an alcoholic. The people I'm talking to these days have seen things and they're well used to keeping secrets. You have to get the devils drunk before you can hear the gossip in Hell. Doctor Doom says I'm just making excuses. She doesn't believe there actually is a story (I can't show her my notes, I'd be off to Saint Pat's in a straightjacket). So she has this picture of me now as a washed-up delusional journo desperately clinging to past glories, pretending that I'm on some great crusade when really I'm just getting pissed with junkies and convicts. I guess from the outside that's what it must look like. Just smile and nod, Patricia. Just smile and nod. Only three more weeks and let's be honest, the judge let you off lightly.

Doctor Doom did have one good idea. She suggested I start keeping a diary to keep track of my alcohol intake. She says seeing it all written down in black-and-white might change my perspective. So I'm keeping a diary. Not to keep track of the booze, but so I have a record before I go to sleep.

Blackout insurance ☺.

September 30, 2002
Meeting with Donal Broy (51) of no fixed abode. Claims to have information about disappearance of a child in the '80s. Lead on Niamh Larkin disapp? Been burned before.

AFTER MEETING: Have to find Tony Prince. Broy claims he's a former garda. Forced off. Booze. Worked as a PI in the '80s. Now down and out. Broy claims he told him he was involved in a child abduction back in '89. Right time. "Little blond girl. Distraught over it."

November 1, 2002
Called all homeless men's shelters in the book. Some knew the name Tony Prince, no sign of him recently. Make another round of calls next week. Ask around the quays.

November 2, 2002
Call from the Morning Star Hostel! Man staying with them under

name Anthony PRICE. Former guard. Asked if he's willing to talk to me: YES.

November 4, 2002
It's not possible. No. Brothers? Am I going mad?

November 6, 2002
Time to process. Just accept what you've seen and figure it out later.

Anthony Price. Male. 62.

Former Garda.

Appearance: Take Barry Mallen, add 15–20 years of rough living. Shocking resemblance.

Manner: Passive. Not "all there." Questions had to be repeated. Hard time focusing.

ME: Trembling through interview. Shades of Lowney. Price: oblivious.

Interview took place in the dining room of the Morning Star Hostel for Homeless Men.

Key points:

Anthony Price forced to leave Gardaí in 1982. Goes into business for himself as a private investigator.

1984: Begun taking repeat business from "Fitt." Says it like I'm supposed to know who that is.

He says Fitt had him investigate a man named Gerry LAND. I asked him who that was. He worked in RTÉ, he says. A producer.

"Why did Fitt want you to investigate a TV producer?"

He said he never asked. He didn't know what the issue between the two men was. Price said it was simple stuff. Trail Land, see where he went and when. See who he spoke to. Once or twice Fitt asked him to search Land's bins. Nothing of use ever found.

He says Fitt convinced Land guilty of something.

"Real bad blood, those two."

I ask him about Niamh Larkin.

Big man, all tears.

Says he didn't know what was going on.

I ask him: Did you abduct her?

No. Not an abduction. She wanted to go with him. Gave him

a big hug. He always remembered that. She ran up to him after school and gave him a big hug.

Why was he at the school?

He had been told to go there and collect the girl. Something to do with Land, that was all he knew. He needed the money.

Little blond girl ran out to him and hugged him and he put her in his own car. Drove off and left her with the father.

I stopped him here. Very confused.

"The father"? You left her with Barry Mallen?

Doesn't know who what is. I ask him who "the father" is?

Looks at me like I'm stupid. "Who've we been talking about? Father Fitt."

FITT=PRIEST.

I draw a picture of the man I saw in Youghal.

"Is that him?"

He nods. Yes. Yes. Yes.

"You're sure?"

Definitely. Yes. Yes. Yes.

MAJOR BREAKTHROUGH

Price left her with the priest. She didn't seem scared. Very calm. (Like she knew him?) Price drove off. Never heard from Fitt again. No more surveillance work.

After Niamh disappearance + various scandals (Brendan Smythe etc.) began to suspect that Fitt had killed child. Couldn't turn himself in, afraid of jail. Depression/alcoholism worsened.

I thanked him and asked if we could speak again. He said yes.

I have the name of Barry Mallen's killer and the killer of his daughter.

Fucking hell. Only solved the bloody thing.

November 11, 2002

No more drinking. Lost too much time.

Early morning 6th November: Four missed calls from un-known number. Later discovered to be from Morning Star Hostel.

Did not answer. Dead drunk. My fault.

Noon 6th November: Call from Morning Star Hostel.

Anthony Price is dead. Heart attack. Found dead in bed.

Devastated. Only witness gone.

Raced down to Hostel to speak with staff. Shrine for Anthony set up. Portrait. Flowers. Candles.

Portrait: Bald, jowly, large nose.
ME: "Where is he? Where is Anthony Price?"
THEM: "Dead. Heart Attack."
ME: "Not him. The man I spoke to. Where is the man I spoke to?"
THEM: "That's the man. Him. You spoke to him."

She ran up to him. She hugged him. She went with him. She trusted him.

Did she see what I saw?

Price looked like Barry Mallen. But only to the people who knew Barry Mallen.

Impossible. Mad?

No more drinking.

Find Fitt.

Diary Extract
File "Skelton. P. #109817"
Archive of the Department of Policy Oversight

MARCH 2003

Betty had been dreaming of floating down a lazy river on a sun-drenched raft, so it took her a few moments to realize that something was amiss when she woke up and saw the nightstand drift past her.

The bed was moving.

She sat up in the darkness, suddenly very awake, feeling for Ashling beside her and finding only empty sheets.

There was a low, mournful grinding sound as the legs of the bed were dragged along the floorboards.

Then, a jolt as the bed reached the saddle of the doorframe and could be pulled no farther. Silence, broken only by the distant sound of drunken catcalls and hooting from the front of the house.

Betty sprang out of bed, throwing on a nightdress and then climbing over the bed into the hallway. A rope, tied to the foot of the bed, ran taut out the bedroom door and down the stairs.

Betty started at the figure that stood at the opposite end of the hallway, cigarette in hand, gazing out the window at the garden below.

"She's giving a show to the neighbors," Etain drawled sardonically.

"Go back to sleep, Etain," Betty snapped, and followed the rope down the stairway.

"It's my fucking house," Etain called after her.

Only until we call an exorcist, Betty thought darkly.

Betty strode out into the garden where Ashling, dressed in a long white T-shirt and underwear, was pulling angrily at the rope tied to her wrist.

Her eyes were glassy and inexpressive but her movement was angry and violent. Betty marveled that her skinny frame had the strength to pull their bed (with Betty still in it) as far as she had.

A group of five or six drunken students, staggering back to their accommodation from the pub, had stopped outside the house to watch, shouting encouragement and lewd, slurred suggestions.

Ashling's bare feet dug into the lawn, tearing up chunks of soft loam. She slipped and fell onto her stomach and kept trying to move forward, digging and clawing over the grass like an animal. The students whooped and laughed. One of them yelled that he could see her tits.

Betty ran out into the garden, slung Ashling over her shoulder, and carried her back into the house, slamming the door behind her. *It's not her fault. Don't be angry. It's not her fault.*

But she still found it cathartic to roughly shake Ashling's shoulders until she woke up.

She was deep in it. It was only after two minutes of shaking her and calling her name and lightly clapping her cheeks that Ashling's eyes refocused and Betty knew that she was looking at her.

"Niamh?" she asked, groggily.

Betty sighed wearily.

"No, love, it's me."

Ashling listed a little uneasily and rubbed her eyes.

"What the fuck?" she muttered, picking at her filthy T-shirt. "Did I go outside?"

"Yup," said Betty. "Almost dragged the bed out with you."

"Shit. I must have scared the bejesus out of you?"

"Go have a shower," Betty said, diplomatically avoiding the question. "I'll put on the kettle."

A gentle blue dawn was rising in the garden.

Ashling, now scrubbed and clean and wearing a fresh T-shirt, sat down at the table and gratefully accepted a steaming mug of tea from Betty.

"I think we're going to need something stronger," she said, after taking a swig.

"You want a coffee?" Betty asked.

"No. I mean like a chain," she said ruefully, raising her wrist to show her the red welts where the rope had bitten her. "If that rope had broken I'd be under someone's wheels right now."

Betty set her own mug down and tented her fingers.

"You need to see someone about this," she said softly. "This is not okay. I mean, it's never been this bad."

Ashling gave a hollow laugh.

"Oh, is that what you think? No, trust me, this is not the worst it's ever been."

"How do you mean?"

"Ask Etain."

"I'm asking you."

"Doesn't matter," Ashling said, shaking her head. "It's just the new job. Stress. It always gets triggered by stress . . ."

She stopped. Betty was giving her the "I know you're lying and I'm not angry I'm just disappointed" look. Deadliest weapon in her arsenal, banned by international law.

"You called me Niamh," she said.

Ashling closed her eyes and gave a deep, frustrated sigh.

"Right. Okay, that makes sense," she said, nodding.

"Ash," said Betty gently. "No one expects you to be over it."

"I do," said Ashling with a touch of flint. "It's been fourteen years, for Christ's sake."

"She was your sister. I don't think you get over that. But you don't have to be . . . under it. Either. Do you know what I mean?"

"Not a clue."

"Just talkin' shite?"

"Complete shite."

"I think you need to see a counselor. I did, actually. When we broke up in college."

Ashling looked at her in surprise.

"Oh," she said, a little embarrassed. "I never knew that."

Betty shrugged.

"Any use?" Ashling asked.

"None whatsoever," said Betty, smiling ruefully. "Complete waste of time."

"Well, I'm sold."

"Still, I think you should try. You might get lucky."

Ashling nodded, and reached across the table. Her pale arm was blue in the dawn light as she took Betty's hand in a firm, warm grip.

"I am lucky," she said simply.

"Me too," said Betty. And she meant it. "Want me to tie you up so you can get some sleep?"

"Nah," said Ashling, yawning. "I'm up now. Might get started on those tapes."

"Oh, want some company?" Betty asked.

"Sure," Ashling said with a weary smile. "That'd be really nice."

They rose together and went into the living room. Ashling took Betty's hand and leaned in and kissed her gently on the mouth and whispered in her ear:

"Happy half-anniversary."

"What?"

"You moved in six months ago."

"Really? Fuck, doesn't feel like it . . ."

"More like ten years?"

"Some days?"

She kissed her again.

Betty had not thought about *Puckeen* for years and yet the rush of nostalgia when she heard the first note of the theme tune was incredibly powerful.

The childhood memories were as clear and sharp as glass, images and sounds taken when all the equipment was still new and in perfect working order.

She was back in her parents' living room, sitting Indian-style on the scratchy gray carpet, a bowl of cereal nestled between her thighs.

Each episode was only twenty minutes or so, and Ashling picked out the video tapes at random, watching each one intently and taking notes.

When Ashling had first brought the tapes home, together with the video player, Betty had been surprised to see that they were all Betamax.

"RTÉ stores all their old episodes on Beta," Ashling had explained as she tried to force the Betamax player and their TV to make friends. "VHS is shite. Poorer quality. Rots away after a few years. Wrong side lost the format war."

The opening titles were scored to an up-tempo piano rendition of the old ballad "*An Poc ar Buile.*" Against a black background, images danced to the music: toy soldiers, dolls, white-faced Pierrots, boys cut from newspapers chased by dogs. Numbers and letters swam in rings. A single eye appeared, blinked like a Venus flytrap, and was gone, to be replaced by the words "PUCKEEN written and produced by Gerry Land."

She had never realized how weird those opening credits were.

In fact, watching the program as an adult, she found them oddly unsettling. There was a dead quality to the cheeriness of the tune and the images. A lifelessness. A chill.

The scene now changed to a bare white set with only a red door and a large black box set on a plinth. The door opened and a man and a woman, both dressed in black-and-white Pierrot costumes, emerged. They took their places on either side of the black box and each gave a wide, coordinated wave.

"Hello, everyone!" said the man.

"Hello, boys and girls!" the woman chimed in with the same high, chirping tone. "Hello, Brian! What are we going to do today?"

"Ah, Brian and Gráinne!" said Betty. "I remember them. Jesus, when's this one from?"

"'Ninety-one or 'ninety-two, I think," said Ashling, a little uncertainly.

She had watched enough episodes to know that it was virtually impossible to distinguish one season of *Puckeen* from another, apart from little clues like the film gradient. The show followed a formula so rigid as to be practically repetition and had done so since its first broadcast. She had seen episodes from the '60s that used the same dialogue as this episode, word for word. The presenters were different, and had different names, but had borne an eerie similarity to Brian and Gráinne.

"I fancied him. Brian," Betty admitted.

Ashling arched an eyebrow.

"Oh really?"

"Just a phase I was going through. He's not still doing it, is he?"

"Why, want me to introduce you?" Ashling teased.

"Fuck, is he actually still doing it?"

"Who do you think hired me?" Ashling asked. "Brian Desmond. He's producing it now. He's my boss."

After graduating, Ashling had put aside any thoughts of working for *Puckeen*. There had never been a response to her letter to Gerry Land and she had assumed that she had been passed over. What surprised her was that she didn't really care.

For years, Ashling had been working toward a single goal with an obsessive determination.

Every choice she had made in her academic life had been leading to that application letter. But when she had finally taken her shot, and missed, she felt only relief.

That was thanks to Betty.

Betty had finally moved in and Ashling's life had become an altogether happier affair. She had always dreaded coming home before, even when she knew Kate would be there to act as a buffer. But Betty had put manners on Etain. She did not seem to have that same fear of her that Kate did. Kate would walk lightly on eggshells around Etain. Betty would put on her boots, stamp around heavily, and tell her to stop being such a bitch. The fact that the two of them now lived in the house meant they could better control Etain's drinking. As a result, Etain mostly stayed in her room and didn't bother them except at mealtimes. For the first time since her father's passing, Ashling had felt at home in her home. She got a job in a call center, taking phone bets for Paddy Power, while Betty had accepted a fixed-term contract working in the folklore archive. Ashling no longer sleep-walked or had night terrors. She got to kiss Betty goodbye every morning when she headed into the college.

Life was simple. Life was good.

Then she had gotten the call from Brian Desmond.

Her mobile had rung while she was on lunch in the breakroom. Surprised to see an unknown Dublin number, she took the call in the corridor.

"Hello, is this Ashling Mallen?"

The voice was soft and shy, with a hint of a Midlands accent. Male. Probably late forties.

"Who's this?" she asked.

"Sorry," he said. He seemed to be the kind of person who apologized reflexively. "This is Brian Desmond. I work in Children's Programming. In RTÉ?"

"Oh" was all she could manage.

"Am I right in thinking you sent an application letter to Gerry Land last year?" he asked. "For the production assistant job? On *Puckeen*?"

Ashling had been leaning against the wall but suddenly stood upright.

No way. After all this time?

"So, I know it's absolutely ridiculous to be following up with you so late but I came across your letter and . . . I was really impressed.

You sound like exactly what I . . . What I mean is . . . I'm sure you've been snapped by someone else but if you're still interested in the *Puckeen* job?"

"Yeah!" Ashling blurted. "Yeah, absolutely!"

"Okay, would you be free to come in for an interview? Say, Wednesday, four o'clock?"

"Love to!"

"Cool! Okay, look, I'll text you the details. Look forward to meeting you. Thanks, thanks a million . . ."

He stumbled awkwardly to the end of the sentence and hung up.

Ashling stood in the corridor, staring at her phone, balanced on a knife edge between dread and white-hot anticipation.

One step closer.

The interview had taken place in a small meeting room on the RTÉ campus. There had evidently been a group in before them as there were dirty plates and brown-stained mugs piled on a table in the corner. Brian apologized for the state of the room as they sat down. She had recognized him on sight. He was a little jowlier now, and his brown hair was well on the way to gray. But he had large, innocent-looking eyes that made him appear younger than his age. He seemed nice in a bland, harmless kind of way.

He was not the kind of person she would have put in front of a camera. He had very little presence for a television personality, even a former one, and seemed to be apologizing for his very existence with every gesture and expression.

He was very obviously attracted to her, and normally she would not have used that.

These were not normal times.

She flirted, she laughed at his jokes. She could practically see his confidence inflate the more they spoke. He was grinning by the end of the interview and talking as if she already had the job.

"So, I'll be honest with you, Ashling, I've been thrown in the deep end here," he said. "So, to have someone with your background who actually, y'know, knows how to run a TV show . . ."

Ashling laughed as if he had said something wonderfully witty.

". . . that's just what I need. And I'm not looking to hire a go-pher. I mean, look. We're not *Fair City* or anything. It's a very small operation. But, that means you will have much more of a creative input than you would if you were working on *Fair City* or whatever. You know? The job's what you make it. And for someone of your age, an assistant producer role, I mean, that's a real feather in your cap. Sorry, that sounded really patronizing . . ."

"No, no, you're absolutely right," she reassured him.

"So . . . what would your vision for the show be? What changes would you want to make?"

Ashling had been preparing for this question for well over a decade. She did not miss her mark.

She launched into her spiel.

More Irish language content. A story segment. New footage to replace the decades-old B-reel of the zoo and the botanical gardens that had been recycled ad nauseum. Perhaps even a new opening credits sequence to rebrand the show. Brian nodded enthusiastically to all her suggestions bar one.

"And, if we really wanted to mix things up . . . maybe actually show Puckeen?"

For a brief second he looked like he'd been cut. Like he'd felt the bite of something incredibly sharp sliding into the soft tissue of his lower back and the pain had not yet overcome the initial shock and confusion. He shook his head. Or, his head shook. It did not seem to be done consciously.

"Ah, no," he mumbled. "Change is great and all that but the show is the show."

"Why do you never show Puckeen?" Ashling asked.

"Creative decision," he said, trying to affect a pale bonhomie.

"Actually," he said, leaning in conspiratorially, "the ignorant fuckers lost the puppet back in the sixties. So they just, y'know, worked around it. I don't even know what he was. I've been working on this show since the bloody fall of Rome and I don't know what the hell Puckeen even is."

"A goat," she said simply.

He froze.

"How . . . how do you know that?"

She stared at him, green eyes as hard and impenetrable as emeralds.

"It's the name," she told him. "Puckeen. Means 'little goat.'"

He nodded uncertainly. "Ah. Right. 'Course.

"Well," he continued, "y'know, Ashling, I'm very impressed. You seem like exactly the kind of person we'd want on the show . . ."

"So . . . are you offering me the job?" she asked, tilting her head coquettishly.

He blushed.

"I, I am. Yeah. If you want it."

She felt numb with joy.

She thanked him effusively and they shook hands. She rose to leave and then stopped and turned.

"So . . . will I be working with you and Gerry or just you or . . ."

"What?"

"Gerry Land?"

"Oh, Christ," he said nervously. "Didn't I tell you?"

She shook her head, confused.

He expelled a breath awkwardly.

"Gerry's dead," he said simply. "Yeah. That's how I . . . that's why I'm here, like. I'm taking over from him. I only found your letter when I was cleaning out his office."

Ashling briefly remembered a great shape standing before her, smelling of hair and sweat. She remembered great hands like pale crabs.

"Oh," she said. "I'm sorry. How did he die?"

Brian had become very interested in the dirty mugs on the other side of the room.

"Ah well," he said. "He wasn't a well man. He was very large. Fried food. Nothing but fried food. And of course with the stress of this job, it put a terrible strain on him."

Ashling nodded. "Heart attack."

"No," said Brian. "No. He shot himself."

Onscreen, Brian and Gráinne stood around the box, their arms extended toward each other, their fingertips touching. There was something ritualistic about it, Ashling mused.

Gráinne and Brian began to chant in unison.

Knock, knock, let us in!
Puckeen, take us for a spin!
Knock, knock, open wide!
Take us to the other side!

Two knocks came from the inside of the box and the lid flew open.

The camera switched to an overhead view of the box and zoomed in to the pitch-black interior. Ashling knew that it would now transition to prerecorded footage of Gráinne and Brian exploring the outside world.

"Bet you it's the zoo," Betty said.

"Hmm?" Ashling murmured.

The pencil hung slack in her fingers. Her eyes were tiny pools of white light reflecting the glare of the screen.

"When they go in the box," Betty explained. "They always go to the bloody zoo. There, see!"

Betty pointed to the screen where a grainy polar bear in a tiny enclosure rocked its head left and right as it paced up and down, slowly dying of boredom.

Ashling looked at the television, where a small child ran screaming through a forest followed sedately by a pike-thin, horned figure as tall as a flagpole and so black that it looked like a crack in the screen.

The child, a blond girl, ran toward the screen and began to pound her tiny fists on the glass, screaming silently for help.

To Ashling it seemed that she was looking right at her.

The horned figure, a widening rent in the world, overtook them and then gently and quickly ate the child as Ashling watched, lifting her daintily by a leg and lowering her into its mouth as she thrashed weakly in the air.

"Yeah," she said. "It's always the zoo."

Many years ago she had learned a lesson. The kind of lesson that became a load-bearing pillar of the mind, never to be moved, never to be questioned.

You never told anyone what you really saw.

No matter how much you loved them. No matter how much you trusted them.

Some secrets could never be shared.

They were back beside the box.

Gráinne stared blandly into the camera.

"That was great fun, wasn't it, Brian?"

Overhead, a floorboard creaked.

"Well," said Ashling solemnly. "Herself's awake."

"She's been up for ages," Betty told her. "She was watching you out there in the garden."

"She needs a hobby."

Betty's eyes lit up. "Oh! I didn't tell you!"

"Tell me what?" Ashling asked.

Betty looked around with an exaggerated air of conspiracy and stage-whispered:

"I think she's got a boyfriend."

Ashling's brain chewed on this for a few seconds before spitting it out as totally inedible.

"No," she said.

Betty shrugged.

"Why do you think that?" said Ashling, with the air of someone about to get into an argument with a flat-Earther.

"I walked in on her using the phone. Which is weird, right? Who does she call? I heard her say 'Pat.' And then she sees me and she hangs up and gives me a look like I caught her in the bath with a courgette. So, you tell me."

Betty grinned mischievously. Ashling didn't find it funny.

Her mother was a mentally disturbed alcoholic. Any man opportunistic or desperate enough to romance her was not someone Ashling was happy to have as a stepfather.

But the fear faded quickly enough.

Since her father had died, Ashling knew that Etain had been less interested in men than Ashling herself, which was an extremely low bar to clear.

Whoever this "Pat" was, she doubted he'd be moving in anytime soon.

GERARD LAND OBITUARY:
A GENTLE GIANT OF
IRISH CHILDREN'S TELEVISION
Gerard Land, producer of the long-running and beloved
RTÉ children's program *Puckeen*, was found dead in his
Kilmainham home on Saturday, February 15. He was
sixty-seven.

Land is believed to have held the record for the longest
tenure on a single show of any producer in the history of
the broadcaster. A lodestar of Irish childhood since the
early 1960s, Land took over as producer of the program
in 1969, replacing *Puckeen* creator Oscar Boland on his
death.

Land was ever insistent that the show remain a place
of stability and reassuring continuity in a hectic, often frightening world. In a rare interview with the *RTÉ
Guide*, Land explained: "There's always terrible things
going on. All kinds of awful things. And the world is
always changing. People are always saying 'Oh, the show's
old hat, you should be doing this and that and whatever.
Get a deejay in or one of those lads.' But I say, what's
wrong with an old hat? Some things should stay the same.
Puckeen will never change. He'll always be there, in the
box, waiting for the boys and girls of this country. He'll
never leave."

"He was a lovely, lovely man," Land's longtime colleague Brian Desmond attested. "Always had a smile and
a wink for everyone. An absolute professional who put his
heart and soul into the show but who always had time for
a bit of a laugh."

Etain delicately cut the obituary out of the month-old issue of the
Irish Times. She carefully studied the picture of the man being eulo-
gized. He was a massively obese hulk, but tall as well as broad, with
a crooked, big-lipped smile as toothy, joyous, and utterly rapacious
as an alligator's maw. His nose was large and crooked, having evidently been broken at the bridge, and she could make out a wen the
size of a button just north of his right nostril. There was something

clownish in the way that thick tufts of coarse black hair stuck out from behind his ears.

She took out a magnifying glass from under her bed and hovered it over his hand, trying to make out the details of the ring he wore. But the picture was black-and-white and of poor quality, and all the glass revealed was that the image was only dots, black on white, like the swarming ants of the *myrekrig*.

So she put the glass away and took out her scrapbook, leafing through pages and pages of cut-out articles until she found a blank space and glued the obituary of Gerry Land in the place she had chosen for him.

She then took the rest of the newspaper and threw it out into the hall, where she knew Betty would find it and pick it up and complain to Etain about leaving newspapers in the hall, which would give Etain the opportunity to completely ignore her.

It was a poor substitute for gin, but she took what she could get.

On the bus into work, Ashling realized that there was still dirt under her fingernails from where she had been clawing the earth in her sleep.

She had had to deal with sleepwalking since childhood. But she had never been so bad that she needed to be tied to the bed to stop her leaving the house. Something was awake in her unconscious mind now, restless and pawing at the door.

She had told Betty it was just the stress of the new job, and the job certainly was stressful.

After her first week, Ashling had come to the realization that, at the tender age of twenty-two, she was producing a television show.

Not officially, of course. But Brian was so helplessly out of his depth in virtually every area that it quickly became apparent that he had not hired her to do her job, but his own. In this way, Ashling was saddled with all of the responsibility of a producer, and all the power and prestige of a production assistant.

The cast and crew were pleasant enough for the most part. The role of the male presenter, what Ashling still thought of as "the Brian," was played by a young actor named Noel, a shy, soft-spoken, harshly closeted former seminarian whom Ashling felt an immediate protectiveness toward. He played the role well enough, but Ashling felt instinctively that he had been cast because of a strong resemblance to a younger Brian.

Gerry Land was dead, but his influence on *Puckeen* still lingered and his vision of the show as a never-changing cycle remained unquestioned. Ashling was shocked to discover that the script for any given episode to be recorded today might be from 1971, with the names of the presenters crossed out and replaced with those of their successors. One script had even been used multiple times, with Noel's name balanced on top of a crossed-out "Brian," itself teetering on top of an obliterated "John."

"Could we not do something new?" she asked Brian.

"Don't mess with success," he had said. "The kids don't notice. They weren't around to see them the first time."

"But you might as well just run the old episodes on repeat. We're just remaking them line for line and shot for shot."

"Don't give them any ideas," he said, glancing anxiously at the ceiling. "Do you want to be out of a job?"

The only other woman on the *Puckeen* crew was the female presenter, Dympna Corrigan. When they had first met, Ashling had tried to befriend her and to subtly hint that if Dympna needed help or an ally, Ashling was here and ready to support her.

After a week, Ashling was actively lobbying to get her fired.

"You *have* to sack her, Brian," she had said as they stood together on the empty *Puckeen* set. The day's shooting had been abandoned and the cast and crew sent home.

Brian, her boss, was standing in front of her, shamefaced like a boy in the principal's office.

"I can't," he said, shaking his head. "She's one of Gerry's. He hired her."

"Brian, it's your show now. C'mon, this can't go on! It's one thing that she treats everyone here like garbage. Did you hear what she said to Noel?"

"Ah, that was just joking, she's always like that . . ."

"That doesn't make it better. It doesn't make it better that it was a joke and it *definitely* doesn't make it better if she says it all the time. It's the way she treats the crew. It's the way she treats *you*."

"Ah, no. Ah, no."

"She's never on time. And when she shows up . . . she was on something today, Brian. She was coked up or *something*. And we lost a whole day! I mean, dude, what does she have to do to get fired? Burn the set down?"

She practically had.

Dympna had arrived, ninety minutes late, swanned onto the set, and proceeded to flub every single take spectacularly. At first she had simply burst out giggling whenever she had tried to give her lines. Then she had spent a few takes seemingly trying to actually deliver the lines but reducing them to mumbled, slurred, run-on gibberish. Then she had launched into some kind of insult comic routine, most of it directed at Noel and his sexuality, and so vicious that he seemed to pale to the color of his costume. At that point, even Brian had had enough. He had raised his voice, slightly, and told Dympna to start acting professionally, please.

This kicked off a furious, eight-minute screaming match as vitriolic as it was entirely one-sided.

Ashling had stood by, fuming silently.

And then she had seen it, out of the corner of her eye.

Everyone else was, of course, riveted to the emotional carnage unfolding in the center of the set. But Ashling's eyes were locked on the lid of Puckeen's box.

Because, for the briefest second, she had thought she had seen the lid move . . .

"FUCKING GOBSHITES," Dympna had spat, and stormed off the set, leaving only a stunned silence in her wake.

"You can't have someone on the crew like that," Ashling said. "She's got to go."

Brian shook his head and smiled sadly.

"Ashling, you're a natural at this, but you have a lot to learn about television."

"What do you mean? It's not like she's some genius we have to put up with. There's a million women out there who could do it and do it better. On her best day, she's *okay*."

"Oh, she's crap," Brian agreed. "Absolutely. Jesus, Gráinne would never carry on like that, not in a million years. What I mean is, Dympna is one of the Untouchables."

Ashling folded her arms. "Meaning?"

"Meaning she got this job through, shall we say, family connections? I can't fire her. I might run the show, but her father runs the *whole* show. Or used to, at least."

"What, her dad's on the board of directors or something?"

Brian smirked. "Or something. Her father did not give her his surname, for the simple reason that his wife is not her mother, do you follow me?"

"Okay. But he's a big deal?"

Brian glanced around conspiratorially and then whispered, "Charlie. Juliet. Hotel."

Ashling's eyes widened in shock.

"Fuck off . . ." she breathed, her face grinning with delight at uncovering such a salacious secret.

Brian tapped his nose.

"Look, you're not seeing her at her best," he said apologetically. "She's not usually like this. Leave her be. She'll be in tomorrow, all apologies."

Ashling gave a look to show that she did not think that was good enough, or anything close.

"Right, thanks, Ash," he said, and turned to leave.

"Oh, Brian," Ashling called after him. "Do you want me to take care of the school tour?"

Brian froze with his back to her.

"What's that?" he said, as if he hadn't heard her.

"We got a memo from upstairs. Apparently some kids are going to be coming in to see the set . . ."

"No," he said. "No. Leave that with me. I'll handle that."

It was the first time she had ever heard him say those words. He had been only too happy to delegate anything and everything, major and minor, to her.

Why the school tour, of all things?

Why did that require the executive producer to take a hands-on role?

Look at your face. Look at your fucking face. What do you know?

"Okay," she said brightly. "No problem. Oh, one last thing?"

"Yeah?" he said, seemingly happy to talk about anything else.

"When you were cleaning out Gerry's office, did you see his production diaries?"

"Production diaries?"

"Yeah."

Brian puffed out his lips and shook his head extravagantly.

"No. No. Didn't see anything like that. Why?"

"I just thought they'd be really useful to have. I want to pitch you some ideas for the show and I thought it would be good to have Gerry's old notes to make sure that everything I'm proposing is . . . y'know. Consistent with his vision."

Vision. It was an odd word for a show about two idiots standing beside a box and talking about a fake goat who'd been AWOL since the 1960s.

Brian nodded approvingly.

"Sounds good. But I didn't see them."

"Any idea where they might be?" Ashling asked.

Brian shrugged. "I dunno. He might have kept them at home, I suppose."

And then, as if that was the end of the matter, he turned and walked off the set.

The sweet, amicable expression on Ashling's face did not last a second past Brian leaving the room.

She turned and found herself staring at the box.

What a grim thing, she thought to herself. *Black. Featureless.*

She realized she had never touched it. It had only ever existed as an image to her.

She had seen it once before in person, before coming to work at the station. She had seen it more times than she could count on-screen. And she was looking at it now.

But she had never actually reached out and touched the thing.

With a feeling of breaking some terrible taboo, she reached out a hand.

Through her fingertips, she got a powerful sense of age and weight. This was not some construction of cheap plywood. This felt like oak, or solid ash. It felt like wood that had been buried in a bog a thousand years ago and then brought back to the surface, weighty and turgid with soil and water and centuries of time.

She remembered that twitch of the lid when Dympna had been throwing her tantrum.

She didn't know why, but she cast a glance around to ensure that no one had come onto the set. She was alone. Just her, the bright red door, the pitch-black box, the empty white space.

Before she had a chance to second-guess herself she placed her hand on the lid and threw it open.

The box was empty. A plain black square, a wart of dried black paint in the corner. Dust.

Well, obviously, she chided herself. *What did you expect?*

Her hands were shaking. There was cold sweat running down her neck.

Clearly, she had been expecting something.

She stood back, and back again.

She kneeled down, like she was genuflecting at an altar. She lowered herself until she was the exact height she had been fifteen years ago.

She had been standing right here.

In her mind's eye she watched as a tiny blond child ran for the box and climbed into it, headfirst.

She remembered the look she had given her, right before she had leapt.

A glance over her shoulder. A sad little smile. A glimpse of love.

Gerry Land had done well for himself, judging by his lodgings.

Just a stone's throw down from Kilmainham Gaol stood his house, a handsome redbrick affair in a leafy affluent South Dublin suburb. She would have expected it to have been snapped up in jig time, but the For Sale sign still stood watch in the overgrown garden months after his death.

Perhaps the estate agent had priced it out of everyone's range.

Perhaps it was not as inviting on the other side of the front door.

She dimly realized that she had no memory of her journey here. Or even deciding to come here.

You're tired, she thought. *Up all night, tugging your leash like a mad dog.*

She felt a rush of excitement when her eyes fell on the large yellow skip in the front garden. Gerry Land had had no surviving family.

The real estate agency, or the bank, or whoever must have thrown all his possessions into the skip to be taken to the dump.

She forced her way through the front gate, its hinges so solid with rust that she worried it might break before it opened.

She clambered up the side of the skip and stood nervously on the edge. It was a good twenty yards long and a small lake of black refuse bags and broken furniture and clothes stretched out in front of her. This would take hours.

"What are you looking for, missus?"

She looked up to see a young boy of around nine years of age straddling a bike and watching her suspiciously through the open gate.

"If you can find me a load of books there's a tenner in it for you," she called to him.

"Books?" he repeated.

"Yeah, like copybooks. Diaries."

He dropped his bike without a care and easily clambered up the side and began eagerly searching through the sea of rubbish.

"Fuck!" Ashling swore as she tore open a bag and was rewarded with the sight of a million pale, writhing maggots and a belch of rotting food.

Tossing it aside, she tore open another and a deluge of European porn mags flopped at her feet like a haul of fish being dropped on deck.

She was just starting to think that she didn't have the stomach for this job when the boy called to her.

"Found them!"

Walking like a woman underwater she stamped across the pile of cracking, snapping, squishing shapes and grabbed the bag that the boy was holding.

Dozens of small black leather-bound books glinted in the evening half-light.

Without a word she reached into her pocket and took out a twenty-euro note and handed it to him.

She leapt off the skip onto Gerry Land's lawn and vaulted over the wall.

"Here! Let me give you your change!" the boy called after.

"Keep it!" she called joyously.

She felt like she could run all the way home.

It didn't last.

* * *

By the time she finally got home she was bone-tired. She told herself that it was just the length of the commute, the stress of the new job, the lack of sleep.

But half the thoughts in her head were mad, now. And the effort of keeping up a veneer of sanity was driving her to nervous exhaustion.

She would not be able to keep it up much longer. The thought of what would finally happen when she committed fully to this idea filled her less with dread than with weary resignation.

What was the point of regret and fear when this was always how it was going to go?

Fourteen years ago she had seen Puckeen's box open and her sister had vanished and reemerged and then vanished again, this time forever.

Since that day Ashling had been on a road with no signposts, and with no exits.

Betty and Etain were both upstairs.

She could hear music faintly through the floorboards, which meant that Betty was studying. Her contract in the archive was expiring soon, but there was a permanent position opening which she had decided to apply for, and she was throwing every free evening she had into preparing for the interview.

Ashling dumped the contents of the bag on the kitchen table and began to organize the diaries by date, starting with the earliest in 1971 and ending with the most recent in 1996. She wondered if Gerry had started keeping them electronically after that, but it didn't matter. The one she was looking for was here.

She opened the first page.

Puckeen PROD DIARY 1989.

The book was handwritten in a surprisingly neat and dainty script with a blue biro. Each entry was a simple description of each episode: cast and crew, budget, script used, etc. Seeing each episode described in this way made it even more explicit how rote and formulaic the series really was.

A few pages in she found a break in the pattern:

SCHOOL TOUR. 31 JAN. 2 (F)*
HEIR FOUND. SCARNAGH RSLVD.

She closed the book with a snap, stood up, and began to pace the kitchen anxiously.

Fuck. Fuck.

She did not know the full meaning of what she had just read but she was sure of this:

The school tour referenced in Land's note was the one that she and her sister Niamh had been part of on January 31, 1989. She also felt certain that "2 (F)" stood for two females, and that she and Niamh had been those two.

Scarnagh. The curse laid upon the family.

When she had been old enough (honestly, when she had not yet really been old enough), Kate had told her about Scarnagh. She did it to exculpate Etain: this is why your mother is the way she is, it's not her fault. Instead, it had just given Ashling nightmares of Feidhlim Lowney for a few months. She didn't know what he looked like, so she would imagine him as a great, terrifying shadow looming at the end of her bed.

Seeing it written down here was like having a dream of being chased by a pack of dogs, waking up, and finding bitemarks on your neck.

Night terrors were becoming concrete and leaving their mark in the physical world.

RSLVD. Resolved?

Scarnagh resolved?

What did Gerry Land mean when he had written those words?

"She's playing her music too loud," a soft voice said.

Ashling looked up to see Etain lurking in the doorway like a vengeful ghost.

"What?" Ashling asked.

"*She.* Is playing. Her music. Too loud," Etain repeated coldly. "*I.* Am trying. To work."

Ashling did not know what "work" constituted for an unemployed, mentally disturbed alcoholic and didn't care.

"So ask. Her. To lower it," she said, mimicking Etain.

"I am not speaking to her," Etain answered primly, with the air of a duchess explaining why the maid was dismissed without references.

Ashling buried her face in her hands. "Did you really come down here to ask me to go up there to tell Betty to lower her music? And, follow-up question, are you five years old?"

"She was rude to me. In my own house."

"She told you to stop leaving your newspapers in the hall. Are you going to do that?"

"She can feck off."

"Then learn to like Alanis Morrissette. Christ knows, I had to."

Etain was staring at the notebooks strewn across the kitchen table.

"What's all this?" she asked.

"Nothing," said Ashling. "Work stuff."

Etain grunted and crossed to the kitchen counter and put on the kettle. Ashling glanced back at the page and a thought struck.

"Mam?" she said quietly. "Can we talk about Scarnagh?"

Etain stopped stock-still.

Her shoulders seemed to sag and her head dipped as if she had been struck. She leaned against the counter, her back to Etain, shrinking visibly.

The kettle grew louder, and louder . . .

Suddenly, Etain snapped off the kettle and turned and left the kitchen without another word.

Ashling heard her march calmly up the stairs, stop, and give an ear-splitting scream of "WILL YOU TURN OFF THAT FUCKING MUSIC!"

In the stunned silence that followed, she could hear her mother's footsteps padding down the landing, and the bedroom door closing behind her.

Am I awake? Am I dreaming?

She could feel the carpet on her bare feet. The hallway was pitch black except for a silver square on the floor where moonlight shone through the window box.

She felt light as she drifted down the stairs.

There was a black pool of something at the bottom step.

It moaned in agony as she stepped on it and it seeped through her toes.

She glanced at her wrist, which suddenly felt painful, but there was nothing there.

I am dreaming. I was tied to the bed.

The realization that this was a dream and that she was aware of that fact thrilled her and terrified her in equal measure. *Anything could happen.*

She walked into the kitchen, which was now three miles wide, and the great windows that looked out onto the garden were the size of cinema screens.

The moon was high in the sky, and brighter than the sun. It cast everything in a perfect silver-white gleam. The whites were blinding. The shadows were pitch.

As white, and as black, as static.

She stepped out into the garden, or rather, she found herself in the garden.

There were two rows of toys laid out on the grass, stretching off into the distance. Two parallel lines of bears and dolls and dogs as far as the eye could see.

Between them, and Ashling's heart seemed to roll in her chest at the sight, was a small blond girl in a white nightdress. She was standing behind a large cardboard box with a thick, crude red cross drawn on the front.

I remember this, Ashling thought. *I know this game.*

"Hi, Niamh," she said to the small child. "Can I play too?"

The child nodded, and passed her a small plastic toy stethoscope.

She spent eighty years or so moving up the line of toys, listening to their heartbeats.

Some were fast and some slow, always tinny and artificial, like the beat of a small drum.

Sometimes she would find one with no heartbeat and then she would have to call Niamh over. Niamh would pick up the patient and tut exaggeratedly with a look of comically broad disappointment and regret and then take the toy away.

She remembered this game. This is what they had thought doctors did all day.

Beside her, the gap in the line of toys had already closed.

How long have I been doing this? she finally asked herself.

She stood up. Niamh was a tiny speck in the very far distance beneath the looming house, as distant as a star in the night sky.

She stood up and walked for a century over the silver grass. Niamh stood behind the box, with her back to her.

"I missed you," Ashling said. "I missed you so much. Did you miss me?"

The child nodded, but did not turn around.

"There's something I need to ask you," Ashling said. "Do you remember the school trip we both took? When they read our names out and said that you and me could look into Puckeen's box?"

Memory bled into the dream and for a moment the moon-bleached garden flickered away and was replaced by the sight of a massively obese man standing in front of a gaggle of schoolchildren. Ashling could see herself, a small, dark-haired waif, hiding shyly behind her sister, who was smiling giddily.

The man was circling his hand over a hat full of names, milking the anticipation of the children like a practiced magician.

Someone very scary and very nice. Someone very good at pretending.

He pulled out a piece of paper and stared at it in mock shock and surprise.

"Well, I never, boys and girls!" he declared. *"Well, I never! This has never happened before in all my years! Puckeen wants to see two of ye!"*

The children squealed excitedly, happy that their odds had doubled.

"And it's a family affair! Puckeen says that he wants to see Niamh Mallen and her sister Ashling, where are they at all, at all?"

He looked around, furrowing his bushy black eyebrows comically, and then gestured for both children to come to him.

Niamh had raced over to him, dragging Ashling by the hand.

They were to be allowed to look in the box.

They would be allowed to see Puckeen, as long as they promised not to tell anyone else what they had seen.

With the way of a dream, she was that small child again. She was seeing through her eyes as Gerry Land brought them onto the set.

It looked smaller than she had expected, and strangely drab and fake.

The box stood before them.

Gerry Land's great hand held her shoulder like a tarantula that had dropped from a tree overhead. She held Niamh's hand tightly.

She was usually nervous; she was a nervous child by nature.

But she was tipping on the very edge of fear.

The box had opened.

"Go and see," Gerry had said. *"Go on and see."*

There was something about his voice that had caused Ashling's legs to seize up and lock. It was the voice that her father used when he read stories about the Big Bad Wolf.

Little pig, little pig, let me come in.

Something not friendly, trying to be friendly.

But Niamh, Niamh had run toward it and dived right into the box like a salmon.

She was gone. She was utterly gone. She had vanished forever.

This is the dream. This can't have been how it happened.

She was back in the garden. Niamh was playing with two dolls on the grass, one dark-haired and one blond.

"That's not how it happened," Ashling said. "You looked in the box and then you and I went home. Together. You only disappeared a few weeks later. You were taken from school. Someone took you from school. Maybe Da. Maybe someone else. But it wasn't when you went in the box. You came home . . ."

The child was looking at her, her face impassive, but perhaps a little pitying.

"But I felt it was wrong," Ashling said, nodding. "Even before you went missing I knew you were gone. Because we were so close and there are some things you can't fake. That wasn't you, was it? That was something else."

The child ignored her and continued playing with her dolls.

"Niamh? Where did you go? Where are you now? No, stop, put them down, put them down!"

She pulled the dolls out of her sister's hand and shook her.

She lolled in her grip like a dead thing.

Ashling let go in shock.

"I'm sorry," she whispered. "I'm sorry, I didn't mean to do that. Can you tell me where they took you?"

The child shook her head sadly.

Ashling was on her hands and knees now.

"I saw you. I saw you in the forest, being chased by the goat. I'm trying to get you back. I've been trying for years. And I'm so close now. I can feel it. But you have to help me. You have to tell me, or show me what they did."

The child stretched out her hand and pointed to the cardboard box.

Ashling nodded, understanding.

The child picked up the box and put it on her head. The shadow cast a perfect black square over her feet, so dark as to swallow them up. She bent her knees, lowering herself down until the box rested on the ground.

After a few moments of perfect stillness, Ashling lifted the box.

The child was gone. In her place, the small blond doll.

Ashling picked it up and studied it.

A raindrop fell on the doll's brow. But it was white and black and buzzing, liquid *myrekrig* dripping down the doll's cheek.

Ashling craned her neck to look overhead.

The huge moon was being swallowed up by great clouds of static.

There was a peal of thunder, or perhaps the noise of the volume on an empty channel pushed to cracking point. She looked around the garden, the rows upon rows of convalescent toys, vanishing in the darkness as the clouds closed in overhead.

That was how the game ended. The rains came and washed the hospital away.

The sky opened and within seconds a flood of *myrekrig* was rising up past her ankles and then her knees. It was so cold it burned.

The toys were washed away.

The trees, the house, the garden were all washed away.

She was struggling to keep afloat on a sea of static.

She screamed and tilted her head back.

She tried to swim but she was too heavy and the rising tide enveloped her.

She awoke, coughing and sputtering and freezing cold on a metal bench.

She staggered to her feet and wheeled around, staring in confusion and terror.

It was dawn and she was standing at the side of a main road.

The RTÉ broadcast tower loomed behind her, black and menacing.

Donnybrook. She had walked across town, asleep, in her night-dress, all the way to the studio. And she had not been mugged, mur-dered, raped, or hit by a car.

That, at least, was comforting.

But then, no one had stopped her either.

She looked at her hand and gave a shriek of shock at the bloody bracelet of torn skin on her wrist where she had apparently just kept walking until the rope had given way. She felt pain in her feet and cursed loudly as she examined her bare soles and found a caked-in carpet of broken glass, cigarette butts, dog shit, and general filth, and what she assumed was blood.

Overcome with cold and pain and fear she keeled over on the pavement and began to weep.

Then, she crossed the road and banged on the door of the near-est house until someone answered, and begged to use their phone.

An ambulance had been called for her and she spent every hour un-til noon being ferried from one cramped hospital room to another, a tiny cell in an indifferent body, drifting wherever the flow took her.

Tetanus shots. Blood tests. Gauze for her arm. Stitches and ban-dages for her feet.

She finally was given a bed and took a few blessed hours of still, dreamless sleep.

She awoke in the evening to see Betty waiting beside her bed, her eyes full of love and concern and giving no hint of the inevitable ut-ter bollocking that would no doubt follow.

Betty waited and listened attentively as Ashling's doctor, a tall, soft-spoken Iraqi with the mustache of a '20s matinee idol, told her that he'd never heard of a case of somnambulism so extreme as what she'd experienced and prescribed her some generic tranquilizers to help her sleep, and advised her to see a psychiatrist as soon as possi-ble for a full evaluation.

Betty nodded gratefully, listening to everything he said.

She was kept in for observation and discharged the next morning.

Betty picked her up and drove her home in silence.

She pulled into the driveway and, just as Ashling went for the door, her hand reached out to stop her.

"Okay, look," said Ashling. "Do we have to do this out in the car?"

"Yes," said Betty firmly.

"Why?"

"Because I don't want to give Etain the satisfaction of seeing me cry."

Ashling laughed, but she could feel herself tearing up.

Oh Christ. This is it. She's walking. And who could blame her?

Betty took a deep breath.

"I know you hate making a big deal out of things—"

Ashling shook her head.

"No, I know—" she interrupted.

"I. Am talking," Betty clarified.

Ashling nodded, and fell silent.

"But waking up and not knowing where you were. Finding the rope with your blood on it. Knowing you'd just strolled off into the night . . . that was the single most terrifying moment of my life . . ."

Ashling kissed her, trying to put all her love and desperation and fear into a single, intimate act.

"That is not going to shut me—" Betty began once she'd recovered herself.

Ashling kissed her again, proving the first one to have just been an opening volley.

Betty was silenced.

"You're right," Ashling whispered. "You're absolutely right. I am so, so sorry."

"What is this?" Betty moaned. "What is happening to you, love? Don't tell me it's the job."

Ashling leaned forward and rested her head on the dashboard.

"It's . . . it's me losing it," she whispered. "It's me just . . . burning down. And I'm so sorry because . . . I've been lying to you this whole time."

"Oh. God," said Betty. "You're straight."

Ashling burst out laughing.

"No! No. Worse. I'm crazy. Like, properly mental. And if I told you the things that I see, every day. The things that I have . . . convinced myself are true. You'd run screaming. And you'd be right."

She looked up at Betty. Love changed how you saw a person. The woman sitting across from her now, she never saw her in pictures or mirrors. That was someone else. This Betty, so beautiful, so full of love and goodness and fierce, loyal protectiveness. This was someone who only Ashling could see in the flesh, before her eyes.

"You're not going to tell me, are you?" Betty said quietly.

Ashling shook her head.

I can't show you that. I'm not that strong.

"Ash. I love you," she said.

Ashling looked away.

"Why don't you like me saying that?" Betty asked.

Ashling said nothing.

"You say it to me all the time," Betty noted.

"I know."

"So why can't I say it to you?"

"Because when I say it to you I believe it."

The words were out before she could catch them.

Betty looked like she'd been slapped.

"You don't believe that I love you?"

Ashling shook her head.

You weren't made for loving.

"That's not what I . . . I know you think . . ."

Betty did not wait to hear another word. She threw off the seatbelt with a snap, opened the door, and slammed it behind her.

Ashling sat alone in the car for a few minutes.

Betty came back out of the house and stood beside her window.

"You can't stay out here, you're sick," she said tersely.

"Okay," said Ashling.

Betty opened the door for her, and supported her into the house. The stitches in her feet were still stinging.

After a simple, silent dinner of waffles and fish fingers, Ashling went to bed and slept as deep and still as a sunken vessel, rusting on the pitch-black ocean floor.

She awoke, or rose in her sleep, to the smell of frying bacon wafting up from the kitchen below.

Betty lay beside her, warm and snoring. Etain had gone to bed before she had.

So who is in the kitchen? she thought to herself with mild curiosity.

She watched herself rise quietly out of bed and pad over to the door.

She realized that she was still asleep, and simply watching herself sleepwalk.

She took comfort in that. If she was simply sleeping, none of this was real and none of it mattered.

The landing was a void, the night outside so dark that not even the small window opposite Etain's door offered so much as a lumen.

With sense memory she crossed the invisible floor and descended into the hall.

The dark patch at the bottom of the stairs moaned low as she stepped on it.

Light was streaming into the hallway through the cracks in the kitchen door but it seemed to have gone sour. It was off-color. Faintly green.

She pushed her way into the kitchen and was hit by a wall of fat and noise and the smell of meat browning and eggs bubbling in grease.

A man was at the stove, four pans hissing in front of him, laden with sausages and rashers and black pudding and white bread and mushrooms and eggs, all roaring at him in so much grease the meal was half soup.

He was as vast as a continent, as wide as he was tall. Forests of tough black hair scrambled for air from beneath his great, pink ears.

He wore the filthy remains of a funeral suit, sans jacket. His pinstripe shirt was gray with mud and one of the straps of his suspenders had slipped off his shoulder and trailed behind him like a red tail.

Ashling took her seat at the end of the table. The rope gave just enough.

With a weary sigh like a rockslide cleaving from the earth, the figure piled his bounty onto a single massive plate and placed it on the table across from her along with a large mug of tea, already filthy from the layer of muck on his great hands.

He took a knife and fork, like toys, and began to devour the dripping meal.

She watched him dispassionately, grateful that this was a dream.

For if it was not a dream, the bloody gaping hole in his forehead through which she could see the kitchen clock on the wall might have disquieted her.

Instead, she felt only what the pigs must have felt when they began their journey to this table.

Weary, numb resignation in the face of a world too unknowable, too unchangeable, and too cruel.

The figure took a large bottle of ketchup and emptied it onto his meal.

A flicker of revulsion rose in her stomach and died a moment later.

He seemed to be creeping toward her across the table.

His grease. His filth. His tea. His ketchup. His smell.

It slunk and wafted and slithered over the shiny plastic table-cloth.

He took a large gulp from his mug and she heard the tea pour out the back of his head and hit the tiles with the slap of piss on a back-alley wall.

He tilted his head back and fixed her with a gaze. His eyes were light brown, the color of old money, and with the jagged red hole in his head they seemed a million miles apart.

He gave her a smile that reminded her of the pale maggots winking up at her when she had opened the refuse bag in his skip.

"Do you know me, girlie?" he asked, and his voice had a Dublin accent as thick as tar, deep as a well filled with old plastic bags and empty cans.

"Yeah," she whispered softly.

"Yeah. You're Gerry Land."

The mound before her rumbled with soft, mocking laughter.

"What gave me away?" he asked.

He tilted his head, and the view through the hole shifted from the clock on the wall to the lightbulb hanging over the kitchen. He looked like a cyclops, gazing at her with pale, sick light.

"You're dead," she answered.

"As fuckin' Shergar," he affirmed, then speared a lump of black pudding with his fork and popped it into his mouth.

"Why are you here?" she asked.

"Well, you've grown so much. And Uncle Gerry wanted to get a look at ya," he said, in a tone of voice that made her skin try to curl up her arms and legs.

"Fucking farmers," he said, taking another swig of his tea. He was wearing a massive silver ring on his left hand, which glinted dully beneath a layer of mud. "A farmer would fuck his ma without a johnny for a bit a' land. That's why I don't trust them. And I was right. Here you are. Twins. Twins are always a bollocks to figure out. Should have got Jerry Fucking Springer in. I still don't know if I chose the right one."

"What did you do to my sister?" she asked him.

"Fuck all," he said, with a note of defensiveness. "I'm just the zookeeper, love. I just feed him."

"Him?"

He raised two fingers over his forehead, forming horns. He then waggled them suggestively. "I get the names. They go into the box. And 'they' come out. And you'd never know. They don't last long, usually. And no one ever realizes because they only go 'missing' after they went missing. They only 'die' after they die. That's the beauty of it."

A slow-burning anger washed over her and suddenly the seat, the table, the smell . . . it all felt very real.

"Do you know what, Gerry?" she said. "When you shot yourself, I hope you didn't die right away."

"Now, now. Don't be like that," he said softly. He wasn't angry. She knew he didn't consider her worth his anger.

"It's just a job that has to be done," he said. "It was mine. Now it's yours, isn't it? You're a member of the *Puckeen* family. Mother of all the little boys and girls. Not bad going, for a dyke."

The word might have hurt from someone else. From him, it was barely noticeable. A nugget of filth on a mountain of rubbish.

"Why?" she asked.

She didn't even know what she was asking. She just cast her net as wide as she could and hoped she'd haul something in that might explain something. Anything.

Gerry gave a long, exasperated sigh. The air grew a little thicker. A shiny, emerald-green fly emerged from the moist cavern of his mouth and began to circle above them, its wings emitting a high, torturous whine.

"Because that's how it's always been," he said. "When people turn on the light they think, 'That's because I paid me electric bill.' And when they see the roads they think, 'That's 'cos I paid me taxes.' But when they wake up in the morning. And they're alive. And there's shape and meaning and order to the world. They never ask

themselves, 'Who paid for that?' Deals, deals, deals. Nothing gets
done in this country without someone getting paid under the table."

"Who?" she pressed. "What's inside the box? What is it, Gerry?"

The fly landed on the table and began to wash itself in the pool of
grease spreading out from Gerry's plate.

"Ah well," he said.

He reached out with a terrible deliberateness and placed his massive thumb over the fly. Slowly, he began to crush it. She watched
its legs, tiny black wires, twitch and then scramble as if desperately
writing a last note of farewell and then falling still.

"Now, do you know what that fly was thinking when he felt my
thumb on his back?" Gerry asked.

He leaned forward, and she found herself staring through the
rose-red hole in his head. "When he felt himself breaking open? He
thought, 'What is it?' But he'll never know, will he? And if he did,
could he understand? And if he did, what good would it do him?
Shite all."

He leaned back, and continued eating.

"But it can be killed," Ashling heard herself say.

He shook his head. "No. It can't."

"You said you feed it. It needs to be fed. That means it can starve."

"Buzz buzz buzz," he said mockingly. "Little fly brain thinking
little fly thoughts. It's not something you understand, understand?
You can't stop it, you can't kill it. All you can do is make it angry."

"Fine," she said. "Then tell me how to make it angry."

He put down his knife and fork with an irritated clink. "Do you
really want to die so terribly? Because you will die. So terribly."

"Better than shooting myself," she told him. "Coward's way
out."

For a moment she expected to feel massive hands closing around
her neck as he broke her apart limb by limb.

Instead, he gave a smile. He smiled so wide that his nose and
eyes rolled back behind his lips and it stretched out and out and
out, the smile encompassing the entire kitchen, the entire world.
The universe was darkness, and the filthy, ketchup-slick teeth of
Gerry Land. His tongue lay before her like a dead whale, eyeless
and gray.

And the world laughed, a mocking, awful jeer.

And then the smile folded back and he was again simply the rev-
enant Gerry Land, rotting at the end of her table.

"Cheeky bitch," he said approvingly. "Fine. The box is an altar. What do you do with an altar?"

"Pray?" she asked. It had been many, many years.

"In your church, maybe. Not mine. An altar is for sacrifice. He's a beast of simple pleasures. Sex or violence. Your choice. So . . . if you're willing to be a bold little girl, Puckeen might come out of his box and pay you a visit. It'll have to be something pretty spectacular, though. He's already fed tonight, and that'll last him."

"What do you mean?" she asked.

"You'll find out, soon enough. But he is out and about, taking in the sights. Well . . ."

He rose, wiping the filth on his hands on his equally filthy trousers.

". . . I have imposed on your hospitality long enough."

He began to drift toward the door.

"Gerry?" she said.

He stopped, a black shape in the darkness of the hallway.

"Why tell me all this?" she asked.

When he spoke, his voice was soft and almost regretful.

"Promises were made," he whispered. "Promises were not kept. So, maybe I'm feeling a bit bold, too."

"What promises?" she asked.

"What do you think happens when you die?" he asked her.

She did not need to think.

"Nothing," she said. "Blackness. Silence."

He gave a deep, shuddering sigh.

"Sweet merciful Jesus," he whispered. "We should be so lucky."

"Not hungry?" Betty asked as she set an Irish fry in front of Ashling and watched her turn an emerald green.

Ashling shook her head apologetically.

"I'll just boil an egg," she mumbled.

"I called your work and told them you were sick," Betty said.

Ashling hissed in irritation. "I'm fine."

"Me arse," said Betty firmly. "He said it's fine and to feel better."

"Who?" Ashling asked. "Brian?"

"Think so, yeah. I did get a fierce nostalgic vibe off his voice. Okay, love you."

She pecked Ashling tenderly on the cheek, ran her hand over her buzz-cut hair for good luck, and kissed her again before heading out to the college. She stopped at the front door and threw her head back.

"Oh, by the way, I left a load of panicky messages on your phone Wednesday night before I realized you'd left it here. Please don't listen to them."

"Okay."

"I'm serious, Ash, I got really fucking emotional. Please just delete them."

"I promise."

Once Betty was gone, Ashling took two eggs and put them in a small saucepan to boil. While she waited, she decided to delete the messages.

She had switched her phone off the night before, and when she turned it on it swelled in her hand with light and vibration as the messages came through.

She dialed her mailbox.

"You have . . . SEVEN . . . new messages. To hear your mess—"

BEEP.

"Message. One. From. 'Betty.' Sent. Wednesday. At. One—"

BEEP.

"Sweetie, where are you, please—"

BEEP.

"Message deleted. Message. Two. From. 'Betty.' Sent—"

BEEP.

"Ash, please pick up the phone I am really fucking scared—"

BEEP.

"Message deleted. Message. Three. From. 'Betty.'—"

"PICK UP—"

BEEP.

"Message deleted. Message. Four—"

BEEP.

"Where—"

BEEP.

"Message deleted. Message Fi—"

BEEP.

"FUC—"

"Message deleted. M—"

KNOCK KNOCK, OPEN WIDE

"... I can't keep doing this. You can't keep doing this to me. I can't live like this anymore. We're done. I'm sorry. We're done. We're finished."

Message Six had struck hard and deep.
It felt like a breakup. Even though she knew that Betty had told her to delete the message unheard and had clearly changed her mind in the interim, Ashling had the audio proof.
Betty had broken up with her and the pain was real.
Their relationship had been, for a few hours at least, dead on the operating table.
She wondered whether she should discuss it with Betty or simply pretend that she had been quick enough on the draw.
Who are you kidding? You'll take the easy way, like you always do.

"Message. Seven. From. An Unidentified Number. Sent. Today. At. Two. Forty-Seven. A.M."

If she had not been so numb from Betty calling time, she would not have heard the cold, oddly accented machine voice tell her that the final message had come from a different number.
She almost ignored it. Whatever Message Seven contained, she sincerely doubted it was anything as urgently in need of action as Message Six.
But curiosity, or perhaps simply the need to distract herself from deciding what to do, compelled her to listen.
BEEP.

"... you said I could call you ... You fucking liar ... You said if I needed help I could call you ... You fucking lying bitch you *said* ... Do you know who my father is, do you?! ... It's your job, you're in charge of it ... You're supposed to stop it ... *You fucking bitch, you sent it, didn't you?!* ... I'm sorry ... I'm so sorry ... it's not your fault ... but you have to help ... I need ... please ... Please help me ... It's here ... I can hear it downstairs ... it's moving downstairs . . . and I can't leave the house . . . if I go past the door it'll see me . . . It got out . . . Ah, fuck fuck fuck fuck . . . it's all my fault . . . I'm sorry . . . I'm sorry . . . I'm sorry for what I said . . . Please God no . . . Please Jesus forgive me . . . It's coming up the stairs . . . Shit shit shit . . . I can hear it . . . Can you hear it . . . tapping on the floorboards . . . hard feet . . . Shit I can hear him scraping against the ceiling . . . Ssh ssh ssh ssh sssh sshs . . ."

There was a silence.

With the phone pressed so hard to her ear that it crushed the helix she thought that she could just barely, just ever so *barely,* make out the thin, sickly whine of a door slowly swinging open.

She flinched as she heard a bang that she instinctively recognized as the sound of a phone being dropped on the floor.

She had less luck identifying the sounds that came next.

The scream was plain enough, although it did not sound like a scream a human being should be capable of making.

It was not particularly loud, but in its high, razor-sharp, serrated tone it sounded like nothing so much as a fox caught in a trap. Sheer, anguished, animal terror.

And mixed in there was a sound she could not recognize; a tearing of something tough and sinewy, a great, wet plosive and then a torrent of liquid, like someone dumping a great pot of broth down a manhole.

The screaming was not antecedent to this sound, but concurrent.

The saucepan bubbled over, and the eggs came tumbling out and smashed their half-liquid, half-solid contents out onto the tiles like the brains of defenestrated martyrs.

Ashling screamed in pain as the boiling-hot water splashed onto her bare toes.

While her body did the manual labor of cleaning up the eggs and spilled water her brain tried frantically to digest what she had just heard.

The voice was vaguely familiar but it had been ragged with fear and anger and also slurred and uncertain. It reminded her of a tiny terrier with a big bark, using volume and rage to mask its constant terror.

The words "FUCKING GOBSHITES" arose in her memory and she had her match.

Why had Dympna Corrigan been calling her in a cocaine-fueled panic attack at nearly three in the morning?

. . . You said I could call you . . . You fucking liar . . . You said if I needed help I could call you . . .

It was true that she had given Dympna her number and told her that she could call her if she needed help, but that had been for work problems, not home invasions.

Why had Dympna called her and not the guards?

Must have been off her face, Ashling thought grimly.

Not knowing what else to do, she called the Gardaí and explained that she'd been left a very concerning voicemail and that she was worried a woman might be in danger.

The guard at the other end of the line patiently explained that they would be happy to perform a welfare check on Ms. Corrigan but would need her address to do so, which Ashling didn't know.

Swearing hotly, she hung up and dialed Brian's number, only for it to go straight to voicemail. She then called the main RTÉ switch and demanded to be put through to Brian as a matter of urgency, only to be told that he was currently filming and couldn't be disturbed.

"I need to talk to him *now!*" she practically screamed, too frantic to realize the incongruity in what she had just been told.

Brian actually sounded angry when he finally came to the phone.

"Ashling, what's all this about?" he barked.

"Brian, I need Dympna's home address, please, there's no time . . ."

"What for?"

"Please, just get me her address."

"Fuck's sake. Hang on, I'll ask her. Wait a minute."

Ashling felt gravity flicker briefly.

"What do you mean, you'll ask her?"

"What do you mean, what do I mean? I'll go and ask her if it means so much to you?"

"She's *there*?!"

"Yeah. She deigned to come in today. Will wonders never cease?" he replied.

Ashling leaned against the kitchen counter for support.

"Ashling," said Brian with the tone of a man who's reached his limit. "What the fuck is going on with you?"

Apologetically, she explained the voicemail.

"Ah, she may have been playing a prank on you," he said sympathetically. "She's got an odd sense of humor."

Odd? Try "fucking psychotic."

"How are you feeling, by the way?" Brian asked.

"What?" Ashling mumbled.

"Your sister said you were sick?"

My what?!

Then, realization.

"Oh. No. Betty's not my . . . doesn't matter. Yeah. Bit run-down is all."

"Nearly run down" more likely. Probably more than once.

"Right, right," said Brian. "Well, take care of yourself, just, y'know . . ."

"I'll be back in on Tuesday."

"Great, great," he said, with obvious relief.

After she hung up, she spent a full ten minutes trying to relax and enjoy her day off before getting dressed, grabbing her keys and wallet, and heading for the bus stop.

By the time she arrived at the studio, filming had concluded for the day and the cast had gone home. In the darkened editing room Brian looked up in surprise as he saw her enter.

"Ashling, what are you doing here?"

"I just . . . I just wanted to talk to Dympna. Make sure she was okay."

He gave a sympathetic smile.

"You missed her by a few minutes," he said.

"Did she seem . . . okay?" Ashling asked.

"Yeah," said Brian, nodding. "Yeah, see for yourself."

He gestured to the screen, where Noel was explaining how rain was formed while Dympna pantomimed being the entire water cycle; lying flat on her back as a lake, pirouetting through the air as water vapor, spreading her arms to become a cloud, and then falling to the floor again as rain. She was smiling, Ashling saw. There was a great open grin on her face and her motion was beautiful, graceful, and perfectly poised.

Ashling felt weirdly happy just looking at her.

The woman had been cleansed; of rage, of bitterness, of poisonous self-regard and self-loathing. She seemed like a new person.

Feeling like an idiot, Ashling apologetically told Brian that she still wasn't feeling fit for work and limped out of the editing suite. Feeling acute sick-leave guilt, she stopped by her desk to see if there was anything she could quickly take care of before heading home. Apparently she had missed a call and someone (Brian, by the handwriting) had taken a name and a number and slapped it to her screen with a yellow Post-it. She picked it up and read it.

Beneath the number was a single word: "PAT," and the time that she had missed the call. This morning, evidently.

She held the note in front of her like a detective scrutinizing a particularly ominous clue.

As a formality, she ran through everyone she knew in the studio who might have been calling her and trying to remember if any of them were named "Pat" or "Patrick." There were none, and besides, it was a mobile number, not an internal extension.

She remembered Betty laughing about Etain's supposed boyfriend.

Buddy, she thought darkly. *Dude. My man. It's one thing if I find out you really are trying to fuck my mother. It is . . .* several things *if you think that gives you the right to call me up at my place of work.*

She thought of some choice, cuttingly emasculating swears, put on her most dangerous smile, and dialed the number left to her.

She listened intently as it rang.

"Hello?"

She was instantly wrong-footed. The voice at the other end was female. Old, and lacquered with decades of tobacco and alcohol, but definitely a woman.

"Um . . . hello?" said Ashling uncertainly. "I've a message from Pat?"

There was a splutter at the other end of the line, as if the speaker had taken a swig of something and it had tried to escape through her nose.

"Is that Ashling?" she wheezed.

"Who is this?" Ashling asked.

"God, you must be . . . how old now?"

This is not a family reunion, you are not some aunt I haven't seen in years. Who the fuck are you, woman?

"I . . . I knew your father," the voice at the end of the line whispered, in the kind of harried, confessional tone that might suggest that a family tree would soon have to be extensively rewritten. "My name is Patricia Skelton."

Ashling saw, if not the light, then at least a kind of murky glow. The name rang a bell. In her teens, Ashling had gotten it into her head that she would solve her sister's disappearance and had tried to read everything she could find on Niamh's vanishing, as well as Etain's own kidnapping in Scarnagh. The name "Patricia Skelton" had popped up quite a bit.

"The journalist?"

"That's right!" Patricia exclaimed, a little too eagerly, Ashling thought. "Yes, I . . . I write for the *Dublin Herald.*"

Ashling didn't read that paper, and made a mental note to check later.

"Okay. Well, what can I do for you, Ms. Skelton?" Ashling asked.

"I, well, I don't really know where to begin. Has your mother mentioned me?"

"No. We don't really talk that much," Ashling said.

"I thought you lived together?"

"What's your point?"

"Oh. Well, I'll just tell you what I told her. Your father was murdered."

If she had been expecting a gasp or a shriek of surprise she was sorely disappointed. Ashling gave an angry hiss.

"No. No, he wasn't. My father killed himself. There was a full investigation."

"Please, you have—"

"And you need to stay away from my mother, do you hear me? She is not a well woman, she doesn't need you filling her head with paranoid conspiracies."

We have enough of our own, thank you very much. We are full, madam.

"Please don't hang up. Just listen to me. Do you know where I was this morning?"

"Where?" Ashling asked, in spite of herself.

"I was at Dympna Corrigan's house. The Gardaí were called out there. The neighbors heard screaming."

Ashling felt the sickening lurch of suddenly losing control of a situation and being very much at someone else's mercy.

"What did they find?" Ashling asked.

"Dympna Corrigan was there," said Patricia, and from her tone of voice it was clear that she knew the balance of power had shifted. "And she seemed absolutely fine. The Gardaí found nothing amiss."

"Well?" Ashling said, trying not to hear Message Seven replaying in her head at full volume. "So what?"

"I've spoken with your mother. I know you know something is wrong."

"Wrong with what?"

"With everything. With this whole country. With the ones who are really in charge."

Jesus Christ, thought Ashling, *if you start ranting about Jews I swear to God . . .*

"That's why you're there, isn't it? That's why you've spent your whole life working to get where you are now?"

Etain, what the fuck have you been telling this woman?!

"I don't know what you're talking about," she said coldly.

"All right, fine. Just do me one favor. Watch Dympna Corrigan. You work with her. Watch her. And I'll tell you everything I know at her funeral."

Ashling's mouth felt very dry.

"Dympna Corrigan isn't dead," she whispered.

"Yes, she is. She just hasn't stopped moving around yet. Trust me. You'll be told she's dead soon. And it will be so mundane, so ordinary, it'll bore you to tears."

She hung up.

After a few seconds, Ashling had recovered herself enough to search online for the number of the *Dublin Herald.*

"Features?" said a young male voice at the other end.

"Hiiii," said Ashling, feigning a nonchalant drawl. "I was just hoping to speak to Patricia Skelton?"

"Who?"

"Patricia Skelton?"

She heard the voice at the other end give a stifled "*oh fuck*" as if she had inadvertently said something hilarious.

"Does she not work there?" Ashling asked.

"No, no, not for years, no," said Mr. Features.

"Oh. Would you have any idea why she left?" Ashling asked.

"Oh, well. Officially? She left to pursue her writing projects and we wish her well."

"And unofficially?"

"Well, I couldn't really say."

"She went crazy?" Ashling guessed.

Another stifled laugh.

"I'm sure I couldn't possibly comment," Mr. Features said solemnly.

Betty had a naughty smile on her face when she came home and showed Ashling what she had bought in town: a wrist restraint from Miss Fantasia's that was comfortable but with a sturdy, robust design quite belied by the delicate hot-pink ribbon on the wrist.

Betty casually mentioned that she had the full pair of restraints in case Ashling was up for experimenting, and then dropped the subject when she saw that her lover was clearly not in the mood.

The second item Betty had bought was considerably less titillating: a long length of industrial-strength chain. She measured out a length long enough for anyone tied to it to comfortably reach the downstairs bathroom with slack and cut it with bolt cutters, fixing one end to the base of the bed, and the other to the wrist restraint.

And, as a final failsafe, Betty slept on top of her to ensure that if Ashling did sleepwalk again she would wake her immediately.

It was not an issue.

Ashling didn't sleep the entire night.

She was dimly aware that something shaped like Betty was moving around the room and adding colored, formless mass to itself.

I am so tired I can hardly see, she thought. *I'm half blind with exhaustion.*

She felt Betty's lips brush hers and heard the words "Back in a bit, love you."

Stay. We need to talk. We need to talk about you breaking up with me, she tried to say.

But she didn't have the strength or the will. The spirit was weak. The flesh was weak. The entire assemblage was an inch away from collapse.

After Betty had left for a grocery run, she lay in bed and tried to think about nothing.

She fantasized about going to a psychiatrist and being told: "This is what is wrong with you. Take this pill. You are better now."

The last ninety-six hours unspooled in her memory and she could not be sure what had been real and what had not.

Had she really gone rifling through Gerry Land's skip?

Her visitation with Niamh in the garden could not have been real, but she remembered it more vividly than her entire stay in the hospital, which had the loose, gauzy, drifting feel of a dream.

Had she really seen that note in Gerry Land's notebook? "Scarnagh resolved."

The call from Dympna. Clearly imagined.

The call from Pat Skelton. Ditto.

Maybe she could just pretend the last decade and a half (barring the parts with Betty) had been a dream?

By her bedside table, her phone buzzed unpleasantly.

She picked it up and found a text message from Brian that simply said: *Call me pls.*

She dialed his number and he picked up immediately.

"Did you hear?" he said without preamble.

"Hear what?" she asked, and he gave a sigh, either of relief or despair, she couldn't be sure.

"Dympna's dead," he said. "They found her in her flat this morning."

Stop, she thought. *Please just let this madness stop.*

"Jesus," said Ashling. "Jesus Christ, what happened?"

"Ah, ah," he sighed. "You know yourself."

Of course. A fatal overdose of pure, uncut, Colombian You Know Yourself, snorted up the nostril, Ashling immediately thought. The whole station was caked in You Know Yourself, particularly the on-air talent.

If there was a dull, banal way for a young, otherwise healthy woman to drop dead suddenly, that was it.

She could almost hear Patricia Skelton laughing.

It will be so mundane, so ordinary, it'll bore you to tears.

And then, Gerry Land's voice, as if joining a chorus. "They don't last long, usually. And no one ever realizes, because they only go 'missing' after they went missing. They only 'die' after they die. That's the beauty of it."

That's the trick. It kills. It leaves a double behind. A fake. Like a cuckoo's egg. And then the double dies or goes missing. A perfect crime. How do you kill something like that? That clever, that cunning, that powerful? Something that far above you on the food chain? How do you stop it? Buzz buzz.

But Dympna had not died like Niamh. There had been no gentle lowering into the box. The thing had come out of its lair, tracked her to her home, and cornered her like an animal.

She remembered Dympna's scalding hate-filled rant and the lid of Puckeen's box vibrating like a pot on the boil.

She made him angry. She made him come out of his box.

When she next watched *Puckeen*, she might see Dympna Corrigan flitting in and out of the trees, a pale, shrieking ghost pursued by a towering horned figure as thin and black as a crack in the screen.

"Listen, Ashling," Brian wheezed. He sounded like he was hyperventilating, struggling to keep panic from overwhelming him. "I know you're off sick but could I meet you for a drink in town? I need to talk to you about . . . about the show. There's . . . Jesus, how do I explain?"

"Just take it easy, Brian," she said gently. "Just tell me."

I have you now. You're so close. You're so close to splitting open and letting all your secrets tumble out, I can feel it.

"We're all going to have to go to the funeral. It'll be the day after Paddy's Day."

March 18. Three days. That seemed indecently hasty, Ashling thought. Wouldn't there have to be an autopsy? An investigation?

"Before the funeral . . . you and I are going to have to meet some people."

The way he said "people" made them sound like they weren't.

The Reverend Father James Fitt
31 Sydney Parade Avenue
Dublin 4
February 24, 2003

Dear Jim,
Just a friendly heads-up from your cousins in Merrion Square.
You have an admirer.
    I've attached a few bits and pieces that you might want to take
a look at (particularly the diary). She has your name, Jimbo. Tsk
tsk. I'd sort that sooner rather than later.

Kind regards
PJM

PS: Following the Six Nations? If we can beat the Auld Enemy,
it's ours for the taking!

MARCH 2003

The morning of Dympna Corrigan's funeral was glorious to the point of perversity. A perfect cloudless cerulean sky domed Glasnevin, and the sun was turning the whitewashed garden wall into a line of brilliant burning blankness. Ashling could hear thrushes chirruping wholesomely in the willow trees next door as she stepped out into the morning air, taking care to avoid having her little black dress molested by the lecherous weeds.

Brian Desmond stood in the driveway, where his car was parked, the passenger door already open. The funeral wasn't for another three hours, but he was clearly in a hurry.

The funeral suit he wore had sharpened him somehow, brought him into focus. He was less soft and flabby-looking. Less safe.

"Where are we going?" she asked as they drove over the Liffey to the South Side, the city still green and glistening from the previous day's festivities.

He shook his head once, as if to say that he didn't have the time or the energy to explain.

The atmosphere in the car was tense and sour.

She felt like a hitchhiker who was picked up on a remote road by someone who had passed where she had said she wanted to get out, and continued to drive in stony silence.

The house that they finally stopped outside did nothing to dispel her worries. They were on Sydney Parade, one of the toniest residential areas in the city, where many of the state's foreign ambassadors had their mansions. The house was not as opulent as all that, but it was still an impressive, respectable-looking red brick that reminded Ashling instantly of the home of Gerry Land.

She was about to get out but Brian laid a hand on her arm.

"Wait" was all he said.

Someone had already arrived at the house and had ascended the stairs.

He was a tall man in his sixties, soft faced, bespectacled, and avuncular-looking, bald to the temples.

He looked oddly familiar to Ashling, as if she had seen him on the news many years ago. Something to do with politics? A newsreader? Some old GAA player of legend, happily soft and fat in retirement, perhaps.

The door opened and the man bowed his head graciously and was admitted.

"Right," said Brian, like a bank robber announcing the start of the job, and snapped his seat belt.

The door was opened by a housekeeper. She reminded Ashling of an oyster in its opened shell, pale and shy, blinking blindly in the harsh sunlight. She was about Ashling's age but dressed as austerely as a Quaker. Her blond hair was tied back in a sharp bun and her eyes were sad and listless. On her finger was a ring, silver, and quite out of place with the rest of her attire, which had no jewelry or ornamentation of any kind.

She looked away as they entered, and ushered Ashling and Brian into the main hallway.

It was an old Georgian house, thick and cold, and Ashling felt an instant chill as soon as her shoes touched the black-and-white-check tiles of the hallway.

There were two figures standing outside a wooden double door at the end of the hall. The first was the faintly avuncular figure that had gone before them. Up close he was even more maddeningly familiar, and monstrously tall in the narrow hallway. He gave them both a welcoming, generous smile as he saw them come in, and extended a paw with a large, gaudy gold ring and proceeded to crush the life out of Brian's hand.

The other man remained where he was at the end of the hallway, his pale features soft and indistinct in the gloom.

Ashling remembered a family trip to Kerry many years ago where the four of them, her father and mother and Niamh and her, had taken a boat out to the Great Blasket Island.

As they had waited on the tiny rocky jetty to get into the boat, Ashling had seen a great, pale shape, a shimmering oval, circling below the boat, deep in the bay. She had pointed a pudgy finger at it and asked her father what it was.

A shark. That's a shark, love.

He stepped an atom closer and she saw that he was wearing a black clerical suit and white dog collar.

The priest for the funeral? Ashling wondered to herself. *What is going on here?*

She noted that neither of the two men, either the priest or the gold-ringed man, had acknowledged her. The priest gestured silently toward the double doors and vanished into the room without a word. The large man clapped Brian warmly on the shoulder and led him in.

"Wait out here," Brian whispered. "I just need to talk to these lads."

The doors closed behind them and she was left alone in the hallway, the housekeeper seemingly having disintegrated and blown away.

She looked at the door.

Slowly and so, so carefully, like a woman trying to hear the heartbeat of a sleeping tiger, she laid her ear on the door and held her breath so that she could hear every word coming from within.

"Well, Brian?"

"Yeah."

"Well well well. *Aililiú, tá an poc ar buile,* eh?"

"Yeah."

"Now before, before anything at all, Brian, I think we should both thank Father Fitt for agreeing to host this little parlay, don't you think?"

"Yes. Yes, thank you, Father."

"Of course. The Diocese is always happy to facilitate cordial relations between the three houses."

"You'll learn that about us, Brian, we're fierce polite. Fierce polite, when we're not trying to bloody murder each other, ha ha! Isn't that right, Father?"

"As you say."

"Now listen, Brian. Brian. You're not a family man, are you, Brian?"

"No."

"That is terribly unfair. I mean, I hate to speak ill of the dead but didn't Gerry Land make an absolute fucking hames of things? And you left to clean up the mess? No one blames you, Brian, I want to make that absolutely clear. We all know you've been dropped in the soup."

"That's very good of you to say."

"No ill will. But . . . well, we have a problem, don't we? And I hate to say it, but it looks like you're the man who's going to have to sort it out."

"I . . . I don't know what to do . . . I don't know how to control him . . ."

"Ah, don't be talking. That's no trick. Listen, what is this? March? Next feast is, what?"

"Bealtaine."

"Right. May Day. Here's what you do. Put the show on hiatus. Cancel the school tour. Let him go hungry for a few months. Ah, then you'll see a different side of him. That'll put manners on him, now."

"I don't know if that's a good . . . What's to stop him—"

"Listen, Brian. Let me be perfectly honest with you. No one at this table wants a war. As far as we're concerned, the workday is over and we're half out the door. We're very anxious to move on to pastures new. But this . . . Jesus Christ. Using the Malacht on poor Dympna. Someone who was under the explicit protection of the Department. See this ring, Brian?"

"I do."

"Do you see it?"

"I do, yeah."

"It means something. It's a promise, to protect our own. And he doesn't respect that. He thinks that he can do what he likes. He thinks he can thumb his nose at the Department and you muggins here, you're left to sort it out. And it's terribly unfair to you, Brian. I know it. But, ha ha ha, I guess what I'm saying is, you're playing in the big leagues now, sort your fucking house out so I don't have to go over there and make you watch while I eat your fucking skin. Comprende, kemosabe?"

. . .

"Yeah."

"Good man. Father, do you have anything to add?"

"Yes. I think this incident has once again demonstrated the folly in having the box be solely under the control of the Station . . ."

"Ahhhh . . . I knew it was coming. Well now, Brian, didn't he do well to hold off this long? Sure the holy rollers have been wanting to get their hands on that box since God was a child, don't listen to a word he says now, stand firm."

"I would not, of course, imply that the Diocese would take ownership . . ."

"Heaven forbid!"

"I simply note that we all face challenges. And that An Púca's ability to create changelings is of great utility. And would be better used in service of all three houses, not merely the Station."

"You manage well enough, I think. You and your reverend fathers?"

"Indeed, just as the Department has its own assets. But there have frequently been instances where the ability to create a decoy would have made my work significantly easier. This morning, for example."

"Oh, let me guess: Skelton?"

"Indeed. The reverend fathers discovered her in the garden early this morning."

"Jesus Christ. Patricia Skelton. How the mighty have fallen. Where is she now?"

"In the basement."

"Ah, and they'll come looking for her, won't they?"

"Indeed. And they shall find no trace. But I would rather they did not look at all. I would much rather Patricia Skelton (or rather a Patricia Skelton) had left my home, satisfied that there was nothing untoward to report. Wouldn't that be better for all of us?"

"He's fierce convincing, isn't he, Brian? Almost had me agreeing with him. Shame he doesn't preach. Anyway, that's to be tabled, I think. Come here to me, Brian. Who is that stunner you have waiting out in the hall?"

"She's my assistant producer. I was hoping to give her a ring. I need your approval, obviously."

"Now, Brian, that is a big commitment. A very big commitment. You want to bring her into the circle? Are you sure, son?"

"Yeah. I need her help. With everything. I want to bring her in."

"My my my, what do you think of this, Padre? Moving awfully fast, aren't they, these young people?"

"The Station has proposed a candidate. It is for us to assess her suitability. That is all."

"Well said, that man. All right, send her in and let the dog see the hare."

Brian rose from the table and opened the door. The hallway was empty.

He looked back at the two men seated at the table, his jaw hanging stupidly open.

Utterly unperturbed, Father Fitt rose and walked into the hallway, casting a conscientious gaze around the entire space, as if ensuring that Ashling was not hiding under the tiles or hanging from the ceiling like a lizard.

"Please be seated," he said to Brian. *"I shall attend to this."*

The house was a cold, dark intestine, an unending labyrinth of twists and turns packed into a seemingly finite space.

She knew she only had minutes, maybe seconds, before they discovered her absence.

She didn't have a plan.

She had just known, as soon as she had heard that Patricia Skelton was in the basement, that she had to get her out.

It should not have been possible to become lost in a house this size. But still the cold, empty, brutally austere hallways with their dark wooden doors, pale blue walls, and black-and-white-tiled floors twisted and turned before her. There was no sound but the clipping of her shoes on the hard tiles and her own high, wheezing breath.

Where is the fucking basement!?

As if on cue, she rounded a corner and found herself at the top of a stairwell.

There was a door at the bottom, unlike the others she had passed.

This one looked like the door of a Victorian bank vault, as thick as a wall and solid iron. There was a large, mighty-looking lock on the door, but she could see a key hanging on a hook on the wooden lintel within easy reach.

Not a door for keeping people out. A door for keeping someone in.

She wanted to call out Patricia's name but she couldn't take the risk. The housekeeper might hear. Or the priest and his guests. Or the "reverend fathers" he had mentioned.

She could feel her odds of getting safely out of this house narrowing to the width of a molecule.

She took the key and opened the door.

It swung open with the terrible finality of a tree falling. Below her, rough concrete steps descended drunkenly into near-total darkness.

No banister.

No light.

And she was, for once, wearing heels.

Trying not to become unbalanced (in every sense), she took a deep breath and descended into the basement.

When she reached the bottom she took out her phone. The tiny screen was able to give her a small haze of piss-green light that meant that she was not completely blind.

Around her, on all sides, were shelves with ancient, heavy cardboard boxes. Like the hallway upstairs, the basement seemed impossibly vast and labyrinthine.

She made her way through the narrow corridor between the shelves, hoping desperately that she would be able to remember her way back.

She could hear something, now. Beneath the low hum of distant morning traffic. A sound that was both mechanical and somehow organic. It reminded her of the sound of a rabbit eating a thick leaf of cabbage, the small sharp incisors rendering the moist flesh into shredded pulp.

"Pat?" she whispered. The noise stopped with a suddenness that seemed to deny it had ever existed.

Her foot touched something soft. She shone her phone down and felt a quick hit of relief. It was a piece of fabric. A rag. No, too fine for that.

Bending down, she picked it up and ran the tiny square of green light over it.

It was a sleeve.

From a woman's jacket. Pink.

An elegant, clean line until it reached the shoulder where it ended in a jagged, violent tear.

Her hand touched moisture and she dropped it in revulsion.

* * *

Something stirred behind her.

Whatever it was, she knew she wanted it in front of her rather than behind her. She swung the phone around and braced herself to see whatever was waiting for her.

She was not ready.

The body . . .
　The remains . . .
　The remains of a body lay on the basement floor.
　Her brain retreated into sick, mad humor to cope.
　She gave a laugh, a high frantic prairie dog yip.
　Patricia Skeleton. Patricia Skeleton. Hahahaha. Patricia Skeleton. Ha!
　Over the skinned carcass two hunched figures gazed up at her. Their heads seemed to float in the air on tendrils of black tar. One of them still had a thick square of thigh flesh dangling, moist and dripping, from the thin line of its mouth.
　She ran. Heels be damned, she ran.
　She could hear the darkness twitching and scuttling behind her and would swear until the day she died that she had felt a thin, dirty nail scrape the back of her closely shaved scalp.
　She raced up the stairs, expecting any minute to feel a bogey man's hand reaching out of the darkness to grab her ankle.
　She emerged into the hallway, which now seemed as bright as the Arctic, and slammed the vault door behind her.
　She twisted the key in the lock and collapsed to the floor, screaming silently into her hands.
　She allowed herself five seconds to feel it all.
　Then she stood, straightened her dress, and walked up the stairwell and into the hall.

The priest stood at the end of the hallway, the lens of his glasses gazing dully at her like the eyes of a doll.

What you do next will decide whether you live or die, she told herself.

Unasked for, the sickly green image of the decorticated carcass of Patricia Skelton appeared in her mind's eye.

Act. Act better than you have ever acted in your life.

Her face broke out in a huge smile showing all the relief she did not feel. She dropped her shoulders to look shorter, she wrapped her voice in candy floss.

"Hiiii, Father, sorry, sorry, sorry. I got lost looking for the ladies', you have suuuuch a beautiful home here but it. Is. A. Maze! How do you find your way around?"

He studied her in silence for five appalling seconds. Then he spoke. *"I find it helps to bring a map. The facilities are this way, Miss . . ."*

He paused, and his pale brow, which seemed to have the texture of new soap, furrowed slightly.

"It occurs to me we have not been introduced. What is your name?"

"Oh, Ashling. Ashling Mallen."

"Mallen . . ."

The furrowed brow again, deeper this time, and she felt whatever reprieve she had won evaporating.

She sidestepped him daintily, meaning that she was no longer between him and the basement door.

She walked back up the hallway, feeling his gaze settling on her like ashes.

"Sorry, the bathroom?" she chirped cheerfully.

"Third door on the left. Up the stairs. First on the right. You mustn't miss it," he quietly called after her.

Brian was close to hitting her. She could tell from the furious glare he shot her when Father Fitt led her into the study where he and the man with the gold ring were seated.

She made an obsequious apology to all three men and Gold Ring waved them aside with hearty noblesse oblige.

"So, Ashling. What in the name of God is all this about, I'm sure you're asking?"

"Well, I won't say I'm not curious," she said, with her most winning smile.

That's it. Smile. Smile your way out of this deathtrap.

"I'll bet," said Gold Ring with a wink. "Well, the three of us,

along with many others, are members of a certain fraternity. A . . .
philanthropic organization, you might say."

"Are you masons?" she asked.

"We're not, no. God, Father, can you imagine? That might get
you in a bit of hot water, mightn't it?"

"Quite."

"What's your cause?"

"Sorry, love?" Gold Ring said, his eyes sharpening slightly. A
man who did not like being asked questions.

"You said you're a philanthropic organization. What's your
cause?"

"Life," he said, gesturing expansively. "And death. And everything in between. You might say we keep the sun hanging in the
sky and the seasons on schedule. We keep the whole bloody country running, it feels like sometimes."

"Sounds very exciting."

"You think so?"

"Absolutely."

"Would you describe yourself as a pragmatist or an idealist?"

"I'm someone with ideals, who's not afraid to use pragmatism to
realize those ideals."

Gold Ring burst out laughing and turned to Brian.

"You bloody coached her, didn't you? Come on, fess up!"

Brian shook his head. His anger seemed to have dissipated. He
was just happy she was doing so well.

"Are you vegetarian, Ashling?" he asked.

"No," she said.

"Good woman. I don't trust vegetarians. I don't trust anyone
who doesn't understand that the best things in life demand sacrifice. Preferably someone else's. Gerry Land understood that, may
he rest in peace."

"He was a great man," Ashling said.

"He was. He was. None finer."

This, Ashling realized, was a man who enjoyed lying. He took
hearty pleasure in pushing mountains of bullshit on top of you. It
was a sport to him.

"Now, Ashling, our little group has certain rituals and traditions
that I'm sure to a young modern woman like yourself will seem
very passé or whatever they call it. But will you indulge a couple of
aul fellahs?"

"Sure. What do you need me to do?"

"Well, I think Brian has a ring for you there, don't worry! It's not what you think, heh, heh, heh."

Brian had produced a small ring box from his pocket. He opened it to show it to Ashling. A large, silver affair. A woman combing long tresses that morphed into a flurry of cawing ravens. She realized that she'd seen one just like it on Father Fitt's housekeeper. Father Fitt himself was wearing another, but in bronze. And Gold Ring's one was different only in color.

"You don't have to wear it. In fact, we'd prefer if you didn't. But keep it on you. As a token. As a sort of—"

"*I object.*"

Gold Ring shot an amazed glare at Father Fitt.

"Come again, Padre?"

"*Forgive me, but this is reckless. Miss Mallen has not been sufficiently vetted. The Diocese rejects her admission at this time.*"

He folded his soft, fleshy hands, like a newsreader who had reached the end of his monologue.

"The Station has vouched for her. Isn't that enough?" Gold Ring asked.

"*It is not,*" Father Fitt said blandly.

Gold Ring made a face and shrugged to Ashling and Brian.

"Sorry, kiddos. It has to be unanimous. See you at the funeral, then?"

"What the fuck did you do?!" Brian swore at her once they were back in the car.

She kept her hand on the car door handle in case she needed to bolt.

"Nothing! Jesus Christ! I told you, I needed to go to the jacks and I didn't want to disturb you and I got lost, I'm sorry!"

He deflated and started to bang his head against the steering wheel.

"Fuck," he said. "Fuck! I can't do this on my own. I really needed them to say yes."

"Look, Brian," she said. "I don't know what the hell all this is about, or why it's important to you, but if you just told me . . ."

He shook his head vigorously as if she'd just suggested he try cannibalism.

"No, no, no. Don't even say that," he said, starting the engine and pulling away from the pavement as they began their journey toward Glasnevin Cemetery. "Don't even think it."

She remembered nothing of Dympna Corrigan's funeral. Her mind was a haze.

She saw Gold Ring and Father Fitt standing by the graveside, but thankfully Brian didn't approach them, nor they him.

After the burial she'd tried to cry off, but Brian had insisted she come with him to the afters, which were being held in a local pub.

They stood in the beer garden under some woodbine, and Ashling tried to listen to Brian's rambling while shooing wasps away from her cider.

After the day she'd had, she couldn't decide if alcohol was the last thing she needed or the first.

Drink first, rationalize later.

"I don't know about sizes," he said.

She stared at him blankly.

"Sizes?"

"Women's clothes," he said. "But you and Dympna, you'd be around the same size, wouldn't you? For clothes?"

Baffled, she tried to recall. Dympna had always worn heels but now that she thought about it, they were roughly the same height and probably the same build too.

"I . . . guess?" she said.

"Great. Great," he said, and slurped from his pint hungrily.

"Why?" she asked.

"You have a theater background, right?" he said, looking at her like a drowning man seeing a sturdy piece of flotsam just over the next wave.

She realized what he was about to ask her.

"Brian, she's not even *cold*," she whispered savagely.

He buried his face in his hands.

"You don't understand," he moaned. "We have to start shooting again, we've lost too many days already, we're way behind and it's that fucking cokehead bitch's fault!"

Ashling frantically scanned the garden to make sure no one, particularly anyone from Dympna's family, had heard him.

The coast seemed clear.

It had been particularly brutal to hear it from him. Soft, mild-mannered Brian.

Betty would be heartbroken.

She lowered her voice, and hoped Brian would follow her example.

"Brian. One of our lead actors has died. We suspend production. We wait a month or two. We recast."

He shook his head, his hands tugging the skin of his face taut. His lower eyelids yawned open, pink and wet like the mouths of baby birds.

"Not on your life. No no no no no. You don't know what you're saying. You have to do it, Ashling. I'm begging you on my hands and knees. Please tell me you'll do it."

"Why me?" she asked.

"Because I trust you," he said. He had not checked the environs before cursing Dympna Corrigan at her own afters, but now he looked around very carefully.

They were alone.

"You looked inside the box, didn't you?" he whispered.

She felt like she was confessing to a murder.

"Yeah," she said.

"What did you see?" he asked her.

"Nothing," she said. "It's empty. Isn't it?"

"Ah, no," he said. There were tears in his eyes, and a grim smile on his face. "Ah, no. Don't be having me on. You've seen it. I know you have."

She said nothing. But she gave the slightest, most imperceptible nod.

"Ashling," he whispered. "You won't leave me alone with it? I need you. Tell me you'll do it."

She couldn't think. She couldn't speak.

She opened her mouth, hoping that something would come out.

Instead, something went in.

Brian Desmond suddenly leaned over and kissed her, sticking his tongue deep into her mouth.

He brought with him the taste of cheap beer and the smell of fear sweat.

Without thinking she gave a scream and clawed at his face and he shot back like he'd been hit with an electric shock.

She backed away, keeping him locked in her sights, knocking

against tables and barstools like a ricocheting bowling ball until she was far enough away that she could turn and run without him catching her.

On the bus ride home she tried to explain to herself why she was still trembling.

It was not the first time she had had to fend off unwanted advances.

There had been one night in her first year when an ag student she had been dancing with had suddenly groped her and stuck his finger inside her. She had kneed him in the testicles and kept on dancing and stayed out until five in the morning.

What was it about Brian Desmond's unasked-for kiss that had left her a shaking wreck?

The need.

The desperate, piteous need in his eyes and his voice and every atom of him.

He would have devoured her body and soul if she had let him.

Ashling understood need. In a way, it was the thing she trusted more than anything else.

Tell me you need me, she had always told Betty.

But I love you.

Tell me you need me.

Why?

Because then I can believe it.

She believed in Brian's need for her, all too well.

She remembered the desperate, pleading look in his eye.

You won't leave me alone with it?

But you are "it," Brian, she thought. *You and him. The zoo. The keeper. The beast.*

Betty did not complain when Ashling grabbed her the second she came through the door and kissed her like a sailor on VJ Day.

"Good day?" she asked between mouthfuls.

"No," said Ashling. "Complete opposite. Come here."

She led her to the couch and straddled her and kissed her neck and chest.

Now Betty was worried. Some people drank their problems away, and some got high. Ashling's drug of choice was sex. She was the only person Betty knew whose sex drive increased with depression.

"What's wrong?" she asked.

"Nothing," Ashling said. "Just a really shitty day."

That gave Betty a flash of inspiration.

"Oh hey, well, I know something that might make you feel better. Want to see a magic trick?"

"Eh, sure?" Ashling said with a bemused smile.

"Okay, show me your phone for a second."

Unthinkingly, Ashling reached into her pocket and found nothing there.

Wait . . . where did I leave it.

She felt a stab of pure black terror.

She had had her phone in the basement. She had used it to light her way. That's how she had seen . . .

She had dropped it.

She had dropped her fucking phone in the basement.

In his basement.

With them.

If he found it he'd know . . .

"Abracadabra," said Betty with a proud smile, and produced the phone from her pocket.

Ashling looked at it like she'd just pulled a gun.

"Where did you . . ."

"So I tried calling you today to see how you were and this guy answers the phone and he says he just found it on the street. He drove all the way out to Belfield to give it to me."

"You met him?"

Oh no no no no.

"Yeah. He was a priest actually. I offered to cover the cost of the petrol for coming over but he said he was happy to do it. Dead sound, for a priest."

Ah, love. Isn't that why we're together? Your sterling judge of character?

"That's what was bothering you, right?" Betty asked. "You'd lost your phone?"

"Yeah," said Ashling wanly. "Yeah, that was it."

* * *

After dinner Betty retired to their room to study and Ashling sat in the living room, staring at the phone with a glassy expression.

She picked it up, and began to scan through the list of contacts. As she had guessed there would be, she found a number she did not recognize, the name in the contact simply listed as "F."

She pressed the button to dial.

It was answered, and a voice at the end began to speak, without preamble. *"Firstly, I must give you fair warning. If I ever find you on my property unescorted again, I shall deal with you in the manner which you have already witnessed in respect of certain other parties. Vices are often passed down in families. Your family, for instance, has an unfortunate habit of involving itself in matters that do not concern it. I would advise you to break this cycle."*

Ashling felt her fingernails digging into the flesh of her palm.

You did him in, didn't you? Patricia was right.

"And secondly, I would advise you not to accept any ring offered to you by Mr. Desmond. Or Mr. Land, for that matter."

"Gerry Land is dead."

"I am sure he told you so. Regardless, never forget that he is your enemy."

"And you're my friend?" she croaked, in a voice hoarse with bitterness.

"No. But I am not your enemy. I will say it once more. Do not accept any ring that is offered to you and, if possible, stay as far away from the box as you can."

"What is it?" she whispered. "What's inside the box?"

"Good evening, Miss Mallen."

The line went dead.

She deleted the number from her contacts. An exorcism.

She sat in the kitchen with a cup of tea, trying to force the last few days with all their horror and confusion and doubt into a neat box.

Pat said she told Mam that Dad was murdered. I need to talk to her.

She stood up to wash her mug out, and as she passed the sink she noticed a long black rubbish bag stuffed untidily behind the yellow-and-blue bottles of bleach.

With a start, she suddenly realized the obvious:

The stack of Gerry Land's production diaries was gone. Someone had stuffed the bag behind the sink, and taken the books.

She heard the creak of a floorboard coming from upstairs.

She had not set foot in Etain's room for many months. Ever since Betty had moved in, Etain had retreated to her own bedroom and rarely came out except for meals and other essentials. Ashling only felt a little guilty at how much she preferred it that way.

She did not know what to expect when she stepped into Etain's room, but the first thing she saw was one of the production diaries lying on the floor, a page having clearly been torn out of it.

Her temper flared.

"Mam! What did you—"

She stopped dead.

Etain was crouched on the floorboards, working feverishly on a massive scrapbook of newspaper clippings that was open in front of her. Gerry Land's production diaries were strewn about her, like empty nut shells, their bounty devoured. As she stepped closer, Ashling could see that each newspaper clipping had a page from one of the diaries affixed to it. She began to read them:

SCHOOL TOUR. 31 JAN. 1 (m)
ACPTD.
SCHOOL TOUR. 30 APRIL. 1 (f)
ACPTD.

The first one Etain had glued to a newspaper cutting about a young boy killed in a car accident in the spring of 1973 in County Donegal. The second, to an account of a girl trampled by a horse in Longford later in the same year.

"Mam, what is all this?" Ashling said, in a horrified whisper.

"Takes your breath away, when you see it all in one place," Etain murmured.

She flipped forward, slowly, through pages of newspaper cuttings of dead children, ill children, missing children, until she reached a leaf with a large clipping, a page-one headline.

LITTLE NIAMH: GARDAÍ APPEAL FOR WITNESSES

Ashling gazed at the photograph beneath the headline, her mother and her sister smiling happily on Dollymount Strand. Beside it, Etain had pasted a page from the notebook:

SCHOOL TOUR. 31 JAN. 2 (F)*
HEIR FOUND. SCARNAGH RSLVD.

I thought we were special. I thought we were the only ones this has happened to. But it went on for decades.

She stopped herself. She remembered Brian Desmond freezing cold at the idea of her taking over the school tour.

Leave that with me. I'll handle that.

Went on for decades? It's still going on. It never stopped.

"Wasn't she only beautiful?" Etain murmured, her gaze fixed on the image of her younger self holding her only beloved daughter.

Ashling felt as if she was looking at her mother through layers and layers of cold glass.

Without looking around, Etain asked: "Where did you find these, Ashling?"

"I . . . um . . . I found them in a skip. They belonged to a man called—"

"Gerry Land." Etain nodded.

She leafed through the scrapbook until she came to the final page. There, she had affixed Gerry Land's obituary as the capstone to her work, the drawing room revelation, the final chapter.

"Did you know him, Ma?"

"We met," Etain said quietly. "Once. No. Twice."

Unconsciously, she glanced down at the stump where her ring finger had once been.

She stood up and straightened her nightgown.

"You've done good work," she said to Ashling. "What's next?"

"I don't know," Ashling said. "I have to stop this."

She gestured to the bulging scrapbook.

"But I don't know what 'it' is. Not really. I don't know what I'm looking at."

"Don't lie to me, Ashling," Etain whispered coldly. "Come away, oh human child . . ."

Folie à deux, Ashling thought. *Finally, a mother-daughter activity we can do together.*

She felt an impulse to simply leave the room. Forget everything she had seen, shut the door on all this madness, and pretend to be a normal woman.

But the dreams won't stop. The sleepwalking won't stop. The guilt won't stop.

She remained where she was.

"Did you know, Mam?" she asked. "Did you know that wasn't Niamh that came back from the school trip?"

"No," Etain answered. "I didn't know. But she felt wrong. I felt the same way looking at her that I felt . . ."

She dropped her gaze. She sometimes knew when she was being too cruel.

Ashling nodded, because it was that or let the tears start to flow.

"Yeah. Yeah. Okay. Why did they take her?"

Etain shrugged limply.

"We never ask why. We never have."

"What do you mean?" Ashling asked.

Etain lifted the scrapbook and let it drop to the floor with a weighty thud.

"The opening chapter," she said darkly. "The tip of the rubbish heap."

She stalked to the door, stopped, and looked over her shoulder at her daughter.

"Never have children, Ashling. That was my mistake. Never have something that you can't afford to lose."

She remembered watching her sister walk toward the box while she stood rooted to the ground, unable to understand why no one else could sense the raw hunger and *need* that emanated from it.

It should have been you.

She wondered when her mother's voice had become her internal monologue.

Perhaps it was part of getting older.

Yes. It should have been her.

It still can be, she told herself.

You've danced around the edge of the box long enough.
Time to fall.

She prepared her goodbyes.

She recorded a voicemail to Kate, short but from the heart: "You saved my life. I can never repay you for everything you did for me. I love you so much. I'm sorry I couldn't be a better daughter."

Betty had already gone to bed, exhausted from her studies. She wanted to wake her up, and kiss her one last time. But Betty would know something was wrong, would intuit what she was about to do, and chain her to the bed to stop her if she had to.

Instead, Ashling tried to write a letter and wept with frustration when she realized that beautiful flashes of inspiration did not magically occur even when you needed them most desperately. The words wandered dumbly on the page, stunned and meandering like sheep without a dog to guide them. In the end she simply wrote: "I love you. I love you. I love you. I always will," and left it on her pillow.

She poked her head through Etain's door and said, "Ma, I'm going out," and closed it behind her, no answer sought, none given.

Brian Desmond woke up in a cold sweat to the sound of his phone vibrating waspishly on his bedside table.

Blearily, he stared at the screen.

Three A.M. *Jesus Christ, who is calling me at three* A.M.*?*

He didn't recognize the number. He answered.

"Hello?" he croaked. His mouth was a swamp of phlegm and bad breath.

"Hi, Brian," said a voice on the other end. Silky and low.

"Who's this?" he asked, baffled.

"Mmmmm," she purred. "I'm insulted. Was it not good for you?"

"Ashling?" he wheezed incredulously.

She murmured softly in the affirmative.

"I need you to come to the studio."

"Why?"

"Come to the studio."

"It's . . . it's three in the *fucking morning!*"

"Couldn't sleep."

"What?"

"I can't stop thinking about you," she said.

He remembered the look on her face as she had pulled away from him in the beer garden.

Loathing and disgust and hatred and fear and just a little, tiny flake of pity to top it all.

Perhaps she couldn't stop thinking about him. But he doubted it was in the way her tone suggested. And then she said it:

"I want you to fuck me. In the studio. On the box."

She gave a beautiful, sultry, faintly mortified laugh.

"Isn't that crazy?"

As soon as she mentioned the box, his blood ran cold.

"That's not funny," he said.

"It's actually been a fantasy of mine. For so very long. I actually think that's why I applied for the job in the first place. I'm here. I'm here now. I've had a little bit to drink. And I have a surprise for you."

He hadn't had an erection like this since his teens. He felt light-headed and giddy but he was still not quite enough of a fool.

"No," he said. "It's a prank. You're making fun of me."

If that was true, he knew, he should simply hang up now. Consider them square for what he did at Dympna Corrigan's afters and never speak of it again. But he hung on the line, because, of course, he wanted to be convinced. Ashling did not leave him waiting.

"If you come over right now I will let you do whatever you want to me," she said. "You can take me however you want. On my knees. On my back. I'll be your slave. I'll be your toy. The memory of the things I let you do to me will keep you warm for the rest of your life. But if you don't come over, I'll never make this offer ever again. We'll work together for *years . . .*"

She dragged the word out, tauntingly.

"And I'll never breathe a word of it. And you'll spend all those long, long years knowing you could have had me tonight. And you didn't. You have one hour. Get over here."

She hung up.

He stared at the phone in numb disbelief.

If she was in the studio, drunk, he should go over there.

Make sure she didn't hurt herself.

You're fooling no one, he thought to himself as he hurriedly threw on his clothes.

She had lit the lights.

The set stood before him in its perfect, almost surreal austerity. The white background. The red door. The black box.

Like a man wandering through a graveyard at night, straining for any sound, he stepped through the door onto the set and looked around for her.

"You were right," he heard a voice say. "It does fit. But I had to make some alterations."

He turned to look and his jaw went slack.

Ashling Mallen stood before him, wearing Dympna Corrigan's Pierrot costume, hat and all. White, with four large black wooly pom-poms running vertically down the front.

In her left hand she held a very large, very sharp-looking pair of scissors.

It took him a second to realize what she had done. She had cut a large square hole in the crotch of the costume.

A black, curly, resplendent bush peeked out at him through the hole.

Absurdly, all he could think of was how nicely it lined up with the black pom-poms.

"Hello, Brian," she said. "What are we going to do today?"

"You're really here," he said, as if he couldn't trust his own eyes.

She sauntered over to him, until she was under his chin, looking up at him.

"Well, I wouldn't lie to you. Not in front of Puckeen. He wouldn't like that."

She kissed him and all of reality for a moment shrunk down to the sensation of thin, perfectly formed satin lips brushing his own, a small, delicate tongue exploring him.

A black shape loomed in the corner of his eye.

The box. You bloody fool, you are right next to the box.

He put his hands gently on her shoulders and pushed away.

She looked up at him, hurt and confused.

"Can we . . . go somewhere else?" he pleaded.

She rolled her eyes and began to walk away.

He threw caution to the wind and grabbed her by the arm and pulled her back and kissed her again, rougher this time.

"Here's fine," he said between mouthfuls. "Here's fine."

She felt limp in his arms. She wasn't kissing him back. She was just standing there, letting him take what he wanted.

He found he didn't care.

"You're fucking nuts, you know that?" he told her.

"Didn't stop you," she noted.

"You get to my age. You don't pass an offer like that up," he admitted.

"You were desperate," she said.

"Yeah."

She leaned in and bit his ear and whispered: "Me too."

The scissors were so sharp he didn't even feel them until they struck something thick and meaty inside him, and then the pain burned him alive.

He flung her back, knocking her roughly against the black box, which did not so much as shudder. He looked at his hand, wet and red as a flag, and suddenly his vision began to snow over and he collapsed to the ground.

She stalked over him, a blur of white shapes and black spots with a red spike in her hand.

Everything below his nose was a sea of red.

"AW, JESUS! WHAT DID YOU DO?!" somebody howled in his voice.

"I stabbed you," she told him dully.

"I KNOW YOU FUCKING STABBED ME! WHY!?"

She shrugged.

"That's not what you asked."

She came closer and he had a sudden premonition she was going to stab him again.

He put up his hands and began to beg.

"Listen to me . . . listen to me . . . I don't know why you did this but I swear . . . I didn't do anything . . ."

"I'll tell you why," she said, and she kicked him savagely in the face.

He swore and wept and tried to grab her legs but his hands were too slick with blood and his grip was too weak.

She stood on his chest and he felt his ribs creaking like the springs of an old mattress.

He couldn't breathe.

She stepped off and pointed to the black box.

"He put my sister in that box. And something else came out."

The box. He felt a sudden rush of sour hope. If he could just stay alive long enough . . .

He shook his head and croaked.

"I don't know what you're talking about . . . you're fucking *mad*!"

Suddenly she was inches away from his face and he could feel the tips of the scissors, one in each nostril. Her eyes were hard emeralds, her pupils were tiny points. Black as pinholes.

"They go in the box. Something else comes out. I've seen his notes. There have been hundreds of them. There have been *hundreds* of them. And I see them, Brian. I see them every day. I'm the only one who can. And you had to know. You had to know what he was doing. You had to know."

His lips began to move and he heard himself say:

"I don't know anything about that. I swear. If it happened, it had nothing to do with me. Maybe Gerry was up to something. Maybe. But if he was, I swear I didn't know."

He fell silent.

A minute crawled by, in which empires must have risen and fallen, and risen again.

She leaned in, gently, as if to give him a kiss.

"I don't believe you," she whispered.

And then she gave a scream that sounded like it came from a thousand throats and the scissors fell from heaven like a red thunderbolt into his heart.

He died at once.

Ten minutes later, she stopped plunging the scissors into his chest.

She had reached the concrete floor, and broken the tips.

She was coated in his blood, saturated.

She had gone swimming in the man.

A thin string of panic was pulled through her mind: *What the fuck did you do what the fuck have you done Jesus Christ . . .*

She burst out laughing.

She felt giddily happy, as euphoric as a child at a birthday party. She danced merrily around the set, leaving perfect red footprints on the white floor.

She leapt over Brian's body, like a Lughnasa reveler leaping over a bonfire. She felt like she was leaping ten feet in the air. She was in moon gravity. Nearly flying.

She spun and danced and whooped and did sloppy, joyous pirouettes, casting droplets of blood from arms and legs, and made art on the blank white floor.

Knock.

Her knees gave out from under her. She rolled and landed on all fours and stared madly all around.

Knock.

A second strike. This time she was looking right at the box and knew, without any doubt, that there was the source of the sound.

She became very still.

Her heart stopped.

Her blood ceased to flow.

But she still watched and waited.

The lid of the box opened. Slowly. Gently. Raised by an invisible hand.

There was no sound in the universe.

She stared at the lip of the box, waiting to see. Waiting to see.

The first tip of the horn she was almost prepared for. She did not scream.

It rose, it rose.

Dimly, she recognized that she was looking at the head of a goat. Black, and dead.

Nevertheless, it stared at her with eyes the color of old coins.

It rose, it rose.

The goat's head was now suspended atop a neck of obsidian, weeping flesh. The rest of its body was pouring out over the lid of the box like an overflowing sewer.

It grew across the room like cancer grows, soft tendrils snaking and touching and taking hold.

She could not understand what she beheld.

Buzz buzz, she thought.

She was now surrounded by it, an island in a lake of pure abomination.

She gazed up into those dead, dull-golden eyes.

She heard its flesh hissing and tearing as its mouth opened to devour her.

As its jaws closed in upon her she sensed, at last, something that she understood.

She sensed its need.

It needed her.

She was accepted.

She fell.

She fell like a coin thrown down an endless well.

She did not know how long she fell or when the darkness began to shimmer and form shapes.

Tall dark shadows were all around her. She realized that they were trees, gray and hazy in the murk.

Suddenly, she was no longer falling, but running.

Gravity had slipped and fallen on its back.

It's a forest, she thought to herself. *I know this place. I've seen the goat stalking these woods.*

She willed herself to stop running and placed a hand on one of the boughs before her. Her hand was not her hand. It looked different. The arm was shorter, paler, fleshier. She knew it but she did not know how.

She walked forward but now her gait was ungainly and stumbling. She felt drunk. Her legs seemed shorter than usual, her body more top-heavy.

She looked down and saw a chest larger than her own heaving with every breath.

Her hands flew to her head and she felt hair, not her own prickly, buzz-cut tennis ball but thick curls that became dislodged and fell about her eyes like russet drapes.

This is not me. This is not my body. Who am I?

Her mind shrieked and panicked but she remained perfectly quiet. There was something about these woods. A wise traveler would remain silent.

Trembling, she wandered on through the forest until she came to a clearing.

There, as if waiting for her, were three tiny, identical cabins. They stood in a circle, their backs to each other.

She walked around the perimeter. Each house rose in her view and then declined to be replaced by another. She was soon completely disoriented and realized she could not tell where she had emerged from the forest and which cabin she had been facing first.

She supposed it didn't matter.

She approached the one before her.

She looked at the door, a handsome thing painted Christmas red.

Engraved on the lintel was an intricate woodcarving of a woman combing her hair, which was transforming into a flock of crows.

The door opened, and she stepped inside.

* * *

Suddenly she was standing in her own living room. She gripped the armchair in front of her.

Was it possible? Was she actually home?

But as she looked around she realized that the room was different from how she remembered it. Immaculately tidy. And, while she recognized much of the furniture, it was arranged in a different configuration.

There were no pictures of Niamh on the mantelpiece and there were twenty volumes of the *Capuchin Annual* on the bookshelf that she had never seen before.

The door opened and Ashling turned to see her mother entering the room.

No.

This woman was not quite her mother.

Too thin. Too short.

And with a face even more weathered by suffering, if such a thing was possible.

The woman gave her a thin, appraising smile.

"Sit down, child," Mairéad Larkin said. "You're in your granny's."

"What is this place?" Ashling asked as they sat across from each other in the dim, immaculately clean living room.

"Heaven," said Mairéad. "Can't you tell?"

"Don't mock me," said Ashling.

Mairéad made an exaggerated face, as much as to say that she wouldn't dream of it.

"It's my heaven," she clarified. "My little space. My nook."

"Who are you?" Ashling asked.

"Don't you recognize me?"

"Mairéad Larkin is dead.

"So are you."

"Why do you look like her?

"It is certainly not by my choice. Your mind is no longer constrained by your senses in the world it creates. You have no senses anymore. Your eyes, your ears, your little fingers. They have all been eaten up."

"By the goat," Ashling said numbly.

"*An Púca, más é do thoil é.*[*] So now your mind is free to create the world around as it sees fit. Yourself included."

"What do you mean?"

Mairéad sighed and opened an old-fashioned purse that she kept by her side and took out a tiny compact mirror. She handed it to Ashling.

Ashling opened the mirror and finally saw why she had felt so alienated from her body.

She knew the eyes that stared back at her. Indeed, she loved them. But they were not hers.

She stared at Betty's face in the mirror, her lips trembling, her eyes wide in shock. She wanted nothing so much as to comfort herself. It distressed her deeply, seeing Betty so distressed.

"Why . . . why . . ."

"A common response, for a weak soul. You reached out to the one who gives you the greatest feeling of comfort. Your soul is clinging to hers now, practically welded to it."

"How . . ."

"You have left flesh behind. If you stay like this too long, you will become her. Her memories will start to fill your mind. You will hear her voice in your thoughts. You will cease to be you. Well. That's love for you," she said, taking the mirror back and closing it with a conclusive snap.

It was true. She was already remembering places she had never been and people she had never known. She was seeing herself, walking through doors, smiling over the breakfast table, sleeping an inch away from her own face.

Is that how she sees me? How can that beautiful person be me?

"Come," said Mairéad, rising and brushing her dress. "We eat dinner early here."

She was sitting at a great black table in the middle of a field, and she had not a clue how she had gotten there.

A winter wind blew softly over the table like a languid snake, chilling her gently.

---

[*] "The Púca, if you please."

Mairéad sat across from her, now dressed in mourning black with an elegant veil masking her features.

The thing dressed in her grandmother's skin looked out at the field.

The field had been carved into the wild landscape with a surgical harshness. A great gray razor-sharp square cut into the wilderness. Within its borders stick-like figures, tiny ants in the distance, toiled away reaping what looked like wheat.

Ashling's mind chose to render them as human, but only just.

"You would not believe the state this place was in when we first came here. Haven't we done well?"

"We?" Ashling asked.

"My sisters and I. They shall be joining us presently."

They waited.

Ashling's mind felt like a pot that was bubbling over. Too many thoughts. Too many memories. Betty's life. Betty's past. More and more of it filled her. She was starting to lose her sense of self.

She looked up and was only mildly surprised to see three women sitting across from her where before there had been one.

The newcomers, like Mairéad, went veiled and in black.

"We have a guest?" one asked.

"Yes. Behave yourselves. Both of you," Mairéad said.

They lifted their veils to get a better look at her.

In the split second between their veils being lifted and her mind assigning faces to them she saw them for what they were, or something close.

But when she had regained consciousness she found herself looking at two very familiar faces.

To her left, her mother. To her right, a face even more familiar. The one she saw in the mirror every morning.

Thoughts began to bubble in the back of her head. Strange thoughts. Thoughts that were not hers.

Three women. Mother. Maiden. Crone. I know them.

Names began to surface in her mind.

Neimhann. Badbh. Macha. Three as one. The Mór-Ríoghan. Goddess of slaughter and sovereignty. Phantom Queen.

How do I know that? Ashling wondered.

I know because I know. Because I know and that means Ashling knows. I mean, I know because Betty knows. Even if she's not here, she's here. That's something.

"We're not going to feed it, are we?" the thing with her face asked innocently. "What's the point?"

"Manners," said Mairéad coldly. "Ah. Dinner is served."

You are in the otherworld, Betty's thoughts told her. *DON'T EAT. DON'T DRINK. OR YOU'LL NEVER LEAVE.*

Suddenly, the light faded and Ashling looked up in wonder as a massive flock of crows, a thousand or more, circled over the table like a pestilent cloud, their cawing so loud and cacophonous that she could feel her bones rattling.

A dead mouse, or rather, the rear half of a dead mouse, dropped in front of her with a moist thud. Then the rain began. Great wet red slabs of carrion and offal and dripping entrails dropped onto the black table until there was a layer of rotting, stinking flesh half a foot thick. The three women seemed to flicker and stretch. Their jaws opened like pythons', six new pairs of arms seemed to spring from the folds of their dresses, and within moments the meat had been gorged and the table cleaned.

"Not hungry?" the thing that was not Etain asked, wiping a rosette of blood from her lips and chin.

Ashling simply stared in mute horror.

"Not to your taste?"

She shook her head.

"I don't blame you. There has been indeed a decline in the quality of the cuisine," Etain said pointedly.

Mairéad gave a polite cough, as if she could very easily say something rather cutting but was electing not to for the sake of familial harmony.

"It's not my fault," the thing with Ashling's face said petulantly.

This is what my mind chooses to give my face to? A spoiled monster?

"It is no one's fault," said Mairéad reassuringly. "The land has run its course. We have overstayed our welcome. We must move on. Find a different place to harvest."

"More children?" Ashling asked.

The three women looked at her curiously from across the table, as if she were an infant in a high chair who had said a three-syllable word.

"You harvest children. You bring them to the box. You bring

them here. And you replace them with changelings so no one notices. Why?"

Mairéad simply smiled.

"Where is my sister?" Ashling demanded coldly. "Where is Niamh?"

"Ah, that one," Mairéad murmured sadly. "Such a disappointment. And meant for such great things."

"We send our children down into the world. To keep things running," Etain said.

"Changelings?" Ashling asked.

"No. Real flesh. Flesh bred with flesh. A union of your world and ours."

You weren't made for loving, Ashling. You didn't come from love.

"They live their lives, they die, and they return here. But some years ago, something went awry."

"Fucking Gerry Land. Fuck him," Ashling's double swore. Her elders tutted disapprovingly.

"Now, we must not forget his many years of good and faithful service," Mairéad said magnanimously. "For decades he provided for our table. But he was getting old, and the time had come to send his successor down into the world to be born. And Gerry Land did a very bold thing. He decided that he was not going to be replaced. He had become rather enamored of life as a human being and its concomitant pleasures. Everyone at this table can empathize. Human life is quite delicious. But while he was arranging the conception of his successor, he betrayed the location of the joyous occasion to a rival house."

"A rival house?" Ashling repeated. "You have rivals?"

Etain and Mairéad tittered indulgently.

"We three have our houses down there. Our agents," Etain offered. "And of course, as is inevitable, rivalries form. They jockey for power and influence. They engage in horseplay. They think they serve three different gods, when in truth we are one. They are all on the same side. They are all working toward the same goal."

"But, as with all horseplay, sometimes it becomes serious and someone gets hurt," Mairéad said solemnly. "Gerry Land betrayed the location of his successor's arrival to the Diocese, and they attacked the house, killing all they found. That was unforgivable. We only discovered Land's duplicity many years later."

"I was raging," Ashling heard her double mutter.

"But, all was not lost. As it happened, we had been contacted by an enterprising young man who offered to breed a second successor for us, who subsequently survived. This child would have replaced Gerry Land when she came of age."

Ashling felt like a death sentence had been pronounced on her. A terrible weight of dread. But also, a curious relief. The uncertainty was over. She at last knew the truth, awful though it was.

It all made sense. It explained everything. Scarnagh. Her mother. The way she had always felt different and off and *wrong*. Her sleep-walking toward the box.

"Me," she whispered. "It was me."

Her face fell as all three women burst out into cruel, hoarse laughter.

"No, Ashling," said Mairéad with pitying warmth. "You were simply a tagalong. An unexpected squatter. Niamh was ours. Our golden child. You were . . . nothing."

"Bloody nuisance, that's what you were," Etain grumbled.

"True," Mairéad agreed. "Niamh was very fond of you. Too fond. Always a risk when our children are raised with siblings. They tend to go native."

"So into the box with Ashling! Into the box!" Etain cackled, as if telling a story to a child.

"Your name was given to Gerry Land. You were to be put in the box. But . . ."

"Fucking Gerry fucking Land . . ." the false Ashling hissed.

"We didn't realize, you see. That he had turned on us. And he put Niamh in the box instead. So he finally got his wish. His successor was gone forever."

"It's your fault!" Ashling saw her double snarl at her. "She did it for you! She went into the box to save you! She loved you that much. Why do you ruin *everything*?"

The world seemed to be melting away into fuzzy static. Harsh lines were evaporating and there was only chaos and noise.

I have to wake up. I have to wake up. This can't be real.

"A terrible thing, to have discovered you have eaten your own child," Mairéad mused. "We were quite distraught."

Ashling felt a hatred too big for her soul.

"Just go," the false Ashling told her. "Why are you still here? Just go."

Ashling lifted her head and rage gave her courage.

"Or what?" she spat. "You'll eat me too?"

"We might," Etain said.

"We might never stop eating you," Mairéad added with a smile.

Oh, Grandma, what big teeth you have.

Suddenly, a desperate thought came to her.

"No. You're lying. Niamh's not dead. She can't be. I saw her. She's the one who wanted me to come here."

"Is she?"

"I saw her!"

"Did you? Is there not someone else who also paid you a visit in the night?"

Every time she felt that she was finally on solid ground, the bottom fell out again.

"Gerry Land?"

"He is relentless, that one. When we finally discovered his duplicity we forced him to resign his service."

The false Ashling helpfully mimed sticking a gun in her mouth and blowing her brains out.

"We placed him in the box, permanently. He still served us, crafting the changelings. Poor sad creatures, they never last long, but they serve their purpose. But now he was denied the pleasures of the flesh that he had enjoyed for so long."

We placed him in the box.

Suddenly she realized how much of a fool she had been.

She remembered the eyes of Gerry Land staring at her across the kitchen table, from either side of a shotgun wound. She remembered the eyes of the goat. Brown. The color of old money.

I'm just the zookeeper, love.

You fucking liar. You were the beast. All along.

"He did what men of his kind always do," Etain sneered. "He lied to you. He promised you what you most wanted. Because he wanted your body. And like a little hoor you gave it to him."

Ashling could barely hear her. Her mind was drowning, a lifetime of alien thoughts and memories and emotions overwhelming. She recited simple facts to remind herself who she was.

Your name is Ashling Mallen.

Your father was Barry Mallen.

You mother is Etain Mallen.

Your lover is Betty Fitzpatrick.

You live in Dublin.

You're twenty-two years of age.
You lie to get what you want.
You use sex to get what you need.
You're a coward.
You're a fool.
You have never been loved, and you never will be.
She felt herself again.
"Where is he now?" she asked.

MARCH 2003

For all the mess he had made, Brian Desmond had not taken long to clean up.

She dumped the body and the bloody scissors in the box, where they vanished, never to be seen again. There were buckets of fresh paint on the set, as the white floor needed constant repainting. She took a pot and a roller and painted over the bloodstains.

Easy-peasy.

She loved the smell of paint. That was one of a million and one things she had missed.

She threw back her head and took a deep, harsh breath.

She looked down at what she was wearing, a bloodied Pierrot costume with a large square hole cut out of the crotch.

She would probably have to change. Dublin Bus could be prickly about that kind of thing.

She found her clothes in the nearby dressing room.

She looked at herself approvingly in the mirror, tilting her head this way and that to catch herself at every angle.

"Not bad," she said.

Time to leave. Just one more loose end to tie up.

"Hi, Brian," she said cheerily. "Working late?"

Brian Desmond, very much intact, looked up lethargically in his seat and fixed her with a glassy, uncertain stare.

"Working late," he said dully.

"Good, good," she said. "I'm heading home now, okay?"

"Okay," he said.

"Here's what I want you to do. I want you to go home and call in sick. Spend all day at home watching TV and relaxing and doing whatever you feel like, okay?"

"Okay."

"And then tomorrow night, I want you to come in here with a can of petrol. I want you to lock the *Puckeen* set, douse the box with the petrol, set it on fire, and burn with it. Okay?"

"Okay," he said.

"Good man," she said, patting him on the shoulder.

She left him there, staring dully at a dead fly on the windowsill.

It was very early morning when she exited the studio, and still dark. She wondered if there were any buses still running and, if not, whether she had enough cash on her for a taxi.

There were blue flashing lights just outside the main gate and she wondered if there had been a car accident.

As she came closer she saw yellow hi-vis jackets beneath navy caps and realized that two Gardaí were searching the bushes beside a public bench.

She walked briskly on. One of the Gardaí looked up at her approach.

"Excuse me!" he called.

She hunched her shoulders and sped up her gait.

"Excuse me!" he called. "Ashling Mallen!"

She froze.

Stay calm.

She turned and gave him her sweetest smile.

"Yes, Guard, is there a problem?"

"You're Ashling Mallen?" he said, running up to her, excitement on his face.

"I am," she said patiently. "Is everything all right?"

"Miss Mallen, your girlfriend put in a call to the station at Whitehall. She said you were missing and she was very concerned you might have—"

Ashling put up her hands.

"Oh no no no no. God. I am such a stupid bitch. Sorry. I can explain this. I just, I just went into work and I fell asleep in the office. I literally just woke up now. God, she must have been so worried."

The Gardaí nodded and smiled. Who wasn't glad to hear a happy ending at 4 A.M. on a freezing-cold morning?

"Would you like a lift home?" the second garda offered.

"Oh, that would be sooooo great," she purred.

She sat in the back seat and they drove off.

She watched the city drift by the window, beautiful and golden in the light of the streetlamps.

Home, she thought. *I'm home.*

One of the Gardaí took out a mobile phone and dialed.

"Hello, is this Betty Fitzpatrick?" he said. "This is Garda James Moylen, we've found her, she's absolutely fine. She just fell asleep at work, is all. Nothing to worry about. We're bringing her home now."

He nodded.

"Not at all. Not at all. Glad to help."

Betty Fitzpatrick. Remember that name, Ashling thought. *There will be so many names to remember.*

The three women watched indifferently as she slid from her chair and fell to the ground.

They stood around her in a circle.

"She's not long for it now," said Etain. "So fragile, they are."

She tried to hold on to who she was, pushing back the crushing weight of memories and thoughts that were not her own.

I can't. I'm not strong enough. She was right.

Suddenly, she was blinded by glare. She was lying on her stomach on a small, dandelion-conquered grassy slope that overlooked a football pitch. There was a chemistry textbook open in front of her on the grass.

The book was new and the glossy white pages blasted the light of the sun straight into her eyes.

This never happened to me. This is Betty. I'm remembering being Betty.

She could hear Betty's thoughts running through hers and over hers.

She struggled to concentrate. Chemistry had never interested her and she was distracted by every tiny sound: the breeze in the trees, the lonely mewling of terns overhead, and a lawnmower muttering ruminatively in the distance. She could feel the glare from the pages bringing on a headache.

Suddenly the glare was dimmed and she realized someone was standing over her.

Awkwardly, she twisted around and made out Síofra Ní Caomhánach, a girl from her class, a jagged silhouette against the white-razor sun.

"Hi," she said.

"Heya, Betty," said Síofra. There was no tone to her voice. She did not sound happy or unhappy to see her. Pure acknowledgment.

Síofra awkwardly sat down beside her and lit a cigarette, gazing out over the empty football field.

Not knowing what to say, Ashling glanced back at her book and mentally tried to wrestle the intermediate formation theory into submission.

They said nothing for a few minutes.

Síofra was sitting too close. She couldn't see her face. She could only see the bronze tips of her hair curling over her shoulder and the wafting trails of smoke from her cigarette.

"Betty," said Síofra in a husky voice, "do you want to go with me behind the bike shed?"

Without waiting for an answer she clambered to her feet, dropped the cigarette on the ground, and stepped on it.

"Five minutes, yeah?" she mumbled, and walked briskly away like a spy in a park who'd just made the drop.

She had only been asked behind the bike shed once, by Ronan Heinz in third year, and he had only asked her on a dare.

She had never stood here before, and found it did not live up to its mystique.

If these walls could talk (one of them being the back of the bike shed, the other being the wall of a GAA club that abutted the school grounds) little of what they said would be repeatable. All around her feet were Coke cans, cigarette butts, and broken polystyrene cups.

Not exactly the most glamorous place for your first . . .

First what, exactly?

Ruefully, she realized that it didn't matter. Whatever it was, it would probably be her first.

Going behind the bike shed was an act with no predetermined outcome. You could be going for a kiss. Or a clumsy but earnest fondling. Or you could be going for unprotected sex and an unwanted pregnancy. All had happened before and would happen again.

Well, at least I don't have to worry about the last one, she mused. *Unless things go* seriously *off the rails.*

The thought did not do much to calm her nerves.

She heard a noise to her left, and Síofra was standing there, looking like she was about to be sick.

Ashling or Betty or Ashling and Betty knew exactly how she felt. She was terrified.

Without a word, Síofra slowly and deliberately stepped in front of her.

Ashling, through Betty, was at once very aware of many things.

She was aware that there were grass stains on her knees and elbows.

She was aware that she wasn't wearing deodorant or makeup and that her hair was roughly bundled into a sloppy ponytail.

She was aware that she probably looked less glamorous than she ever had in her life.

She was aware that Síofra was leaning in.

She closed her eyes and suddenly there were two tongues in her mouth.

The kiss was gentle, unsure, and softly awkward.

And she felt like God, outside of reality, looking down on a beautiful and wondrous creation.

Ashling/Betty felt like her blood was glowing white in her veins.

She felt Síofra's hands coming to rest on her shoulders.

Touch me. Touch me all over.

And then suddenly, the world turned to iron.

She heard an angry grunt from Síofra and those hands that had been resting softly on her shoulders suddenly bit down and pushed her back.

There was an audible pop as their lips were wrenched apart and Ashling felt, as Betty had felt, the back of her head strike a hard nugget of paint and stone on the pebbledash wall behind her.

That would scar. That would draw blood.

She stared at Síofra in shock and confusion but in truth she knew exactly what had happened.

She could now hear the Two Marys and Annie chattering

excitedly at the side of the bike shed where they had been hiding, silent as hovering kestrels.

She winced in pain as Síofra trod on her foot in her haste to run out into the sunlight and bray, "SHE IS! SHE IS! TOTAL LEZZER! SHE IS!"

She heard them running off, laughing with fear and astonishment at their own cruelty.

She slumped to the ground. Her vision seemed to be filmed on video, grainy, colorless, and transparently fake.

She knew that soon she would feel something. The cut of a whip across her heart.

But for now she simply laughed.

She did not yet feel like she was the one it had happened to. She felt like she'd just watched someone have a piano dropped on them from far away. Tragic, but also grimly hilarious.

And as she sat slumped in the filth behind the bike shed she spoke to herself aloud.

"Well. That was the worst thing that has ever happened to you, wasn't it? Yeah. Yeah, it was. Gonna scar you for life? Sure will. You're probably never going to trust another human being again, will you? Probably not. Probably not. Fuck. Fuck me."

And yet a part of her that was not her was silently crying out.

I'm sorry. Sweetheart, I'm sorry. I love you. I love you. I love you. I always will.

The memory faded and others came to take its place.

She saw her first day at college and meeting the gorgeous girl with the dark buzz-cut hair and pierced tongue who flirted her into joining the drama society.

Fuck off, I never looked that good.

She was lying in bed in darkness, and the buzz-cut girl lay on her chest, as still and heavy as a layer of turf.

Ashling kissed her sleeping lover on the forehead and swore a silent oath.

I will always protect you. I will always love you.

It was a foolish thing to think. They'd been together three months.

Fuck it, thought Ashling. *I know what I know.*

❖

With a wail she sprung up and the three *morrigú* actually started back in shock.

"Jaysus," said Etain. "Will you look at that, now?"

Ashling felt the change instantly. Her hands flew to her hair. Short, prickly. Her chest was flat once more, her arms sallow and lean. She was herself again.

She opened her mouth and screamed in fury and bitterness and regret.

She hadn't known.

Betty loved her. Betty had truly loved her.

She had never really allowed herself to believe it.

She had never believed it could be possible.

But Etain had been wrong about her.

She had come from love.

She had been made to be loved.

She had been loved.

And she had left it all behind.

"Doesn't it warm your heart, a love like that?" Mairéad said. "That's the real thing now."

"Such a pity," Etain noted with an air of regret.

Ashling looked up at them, pleading.

"I have to go back," she begged. "Please. Please let me go back."

"No sooner are you in than you want to go back out," Etain tutted. "Like a cat, you are."

"I *have* to go back," Ashling insisted. "Please. What difference does it make to you?"

"Ah, but you're already back, don't you understand, girl?" Etain said.

Ashling thought for a few seconds and then it hit her.

Gerry makes the changelings.

"He's walking around in your skin," the other Ashling mocked her. "Touching with your hands. Smiling with your teeth."

Ashling took a second to digest this.

Suddenly she leapt forward and grabbed the figure of her grandmother by the shoulders.

"No! No! Not him! You have to send me back! You have to send me back!"

Betty is with him and she doesn't know, she doesn't know it's not me . . .

Oh God.

Oh God.

"Child," said Mairéad quietly. "Remove your hands or they shall be removed for you. And from you. You're forgetting the most crucial point."

Ashling released her and tried to, if not remain calm, at least panic quietly in one place.

"The changeling is not made to last. It will soon sicken and die. He knows this. He will do whatever he can to forestall it. You have seen the carving over my door. Have you seen that design anywhere else?"

Ashling's mind raced.

"The rings."

"The rings."

"I've seen them, Gerry had one. And . . ."

"Etain Larkin. Correct. Gerry Land needs that ring. He will do anything to anyone to obtain it."

Ashling remembered the warning she had received from Father Fitt, to accept no ring that was offered her.

"Can we stop him?"

"Perhaps we do not want to. When he puts on that ring it will sustain his body for years to come. He will feed on us, as all children feed on their mother. But what if we were to send him something a little, indigestible?"

Etain and the false Ashling laughed and danced merrily.

"Yes! Yes! The Malacht! Let's see him eat that!" Etain hooted, clapping her hands.

"What are you going to do?" Ashling asked desperately.

"The question, child, is what are you *willing* to do?" Mairéad asked. "To save Betty, what would you be willing to do?"

"Anything," Ashling said. And she knew it was true. "I'd die for her."

"Dying is easy," Mairéad said dismissively. "What we are going to ask of you is so much harder than dying."

Ashling swallowed nervously.

"What is it?" she asked.

"The opposite."

Betty threw open the door and when she saw Ashling her face creased and she took her in a bear hug so strong Ashling felt her shoulders creak.

"Oh baby, baby, I'm sorry," Ashling cooed, and she kissed Betty with so much tongue that the Gardaí looked away, embarrassed.

Betty returned the kiss and wondered why joy felt so much like disgust.

She didn't want to admit to herself that something felt wrong, when all her worst fears had just melted away to nothing.

She invited the Gardaí in for a cup of tea but they politely refused and went on their way.

As soon as the door had closed she rounded on Ashling.

"What the fuck is this?!" she yelled, shoving a piece of paper in Ashling's face.

Ashling quickly scanned the writing and found nothing objectionable.

"What, it's a love note?"

Betty stared at her as if she was mad.

"You gave Kate a nervous breakdown!" she exclaimed. "She was calling me in floods of tears because she couldn't reach you! She's flying over tomorrow morning!"

"Kate? Is she? Kate?"

"Ashling," said Betty, as if trying to explain to a child why they can't run in front of traffic. "We thought you were going to *kill yourself!*"

"Oh, sweetie, sweetie no, no."

Ashling hugged her tight and Betty felt her hands moving down her back.

What the fuck is wrong with you, it is not the time for that, she thought, and gently but firmly broke the link.

She still felt like crying and she didn't know why.

Ashling was home and safe. Why did she still feel like she had when she first found the note on her pillow? Why had the awful, icy-cold panic from that phone call with Kate not thawed?

Shock, she told herself. *You're just in shock. Go to bed.*

She called Kate to let her know the good news and knocked on Etain's door to tell her that Ashling was safe and received no answer.

She caught Ashling watching her undress for bed and it felt like she was being slowly peeled.

An awful thought crossed her mind:

Maybe you've just fallen out of love with her? Maybe you're just done?

She cast the thought out of her head at once and lay beside Ashling.

"Too tired, sorry," she mumbled as she pushed Ashling's searching hands away from her chest.

"No, stop!" she hissed when they returned.

The hands retreated, but to her dismay she could sense a tension in them, as if she was simply waiting for her guard to be lowered before trying again.

For the first time since they had been together, Betty waited until she was sure Ashling had fallen asleep before drifting off.

"Morning, Etain," Betty croaked from where she was slumped against the coffee pot.

Etain froze the second she entered the kitchen.

Christ. I must look worse than I feel, Betty thought.

"Sit down, Ma," Ashling said from the kitchen table where she was eating a hearty breakfast of eggs, bacon, and rashers.

Is it just me or has her accent gotten stronger? Betty mused to herself.

Without a word, Etain sat down across from Ashling.

Betty set a plate with an Irish fry in front of her.

Etain picked up the fork and a sharp little steak knife, but did not begin to eat.

Betty took a swig of her coffee and glanced at the time.

"Shite," she said. "Gonna be late. Bye, love."

She bent down to kiss Ashling and pulled away before she got more than she wanted.

"Bye, Etain. Be good."

Etain said nothing.

Betty noticed the tension building in the room and decided that whatever needed to be aired between the two of them, she would rather not be in the room when it started.

They listened to the metallic scrabble of Betty taking her keys from the hallstand and heard the front door close behind her.

* * *

There was silence.

"You know what?" said Ashling. "She's some woman. If I still had a cock I'd be halfway through her."

He turned and glanced at Etain.

She stared back at him, and did not blink.

The knife was gone.

"Did you drop your knife, Ma?" he asked.

He had to credit her, she moved so fast the knife was only an inch from his eye before he caught her wrist and forced her back. They arm-wrestled on the table for a few moments until she gave a scream of pain and the knife clattered to the ground.

He pushed her back onto the kitchen floor and kicked her solidly in the stomach as she lay gasping.

"Bet you wish you'd listened to me now!" he roared, and kicked her again. **"Didn't I tell you to fucking kill her?"** he bellowed. **"Didn't I FUCKING TELL YA?"** He picked up the knife and grabbed her by her hair and held the blade under her nose. **"Where is the ring? Where is the ring, or do you not want your fucking nose, is that it?"**

Etain laughed, cackled with glee.

"Look!" she crowed, holding up her hand with the missing digit. "Did you think I'd keep it after that, you bloody fool!"

"Where is it now?" the thing in Ashling's skin growled at her.

"Somewhere out in the garden, I threw it away. Ugly fucking thing anyway."

With a growl, Land pulled her up by the roots of her hair and dragged her out into the garden.

He threw her roughly onto the grass.

"Five minutes," said Land. **"You have five minutes to find it. Or I will cut the rest of them off you, and that'll just be for starters."**

She watched her grandmother peel away to reveal the thing beneath.

As did her mother, and herself.

She saw feathers, black as night. She saw mottled fleshy feet, claws that could cut through her like paper. She saw beaks and wings. She felt the hunger.

But she could not see the whole, any more than a fly could see past the thumb pressing down upon it.

They towered over her.

But she was not afraid. Fear had been burnt out of her.

"Do it" was all she said.

The thing that had taken the form of her grandmother croaked a single word, like a crack in the Earth.

WAIT

Etain pawed on the ground under the hedge where she remembered, dimly, through a haze of agony and adrenaline, tossing her own severed finger with the ring on it all those years ago.

"Two minutes," she heard the thing that wore her daughter's face call out behind her.

She could search for hours and never find it.

It could have sunk into the earth, it could have been taken by magpies or rusted away or—

She felt her finger close on a cold, rough hoop and she whooped with joy.

Oh my God. I've found it!

Unable to believe her luck she pulled the ring out, snapping a twig in the process that she realized could have been her own finger bone.

Panting heavily, covered in dirt and twigs and grass, she rose unsteadily to her feet and held out the ring.

She suddenly realized her mistake as Land lunged at her with the knife.

She dropped the ring and dodged left, hoping that Land would prioritize finding the ring in the grass, which might buy her a few precious seconds.

She was right.

Land dropped to the ground like a cat, pawing desperately in the grass until he found the ring of Badbh.

With a look of gleeful relief he slipped it onto his finger.

NOW.

They pounced.

Three white-hot points of pain entered her body.

Their beaks tore her flesh from her bones.

Being eaten was much easier the second time.

And then, suddenly, agony.

She was in a dark place, so cramped that her arms and legs were wrapped and folded around her. She tried to scream but her mouth was full of fluid.

Her mind became a perfect point of white, total panic.

I am going to die.

Either I will be crushed, or I will drown.

And I will do it in total darkness.

Etain ran into the kitchen and locked the door behind her.

A massive boulder from the rockery flew through one of the large kitchen windows and smashed into the food press, sending rice and lentils cascading all over the tiles.

Knife in hand, Land leapt in over the now empty window frame and stood between Etain and the door to the hall.

He raised his hand to show her the ring, now snugly screwed to his finger.

"Cheers, love," he said.

He grabbed her by the neck and slammed her against the wall. Through a haze of stars, Etain watched her daughter's face, twisted with so much hatred and rage that it was no longer human.

"When I think of all the trouble you've caused me. You and that cunt Lowney. How does it feel to die for a fucking field? Did you know that? He sold you to them for a field. That's all you were worth."

Etain found the strength to rake his face before Ashling pinned her hand back to the wall.

"Ah, don't be like that, Ma," he said, grinning viciously at her through the veil of blood on his face. "I saw you at it. You loved every minute, you dirty b—"

Ashling suddenly gave a scream and Etain felt the grip on her neck weaken. She fell to the floor, gasping as oxygen returned to her starving body.

The thing that was not her daughter was rolling on the ground, howling in agony.

Suddenly, his belly swelled and ballooned until it looked like he was on the very verge of giving birth, a month past the due date.

But it still grew.

The skin of his stomach stretched until the mass was hanging past his knees.

He screamed in pain as his flesh tore and his innards were crushed. He was being opened from the inside out.

Etain watched as he feebly tried to pull the ring off.

As if that would have done anything but prolong the agony now.

He was dead by the time the belly burst and a figure, thin, naked, and screaming, emerged and flopped onto the kitchen floor.

It lay on the tiles and howled and howled like an animal. But the voice was human.

Etain screamed with it.

She wept with the thing that had emerged into the world, naked and covered in blood.

She wept for Barry and for Niamh and for Ashling and for herself.

Trembling with the cold, blind with the blood and bruising of its awful birth, the creature crawled toward her, trailing blood and viscera behind it in a snail's trail.

It reached out its hands to her, pleading, begging to be held.

And when Etain looked into its face, she saw, at very long last, her daughter.

She took her in her arms and carried her to the bathroom and let her sit on the floor of the shower and held the showerhead over her to wash her clean.

Ashling was still crying half an hour later.

But she was clean, at least.

As Etain dried her gently, Ashling asked in a voice shaking and hoarse:

"How did you know it wasn't me?"

"Do you think I'm a fool?" Etain asked. "We've met before, him and me. I told you."

"When? What happened?"

Etain looked away and Ashling followed her gaze to the bathroom door.

It was the replacement door. The one they had had installed after Kate had broken the old one with an ax to reach her.

"When you started telling me that you were seeing . . . that you'd seen her. In the telly. I heard him. I heard his voice in my head."

Ashling stared at her in shock.

"You heard Gerry Land?"

"More than heard him. Felt him. Felt all of him. I could smell the breath on him. Still can."

"What did he say?" Ashling asked.

"Well . . ." said Etain slowly. "When I heard what he had to say I locked you in the bathroom, threw away the key, and cut the ring off me, so just take it he wasn't chatting about the weather."

Ashling leaned her head back against the wall of the shower and closed her eyes.

She felt at once both heavy and light.

"Jesus Christ. Mam. Thank you."

"Arrah, whist," her mother said airily. "That's the best thing I ever did for you and that's a poor shout."

Ashling took her hand in hers and squeezed it tightly.

"I love you, Ma," she said.

Etain looked at her and it was like she was seeing her for the very first time.

"Aw fuck, I'm sorry, love," she wept, and threw the towel around her daughter and held her close and they cried until everything but love was washed away.

* * *

She dried Ashling and dressed her in pajamas and put her to bed, stroking her hair until she fell asleep.

Then she went downstairs and gathered up the skin and bones and viscera and filth of Gerry Land and put them in a rubbish bag.

And then she took it all and buried it at the back of the garden, beneath her least favorite tree.

MAY 2015

On the morning of May 22 Ashling called her grandfather.

It had been over a year since she had spoken to him but not for want of trying on her part.

He still lived on the farm and was in excellent health for his age but he was difficult to reach, now.

Some men needed their wives to tether them to the world of the living.

Widowed, they became silent and solitary, like a tree on a hill.

So she was pleasantly surprised when the phone was answered and she heard his soft, creaking voice on the other end.

They talked for around twenty minutes and she could not be sure that he remembered exactly which of his great brood of grandchildren she was.

But they chatted pleasantly of nothing in particular until at last he made his excuses and told her that he had work to do on the farm.

"Okay. Love you, Grandad."

"Love you too," he said. "Good luck today."

He hung up and she stared at the phone with a baffled, joyous smile.

Good luck today.

Well. Couldn't people surprise you?

They went down early to vote, all four of them.

Their duty done, Ashling and Betty headed off to work and Etain and Kate walked slowly back up the road they had grown up on.

Kate, who had flown back from London just for the big day, cooked dinner that night. As they sat around the table Ashling and Betty nervously discussed shy voters and overconfidence and polling errors and Etain told them not to be such a pair of old biddies because the papers had said it was a sure thing and Betty fixed her with a gimlet gaze and said:

"I swear to God, old woman. If you jinxed us . . ."

They slept. Somehow.

In the morning Ashling woke to hear her phone ringing and answered to hear a voice she hadn't heard in years. Gemma had dug up her number to wish her the best of luck. They talked about how much they missed each other and how they should never have lost touch and promised to meet up for drinks that very night to celebrate or plot the destruction of the Irish state, as events required.

They did not have to wait long.

At 10 a.m. Betty walked into the kitchen where Kate, Etain, and Ashling sat around the table drinking tea in silence like family members in a hospital café waiting for news of the surgery.

They looked up at her.

She said nothing, and simply nodded.

Mania. Whooping. Cheering. Dancing. Kissing.

Without another word Ashling took Betty's hand and ran with her up the stairs to their room.

They faced each other, smiling shyly.

"Should I?" said Betty. "Or . . ."

"I dunno," said Ashling. "I've never done this before."

"Well, you're never going to do it again. So, get it right," said Betty.

"Okay, on three?" Ashling asked.

"On three."

They counted to three and knelt before each other.

In unison, they reached into their pockets and both took out small, plain rings.

"Ashling . . ." said Betty. "I love you."

"I love you too," said Ashling.

"And I want you . . . will you be my . . ."

"Yeah," said Ashling, getting the words out while she still could. "Yeah."

"I will."

"I will, yeah."

They sat on the couch, wrapped in each other all through the night. At first they made plans, talked about venues and guest lists and the impossible, unimaginable cost of it all.

But finally they settled into comfortable silence in front of the TV with Sky News left on to keep it real.

Ashling felt Betty grow heavy and warm in her arms as she drifted off to sleep.

In the kitchen, Etain and Kate sat at the table, still drinking tea.

"What about you?" Etain asked her sister.

"What about me?" Kate replied.

"When are you going to find someone and get out from under me feet?"

Kate laughed. "Bit late for that."

"What are you talking about. You could be a, what do they call them? A puma?"

"A cougar?"

"Get yourself a toy boy, Kate. We'll make it a double wedding."

Kate laughed again, and sighed.

"No," she said. "I think that ship has sailed."

"You're not that old."

"That's not what I mean. Looking back, I've started to realize that there was only ever one man for me."

Etain took a sip of her tea.

"Ah. And what was the problem?"

Kate looked up at her sister.

"I wasn't the woman for him," she said. And shrugged.

Etain nodded, and together they drank a silent toast to the spirit in the room with them.

It was past midnight when Ashling awoke on the couch. Her phone had buzzed. She slowly climbed out from under Betty and kissed her forehead and laid a blanket over her.

She looked at the phone and saw a single text message from an unknown number.

One word: *Outside.*

He stood a respectful distance down the driveway.

He looked older, his hair turned white, and his soft round features were now somewhat saggy.

The light from the hallway turned the circles of his glasses into opaque golden barriers, shielding his eyes from view. So much the better.

"Good evening, Miss Mallen," said Father Fitt. *"I hope you are well?"*

"What are you doing here?" she asked him.

"Saying my farewells. Might I come in?" he asked.

"You might not," she replied.

He gave a thin, bland smile.

"As you wish. I see you disregarded my advice twice over," he said, gesturing to her hand.

On one finger there was the engagement ring Betty had given her. On another, she wore her mother's engagement ring, the silver ring of Badbh that she had kept on her every day since her return.

"There is a pleasing symmetry to it. You went to the other side because you believed you were a changeling when you were not. And it was only by becoming a changeling that you were able to return here and live as a human being," the priest mused.

Ashling was not in the mood.

"What do you want?" she said curtly.

The priest gave a slightly melancholy sigh.

"We're leaving. All of us. Our time here is over."

She should have felt relieved. Liberated. But instead she felt a slow dread creeping up her back like ivy.

"What happens then?" she asked.

The priest cast his head back and looked at the few stars strong enough to peep through the lamplight-soaked night sky.

"I think you know," he whispered. *"You can taste it in the air, can't you? Bile and blood and ash."*

"How long?" she whispered.

He looked back at her and for a moment, oh, for the briefest moment, she saw something that might be sympathy.

"If I may offer some advice, I have always envied those who knew not the hour nor the day of their ending. Time is not stone. Days can be years if lived wisely. Years can be lifetimes. Find your joy where you can. Live now. Live well. And speaking of, I wish you to have this . . ."

He reached into his pocket and took out something small. He tossed it gently to her and she caught it easily.

It was a ring, in design identical in every way to the one she wore. But it was not silver. It had been scorched black, as if by fire.

"They do not last forever," the priest explained. *"The ring you wear will eventually weaken and fail and will offer you no more protection. Someone who I had come to regard quite fondly was in your exact situation. I went to Scarnagh to find that ring that you hold there. I found it but . . . regrettably, it was too late."*

She remembered the blond housekeeper and her silver ring. She stared at the priest. Hard to tell with someone who wore all black, but he was in mourning. He looked almost human.

He gestured gently to the ring in her hand. *"It belonged to a remarkable woman. Very strong-willed. It was scarcely worn. It will keep you alive for many years."*

"How many?" she asked.

He shrugged. *"I cannot say. You will not know the day nor the hour. Who does?"*

That only left one question.

"Why?" she asked.

He gave another smile. *"I told you once before. I am not your enemy, Ashling Mallen. I never was."*

He turned and walked away into the darkness.

The black of his suit married the night and he became invisible. His footsteps faded away up the leafy avenue toward the park and the river, darkly whispering its rumors.

She stood guard upon the doorway, until the priest had gone.

A NOTE ON IRISH FOLKLORE

To any reader who wishes to learn more about the incredibly rich, bafflingly under-exposed world of Irish mythology I would recommend *The Irish Storyteller* by George Denis Zimmerman, *The Lore of Ireland* by my former tutor the late, great Professor Dáithí Ó hÓgáin, *Over Nine Waves* by Marie Heaney, and, if you can lay hands on them, the works of Seán Ó Súilleabháin (unfortunately out of print).

I would, in fact, recommend just about any book touching on the subject except the one you are currently holding. I tried, where possible, to keep the lore accurate. But where accuracy stood in the way of telling a good story, I chose story every time. The only consolation for my aching conscience is that, in this respect, I was no different from any other Irish storyteller throughout history. Still, it has to be said. Hopefully this work got you interested, but take nothing you read here as gospel. The book's depiction of the Morrigan, to take but one example, is such a mishmash of authentic Irish lore, H. P. Lovecraft, Stephen King, and my own invention that if you wish to learn about Herself you're better off striking everything you read here from your mind and starting afresh.

One thing that I can't take credit/blame for creating is the peculiarly horrific story of Etain's encounter with the corpse and everything that came after. Versions of this story are very ancient, indeed; no less an authority than Séamus Ó Duilearga himself called it "one of the oldest Irish folktales to come down to us." The version that inspired *A Corpse on the Road* (the stage monologue that eventually became the Etain sequences of *Knock Knock, Open Wide*) is called *The Devil's Son as Priest* (classified as Aarne Thompson Index Number 0764) and was originally told by none other than the legendary Irish storyteller Peig Sayers.

Sayers has often been unfairly held up as a scapegoat for the failure of Irish language education policy in the Republic of Ireland, as her autobiography, *Peig,* was a core syllabus text for many years. It is my personal opinion that if her presence on the curriculum had consisted less of accounts of the bleakness of Irish peasant life at the turn of the century and more farmers' wives cuckolding their husbands with corpses possessed by the devil, the Irish language would be in rude and glowing health today.

Ah well. The century is still young.

ACKNOWLEDGMENTS

I have an aunt Mary, who is lovely. This is not surprising. I'm Irish. If, through some exceptional circumstances, you are born without an aunt Mary, one is provided for you by the government along with your birth certificate and book of grievances.

My aunt Mary sent me a text shortly after the publication of my first book, *When the Sparrow Falls,* congratulating me and asking how the second book was coming.

"Is 'the difficult second album' a thing with books as well?" she asked.

I assured her that it absolutely is.

This book was many things. It was my first novel as a full-time writer. My "stay-at-home dad" novel. My "prove the first one wasn't a fluke" novel. My Covid novel. It was absolutely a difficult second album (why do I get the feeling that a future version of myself, trapped in some hellish nineteenth draft, is looking back on this sentence and laughing bitterly?).

"The harder the novel, the more people there are to thank" isn't a saying. But it should be.

In a just and fair world, every writer would have Jennie Goloboy as their agent. Unfortunately, this is not a just and fair world and you can't have her.

Huge thanks to Will Hinton, my editor at Tor and fellow "kids in a pandemic–haver." Future generations will never know the struggles we overcame, brother.

Thanks to Oliver Dougherty, who cried for Betty and Ashling.

To Alan Markey, who, as we commiserated over a coffee after RTÉ canceled our really cool little horror short about the possessed kids' show, suggested I turn it into a novel. See, Alan, I always listen to you eventually. Sometimes it just takes a few . . . years.

To Caitríona Uí Ógáin, for very kindly allowing Daithí to make an appearance.

The canny reader will have picked up that this ostensible horror novel spends a lot of time focused on the day-to-day of life in a student drama society. That same canny reader will probably have realized that this novel is at least partially autobiographical. Dramsoc was, in many ways, where I became myself, and while Betty and I have some pretty obvious differences (I'm not a redhead), we both learned to be writers, friends, and lovers in that wonderful little cult. Too many people, too many friends to list (although some of them do poke their heads in here and there in these pages). I love you all. As a final word, while the Dramsoc depicted here is fictional, it's perhaps not as fictional as you might think.

In other words: yes, Virginia. There really was a giant papier-mâché vagina.

My wife literally just chimed in to complain that it was actually a vulva. I'm leaving this in the acknowledgments. It's going to print. It's going to be in every edition. I hope you're happy, Aoife.

To my wife, Aoife, for her constant love and support or whatever.

Lastly to Anna Bale, formerly of the Irish Folklore Department of UCD. Thank you for all the deep dives into the folklore archive. Thank you for instilling a love of these stories in me. Thank you for forty years of love, support, and friendship.

Thank you for being my mother.

That last one most of all.